I stopped speaking now and listened to the sound of the land around me. I felt its air on my skin and I breathed its scent into my lungs. I let Brasil seep through my pores and fill every part of me. There was so much I hated about this country and yet there was even more that I loved. Despite what it had done to me, I couldn't imagine myself anywhere else.

Paulo chewed his bottom lip and looked at me. For a long time he didn't say anything. Then he shook his head and spat into the dirt.

'And I let you get involved with Da Silva,' he said. 'God forgive me.'

'No.' I shook my head. 'There *is* no God. The things that happened in Roraima . . . No God would do that to his people.'

For eighteen years, Dan Smith followed his parents across the world to countries in Africa, Asia and South America. He has been writing short stories for as long as he can remember. *Dry Season* is inspired by the four years he spent living in the interior of Brazil. He now lives in Newcastle with his family.

DRY SEASON

DAN SMITH

PHOENIX

A PHOENIX PAPERBACK

First published in Great Britain in 2010
by Orion
This paperback edition published in 2011
by Phoenix,
an imprint of Orion Books Ltd,
Orion House, 5 Upper St Martin's Lane,
London WC2H 9EA

An Hachette UK company

1 3 5 7 9 10 8 6 4 2

A CIP catalogue record for this book
is available from the British Library.

ISBN 978-0-7538-2932-5

Typeset at The Spartan Press Ltd,
Lymington, Hants

Printed and bound in the UK by CPI Mackays,
Chatham, Kent

The Orion Publishing Group's policy is to use papers
that are natural, renewable and recyclable products and
made from wood grown in sustainable forests. The logging
and manufacturing processes are expected to conform to
the environmental regulations of the country of origin.

www.orionbooks.co.uk

For Divya

Acknowledgements

If I can interrupt for one moment, I'd like to extend sincere thanks to my agent Carolyn Whitaker who helped give this life. She says it how it is, and every writer needs that. Thanks also to Jon Wood, Genevieve Pegg, Jade Chandler, and all the others at Orion who have helped put this book into your hands.

I raise a glass to the people of Mato Grosso who inspired this novel – the good ones who worked so hard, and the rogues who added colour.

A nod and a warm smile for my parents who took me to the places that are always in my thoughts.

To my first reader, my wife, for unwavering support and tolerance of my inability to remember . . . well, anything, I offer this: *Dry Season*.

April 1986

1

It was late, and I was dreaming of fire when she came banging on my door. She was shouting and whispering at the same time, pounding like she was never going to stop. The sound of her voice saying, 'Sam! Sam!' and the padded thud of her palm slapping the cracked paint, rattling the wood in its frame. 'Sam! Wake up!'

Blinded by the night, I pushed myself up with one arm, turning my head towards the insistent, unfamiliar voice.

'Sam! Wake up, Sam!'

I squeezed my eyes shut and pinched the bridge of my nose. I breathed hard to clear my head.

'Sam!'

I threw off the thin, discoloured sheet and dropped my feet onto the cool concrete floor. The room spun in darkness when I stood up, and I put out a hand to steady myself against the warm air, stumbling until my palm was flat on the powdery, whitewashed wall. Leaning like that, I shook my head and cleared my throat. My heart was thumping, my senses were dull, the taste of my dream still in my head, the smoke still running in my blood. I always remembered my dreams; especially the bitter ones. The ones that showed me fire and pain and death.

I steadied myself for a moment longer, hanging my head, breathing hard from the effort of having risen from my bed.

The hammering on the door continued, jarring my brow like the steady beat of a drum, her voice biting into me. I had to make the sounds go away, so I took another deep breath and moved to the door, pulling back the heavy bolt which was the only thing keeping it shut. 'Stop banging.' I tugged at the handle, pulling the door over the spot where it stuck against the floor. 'For God's sake, stop—'

'At Manolo's. You have to come,' she said, crossing herself. 'He's dying.'

I didn't recognise the young woman, but she knew me. Everybody in São Tiago knew me.

I leaned one hand on the door frame and looked down at her, feeling the cool draught on my half-naked body. 'What? Who's dying?' The drying sweat made my skin tighten into pimples. Somewhere behind her, beyond what was visible in the night, I could hear faint voices and music, the sound of samba coming to me, stretched and crackling because the tape had been played over and over. But even as I listened, the music stopped and the sound of the cicadas folded in to fill the void. They seemed loud that night.

She didn't answer my question right away, her eyes not knowing where to look, so I asked her again, 'Who's dying?' and as I began to focus, I could see that she was quite beautiful. Young. Dark-haired. Not much more than a girl. The whites of her eyes were clear in the half-light of the cloudless night. One strap of her cheap red vest had slipped down to touch her upper arm. Her skirt was short, her legs were bare, and I could see one or two healed sores on the dark skin. She wore shabby green flip-flops on her stained feet. When she looked at my face, she said, 'Please. You have to come now.'

I ran both hands through my hair and rubbed some life into my face. 'OK, OK. *Calma.*' I moved back into the room and pulled on a pair of old jeans, asking again, 'Who's dying?'

'Come,' was all she would say. 'He's at Manolo's.'

I picked up a shirt, throwing it over my back, leaving the buttons free at the front, and the girl grabbed my hand in hers.

I knew the way to Manolo's café, it was less than a minute's walk and I could even see part of it from my place, but I let her take me by the hand, pulling at me like a mother leading her child. My shirt opened as we went, each side wafting back in the breeze that came off the river during the night. It was refreshing after the stale heat of my tiny room.

As we came past the old bakery and rounded the corner, I saw the lights from Manolo's. Bare bulbs hanging from the steel skeleton which supported the awning over his café, the raised concrete floor grey and worn. The lights were on, so I knew it was before midnight, because that's when the electricity went off. If I'd stopped and listened over the sound of the cicadas, I might have heard the faint chugging of the diesel-powered generator which I had learned to ignore.

A small group, most of them men, was gathered by one of the tables, and I recognised all of them, though I didn't know all their names. Voices babbled in confusion.

'He's here,' shouted the young woman who was dragging me. 'He's here.'

The group looked over to watch us arrive, their voices becoming silent. I could hear the whisper of the river as the girl pushed me forward at the last moment, the people ushering me amongst them and directing me into the café. I allowed their hands to be on me, to push me in whichever direction they wanted, and then I stumbled under the Coca-Cola awning and stepped into the dark blood.

It was at least an inch deep by now and had already begun to solidify like pudding. My foot broke the rubbery surface and sank into the thick liquid. It crept over my flip-flops and slid between my toes. It was still warm. My stomach turned and alcohol-tainted acid jumped into my throat. I swallowed hard to keep it down, and wondered what they expected me to do.

The people parted in front of me, giving me a route to the man who was lying on the floor. He was on his side with his knees pulled up towards his chest. His face was buried in the folds of material where his shirt had ridden up. Both hands were pressed into his abdomen, making it impossible to see where he'd been hurt. The smell was strong and metallic; just like it was on the days when the *fazendeiros* butchered their cattle.

An overturned chair lay behind the man, its steel frame splashed silvery red. On the table there was a deck of cards dealt into four hands, a bottle of cheap *cachaça* with a red and gold label, brand number Fifty-One. The seal was broken, the cap missing, and there was no more than an inch of liquid left in the bottle. There was also a pile of money and a knife. The knife was stained with blood.

'What's his name?' I said, kneeling down and turning the man's head so I could see his face.

'Eduardo,' said a voice. 'Or Edson, maybe. He works for Da Silva, I think.'

'You think?'

'Just give him his rites.'

I lifted my eyes and saw it was Manolo who had spoken of rites. 'You know I can't do that, Manny. Anyway, this man needs a doctor,' I said, 'not a priest. He doesn't need rites.' I looked around. 'Any of you people call for Paulo?' I watched their silent faces but nobody answered, not even a blink. 'You,' I pointed at the girl who had dragged me to the café. 'What's your name?'

'Alicia.'

'Alicia, find Paulo. You *do* know who he is, don't you?'

She nodded.

'Then find him and bring him here. And hurry.'

She turned and ran; glad to be away from the smell of the blood.

6

I watched her disappear into the darkness beyond the lights and then I looked back at the dying man, saying, 'Manny, bring some towels.'

Manolo disappeared into the building with the corrugated roof at the back of his café and returned carrying a handful of linen. It wasn't clean but it would do.

'Press them here,' I told him, pulling him down to kneel beside me in the blood. I placed his hands on the man's abdomen. 'Hold it tight,' I said.

Manolo hesitated, held back for longer than he should, but then nodded once and did as he was told. I leaned over so my mouth was close to his ear.

'What happened, Manny? Who did this?'

Manolo refused to look at me.

'What happened?' I said through clenched teeth.

Manolo spoke in a quiet voice. 'There was a game, Sam. He was cheating.' His eyes wouldn't find mine. Instead he focused on my nose and then on my chin.

'And this is how we punish a cheater in São Tiago?' I said. 'We stick a knife in him and give him his rites?'

Manolo shrugged.

'Whose knife is it?' I asked.

His eyes met mine for a second and then flicked away, so I looked to those standing around us. 'Whose knife is it?' This time louder, but still no one replied. 'Who did this?'

'There is no knife,' said Manolo.

'What?' The words caught me by surprise and I let my eyes linger over Manolo's face for a moment before I looked back at the empty table. Only the cards and the *cachaça* remained. No one spoke inside the café. The only sound was the gentle sigh of the river behind us, and the constant chorus of the cicadas. When I turned back to Manolo, our eyes met and I knew, right then, what he had done. 'Manny?'

Manolo leaned across the bleeding body and whispered in my ear. 'Forgive me, Father; I have sinned.'

But forgiveness wasn't mine to grant. 'I can't. Manny, I . . .' Just as rites were not mine to give.

'I acted in anger, Father.'

'Manolo—'

'I struck a fellow man. He may die. Forgive me.'

Just the river. The cicadas. No words from me.

'Absolve me,' Manolo said. 'Forgive me.'

I shook my head and looked down, looked away, looked anywhere but into Manolo's eyes. Then I turned away from him, showed him my back as my throat tightened and my hands trembled. I shook my head again and searched my mind for an answer I didn't have. I couldn't forgive Manolo for what he had done.

And then the moment was broken by the sound of footsteps bringing Alicia and Paulo out of the night. Paulo was still drunk, looked worse than I felt, but he sobered up when he saw the blood. He had to. He was the only one who could save the man's life.

He went straight to work, kneeling in the jelly, feeling for a pulse, searching for a wound, asking me, 'What's his name?'

'Eduardo, we think.'

Paulo glanced at me. 'Well, we can't move him far, he'll die for sure.'

I swallowed hard. 'You think we can save him, though?' I was trying not to think about Manolo's confession.

'A doctor and a priest,' he said. 'How can we fail? Together we're more or less God.'

I raised my eyebrows at Paulo and shook my head, but he just put his bag onto one of the tables and pointed at two old men, saying, 'You two, pull those tables together. And you,' he pointed at Alicia. 'Go back to my house. There's another bag by the door. Bring it straight here.'

Alicia turned and ran but Paulo called after her. 'Bring *every*thing,' he said. 'Bring *every*thing you can find.'

She hurried into the darkness.

2

We chased the people away and hung sheets from the awning to keep out the dogs and the dust. Only Manolo waited, staying back, perched at the table in his room behind the café, leaving the door ajar so he could watch us work. He remained silent, doing nothing but sitting, his gaze like a weight on my back.

Between us, Paulo and I lifted Eduardo onto the tables which the men had pulled together, and we tore off his shirt and his trousers. Paulo took a scalpel from his bag and began to cut. Eduardo didn't mind, he was dying anyway.

Paulo's face was firm and concentrated like I'd never seen it before. I'd known him since he'd come to São Tiago, and I was used to seeing my friend drunk, dancing and laughing by the barbecue, but as I watched him work – pressing, cutting, searching and stitching – I did everything he told me to do.

'Put your finger here,' he'd say. 'Not too tight,' he'd say. 'That's it,' he'd say. And all the time, his eyes were down, looking inside the dying man.

When the electricity gave out on us, I called to Manolo to bring storm lamps, as many as he could find, and he blundered around us, clanking the metal bottles and lighting the mantles. He muttered about forgiveness, about confession, but I ignored his words. The hiss from the gas drowned the other sounds of the night and brought strange insects to lurch around our heads and hands.

We worked under the Coca-Cola awning for hours and the sun was orange around our makeshift tent when Paulo was finished.

'Will he live?' I asked.

Paulo was stitching the wound in the man's abdomen and he looked up with reddened eyes. His shirt was washed in blood. 'I've done my part,' he said. 'Now you do yours.'

'Mine?'

'Pray for him.'

I managed a half smile. 'But will he live?'

Paulo returned his focus to the wound and shook his head. 'I doubt it. Maybe with rest, but . . .' He cut the stitch and stood back from the table. 'We'll take him to yours. He can sleep there.'

'Why not yours?' I needed to sleep, too. 'Why mine?' I only had one room; just one bed.

'Yours is closer.' Paulo glanced up at me over the body.

I hesitated, and then gave in. 'Of course,' I sighed.

So we carried him back to my place.

It was more or less as I'd left it when Alicia came to me. The door was still open and the bed was still unmade. There was a skinny white cat asleep on the pillow but it wasn't mine, not sure I'd even seen it before, so I woke it up and shooed it away. On another day I probably would've let it stay.

My room was small, with a bed at one end and a table and chair near the door. A bookshelf, half empty; a fridge, rusted and clunky; a stove, blackened and almost useless. It smelled of concrete dust and whitewash, maybe even a hint of garlic and sweat. A bare bulb hung from the ceiling and the top of the wire was matted with spider webs and dead mosquitoes. On the furthest wall hung a calendar with a tasteless representation of Christ printed on it. Standing with his arms outstretched, his fingers in the nailed position, a wide, gold halo shining around the back of his head. Every year it was replaced when Father

Mateus sent a new one from São Felix, the only contact I still had with that part of my life.

We laid Eduardo on my bed and left the shutters closed so he could rest. We washed his blood from our hands in the cracked corner basin, and when we were clean, I found a couple of T-shirts in a drawer, and threw one to Paulo. On the front it had a picture of giant red lips and a great rubbery tongue lolling between them. On the back there was a list of The Rolling Stones' tour dates. It suited Paulo's heavier figure better than it had ever suited mine, and it gave him the appearance of a roadie, the way it matched with his moustache and his unshaven cheeks.

I took a couple of bottles from my old fridge that hummed and rattled louder than it should, and went outside. I sat down, opening the beers on the edge of the step, slamming the palm of my hand down on them so the golden lids flipped off onto the ground. I left them to lie in the dust, the words 'San Miguel' staring up at today's new sun.

'*Saude.*' We clinked wet bottles and drank.

Paulo wiped beer from his thick moustache, took a dented packet of cigarettes from his pocket and offered it to me. I thanked him and put one in the corner of my mouth, sucking it unlit, tasting the dry tobacco. He scratched a match on the step, the first waft catching in my nose, and he reached over to light my cigarette, cupping his hands around the flame even though there was no wind to blow it out. A habit almost as hard to break as smoking itself.

I accepted the light before Paulo lit his own and flicked the match onto the street where it died. 'What is it makes someone do that?' he said. 'Stick a knife in another man, I mean, just because he's cheating at cards?'

I told him it was the *cachaça*, saying, 'Everybody knows that.'

'Yeah, but I wouldn't stick a knife in you no matter how drunk I was, Sam. And sometimes you really piss me off.'

I smiled and leaned forward, resting my elbows on my knees, wondering why Paulo even needed to ask such a question. He had been here almost as long as I had. Came from Brasilia to work as a doctor in a small hospital near Vila Rica, set up by one of the banks to service some of the initiatives it was running. But Paulo drank too much and they fired him. For a while he drove around the frontier towns offering advice and treatment from the back of his car. When his money ran out and the supplies were gone, he sold the car and bought a place in São Tiago where he did what he could for whatever money there was to be had. And here he stayed; in a place that grips you like a dirty drug. So now he was just like the rest of us. São Tiago was his home, and here it didn't matter whether you were a doctor, a murderer, or a priest. We were all just faces in a town full of people who had no reason to go back. And Paulo knew the way things worked as well as I did.

We enjoyed the early morning warmth in silence for a while until Paulo said, 'The top of his liver was sliced off.' He tapped ash onto the dirt between his feet and followed it with a ball of spit that soaked into the dust. The night had left a bad taste in his mouth, just as it had in mine.

From where I was sitting I could see between two small buildings and across the empty main road to Manolo's café. I could see the pale blue hut with the corrugated roof and the letters across the front. Faded pink capitals, telling us *Bar e Restaurante* and underneath the words *Café São Tiago*. There was one end of the Coca-Cola awning, too, protruding from the light green bakery which blocked the rest of my view. The canopy was a happy and shameless red against the caramel river behind it, where the sun was teasing the surface of the water. Manolo was there, under the shade, clearing away the thick, bloodied dirt with a shovel, and I could hear the scraping as the metal dug into the ground. The sounds reached me a fraction of a second after he made them. I knew that later he would be

13

serving food again; preparing it in his kitchen behind the café. He'd sit at the unwashed table, slicing tomatoes and cucumbers, cutting them even thinner than his conscience. I wondered if he'd use the same knife.

Paulo sniffed hard. 'You know, don't you?'

His words surprised me and I turned to him. 'Know what?'

'Who it was. You know who did it, don't you?'

I stared down at the step.

'So, come on then, who was it?'

I was quiet.

'What's wrong? He threaten you?' Sitting forward now, turning his face towards me.

I looked back to the café, saying, 'No, nothing like that,' and allowed my eyes to settle on Manolo.

'What, then? What . . .' he followed my gaze and stopped. 'Manny? No way. It was Manolo?'

I half laughed, blowing smoke through my nostrils, and squinted my eyes against the glare of the sun. 'He confessed, if you can believe that.'

'Shit, what did you do? Did you absolve him?'

'What d'you think? Of course I didn't absolve him. I have no more right to do that than you do.'

We were quiet for a moment, thinking about what had happened. Both of us seeing the blood.

'So.' Paulo broke the moment. 'You going to tell José?'

'He can't do anything.'

'Still needs to know.'

'He already does.' I stood up, stretching my legs and taking a few steps out onto the road in front of my place. 'He was there. Drunk as usual.' In one direction, the red dirt track limped its way to Vila Rica and beyond, but in the other, it was at a right angle to the main drag through São Tiago, the empty street which lay parallel with the river. I had a better view of the café now, and beneath the awning, Manolo stopped what he was doing for just a second and glared over at me between the other low-roofed buildings. He touched his hand to his forehead, a movement which hung there in time, a freeze-frame, and then he turned away and went back to shovelling the sand which he'd used to soak up the blood.

I shook my head and crept into the darkness of my room to take another beer from the fridge. When I stepped back out into the sunshine, I closed the door behind me. 'All José has is a bike and a rusty gun,' I said, sitting down beside my friend. 'He doesn't even have a jail, where's he going to keep a murderer? In his house?'

'That's his problem. He's the policeman.' Paulo shifted, uncomfortable on the concrete step. 'Maybe he'll go up to São Felix, tell the police up there.'

'So they can come and beat Manolo to death?' I snorted and a little beer went up my nose, making it sting. 'More killing? Throw him in the river with a concrete block tied to his feet? Or maybe hang him from a tree and light a fire underneath him? You know what those people are like.' I thought for a second, looking down at the bottle I was holding in my hand. Then I shrugged and said, 'Maybe I should've just forgiven him. He *is* supposed to be my friend.'

Paulo shook his head. 'Let him go to hell. Make him sweat.'

'Yeah.'

'Just think what would've happened if we hadn't been here.'

'But we *were* here.' I slapped Paulo's shoulder and drank from my bottle. This wasn't the conversation I wanted right now. 'If we hadn't been,' I said, 'then I guess he'd be buried by now. Dead *or* alive.' It was my second beer and already it was nearly empty. 'Like Sandro, poor bastard. Buried him alive.' The alcohol was going straight to my head now I was more relaxed and the adrenalin from last night had subsided. 'Found him in a coma and stuck him under the ground.'

'We don't know that. Not for sure.'

My mind slipped back a year, to the day Paulo and I returned from a fishing trip, a weekend on the river, to hear about Sandro. He wasn't a friend, just another face in São Tiago, but we knew who he was and we knew how much he liked to drink. Paulo himself had found Sandro one morning, passed out on the main street, lying face down in a pool of vomit and blood, his nose broken because he had fallen on his face when he collapsed. I imagined him falling like a tree, stiff and straight, no attempt to protect himself, face first with a wet slap onto the hard road. Paulo brought him round, helped him recover, only to see him do it again, more times than he could remember. That weekend, though, the weekend we were away, José found him. Our policeman found him lying on the beach, said he'd choked on his own vomit and pronounced him dead. It was the dry season, temperatures rising to forty-two degrees and no one wants to leave a body for too long in that heat, so they took him out to the cemetery and they dug a hole for him. No box, no ceremony, just a hole in the ground and red dirt piled on top of him.

'You know, I still think about that,' said Paulo. 'Makes me feel . . .'

'Let's *not* think about it,' I said. 'Let's drink and relax. Forget it all. I don't know why we care so much about these people.'

The sun was well up now and its light bounced off the scruffy whitewash that was painted on almost every building I could see. I scanned out towards Manolo's again. He'd finished clearing up and was preparing the tables, wiping them with a dirty cloth.

'I bet this kind of shit never happened in England,' Paulo said.

'I can hardly remember,' I told him.

Paulo and I drank more beer and our conversation turned in a hundred different directions. We talked about São Tiago, about Jose, about women and sex and football. We talked as the sun climbed in the sky, minute by minute, second by second, until it reached its centre point and focused on us like ants trapped under a magnifying glass. And when all the beer was gone, Paulo stood up and swayed a little. 'It's too hot here,' he said. 'Why does it never rain?'

'It'll rain when it rains,' I said. 'And then you can complain about *that*.'

'We should go check on Eduardo.'

'If that's even his name.'

'Yeah. And after that, we'll go to Manolo's and get another beer. Maybe something to eat.'

I touched the bottle to my forehead, but it was empty and warm, the coolness long since gone. 'Manolo's?' I said. 'After what happened last night?'

'Was it last night? Shit, it feels like it might've been ten years ago. Anyway, he's cleaned it up, we saw him.'

'Hmm.'

Paulo waited for me to say something else, tell him what I wanted, but I stayed quiet so he asked me, 'Look, do you want another beer or not?'

'Of course.'

'And do you have any left in your fridge?'

'No, but you're talking about Manolo's, and after what happened . . .'

'OK, then if we can't go to Manolo's let's go somewhere else, how 'bout that?'

I looked up at Paulo. 'You're trying to be funny now?' There *was* nowhere else and he knew it. Manolo's was the only place to drink in São Tiago. One hardware shop, one baker, one mechanic, one general store, one café. People didn't come here to start a business, they came for other reasons. It was the last place to run on a long and lonely road, and I'd never met a man in São Tiago who hadn't been running from something in his life – or maybe from life itself. In that respect, we were all the same.

'Then come to mine,' Paulo said. 'I've got some steak in the fridge and a handful of beers. We can get some more from Manolo tomorrow. How's that sound? Today we boycott his café, tomorrow we forgive him.'

I wondered what had made him choose that word. Forgive. It made me think of all those eyes watching me in the café, seeing me turn my back on a friend, and there were a hundred things I thought I should say to Paulo, but what I said was, 'You forget I've tasted your cooking.'

That made Paulo snort. 'Then we'll barbecue. You can bring your special seasoning.'

So we checked on Eduardo, left him sleeping, and went to Paulo's house. We barbecued outside on the street using a blackened oil drum which had been cut down the middle and welded to a thin metal frame. By three o' clock we were fed and drunk. We sat side by side under a golden San Miguel parasol, on chairs made of metal and wound with electric-blue plastic. When people passed us, we smiled and waved. People waved back.

We drank Paulo's beer until there was nothing in his fridge but a slice of baitfish, half a cup of cooked rice and a container of *farinha*. With nothing left to drink, I closed my eyes and dozed for a while, forcing myself awake when I began to see blood in my hazy daydream.

I stretched my arms and nudged Paulo. 'Eduardo,' I said. 'We better check on him again, don't you think?'

3

I put my palm flat against my front door and shoved. It always stuck a little in the frame and I half-thought I should fix it. The white paint was blistered from the heat and it flaked onto the sleeve of my T-shirt, some of the cracked edges scraping against the skin of my arm.

The door swung in halfway and then caught on the uneven floor. Dust swirled up into the fingers of late afternoon sunlight which crept through the slats in the shutters, and the stale air rushed to escape around me. It smelled worse than usual. I reached in and slid my hand along the wall until I found the light switch.

I didn't need Paulo to tell me Eduardo was dead.

He was on the floor, lying in much the same position as he had been in the café, except now he was still and made no sound. Naked, but for a pair of shorts, his face was turned towards me but he wasn't seeing anything. His eyes were rolled high in his head and only the whites were visible. They were dry, like they are in the severed head of a baitfish in the bottom of the canoe. His lips were parted slightly and I could see the tip of his pink tongue.

Paulo pushed past me into the room, going straight to Eduardo and kneeling beside him, touching his fingers to the pale neck and lifting a wrist. He shook his head and dropped the hand, allowing the knuckles to rap the floor. He pulled at the skin under Eduardo's eyes and leaned closer to his face, while making a tutting noise like a mechanic about to tell me I needed a new carburettor. Paulo shook his head again and heaved the body over so he could inspect the wound. 'Shit, he tore the stitches.'

When Paulo took his hands away from Eduardo, the body flopped back against the fridge door.

I sat down on the corner of the bed and put my elbows on my knees. I covered my face with my hands and breathed in the smell of barbecue which was still on my fingers. A smoky blend of charcoal and cooked meat.

'Maybe he was looking for something to drink,' said Paulo, still squatting by the body, undisturbed by its closeness. 'Trying to open the fridge. Who knows.' It wasn't the first time either of us had been this close to a corpse, but even though I had seen much worse, I had to force myself to focus on Eduardo.

'We should have left some water for him.' I sighed and removed my hands from my face. 'Why isn't there more blood?'

Paulo looked round at me, the sweat on his forehead and cheeks shining in the strange orange mixture of sunshine and electric light. He shrugged and stood up. 'There wasn't much left, I guess. Manolo emptied most of it and shovelled it away.'

I lit a cigarette and offered one to Paulo, who shook his head and gazed down at the corpse. 'It isn't our fault,' he said. 'There wasn't anything we could do. Not really.'

'Except leave some water. And maybe check on him a little earlier?'

Still watching the body, Paulo told me it didn't make any difference. Eduardo had been dead a while now. If we'd come an hour earlier, two even, he still would've been dead. 'We didn't kill him,' he said. 'Manolo did that when he slid the knife into his belly.' He'd lost too much blood, there never had been much hope for him.

'So much for the doctor and the priest.' I stood up and went to the door, wondering if Eduardo was married, if he had children, and if he did, who would tell them he was dead. I tried not to care, not to think about it, to push it from my mind just like I did with everything else, but even when I closed my eyes, I saw the blood. It made me think about Roraima; about the bodies strewn amongst the ashes. Many of them had borne the same white-eyed stare Eduardo now had. 'Why does everything have to be like this?' I said in a breath. 'Everything turns to shit.'

'It wasn't our fault.'

'It never is, but it still always ends in blood.'

'We didn't kill him, Sam.'

From where I was standing, I could just about hear the river, and I wanted to see it, knowing somehow it would make me feel better. But Manolo's café was in the way and that angered me. It was Manolo's fault I couldn't see much more than a glimpse of water now all the tables were set up. The white paper covers held down by a few half-empty bottles of ketchup, all the tables free except one. *Gringos*, probably *Americanos* from the look of them, with their red foreheads and their money. Three of them. They were lounging in their seats, their feet in the spot where Eduardo's blood had drained away, and they were stuffing themselves. Steak, the smell of frying coming from the café. One or two tourists sometimes came at the beginning of the dry season when the waters were low and the temperatures were still bearable for their pale, puffy bodies. That's when the fishing was best. They never stayed long, though; a week was always enough for them. Seven days of adventure and then back to civilisation, high-rises and patent-leather loafers.

In the still afternoon, I could hear the murmur of their voices but no words.

Paulo put a hand on my shoulder. 'Sam, there wasn't anything more we could've done.'

I took his hand away and sat down, so he pushed past me and stepped out onto the road. He turned around to give me one of his looks. Him standing, me sitting.

'Don't,' I said and lowered my head to stare at my feet. I noticed there were still traces of dried blood between my toes, and I spoke to them, saying, 'You really reckon he would've died anyway?' I squinted up at my friend, standing there in my Rolling Stones T-shirt, that big red tongue still lolling across his belly. 'If we'd come earlier, I mean?'

He dug his hands into his pockets, 'I don't know, Sam. Maybe.' His arms were tight against the side of his body. 'Maybe not.'

'Ah, what difference does it make?' I stood up and walked away, my head full of beer and blood and death. I didn't know where I was going or what I was going to do, but I knew I wanted to see the river. Seeing the water always made me feel calmer. But as I headed towards the sandy bank, Manolo came out of the hut at the back of his café, catching the corner of my eye, a flash of yellow and green. Manolo in his football shirt. He owned a number of identical shirts and no one had ever seen him wear anything else.

My flip-flops slapped at my heels and I felt the dust flicking up against the back of my trousers as I crossed the road. Manolo didn't see me, he was too busy with his customers, laying down a fresh plate of beef and *fritas*. The *fritas* golden, and smelling of cooking oil. There was salad on the side, the tomatoes sliced thinner than cigarette papers.

The *Americanos* at the table stopped eating as I came under the awning, the sound of my flip-flops clicking. They must have seen what was in my eyes because they sat up in their seats, ready to watch the show. Manolo saw their reaction and turned to me.

'He's dead, Manny. The poor bastard died in my bed because you stuck a knife in his guts and bled him dry.' I tightened my

22

fingers into fists, wanting to hit him, feeling the rage building. 'That makes you a murderer.'

'Most of your friends are murderers,' he said, making me stay my hand. 'Or whores. You forgive *them*.'

'They don't make me a part of it,' I whispered through clenched teeth.

'It's your job.'

'It's not my job to make you feel better. I'm not here to give you a way out. You're going to have to live with what you did.'

'You're no better than I am, Sam. Look at you. Look at what you're doing right now.'

I glanced across at the three *Americanos*, seeing the way they watched me. The one nearest to me had reached down to put a hand on his own hip, an unconscious reaction to the violence being played out in front of him. A man who was accustomed to seeking the reassurance of lead and steel in the face of danger. All I saw was the expression on their faces, as if I were the threat. I was the one intimidating another man, my fists raised. I was the aggressor now; the one intending to draw blood.

I thought about Manolo's words. He was probably right. Acting this way, I was no better than he was. I lowered my fists and took a step away from him. 'Screw you, Manolo. Screw you and damn you to hell,' I said. 'You murdered that man and you made me a part of it.' Then I turned my back and walked away.

4

'I thought you were going to hit him,' said Paulo. He was leaning against the door frame of my place. The door was open, Eduardo was on the floor.

'So did I.'

'What stopped you?'

I didn't answer. I stared at Eduardo. Paulo had turned him onto his back, straightened him, closed his eyes and his mouth. He looked more peaceful that way.

'We should call Jose,' Paulo said. 'Have the body removed.'

'No. Leave him where he is. I'll take him to Da Silva's place in the morning.'

'The *fazenda*?'

'Someone said that's where he worked.' But no one had come for him. No one had asked about him.

'It's not your job, Sam.'

'I want to,' I said. 'It's the least we can do for him.'

Paulo shook his head and sighed. 'We need to move him, then. Until morning.'

'And put him where? In the street?'

'I don't know. Maybe—'

'It's late,' I said, looking away. 'And it'll be dark soon. We're tired and half-drunk. This man is in no hurry. Let him rest here. I'll sleep at yours tonight.'

Paulo tried to argue, but I'd made up my mind, so I took the sheet from my bed and threw it over the body, then we went back to Paulo's place and slept a few hours, leaving Eduardo laid out in my room. When we woke, we went back and opened the windows and the door to chase out the flies. Paulo helped me dress the body in some of my clothes. A T-shirt and trousers, both of us struggling with Eduardo's rigid limbs. After that, we wrapped him in old sheets and left him on the floor while we went round to Papagaio's place. Papagaio was the only man I knew who owned a car, and I was going to need one to take Eduardo back to where he belonged.

Together, the three of us lifted the body into the back of Papagaio's white Beetle. Eduardo was not a big man and we could easily move his dead weight, but the car only had two doors and the sheets kept snagging as we struggled to lay him on the back seats. By the time we had finished, Paulo's breathing was heavy and the front of his shirt was dark with sweat. He wasn't labour fit like Papagaio, nor was he lean like I was, so hard work and hot weather always conspired against his heavier frame.

'Thanks for this,' I said to Papagaio. The car was his pride and joy.

'You sure you want to do this?' he asked. 'It isn't your job.'

'What else can we do?' I pulled the sheet back over Eduardo's sunken face and stood up to wipe sweat from my brow. 'Leave him for the insects?'

'Someone will come for him.' Papagaio pushed the battered straw hat back on his head. 'You leave him by the road outside town, and someone will come for him.'

'Who?' I said. 'His wife? Maybe his children?'

'Some of Da Silva's people.'

'They won't come,' I said, and Papagaio knew I was right. He used to work for Da Silva, he knew how little care they had for their people and he knew the kind of people they employed. Drifters, *pistoleiros*, anybody who came seeking work. Nobody

25

cared much for these people, their lives meant next to nothing. A man could be shot, cast into the jungle and forgotten. 'I have to take him there.'

'It's not a good place, Sam,' Papagaio insisted. 'The Da Silvas are not good people.'

'I know.'

Papagaio sighed. 'OK. Well, make sure there's no blood on the seats.'

'There won't be any blood,' Paulo told him. 'He doesn't have any left.'

'And come straight back,' said Papagaio. 'If you're not back in two hours, I'm coming to get you.'

I reset the front seats into position and slammed the passenger door. 'I'll be fine.'

'Let me come with you,' said Paulo.

'No.' I glanced over at the river. Beside it, on the bank, Manolo's café remained closed, not yet open for the day.

'Then at least let Papagaio go with you, he knows those people.'

I shook my head and continued to watch the café. 'I know them too,' I said. 'People like them are all the same.'

'You sure?' said Papagaio. 'You don't want me to come?'

The red Coca-Cola awning was rolled into a tube, the end hanging loose over the steel skeleton which supported it. 'I hope he had trouble sleeping last night.'

'Sam, let—'

'I'll see you later,' I said and climbed into the driver's seat. I closed the door and started the engine, but before I could move away, Papagaio ran around the front of the car and yanked open the passenger side.

'Take this,' he said. 'It'll make me feel better.' He pulled a pistol from under his shirt and offered it to me.

'No, Papagaio,' I said. 'Thanks but no.'

*

26

With the windows down, I drove out of São Tiago and nego-tiated the narrow plank bridge at a crawl. Two unconnected and unsupported beams spanning a gully several metres deep, crossing it always put me on edge. If I turned even a few inches to either side, the car would lose its grip and the wheels would be spinning on air. There weren't many vehicles on the roads around São Tiago but, at least once a year, someone would pitch into the channel. Someone from out of town usually, one of the salesman who came here from time to time selling drinks or cigarettes from the back of his truck. Broken bones, bruises and dented pride were usually the worst injuries, and people would rally around to help pull the vehicle from its early grave. No one had ever thought to build a stronger crossing, because no one ever thought to make *any*thing better. Progress was not a word that was uttered often in São Tiago. Here, we just accepted things the way they were.

On the other side, one or two kilometres from the bridge, the road split and I took the right turning. This road was much the same as the one which ran on to Vila Rica, except this one veered north, in the direction of Marabá and Imperatriz. It would never reach either of those places, though, because the Da Silva ranch was the sole destination of this path of muck threading its way through the flattened landscape. I didn't know how much of the scrub here had been forest and how much of it had always been this way, but it stretched as far as I could see, nothing but yellowed grass on red soil, the dirt road lined with bleached fence posts. It was grazing land but I couldn't see any cattle; the expanse of nothingness reserved for the animals to roam was too wide and too open for them, the soil becoming barren soon after deforestation. Within a few years of burning, nothing could grow in the dust.

For twenty minutes I saw no sign of life except a small gathering of vultures sunning themselves in the crook of a solitary tree. They were shabby birds, unmoving in the sun, wings spread amongst the stripped branches. I passed them without turning my head, my thoughts fixed on taking Eduardo to the ranch and erasing him from my life.

Eventually, I came towards a low, whitewashed wall, behind which stood trees and dusty palms, a hint of faded green against the scorched land. As I approached, I could see a break in the wall, a gate wide enough for three trucks to pass side by side, with an arch rising over it. Across the top of the arch, in weathered letters, the words *Fazenda Da Silva* told me where I was.

I passed under the arch, overtaking a couple of riders slouched in the saddle, small hats secured with tight chinstraps, well-used rifles slung across their backs. They held up a hand in a lazy gesture of acknowledgement.

Just beyond the trees, away to the side of the main building, there was an extensive run of wooden fences and metal gates, a maze of corrals where one or two cattle were being prodded and jabbed by men like Eduardo. To one side of them, a hut built from uneven pieces of wood crouched like a tired animal.

The main house itself was by far the biggest building I had seen since coming to Mato Grosso. Like everything else, it was whitewashed to reflect the sun, its brightness stark against the deep red of the earth.

There was a large circular drive at the front of the house, the centre of which was planted with yellowing grass. In the middle of the grass, a grey stone fountain stood idle. An old man, his skin like elephant hide, his orange trousers torn down one side, was aiming a hose at the ground. He had one finger jammed over the end to make the water shower onto the grass. As I approached, he stopped and pushed back his battered leather hat, glancing our way, but saw nothing that interested him, so he moved the hat back over his brow and continued.

The front of the house was lined with freshly dug beds, the

flowers colourful against the whitewash, and tall palms offered limited shade.

I stopped the car directly at the bottom of the wide concrete steps leading to the front veranda, and switched off the engine. I waited for a moment, the air quiet now, and listened to the gentle ticking of the car, the song of the cicadas, the spray of water falling on the grass behind me. I closed my eyes and tried to forget the past hours which had pushed all other thoughts from my mind. I wondered if blood and death was all I would ever know.

I was roused from my thoughts by a voice at my side and I turned to see a young man's face leaning towards the open window.

'What you got there?' he said, moving to one side and peering into the back seat. I turned to follow his gaze and stared at the bundle of sheets. Paulo and I had tried our best to cover Eduardo, but the roads were uneven and the car was old. One of Eduardo's feet was now visible; a dark, dusty, hardened foot, the toes crusted with flaking blood.

'I brought him from São Tiago,' I said. 'There was a fight.'

The man nodded his understanding and moved away so I could open the door and climb out of the car. I popped the catch and slid the front seat forwards while the man shouted to some of the other *vaqueiros* to help.

The old man with skin like an elephant dropped the hose and sauntered towards us, while two other men came across from the corrals, none of them in any hurry.

The man who had first spoken to me climbed into the car and pulled the sheet to one side so he could see Eduardo's face. His skin was waxy and pale now, it had an unreal quality to it. His eyes were dry and dead.

'It's Eduardo,' the man said. 'Come on, let's get him out.'

I stepped back while they dragged the body from the car and heaved it onto the ground at my feet. There was no respect for the dead here. They stripped the sheets from him and rolled him onto his back by the tyres of the car. They studied him for a moment, talking among themselves, lifting the red T-shirt we'd put on him, pulling down the top of the trousers, inspecting the torn wound in his abdomen.

'Is he married?' I asked. 'Does he have a family?'

'What happened to him?' A woman's voice this time, making me turn to see who had spoken.

Senhora Da Silva was standing at the top of the steps to the main *fazenda* building, one hip dropped, a hand placed upon it, manicured nails at the end of long fingers. She was wearing jeans which were cut off high on her thighs, a shirt with no sleeves, white shoes with straps snaking around her ankles and creeping up her calves where they were tied in a bow. She had all the coveted colouring of a pale-skinned *morena clara*. Light brown hair pulled back in a loose ponytail, lips painted, olive skin tight around her cheekbones. Not beautiful, not ugly, a little weight around her stomach and thighs, but just enough to suit her and not make her heavy. She didn't have the appearance of a person who could order an execution, though I wasn't sure such an appearance existed, but I knew there was no way to count the deaths she and her husband had caused.

As soon as she spoke, the men who were busying over the body stopped and became quiet. They stood as if to attention and turned their heads towards her but lowered their eyes.

I went to the steps to meet her, putting a hand to my brow, shielding my eyes from the glare of the whitewash as I looked up. 'Senhora Da Silva, I'm—'

'I know who you are,' she descended the steps and came close. 'You're the *gringo* priest.' She didn't offer her hand or any other form of greeting. Instead, she waved her fingers in a dismissive gesture at the men by the car. They lifted the body and carried Eduardo away.

'What happened to him?' She was unafraid to stare right into me.

'A fight,' I said. 'There was a fight over a card game.'

'So you killed him?'

'No. We tried to save him. The doctor and I.'

'Do you know who *did* kill him?'

I glanced back at the men carrying Eduardo, watching them take the body into the hut by the corrals. I wondered what such men might do to Manolo if they knew it was he who had put the knife into their friend. 'No. I don't.'

'So you just gave him his rites and brought him to me.'

'Something like that.' They closed the door behind them and Eduardo was gone.

'Well, you must know by now that people die here every day. It's nothing new.' A bored expression came over her and she stifled a yawn. 'I have other *vaqueiros*.'

'Was he married?' I asked. 'What about family?'

'I don't know,' she said. 'Does it matter? He's dead, like this whole place. There's nothing anyone can do about it now. Not even God.' She looked at me again and tried to show concern. 'You think me callous.' It wasn't a question and she didn't give me time to reply. 'No matter. The men will take care of it,' she said. 'If he has family, they'll take him to them.'

I glanced over at the wooden hut and wondered how these men took care of each other.

'But perhaps we should talk about it further,' she said, changing her tone. 'You should come in, have a drink. You must be tired.'

'I can't,' I said. 'I have things to—'

'I insist.'

'Really, Senhora Da Silva—'

'Catarina,' she said, looking me up and down like she was inspecting me.

Her interruption made me falter. Catarina was an

unassuming name for a woman with a fearsome reputation. I tried to smile. 'Really. I have things to do.'

'Another time, then.'

'Maybe.' But I came to São Tiago to avoid people like her. I didn't want to drink in her house any more than I wanted to be bitten by a jararaca pit viper.

Catarina Da Silva followed me back to the car and waited as I climbed in and shut the door. Then she bent down, placing her hands on her thighs and peering through the window. 'You must come again,' she said. 'It would make a change for me. A *gringo* priest. I bet you have some stories to tell, eh?'

'Perhaps,' I said and started the engine. I raised my hand in brief farewell and pulled away without another word.

As I passed the corrals and headed out onto the road, the door to the shed opened and the old man with the elephant skin came out. He was wearing my old trousers. The man behind him was wearing my red T-shirt.

5

Coming back to São Tiago, I kept the speed up and the windows down, so when I arrived, my face was dry from the warm wind. I dropped the car back at Papagaio's place and threw the keys into the glove compartment where they lay amongst the cassettes and .38 calibre pistol cartridges. I walked away from the river, towards the back of town, and within a few minutes I was standing outside Ana's place. It was larger than mine, a two-roomed, flat-roofed house with a porch at the front. The building was painted pale green and there was faded black lettering stencilled across the front. *Costureira*.

I paused for a moment, standing across the street and looking at the building in which Ana lived and worked. I remembered the first time I'd come here, brought some old jeans with holes in the knees, paid a few coins for the seamstress to patch them up. She did the job quickly and with pride, and she was so friendly when I collected them, I found myself searching for other clothes that needed to be fixed. She had an air of calmness about her that made it a pleasure to be in her company and as time passed we became close friends. I was drawn to Ana in a way I found hard to understand, and as a man who had lived so close to God for so many years, I told myself my interest was only in friendship. But, of course, everything changes and I had come to understand that, more than anything else, I was just a man. And as a man, my needs were as primitive or elevated as any other man's.

Everybody knew who Ana was, what she used to do, and almost everybody wore clothes which she'd made or mended in one way or another. She had been in São Tiago longer than I had, a product of unmarried parents who never wanted her. Her father was a drifter whose name she didn't know; her mother long gone, hidden under the soil of the cemetery between here and the airstrip when Ana was just fourteen. Ana's life had been hard and she had sold herself to survive. She started by giving men the only thing she had that they wanted. She had no money and no alcohol, so she gave them her body in return for their cash so she could make something else of herself. Now she took care of São Tiago's men in a different way. She kept them clothed.

I patted a dog that was sitting in a doorway, and then crossed the deserted road to the green building. I went into the shade of the porch and knocked on the screen door. Her face appeared at the netting almost immediately. Her features blurred behind the gauze.

'Ana,' I said, and she swung open the door.

She was dark, *morena*, her skin the colour of sweet mocha. Her black hair hung in loose curls, falling about her shoulders which had borne so much weight. She stood straight, proud, her head up, her brown eyes hard but kind, her mouth always threatening to twist into a smile. Perhaps not conventionally beautiful, Ana carried a light about her that made people feel good. She had a way of making things seem better than they were, and it was always easy to be with her.

The pattern on her dress was faded to almost nothing, scrubbed so many times between soap and stone, but the worn cotton sat well on her slender hips, tight around her narrow waist, hanging loose above her darkened knees and bruised shins. Her feet were bare, as they always were when she was in the house.

She stepped back to let me in and I moved past her, waiting while she closed the door behind me. The familiar two-room house carried the smell of cooking and concrete dust which immediately made me comfortable. Ana led me to the kitchen. The rough wooden table in the centre of the room was busy with rolls of cloth and piles of clothes waiting to be mended. Needles and scissors. Tins containing reels of cotton. An old iron and a lopsided ironing-board lay idle beside a well-used sewing machine.

'Busy as always.' I gestured to the materials.

'I'll never be rich.' She took two small cups from a cupboard and filled them with coffee as she spoke. 'But all these men without women . . . I think some of them treat me like their mother.'

She handed me one of the cups and we went outside onto the small porch. Ana asked me to sit and pulled out a chair for herself. She sat beside me, close, her knees touching mine. We were in the shade, but a single shaft of sunlight found its way through the roofing above us and settled over Ana's hair, turning it from black to brown.

'I thought you might come,' she said. 'Nilva told me something happened at the café last night. There was fighting this morning, too. They say you threatened Manny.'

I told her what Manny had done, how the girl had come to drag me from my bed in the middle of the night.

'You should have called me.'

'No one should have to see things like that.'

'It wasn't your fault, you know, Sam. You and Paulo did everything you could for that man. You've done nothing wrong.'

I told her how I refused last rites, how I'd rejected Manolo's confession. 'It would have been enough for him,' I said, 'for

35

both of them maybe, but I couldn't bring myself to do it. Manny wasn't sorry for what he did; you don't find forgiveness by muttering a few prayers.'

'You couldn't do what he asked, Sam, you were in no position.'

'Was it right of me to want him to burn in hell for what he did, though, for making *me* part of what he did?'

'Anyone would be angry, Sam.'

'Not just angry, Ana. I wanted to punish him. To beat him with my fists. But I stopped myself because I know I'm no better than he is.'

'Of course you are.' She put her hand on mine.

I wondered if Ana's opinion of me would be changed if I told her what happened in Roraima; if I would risk turning her away from me. Many times I had wanted to tell her. Many times I had held my tongue. But any thoughts I had now of confiding in her were interrupted by a familiar voice.

'So this is where the priest comes to dip his holy *pica*?'

Without thinking, I snatched my hand away from Ana and turned to face Manolo. Standing just beyond the low porch wall, he was wearing green shorts and his customary yellow football shirt.

'You like the girls, eh?' he sneered.

Everyone in São Tiago knew about my friendship with Ana, even Manny. There was no secret that she and I spent much of our time together, but now I felt like a child who had been caught stealing, and I stood up with such haste my chair fell back with a crash.

Manolo curled his lip and shook his head at me.

'What are you doing here?' It was all I could think of to say. I was confused by my emotions. The pangs of guilt at having been caught with a woman were giving way to anger.

'I was passing,' he said. 'Going to work.' He sneered at me

with distaste. 'Something you know nothing about. Odd jobs; catching fish? That's not work.'

'Manny, leave us alone.' Ana stood, too, coming to my side.

'The pure priest who can't stomach another man's confession.' He leaned to one side and spat. 'The priest who never led a funeral, never performed a marriage, never gave a mass. But here he is, getting intimate with a whore. *Mula sem cabeça.*' It was an old myth. *Mula sem cabeça*, the headless mule. A woman cursed by God for her love affair with a priest.

I felt my hands tightening at my sides, and my breathing quickened. 'Go away, Manolo. This is not the place.'

'Why not?' said Manolo. 'What other place is there?'

I glanced around without moving my head. Two men I didn't recognise had stopped to watch. They were Indian, Karajá from across the river at Bananal, probably. Their dark, lined skin like cured animal hide, their eyes small and slow. Drunk on the local liquor.

'Manny . . .' I spoke through gritted teeth and stepped towards him so the only thing keeping my toes from touching his was the low wall of Ana's porch.

Manolo looked at Ana. 'I like your whore. She's pretty. A bit old, but pretty. Maybe I can make an arrangement with her. When she's finished with you, I can have a go. It will make her feel better, to be screwed by a real man instead of a crying priest. As long as she's not too expensive, that is.'

I threw my right fist and slammed it into the side of Manny's face. He staggered back from me, bringing his hands up to protect himself. But before he could steady himself, I hurdled the low wall of the porch and launched myself at him. I hit him repeatedly, feeling my knuckles pounding his bony chest and ribs, raking his cheekbones. I swung at his head and his body, forcing him to his knees and then I kicked him onto his back. I fell upon him, sitting over him and using my fists on his face.

Behind me, Ana was calling my name, but I continued to hit

Manny until he managed to raise a foot to my chest and push me away, unbalancing me, leaving me to sit in the dirt, looking at his bloodied face.

'Sam.' Ana crouched beside me and put her arms around me, trying to help me to my feet, but I shrugged her away and watched Manolo sit up.

'What kind of priest are you?' he said.

I stayed where I was while Manolo stood and wiped at his face with the hem of his shirt. He stared at the blood, then looked down at me like I was something he'd found out in the field.

'You're no priest,' he said, backing away. 'You're just the same as me.'

I stayed where I was, sitting in the road, watching him walk away until Ana touched my shoulder, saying, 'Sam.'

I held my hands out in front of me, studying the blood engrained in the creases of my knuckles.

'Sam. You OK?'

'I'm sorry,' I said, getting to my feet.

'Don't be.' She turned me round to face her. 'You wanted to protect me. Don't ever be sorry for that.' Ana reached up with both hands and put them on my face. She looked into my eyes as if there were nothing else she would ever want to look at again. She burrowed into me, searching deep and finding what she was looking for, hoping to touch it, bring it to life, embrace it and keep it for her own. Then she leaned forwards, put her lips on mine and allowed them to linger for a moment before pulling away. It was the first time she had ever done such a thing, and it awoke a sensibility inside me which, for a moment, raised me above anything else.

May 1986

6

Paulo and I pushed the dugout away from the shore and paddled towards the centre of the river. In places, I could see branches jutting from the surface, slight ripples circling outwards as the brown, silt-laden water flowed around them. A few hundred yards from the bank, a hump of sand rose from the river, revealed every year during the dry season when the sun took away the water. Sand so white it hurt your eyes to look at it, and so fine it squeaked when you walked on it. And when this *praia* was revealed, there was partying to be done. Right now, early in the morning, it was deserted except for a few parasols, but later it would be busy. After pay day, everybody in São Tiago came to the new beach, making the most of the low waters. Manolo would set up a bar and there'd be samba on the hot sand.

Paddling south, working against the current, I narrowed my eyes, raising a hand to my forehead and surveying the Araguaia river. It wasn't at its widest here, but it was still wider than three of our scruffy football fields endways on. On the São Tiago side, the white sand gave way to a bank that was a dirty hotchpotch of dry grass in shades of green and yellow, much of which would be submerged once the rains came and the river swelled and burst its banks. From the canoe, I could see how small the town was. A broad main street, known just as the *rua*, running at a right angle to the river. Parallel with the water was another wide street with a row of widely spaced buildings backing onto the water. Manolo's place with the red awning and the pale blue, corrugated box which he used as his kitchen. André's floating hotel, a bizarre and wonderful contraption, was moored a little further down. One or two other buildings painted light pink or lime. On the other side of the street, four or five rows of low, shabby buildings stood in no particular order and for no particular reason. The bank a lilac colour, the bakery yellow, the rest just whitewashed to reflect the sun. A frontier settlement populated by *vaqueiros*, *pistoleiros*, runaways, and people who had stumbled into the place and couldn't escape. A small and unimportant town, sitting in tufts on the red dirt where the forest had been cut and burned in times none of us remembered. Our town was nothing more than a tiny blemish on the vast expanse that made up the central Brasilian state of Mato Grosso. With an area of more than nine hundred thousand square kilometres, the state spread out around us, an explosion of life and death, unfolding itself into the states which surrounded us, emptying itself into Bolivia on its western border. Sprawling from dense Amazonian rainforests to the open savannahs of the west and the pantanal wetlands of the south, the state in which we limped through our lives was one of the most deforested regions of Amazonia. Countless thousands of kilometres of land had been ravaged by fire, gold mining, damming, aluminium processing, logging and cattle grazing. If there was a way to torture the land, it had been tried and tested here, in this enormous, chaotic territory where land was its most important commodity and belonged to whoever was ruthless enough to take it. And although many parts of the state had experienced rapid population growth, countless other areas, like ours, remained small and isolated. Here, in these primitive, anarchic places, violence was a daily occurrence and the law was almost non-existent.

On the opposite bank of the river, at the gasping heart of

Mato Grosso, lay Bananal island, the largest fluvial island in the world, created where the Araguaia river split into eastern and western tributaries. Here, there were protected trees which were still standing, kept intact by the elastic laws which were bound to the island reservation and the Brasilian national park. That's where the fishing was always best.

'It's too hot, Sam, we'll never make it today.' Paulo liked to complain about the heat, it was always on his lips, but it made me feel calm, languid, like there was nothing I needed to do but relax.

'We'll make it, Paulo. We always make it.' I switched the paddle into my left hand and reached down to pick up a rusted margarine can that was idling in the water at the bottom of the boat.

'We should've hired one of André's boats,' said Paulo. 'These Karajá canoes always sink.'

I used the tin to scoop the warm water and tip it over the side of the darkened wood, saying, 'Why pay when you don't have to? It sinks, you know how to swim, don't you?'

Paulo flicked a bug from his shoulder. 'Not when the *piranhas* are eating my toes.'

I grinned and put the tin between his feet. 'Just paddle.'

Once we were beyond the centre of the river, where the current was at its strongest, we headed up towards the bend. I could already see the hint of another beach creeping around the edge of the forest. 'We'll have a beer when we get there.' I patted the top of the red polystyrene cool box which sat in the middle of the boat. 'That'll cool you down.'

Paulo stopped paddling and wiped sweat from his brow. The sun was strong at that time of the morning; it must have been over thirty degrees already, and it was going to get hotter. He bent down and lifted a thick line from the fishing box.

'It'll just snag,' I said. I'd fished on this part of the river often

43

enough to know this was where the vegetation was at its thickest under the water.

'It's worth a try. If I can catch a *filhote* before we get up there,' he pointed ahead, 'then we're going straight home. No more paddling, no more sitting in the sun, no more rice with sand in it.' He shook his head and pulled a face. 'You and your damn bets.'

'You didn't have to come.' I spoke quietly, my words punctuated by the sound of the paddle easing us upstream. 'I *can* fish on my own, you know.' I loved that sound – the dipping of wood into water, the trickle and plunge as it furrowed through – and there wasn't another noise on the river to disturb it that day. Apart from Paulo's voice.

'It's not so good to be out on the river alone,' he grumbled. 'It's not safe.'

'Nice to know you care.'

He made a dismissive sound, like air escaping from a tyre. 'Everyone knows *filhote* is the hardest to catch. Why does it have to be *filhote*? You couldn't have bet on a *piranha* or *tucunaré*?'

'Wouldn't have been much of a bet then, would it?' I'd found my rhythm with the short oar now and I enjoyed the consistency of it, playing it like a comfortable beat in my head. 'Anyway,' I said, 'it's in the bag this time. Old Severino caught one up there last week.' Severino, they said, had killed seventeen men. Shot, stabbed, strangled, drowned. Whatever there was you could do to another human being, Severino had done it, but he was old now, his face like sun-dried tree bark, his muscles wasted. And if you looked into his eyes you saw nothing more than a tired old man who likes to talk and fish. 'Sixty kilos it was, and you should have seen the state of his hands. All cuts and blood, they were.'

Paulo looked down at the line he was holding between his forefinger and thumb. 'Maybe we should get rods,' he said.

44

'Save our fingers. How the hell would I work with broken hands?'

'When do you ever work?'

'I work. Just last week we painted Zeca's place.'

'That was three weeks ago, Paulo, and you don't need good fingers to paint. Anyway, you don't catch *filhote* with a rod. You need to feel him,' I said, really believing it. 'You catch him with a rod, it's an insult. A fish like that, you have to *feel* how he moves.'

'You're so full of shit.'

I beamed at him and took a pack of Carlton from my top pocket, lighting one as I watched Paulo throw out his line. I sat in silence while he fished, but he didn't catch anything, so I took up the paddle again and told him to do the same. We paddled together, and when we rounded the bend in the river, we headed inland.

Behind us, we heard the sound of an outboard motor breaking the tranquillity of the day, and we both stopped paddling. We turned to watch the boat skim past, a hundred metres away, heading further upriver.

'They've got the right idea,' said Paulo, his whole body moving as he turned to follow their course. 'Hired one of André's boats like we should have done.'

I used the paddle to turn our canoe, straining to see who was in the passing boat. 'We can't afford it,' I said.

By the time the wake from the outboard reached us, it had lost most of its energy, but it nudged the side of the dugout, rocking us from side to side.

'You see who that was?' I asked Paulo once the boat was little more than a shimmering speck in the distance, the sun glinting from its metallic hull as it skipped across the water leaving a frothing trail behind it. '*Americanos*, wasn't it? You seen them around?'

'Sure. Everyone's seen them around.'

'Last time I saw three of them,' I said. 'In the café. Today I see only two.'

Paulo wiped his brow on the sleeve of his shirt. 'So? What do you care how many *gringos* are in the boat?'

'You know where they're from? They're not tourists. Tourists would be gone by now. Those men, I keep seeing them. In fact, it seems like I'm seeing them more and more.'

'What's the matter?' Paulo shrugged. 'You worried you're not the only *gringo* round here any more?' He laughed. 'Hell, maybe they work here. Why not?'

'Where?' I said. 'Not for Da Silva.'

'Maybe that new place,' he said. 'Hevea. Some kind of plantation they're building up past the *fazenda*. I heard it's an American company. Makes sense they'd have Americans working there.'

'Yeah, maybe,' I said, starting to paddle again, turning the boat and heading to shore. I looked back at Paulo who was still watching the trail the boat had left in the water. 'Come on, Paulo, that oar looks fat. I think it needs to do some work.'

We left everything in the boat except for the cool box, which we placed at the edge of the water, where the sand was wet. Then we sat down and opened a beer. A few metres behind us the rainforest hummed, everything keeping still enough and quiet enough to preserve its own life. The cicadas were the only things that made a noise, their singing the only constant.

'You think about Eduardo much?' said Paulo.

He died in my room, by my bed. 'No,' I lied.

He considered that for a second and then asked, 'You talked to Ana about it?'

I nodded.

'And what she say?'

'That we should move past it. It wasn't our fault.'

'She's smart. A man like you doesn't deserve a woman like that.'

I tightened my lips and thought about how Ana had kissed them. 'Maybe.' I drank some beer and wiped the back of my fingers across my mouth.

'I think about it all the time. I try not to, but it's always there. That night in Manny's café, it's the only real work I've done in years.' Paulo still looking out at nothing, me not saying anything. I didn't need to tell him I knew how he felt.

'I was thinking about opening a health clinic.' He leaned back, his elbows wedged into the bright white sand behind him.

I turned to my friend. 'Why? What difference would it make?'

He shrugged his face, the eyebrows going up, lips tightening together. 'Been thinking about it for a while.'

'It won't make it go away.' I sighed. 'And what about money? You need money for a thing like that.'

'I can get money.'

'Yeah?' I stood up and went to the boat, wading into the water to lift out the fishing box, calling back to him, saying, 'Then maybe you could get some for me too.' I kept my flip-flops on because I didn't want to stand on anything poisonous. The *arraia* rays had a nasty habit of sitting in the shallows, their serrated spines and spiked tails waiting for you to stand on them. 'We're going to need more lines and hooks.' The shallow water was warm and it felt good against the skin on my calves.

When I was back beside Paulo, sitting in the sand, I opened my fishing box and removed some lines. I always noosed a few hooks before we went out.

'You could help,' said Paulo, sitting up. 'With the health clinic, I mean. We could do it together. You, me . . . Ana.'

'No thanks.' I fixed a couple of lines with lures in case I spotted *tucunaré* by the bank. 'Sounds too much like work. And you remember what happened to Father Jentel over in Santa

47

Teresinha. Shit, he tried to put up one building, the landowners bulldozed the whole town to teach him a lesson. It always ends in trouble. You try something like that, Da Silva will send people to burn it. And you'll be lucky if they don't burn you along with it.'

'It's different here.' Paulo picked up one of the lures, turning it over in his hand.

'No,' I said. 'Landowners are all the same. You didn't see the reaction when Da Silva saw that Eduardo was dead. She didn't care, Paulo. She didn't even know who he was. She just shrugged and offered me a drink.' I thought about the Da Silvas up in their ranch, watching over their people like gods. 'Took me by surprise, though. She wasn't what I expected.'

'Oh?'

'She's attractive, Paulo. Sexy.'

'Yeah? Sexy? In what way?'

'In just about every way, from what I could tell.'

Paulo put his hands out in front of his chest and showed me an enquiring look.

'Oh yes,' I said. 'She's definitely got those.'

Paulo went quiet, thinking about how Catarina Da Silva might look. 'She have long legs?' he asked after a while. 'I like long legs.'

'Long enough to reach the ground,' I told him. 'But it's not the same ground you and I walk on – at least I reckon that's what she thinks. She's way out of your league. Anyway, she might look good, Paulo, but that doesn't make her a good person. Like I said, she didn't care one bit about her worker.'

'Then we'll be the ones to care,' said Paulo, dismissing the unattainable from his mind. 'It'll be good for you. It'll be good for both of us.'

I shook my head and tied a line with a steel leader so the *piranhas* wouldn't bite through when I caught them for bait. 'Why should we be the ones to care?'

'If you're worried about the Da Silvas, we can go up there, tell them what we're going to do. That way there's no surprises.'

'I'm not interested.' I kept my eyes down and my hands busy, only looking up to sip the beer which was already starting to warm in the sun. I was thinking I should have come alone. 'Not in building a clinic. You want to do it, do it, but leave me out of it.'

'With a health clinic, a nurse, the right equipment, we might've saved Eduardo.' Talking more to himself now than to me. 'He might still be alive. Sandro, too.'

I tucked my knife into the waistband of my trousers and stood up. I dusted myself down and loaded everything back into the dugout. With my feet in the water, I turned to Paulo and said, 'You coming to catch some fish, then, or what?'

7

We stayed on the river until after midday but the deep water was quiet, and there was no sign of my fish. Once or twice I thought I had a bite but it was just debris snagging at the lines. If I tugged too hard and the hook caught tight, I cursed myself for having to cut the line, but I always expected to lose a few that way.

I'd hooked my fish once before, felt his weight on the end of my line. That's why I thought of him as mine. Like we had a connection. We were pitted against each other; him under the water, me on top. He'd pulled the nylon so hard it cut into the flesh across my fingers, taking it all the way down to the bone before it snapped and the fish was gone. I'd bought thicker line and my hands were harder now. Next time he wouldn't be so lucky. One of these days, I would bring the fish in. The *filhote*. I would bring him in and show him.

Filhote is just fry until he's around fifty kilos, and after that he's properly called *piraíba*, a Tupi-Guarani name that means 'the mother of all fish' – or 'evil fish', depending on who translates it. Out there, though, everybody just called him *filhote*, figuring it didn't matter what name you gave him. What mattered was the catching, not the naming.

As a catfish, you wouldn't expect him to come so close to the surface, but sometimes he likes to show himself. Maybe he comes to a sandbank that rises on the bed of the river, forcing

50

his bulk close to the surface, his shimmering grey skin coming slick and wet from the brown water, the sun reflected on his back. Or maybe he just likes to show the world how big he is. Either way, whatever it is that makes him come to the surface, one came on that day; the day that Paulo first mentioned the health clinic that would bring death into our friendship again.

The fish surfaced not far from us, silent except for the slight disturbance in the water, his shape almost the length of the canoe, and we paddled towards him and fished there for a while, right in the spot where we'd seen him. I baited my hook just how *filhote* likes it, and I dropped it into the water where he'd surfaced, but he'd either moved on or he wasn't biting that day.

I spoke my thoughts aloud. 'Maybe he's not hungry.'

'I am, though,' said Paulo.

'Huh?'

'Hungry.' He put the palm of one hand on his stomach. 'I'm hungry even if he isn't. It *is* nearly one.'

I looked at my watch but it had stopped at a little after eleven o' clock. I wound it up and stared across the river towards the bank where a small tributary cut away from the main channel. The sides were a couple of metres high, exposed roots protruding from the sheer face of cracked and dried mud. The jungle undergrowth was spilling over into the river, it was thick and dark, but the canoe would slip through with ease.

'We'll head over there,' I said, pointing. 'There's bound to be *tucunaré*.' It was an aggressive fish that loved the cool shade amongst the flooded timbers. He was good to eat, too.

We glided amongst the branches, ducking beneath the greenery and flicking the bugs from our shirts. Here the still waters were clearer and shallower and I could see fish just below the surface, their scales flashing in the shafts of light that cut through the foliage above. We stopped paddling, allowing the boat to settle, and then we used lures, throwing them out and whipping them back towards us. The first I caught was almost as big as my forearm and enough to feed both Paulo and me. He was a beautiful creature. Silvery-green on top, orangey-gold underneath, three black stripes like a tiger's dropping vertically from his back to his belly. On his tail fan, a false eye, bigger and lighter in colour than the ones which had allowed him to see my lure so clearly. He fought even when he was out of the water, jumping and flapping against the sodden wood in the bottom of the dugout, so I took my knife and pushed it through the top of his head with a wet crunch.

We stayed to catch a few more, then headed back to the beach where we'd left our gear. As we paddled, I looked down at the fish lying in the water at the bottom of the boat, staring up at the sky with dead orange eyes rolled back in their heads. It made me think of Eduardo.

When we reached the sandy bank, I retrieved the cool box from the shade of the forest. I opened a couple of beers and took out some plastic bags. I cleaned and bagged all but one of the fish while Paulo started a fire, the smoke coming over, stinging my eyes as I worked. By the time I'd filled the cool box with *tucunaré* for the *festa*, the fire was hot enough to cook. We boiled some rice in an old tin pot and barbecued over the wood once the flames had died down. The cooking flesh smelled better than it ever tasted, but it was still good and it filled our stomachs.

After we'd eaten, we drank beer and gazed out at the tip of São Tiago. The town looked small. Somewhere out on the river, the faint drone of an outboard drifted across the water and I wondered if it was the *Americanos* returning from their trip. I hoped they hadn't caught my fish.

'Why d'you stay?' asked Paulo.

'In São Tiago?' I shrugged and threw a handful of sand at the water. 'There's nowhere else to go.'

'You could take Ana,' he said. 'Go somewhere else and leave

all this right where it is.' He paused, waiting for me to speak, but I didn't. He lay back, his voice dropping like he was talking to himself. 'You don't need any of this.'

Out in the water a couple of *boto* surfaced and blew spray into the afternoon. Their backs arched, pinkish-grey against brown, as they took another breath and slipped back out of sight. The river dolphins were still common here, but they wouldn't last long if the mining continued upriver.

'It's what she wants, isn't it?' said Paulo. 'For you to be together. Properly, I mean.'

'Is it?'

'You mean you never asked her? Never told her how you feel?'

'It's not so easy.'

'Of course it is. You just say the words.'

Just say the words, I thought, like it was just words I should have said to Manolo when he asked for my forgiveness. Or like it was just words I should have said when they made me see what they had done in Roraima; made me listen to the screams that still haunted me. Paulo made it seem so easy, like words are just sounds that pass over our lips.

'*Mula sem cabeza*, that's what Manny called her. She doesn't need that, Paulo, she deserves better. She's worked hard to get away from that kind of life, I don't want to drag her back down.'

'No one else sees it like that. People are happy for you, Sam—'

'People make too many assumptions.'

'. . . and Manny's just sore because you wouldn't open his way to heaven. I can't think of anyone better suited than you and Ana. A lapsed priest and a lapsed pro—'

'Don't say that.'

Paulo gestured an apology. 'Anyway, what do you mean by too many assumptions?'

I shrugged. 'Some people see things that aren't there,' I said. 'Not yet anyway.'

'You're talking about you and Ana?'

I nodded, wanting to change the subject, but wanting to talk about it at the same time. My emotions for Ana were growing stronger, moving well beyond mere friendship. I had begun to think more and more about how it would feel to hold her, to have her warmth against me, but something always held me back. A lapsed priest and a lapsed prostitute, just as Paulo said. I had issues with my former profession, traces of certain beliefs and indoctrinations which still tainted my blood and clouded my vision. And similarly I was afraid that Ana would think I spent time with her for only one reason: lust. All over the world holy men had a reputation for their lack of adherence to the bonds of chastity, and this place was no exception. As Manolo had already illustrated, the notion of a priest's infidelity with a woman was a common one. There was even a myth to warn of the dangers of such union. But *Ana* had kissed *me*. And when I thought about the way she had kissed me, these things ceased to mean so much. The man had enjoyed it and, even though the priest tried to poison it with guilt, something turned over inside me like I was a young man, falling in love for the first time.

'Anyway,' I said. 'After what I did to Manolo . . .'

'Anyone would have done the same.'

'Maybe,' I said, thinking about that kiss again, and how Ana had looked into me, reached inside. 'But I don't feel bad that I hurt him.'

'Nothing wrong with that.'

I smiled at my friend. 'You're right. Bastard deserved it.' I made a fist and looked at my knuckles. It had felt good to hit Manny, make him suffer a little for what he'd done. Talking about it, though, I wondered if Manolo ever thought about the life he had taken. I imagined him trying to sleep, haunted by what he had done, but I knew it wasn't so. Manolo would sleep as he had always slept. A place like São Tiago did not breed men with heavy consciences.

8

We watched the sky darken, then we finished our beers and packed up, going back onto the river when the sun had dropped in the sky. We let the current take us back towards São Tiago where people were starting to gather on the *praia*. As we grew closer I could hear the steady beat of samba; a pleasant, familiar rhythm, each song always sounding the same to me.

I could see Manolo but I was too far away to see the bruises on his face. He was setting up a bar behind the two long tables which he brought over every year when the beaches came. There was a small lean-to with a few rough poles and a shaded roof made from woven dried leaves. He'd arranged a couple of plastic tables with parasols and was lining up cooler boxes which were filled with beer and lime juice. A group of four or five people was close to the water's edge, drinking *cachaça* straight from the bottle. One of them was Papagaio; tall and sinewy with shining black skin. He stood up and walked into the water until it covered his ankles and darkened the bottom of his tight blue trousers. He was wearing one of his best shirts, the kind a businessman might wear. It was open at the chest, collar spread wide, and his beaten straw hat was pulled down over his afro. In one hand he was holding a guitar by its neck. He raised his arms, dangling the guitar, and waved to us, so I steered the boat towards him.

When we reached him, Papagaio pulled the boat onto the

sand and held out his hand to help me up. I stepped into the water and he put his arm around me as we walked a few steps onto the beach.

'Sam, Sam, Sam,' he said. 'No *filhote*, Sam. No *filhote* in the boat. No *filhote* for the *festa*. Looks like you're better with your fists than you are at fishing. What were you doing out there, amigo? Playing with each other? Teaching each other a few new tricks?' Papagaio spoke quickly, even more so when he was drunk, and sometimes it was hard to shut him up. 'You lose the bet again. Shit, Sam, you *always* lose the bet.'

'Since when did you play the guitar?' I said. 'You can't even whistle in tune.'

'And *you* can't catch *filhote* from the look of it, so don't pretend you forgot our bet. You go out there saying this is the day, this time you'll come back with something to make me cry, but then you come back with what, hmm? Nothing. *Nada*. Only thing you do that makes me want to cry is when you load bodies into the back of my car. Driving up to Da Silva's place in my little Beetle with—'

'There's *tucunaré*,' I said, not wanting to think about Eduardo. It was all still too clear to me. It had reopened too many doors.

Papagaio stretched out his arms and raised his face to the sky. 'Ah, there's *tucunaré*, he says, as if it's the same thing.' He put his arm around my shoulder again and lowered his voice. 'Well, *tucunaré* is good, Sam, it's very good, but it's not *filhote*, is it? Our bet was for *filhote*.'

Papagaio was one of my two best friends; the warmest cold-blooded killer I knew. We called him Papagaio because it meant 'parrot' and he talked so much. Also because no one knew his real name. He was a true native, a fusion of Karajá Indian and Afro-Brasilian. His mother was descended from African slaves, and his father had walked out of the jungle when he was fourte, returning when he was eighteen because he couldn't bear to live without the trees. Working as an electrician in Goiânia, Papagaio decided he wanted to discover himself, so he came to São Tiago to learn more about the Karajá who lived on Bananal Island. His mother died young and the city held no grip on him with its racism and its exclusion, so he wanted to find his roots. But the way his father's people lived didn't suit either, so he looked for work with the *fazendeiros*. For local landowners Marco and Catarina Da Silva, Papagaio had kept the labourers in order, and he had no problem talking about the things he'd done. He had killed more men than he could count on his fingers and toes, and I often asked myself how it was I could have such a friend after the things I'd seen in Roraima. But I knew Papagaio before I knew of his past, and you can't tell a killer from the look in his eyes or the expression on his face. You can't tell by the way he talks or the way he moves. A man like Papagaio carries his darkness locked in his head and his heart, and he only brings it out when he needs it.

I have no idea where my friend learned his skills as a *pistoleiro*, perhaps it was natural talent, but when I asked him why he didn't work for Da Silva any more, he just said he'd had enough. So, one day when he was ordered to shoot a man who couldn't work, he refused to take out his gun. He shook his head when he told me, saying if they'd asked him to do it the day before, he would have shot the man dead and gone for his lunch. He couldn't explain the change, it's just how it was. The others were prepared to do it, though, so they drew their sticks and machetes, and they went to work while Papagaio walked away.

'We *nearly* caught a fish, didn't we, Paulo?' I said loudly, handing Papagaio a few notes to cover our bet. It was all I had left from the last catch I had sold to César.

Papagaio pocketed the money, quiet while he processed the joke, and then his face lit up. 'You mean he snagged again?'

said Papagaio, more proud he understood the joke than anything else.

I nodded. 'He snagged again. Lost at least six hooks,' and Papagaio laughed loudly, taking his arm from around me and bending double. A healthy sound, contagious and friendly, not what you'd expect from a man who used to make his living killing other men. When he put his free hand on his knee to support himself, the sinews tightened and twitched in his forearm. 'Ah, Paulo, we'll make a fisherman of you yet.' He straightened up, dropped the guitar and moved to help Paulo.

'I'm a doctor.' Paulo heaved himself from the boat and lifted the cool box onto the sand. 'Not a fisherman.'

'Then you're in the wrong place,' said Papagaio. 'Come on then, *doctor*, come and drink some *pinga* with us.'

By nine o' clock most of São Tiago was on the beach and by ten o'clock *every*body was. There was even a group from the *fazenda*, drifters and regulars, playing cards and drinking *pinga* at a table near the bar.

Ana was there, sitting with some of the women by the spot where the canoes brought them over from São Tiago. Close to them, a group of young men was swimming in the murky waters, not caring about the dangers beneath.

'Come on, Sam, let everyone see you together. You know what it's like here; anything goes. They talk for a while and then they forget. People wouldn't care if you fell in love with a horse.'

'Who said anything about love?'

Paulo laughed and we went over to Ana, Papagaio coming with us, immediately smiling at the other women, taking one of them away to join the dancers. I watched him go, admiring his lack of restraint, then I turned to Ana who kissed my mouth and handed me a beer. 'You smell of fish,' she said. 'I'm beginning to think I'll never get used to it.'

'Is it bad?' I said.

'No.' She kissed me again, parting her lips a little, not caring who was watching. 'Not really. Not that bad.' She took her mouth away from mine before I needed to decide whether or not to return the kiss. I could taste her on me and it made my heart beat a little faster when I thought how it might be to take her home, across the river right now, and close the door behind us.

Paulo put a hand on my shoulder and spoke into my ear. 'See,' he said. 'Look around you. No one is interested.'

There were a few faces at the party I'd never seen before so I guessed they must have been workers from the new plantation over at Hevea. Even the *chefe*, a *gringo*, had come to the party. Someone said he was English not American, but, either way, he didn't look like he belonged. He was the new guy at the party, the only one who wasn't drunk yet. His shirt was too clean, his trousers too new, and maybe he still had his foreign inhibitions, but it didn't make any difference, nobody mattered much. Everybody was welcome, and it wouldn't be long before he was sucked into the way of life just like everybody else.

His was not the only pale face at the party, though. There were three others, two of whom I had seen earlier that day on the river. They were the men who had been sighted regularly in São Tiago these past weeks. But these *Americanos*, as I called them, were not like the *gringo*; these men had something very different in their eyes and about their manner. An untamed edge that made them more at home in a town like ours. The *Americanos* looked as if they belonged in a place like São Tiago.

They were with the *gringo*, that much was clear, but they did not seem to spend much time talking with him. Instead, they stayed together, sitting apart from everyone else, drinking Coke straight from the can. They watched the crowd but did not speak to anyone; hardly even spoke to each other. I watched them for a while, seeing how their eyes kept flicking back to the *gringo*, wondering how they would react if I approached them. After a while, though, I grew bored watching them sip their Coke and sit, motionless, so I moved on, dismissed them from my mind. I assumed they were there to protect the *gringo*, and it made sense to me that an ordinary man, coming to a place like this, would want someone extraordinary to watch his back.

When the sun was gone, they lit the bar with half a dozen storm lamps, and someone turned the music up as far as it would go to cover the hiss of the gas bottles. The old player was clunky and tinny and the tapes were stretched but the beat played just fine. The women danced alone if they had to, but one or two of the men could samba well enough, their bare feet scuffing in the white sand. After some persuasion and a few more beers, even I danced for a while with Ana, remembering the few steps I had learned. Our hips pressed firmly together, her thigh between mine, I held her around the waist, my hands feeling the curve of her body through the soft cotton dress. And as we found our rhythm, she buried her face into my shoulder, her smooth skin against mine, rough and unshaven, and she repeatedly kissed my neck as we danced. I enjoyed the way we moved together and I danced for longer than I had ever been inclined to before, but eventually I grew tired and broke away, leaving Ana to continue alone as I watched.

Later, I spent time talking with Papagaio, listening to the same old jokes. I bore the jibes about not catching the fish, about transporting bodies in his car, but after a few more beers and a strong caipirinha I didn't take any notice. It wouldn't be long before he'd be too drunk to make jokes, so I ignored him and watched the dancers.

My eyes followed the women moving to the music, uninhibited and lithe, even the fat ones twisting like snakes in the white glow from the lamps. I spotted Alicia amongst the agitation of supple dark limbs and it made me think of the night she had come to wake me. She was wearing the same dress and she was beautiful the way the thin cotton clung to her skin. Like Ana would have looked when she was younger. She glanced over in my direction and our eyes met for a second before she disappeared amongst the other dancers, enjoying the shameless pleasure of the music.

To one side, I could see Paulo sitting on a plastic-wound chair, drinking beer with the *gringo*. I wondered what they were talking about. They were serious, deep in conversation, but I guessed Paulo would tell me about it later, so I took some meat from the barbecue and went to the water to eat it in peace. I was nearly finished when I heard a collection of voices rise above the general noise of the party, and I caught a glimpse of frenzied movement from the corner of my eye.

Further up the beach, close to where the half-barrel barbecues were now dying, a group of men was crowded in a circle like schoolboys, shouting and encouraging two fighters who were struggling together in the sand. I stood, throwing away what was left of the meat, and began walking towards them as the huddle broke and one of the fighters staggered from among them, holding a hand to his face. I knew who he was. A *vaqueiro* and sometime *pistoleiro* from the *fazenda*, he didn't often come into town, but I had seen him once or twice before on the beach. Papagaio had pointed him out to me because he used to work with him, the two of them never seeing eye to eye. When I asked why, Papagaio simply pinched the black skin of his forearm and raised his eyebrows at me. A black mother and an indigenous father. The colour differences could be subtle, and racism in Brasil was largely unspoken, but it was everywhere. A prejudiced man like João wouldn't have wanted a *negro* counterpart who held a lower position on the colour chart. Anyway, he said, João had a rotten heart. He took pleasure from killing, while Papagaio saw it only as a job and a part of life. My friend told me that João liked to mutilate his victims. He liked to cut out their tongues, remove their eyes and their ears; he liked to use his blade before he would ever waste a bullet.

It didn't surprise me to see that the man who followed him from the circle of agitators was my good friend Papagaio, but it did encourage me to quicken my pace. I understood how far a fight between two such men could go.

Before I reached them, Papagaio feinted to one side and hooked a quick fist to João's jaw, dropping him onto the sand. Even from where I was, I could hear the sound of bone and flesh meeting. The gathering of men voiced their approval of Papagaio's direct hit, but as he stepped back and raised his hands in a defensive gesture, waiting for João to come back at him, I called to him to stop.

'Enough,' I said, coming to a standstill just a couple of metres from the men. My breathing was heavy but my voice was loud enough to make them all stop and turn in my direction. Papagaio looked over at me and grinned, but his grin quickly faded when João took my interruption as an opportunity to spring to his feet. He was not a big man, but he was fit and strong. Men like him spent their days wrestling cattle to the ground. Before I could shout a warning, João had whipped a knife from beneath his loose shirt and lashed out at Papagaio. My friend leaned away to avoid the blade, but the honed edge caught him across the knuckles of his left hand. Papagaio jerked backwards, closing his other hand across the knuckles, and in the semi-darkness I saw black blood seeping between his fingers, dripping in dark patches onto the white sand.

He quickly regained his balance and became still, looking up at João, the two of them keeping their distance, and I saw nothing in my friend's eyes. No laughter, no anger, no pity, and I knew what he had in his mind.

'No, Papagaio. Enough.' I stepped forward as he tugged his revolver from his waistband and pointed it at João's heart.

'You want *this* kind of disagreement?' Papagaio said to João, his voice measured and calm. 'Fists not enough for you? You want lead and steel?'

'Papagaio, put it away,' I said.

'And him?' asked Papagaio, blood still dripping from his left hand. 'What would you have him do?'

'The same.' I looked at João. 'This is no place for it. You're drunk. Both of you. You don't want to do this.' I took another step forward, almost coming between the men, but keeping out of Papagaio's line of fire. If the gun went off, I didn't want to be the one to stop the bullet. 'You,' I said. 'Put the knife away.'

João considered my words for a moment or two, then he pursed his lips and reluctantly hid the knife away beneath his shirt. He knew he had been lucky. If I had not been there, Papagaio would have shot him without another thought. If I had not come, João's lifeblood would be draining into the sand.

'Saved by the priest,' said João, trying to salvage his pride. 'Saved by the hand of God.'

'I think it was you who was saved,' said Papagaio, taunting João by waving the *pistola* at him. 'I have a different God.'

'Give that to me,' I said, putting my hand on the revolver and taking it from him. 'You don't need it tonight.'

'Maybe next time I'll bring one of my own.' João's words were slurred, the alcohol from the *pinga* replacing the surge of adrenalin that would have been raging through him a few moments ago. 'Maybe I'll come down here with some of my friends.' He looked around, seeing all the faces watching him, people laughing. 'You won't be smiling when I cut off your lips,' he shouted.

I shook my head and watched him turn and walk away from us. As he passed one of the barbecues, he kicked out at it, knocking it sideways with a metallic crash, spilling hot coals across the sand. Men scattered in all directions to avoid the flying embers, most of them swearing at João's back before they returned to whatever business had been disturbed by the excitement of the brawl.

I stayed where I was, watching João skulk away, seeing the *gringo* near the bar, the *Americanos* on their feet, all of them watching João with acute intent, each of them with one hand under their shirt. The *gringo* himself looked bemused by the entire incident, unaware of the protective arc that was now dissolving just out of view, the men already stepping away to become just drinkers on the beach as the threat dissipated.

I waited until João took one of the canoes and headed over to the mainland. Then I turned back to Papagaio and hefted his pistol in my hand. 'I'll keep this for now,' I said, feeling more like a schoolmaster confiscating a toy than a priest who had stopped two men from killing each other. 'You can have it back tomorrow. Come on, let's find Paulo, get your hand looked at.'

'I'm right here.' Paulo came alongside me and reached out to take Papagaio's hand. He lifted it and turned it to one side. 'Can't see anything,' he said. 'Too much blood.'

Papagaio pulled his hand away. He lifted the hem of his shirt, bit into one edge to rip it, then tore off a long strip of fabric. He wiped the blood from his knuckles then offered his hand back to Paulo.

'Very sanitary,' he said, taking another look.

For a moment I thought I saw the white of the bone beneath Papagaio's gaping skin.

'It'll need stitching,' Paulo told him.

'Forget it.' Papagaio held the fabric tight in his fist and wound it around his knuckles as a makeshift bandage.

'Let me do it for you,' said Paulo. 'You don't stitch it, it won't stop bleeding.'

'I've had worse.' Papagaio dismissed us with his good hand and made his way back to the bar, leaving Paulo and me alone.

'You know what that was about?' asked Paulo as we watched him go.

'No.'

'And you stepped between them? Guns and knives?'

'Sure.'

'You want to get killed?'

'No one died,' I said and began walking back towards the water.

'And what about him?' Paulo looked back in João's direction. 'You think he'll be back?'

'Don't worry about him. He'll cool off.'

Paulo followed me. 'What am I going to do with you people,' he said. 'Him not wanting treatment, you trying to get yourself killed.'

'I was trying to *stop* people from getting killed,' I said, sticking Papagaio's revolver into my trousers but not liking the feel of it. I took it back out again and handed it to Paulo. 'Here,' I said. 'You look after it. Give it to him later when he comes to have his hand stitched.'

'You think he'll come?'

'He's tough,' I said, 'but he's not stupid. He wanted people to see that. He'll come later when they're looking the other way and the bleeding won't stop.'

'He'll need antibiotics.'

'Then give him some.'

'I don't have much. And what I've got is old and out of date.'

I went to the edge of the water and picked up the beer I had been drinking when the fight started. It was warmer now, but still cold enough to drink. I looked out at the river.

'If I had a clinic, he could go there.' Paulo studied the sand, pushing his toes into it. 'Have you thought any more about that? About the clinic?' He looked up.

'No.'

'You mean no you don't want to help, or no you haven't thought about it?'

'Both.' I drank from my bottle and turned to him. 'There's

no point, Paulo.' I turned and held my arms out towards the crowd and the fires. 'Barbecue; drinking; music. The odd fight. What are you trying to save them from? Looks to me like they're having a good time. What do they want with God and health? They only need us when they *need* us. What you do now is enough.'

'I'm not trying to save them from anything, I'm trying to make life easi—'

'They don't want us to save them. They don't want us to make a difference. It's not why they're here.' I turned away and lowered my voice. 'They want to be left alone to forget whatever it is they've done.' A *boto* flicked its tail from the water and its dorsal fin arched around and then disappeared.

'You're talking about yourself,' said Paulo. 'Not these people. It's *you* who wants to forget. Whatever it was that happened in Roraima—'

'Stop.'

Paulo was silent for a while. No awkward shifting, no hesitating, just silence. We had both known terrible things.

Eventually he spoke, saying, 'Today, on the river, I said you should talk to Ana. I'm saying it again, Sam. Talk to her.' He paused and scooped a handful of sand, letting it run through his fingers. 'She loves you. You know what that's worth?'

My eyes went to our canoe which was still pulled up on the beach, my fishing gear inside. 'I'm going to catch the fish,' I said. 'The *filhote*.'

'Now?'

'Now.'

'But what about Ana?'

I threw my bottle onto the sand and began walking towards the boat.

'Don't be crazy,' Paulo called after me. 'You know better than to go on the river at night.'

I reached the canoe and waded into the water to push it away from the shore.

'You're drunk!' shouted Paulo.

Once the boat was away from the sand, I grabbed a paddle and climbed in. Paulo realised then I was serious and I heard his footsteps squeaking in the sand as he jogged towards me. I was already too far out, though, and he stopped at the edge of the water. 'Sam! Don't be crazy,' he called again, and I saw a few heads turn in our direction. Ana came over to stand beside him. She spoke to Paulo, then cupped her hands to her mouth and shouted something but I couldn't hear, she was too far away and the music was too loud.

They stood on the shore and I watched them until they were just shadows against the lights on the *praia*. Then I turned my head and kept paddling out towards the bend in the river. I took the canoe past the central current and into the darkness, instinctively knowing the feel of the water. When I was near the forest on the other side, I headed straight up, slipping past the reservation on my left. The sound of the water was soothing and the rhythm of my paddling settled to match the faint samba beat I could hear from the *praia*.

Eventually even the music faded and I was truly alone.

9

As the canoe slipped through the flat water, my eyes became accustomed to the night. Above me the sky was clear, not a cloud to hide the stars, and the moon was strong enough to give me a little light. When the *boto* surfaced near by, I stopped paddling and banged the oar against the side of the boat to scare them away. I didn't want one to surface underneath me and tip me into the river.

I'd been moving for some time when I rounded the bend and steered towards the bank, coming out of the current. I pulled a heavy line from the fishing box, baited the hook and stood up to cast it, hearing the lead weight sail out into the darkness and plop into the water. I sat back, holding the line lightly in my hand so I would feel even the slightest touch, and I allowed my mind to crawl over the last few weeks.

Things were changing; I could sense it all around me. There was an atmosphere in São Tiago that I didn't recognise and I wondered whether it was me alone who felt it. I couldn't deny the impression that something new had begun when Eduardo died. Paulo was already looking within himself, putting into words a notion which must have been growing in his mind long before the events in Manny's café. The clinic that was now taking form in his imagination was reshaping my friend, giving him a purpose, making him a stronger man.

And then there was Ana and that kiss. Those *kisses*. The

dancing. Our bodies tight together. It had been many years since I had experienced anything like it, and it brought memories of the pleasures of a young man in another world. When I took my vows, I put such things behind me, but my life had twisted in innumerable ways, distorting itself from the route I had planned. And since meeting Ana, I had wondered for a long time how it would feel to rekindle those emotions. Even now, I imagined I could taste her on my lips, and I knew that it was time for us to follow our relationship along its inevitable and most natural path.

Yet, seeing these changes beginning around me, and believing I knew what they were, I still wasn't convinced that I understood my place among them. I didn't want Paulo to become a different man. I wanted him to be the friend he had always been. And the thought of being something more to Ana than just a friend filled me with fear as much as it did with excitement and expectation.

I fished for a while but I didn't catch the *filhote*, so I put the boat to shore where I'd been with Paulo that afternoon, and I made a pillow with the sand. For a while I lay on my awkward bed, keeping my mind blank, watching São Tiago in the distance. I saw the electric lights wink out when the generator shut down, and I stared at the glow from the gas lights at the party, and the fires from the barbecues. Then I closed my eyes and lay curled in the dark, listening to the slap of the water.

The *boto*'s breathing was loud as they swam downriver, and at some time during the night I heard a turtle drag herself onto the beach close to me. She shuffled and scraped as she dug into the sand to lay her eggs but I stayed quiet and left her to her business.

The night was cold, and I lay unsettled in the darkness, somewhere in the place between sleep and waking. I was dreaming about Eduardo. Reaching him too late, finding him there in the heat of my room, seeing Paulo lifting his hand and letting it drop, hearing the dead knuckles rap on the bare concrete floor. And then the heat intensified, the air around my body sparking and spitting into life as fire began to take hold of everything about me. The flames dissolving the walls to show me the burning forest, but blurring my vision behind boiling tears, allowing me only a glimpse of the shadowy figures running in the smoke and the haze. Sounds were muffled, but I could feel them in my skin, my bones, my teeth. Immune to the fire, I looked down at Eduardo, but he wasn't Eduardo any more, he was a child now, his body almost unrecognisable, his face nothing more than charcoal, his fingers curled into tiny, brittle fists, and I caught sight of what else I was holding in my hand.

I shook my head to chase the dream away, but it kept coming back, like a tune that invades every part of your mind and refuses to let go. So I opened my eyes and stared at the stars above me, trying to clear my mind, to think only of the river and the fish, but Eduardo's face kept coming to me in the darkness. My link to his death had broken a seal on the things I had tried to contain, and with those horrors now disinterred, my mind slipped back to Roraima, to the days I had spent with Father Machado, to the cruelty he had tried to stop. For so long, when I remembered those things, I saw memories played out in my mind as if they belonged to another man, but now I felt every emotion again, smelled the burning and the blood as if it had happened yesterday.

I wondered what Father Machado would say if he could see me now; if he could look down and see into my heart. But I knew he could not.

There is no looking down. The dead are dead.

10

As soon as the sun came up, I stripped off and washed myself in the warm river, wading out in just my flip-flops until the water was at my waist. Back in Roraima, Father Machado once told me that if you take a pee in the water, there's a chance a *candiru* might be attracted by it and swim up inside you, so I held my bladder until I was out. I didn't know for sure if what he said was true, but the thought of having a tiny fish deploying its spikes into my urinary tract and drinking my blood wasn't something I wanted to leave to chance. He'd said that while it was possible to remove, the traditional folk methods were almost worse than just leaving it there. The blockage would probably kill you eventually, so the most effective way to get rid of it, other than amputation, was to force a mixture of juices from the *Xagua* plant and *Buitach* apple into the invaded area. Doing that would kill and dissolve it, but it wouldn't be pretty, and you know there's going to be a trade-off when you squeeze flesh-dissolving substances inside yourself. Father Machado said he'd only seen it happen once, and that the woman in question eventually died from infection. It was the kind of story that stays with you once you've heard it, and ever since I'd learned about that particular soldier of the river, I kept my bladder locked tighter than a constrictor's coils when I ventured into the water.

Clean, awake, and free from parasites, I went to the edge of the forest and relieved myself by the trees, watching the butterflies as they gathered around the damp patch. They came from all directions, a delicate cluster of green and orange and blue, to settle on my urine, and probe it for minerals. Out here, nothing was wasted.

Pulling on my shirt and trousers, I noticed a banana plant growing amongst the foliage so I cut a hand from it and put it in the boat before heading out in the canoe to catch some fish. I caught plenty, but not the *filhote*.

As the morning wore on, eight, maybe nine o' clock, I allowed the current to take me back towards town and when I came closer, I saw a figure sitting out on the *praia* which lay between me and São Tiago. I thought it must be someone left over from the party, too drunk to make the short journey home across the channel, but as the canoe neared the bank I realised it was Paulo. He was sitting with his knees pulled up towards his chest and his arms wrapped around his legs. When I was a few metres away, he stood up to watch me land.

'You're crazy, you know that?' he said as I came closer to the beach. 'Going out like that.'

I think he was too hungover to be any more than just a little angry. His hair was messed up and there was sand pressed against one reddened cheek. There were even grains in his moustache. His eyes were bloodshot and he was still wearing the same clothes he'd worn for the *festa* last night.

'You been here all night?' I asked, staying in the canoe but reaching over the side to steady myself with the paddle.

'Course not. Why the hell would I be here all night?'

I let it pass. 'Come on, let's eat,' I said. 'Get in.'

We paddled together, crossing the short stretch of river in just a couple of minutes, landing the canoe at São Tiago. We collected our gear and climbed the bank behind Manolo's café. The chairs were upturned on the tables and the awning was tied back.

'You could've got lost out there in the dark,' said Paulo as we crossed the road and made our way towards my place. 'I was worried.'

I watched my feet treading the red dust. 'I know that part of the river too well.'

'Well you could've turned the boat and drowned then.'

'I can swim.'

'In the dark? Drunk? With the *jacaré* and the *piranha*?'

'Sure. I wasn't that drunk.'

Paulo stopped and took my arm. 'Do you care about anything, Sam? Do you care about *any*thing?'

I pulled away from him and continued to walk.

'Sam.' Paulo stayed where he was but I kept walking. 'I want you to tell me,' he called after me. 'Do you care about anything?'

'No . . . Yes . . . Probably.'

'So why did you hit Manolo? If you don't care, why did you do that? And how about Ana? Don't you care about her?'

I stopped and turned to my friend.

'So there *is* something.' He appeared relieved. 'She was worried, you know. You should go see her.'

'I will,' I said, rolling my eyes. 'Come on. Let's eat.'

11

I dumped my things and rinsed the fish in the sink before laying them in the fridge. Some I'd keep, but the rest I'd sell for beer money.

We pulled my dented, unplaned wooden table to the open door so we could watch the street while we had breakfast. There were beans and *farinha* which we ate cold because we were too hungry to wait, and after that we had the bananas I'd brought back from the reservation. *Nanicas*, they were, short and sweet with a thin, yellow-green skin. Soft and scented, Ana would have mashed them with oatmeal and honey, but I had neither of those things, so we ate them as they were. I had two while I made a flask of *cafezinho*, the smell of the strong coffee filling my room. When my stomach was full, I poured two small glasses from the flask and gave one to my friend. Then I sat back, sipped my drink and lit a cigarette.

'Don't you ever get bored?' asked Paulo.

'I never really thought about it.' I touched my fingers to the hot glass.

'Don't lie.'

I blew across the top of my coffee and sipped it. It was strong and sweet, the caffeine mingling with the nicotine.

'You need something else,' he went on.

I dragged on my cigarette and leaned forward so my

sun-darkened forearms were resting on the table. 'A *proper* drink, you mean?'

'No, I meant . . .'

'I know what you meant.'

He narrowed his eyes at me.

'And I also know where you're going with this,' I said. 'You're talking about your clinic again.'

He put his cup down. 'It's a good idea, Sam.'

'You're wrong about me, Paulo. I don't want anything else. I don't need change. I'm happy as I am.'

Paulo gave me one of his looks; the kind that says he knows better than I do. 'Want and need are different things,' he said. 'You *need* some responsibility.'

I watched my friend's face and sighed. 'Look,' I said. 'If you need this clinic then go for it. It's a good idea.'

'You'll help?' he looked hopeful.

'Uh-uh.' I shook my head and sat back.

Paulo sipped his coffee, the small glass out of place in his big hands. He tipped it right back, draining it. 'With a clinic, we could've done so much more.'

I glanced over at the fridge and saw Eduardo lying in front of it, his eyes dry and dead. His body was gone now, probably hidden under the warm soil between the town and the airstrip, but his memory was still lying on my grey concrete floor like it was lying across my conscience and refusing to move. 'That's low, Paulo. Too low even for you.' I ran a hand across my face, feeling the sharpness of the beard that was pushing through. I needed to buy a razor from Zeca's but it could wait. I'd have to sell the fish first. 'Don't make this about Eduardo,' I said.

'But that's exactly what it's about, Sam.'

'I don't want to hear it.'

'You telling me it doesn't bother you? It doesn't bother you he died right here?' He pointed to the spot where we had found him. 'Right here, for Christ's sake. In your room.'

I held up a hand and closed my eyes. 'I told you, Paulo, I don't want to hear it.'

He backed off a little, he could see he'd taken the wrong approach, so he sighed and changed tack, saying, 'I was talking to Senhor Swan last night.'

'The *gringo* at the party? The one with the bodyguards?'

'They're not bodyguards, they just work for him. You know how things can get round here.'

'Sure, Paulo, whatever you say.'

'He's a good man, Sam, you should meet him. He's English; one of your countrymen. Ana liked him, too.'

I shrugged and flicked my cigarette out into the street. 'I've met enough of my countrymen. I don't need to meet another one.'

'Well, he wants to meet *you*.'

'Why would he want to do that?'

'Because I told him he should meet you. He saw you break up the fight with Papagaio last night and asked about you.'

'What did you tell him?'

'That you're a good man. That you're English. That you're a priest.'

'Well, one of those things is right, at least.' I smiled and refilled my coffee from the flask.

Outside, Manolo was standing on one of his tables, untying the awning over his café. I hoped his bruises were still hurting and that they kept him from a good night's sleep. When the awning unfurled it nearly knocked him down, just like every other morning. And, just like every other morning, I was disappointed it didn't.

'You were right about Papagaio,' said Paulo. 'I stitched his hand for him. God knows how it looks, though, I was as drunk as he was.'

Reginaldo, the guard from the bank, strolled past raising his eyebrows in greeting while tucking his fingers under his belt and hitching his trousers up over his belly. They immediately sagged again as the weight of his old gun dragged them down. A battered Ford pickup that may have once been white rolled past in a low gear as if it were already weary of the sun.

'Another day begins,' I said.

'Yeah, and I want to make this one count.' Paulo stood up and pushed back his chair. It scraped on the floor and the sound jarred inside me. 'I have to go,' he said. 'I'll see you later.'

'You have to go?' I looked up at him. 'Go where? When did you ever have to go somewhere?'

'Things are changing, Sam. *We're* changing.' Paulo went to the door and stepped out. 'And I want you to play a part.' He turned and held his hand over his brow to shade his eyes from the sunlight. It looked like a mock salute. 'At least think about what I said, eh?'

'Where you going?'

'What do you care?' he said and walked away.

I thought about following him but my muscles were aching from sleeping in the sand and my skin was itching from the insect bites. My chair was hard, but it was the most comfortable place to be so I lifted my bare feet onto the table and balanced my heels on the edge. They were tired feet, as if they belonged to someone older. Like my fingers, they were callused beyond their years, hardened to their manual life.

A few moments later, as I was closing my eyes, I heard shuffling noises outside my door and I wondered if Paulo had come back. Maybe he'd been joking about having to go somewhere and we'd spend the day playing cards and fishing. But it wasn't Paulo, it was a dog. A scruffy old mutt with scars on his muzzle and a limp in his leg. The true colour of his coat was hidden beneath a heavy layer of red dust and grime. His dirty face appeared from one side of the door frame and he peered in. Then he climbed up onto the step with his front paws and sniffed the air before wandering in. He collapsed beside me as if his legs had given way, so I ruffled the top of his head, unsettling the dust from his wiry hair. He smelled of rotting food but I didn't mind.

'Hey, dog. What're *your* plans for the day? Any ladies lined up?'

He blinked his crusty eyes, licked his lips once, and laid his chin on the concrete.

'Yeah, that's pretty much what I thought.'

I gave him a bowl of *cafezinho* to liven him up, he looked like he needed it, and we spent part of the morning together watching São Tiago from my table. For a while I dozed and then I read a book. I'd already read it more times than I could remember. I went out to sell my fish to César, then I had a cold beer, closed the door, and slept. The day was too hot for anything else.

In my sleep, flames danced in my head. Orange and black, flickering behind my eyelids, imprinted onto the soft tissue which tried to protect my eyes from such horrors. In my ears, women screamed my name while their children burned, and the smell of their smoking remains, bone and flesh and enamel, was so cloying and vivid that it caught in my throat, making me cough and waking me with a start.

I immediately sensed that the door was open and I was not alone.

'You sleep like a pig,' one of the men said, before I could even focus my eyes. 'Bad dreams?'

I swung my legs over the side of the bed and rubbed my face with both hands. When I took my fingertips from my eyes, I was looking directly at João.

'You live like a pig, too,' he said, dropping a cigarette onto the floor and crushing it with his foot. 'This coffee is cold.' He glanced at the small glass standing half full on the table-top. Beside it, my knife, still in its sheath. Beside that, a heavy-looking revolver, dull steel, bigger than the one I had taken from Papagaio the night before.

'What do you want, João?' I asked, standing up. My twenty-two was under the bed, but there was no point going for it. He could shoot me ten times over before I could ever reach it. 'I see you already have coffee.'

João was sitting at my table with his dirty feet stretched out in front of him. His lip was fat, filled with blood, and his right eye was bruised. He was wearing a red cap with the Hollywood cigarette logo on the front, his curly hair bulging around the sides. His T-shirt was stained and I could smell the cattle on him from where I stood. I wondered how he could make any comment on the way I lived.

The man beside him was younger, fairer-skinned, sitting upright with his arms crossed and his lips pursed. His wide eyes shifted from side to side, unlike João's hard, lazy stare. I guessed he was new to the business of sneaking into priests' homes and intimidating them.

João picked up the revolver and pointed it at me. He closed one eye and sighted down the barrel before smiling and turning the gun sideways so that he could inspect it. 'Not bad, eh?' he said, running his other hand along the barrel. 'Forty-five. The shells are expensive, but it makes a big hole.'

'What do you want?' I pretended to be unafraid, taking a glass for myself and pumping some coffee from the flask.

'It's new,' he said. 'Well, not new, but it's new for me. Took it off someone just the other day.'

No doubt the original owner was lying dead somewhere. More food for the wildlife. 'What do you want?' I asked again.

João placed the solid revolver on the tabletop and rubbed a hand across his jaw. It was probably still painful after his fight with Papagaio. 'The Senhora wants to see you,' he said, keeping his eyes on mine as I sat down.

'Why?'

'I guess she needs a priest for something.'

I took a sip of my coffee and leaned forward, elbows on the table. 'Tell her I'm busy.'

'Busy being a pig?'

I sighed, no longer afraid. My sleepiness had gone, and I was sure that if João had come to kill me, he would have done so already. 'Tell her what you like, I'm not coming.'

João stood up and collected his revolver. He tucked it into his trousers, saying, 'Come on. Let's go.'

'I already said I'm not coming,' I told him, reaching across to take my knife. 'You tell her, she wants to talk to me, she can come here and talk to me, otherwise—'

João was quick – quicker than me at least – so in my eagerness to retrieve my knife, I didn't see him move. In one swift movement, he thrust his left hand down on mine, pinning it to the table, while his right hand sprung forward to grasp my throat. The tips of his fingers bit into the skin around my Adam's apple as if he were about to rip it out. I immediately began to feel the blood pounding in my head.

'The Senhora wants to see you,' he said through his teeth. 'And she's the one who puts money in my pocket. She wants to see you – she sees you.'

I put my free hand on his wrist and opened my mouth to gasp for air, but his fingers dug deeper.

'I have a truck outside. When I let go, I want you to leave the knife on the table, stand up and walk in front of me. You understand?'

I nodded.

'Good.' João loosened his grip, testing my reaction.

I remained still as he removed his hand from mine, and took his claw from around my Adam's apple. I looked down at my knife, lying on the table, and João kept his eyes on me, his hand moving towards the pistol in his waistband. He shook his head.

'OK,' I said, holding up my hands. 'I'm coming. Let's go see what she wants.'

Moving out of my room and into the late afternoon sun, my attention was drawn to the sound of whistling and approaching footsteps, so I squinted my eyes and looked right. I was surprised to see Papagaio just a few metres away. He was walking in my direction, the bottom of his trousers rolled up, his battered straw hat on his head. He raised a hand to greet me, opened his mouth to call my name but immediately stopped when he saw João and his partner step out from the door behind me. Before João had time to react, Papagaio had pulled his revolver and was pointing it at the two men.

'You OK, Sam?'

'Sure,' I said, waving a hand. 'You can put that away.'

Papagaio hesitated. He shifted his eyes from João to the man beside him, assessing the threat from each of them.

João stayed where he was, but his partner began to inch his hand towards his waist.

'Leave it, Alberto,' João told him. 'Keep it in your pants.' I could see the hatred in his eyes, but he knew that, once again, Papagaio had the advantage.

'It's OK, Papagaio,' I said. 'Put your gun away.'

'What do they want?'

'They're taking me to the *fazenda*,' I said. 'That's all. Da Silva wants to see me.'

'Senhor or Senhora?'

'Senhora,' I told him. 'What difference does it make?'

'Why? Why she want to see you?'

I shook my head.

'And that?' he nodded his head towards me. 'The marks on your throat. You have to have those before you can see her?'

'It's nothing, Papagaio, don't worry about it.' I turned to João. 'Come on, then,' I said. 'Let's go.'

I began walking towards the pickup which was parked on the

other side of the road. 'I'll be fine,' I said to Papagaio as I went. 'I'll see you later.'

Papagaio kept his *pistola* pointed in our direction, but he allowed his arm to relax as we moved away from him.

I tugged open the door and waited for João to follow. He climbed in and shuffled across to the driver's seat before I stepped up into the cab. Now that João was safely in the pickup, I could see that my friend had turned his attention almost solely to Alberto, who remained by the door, watching Papagaio.

When João turned the key in the ignition, he called to his partner. 'Get in. Let's go. I'll kill this *pica* some other time.'

For just a moment, Papagaio took his eyes from Alberto and glanced over to see João behind the windscreen of the Chevrolet. Alberto saw a moment and took a chance. He was young and eager, perhaps thinking he might earn a few extra notes if he killed the mighty Papagaio. So, half shielded from view behind the door of the pickup, he lifted the hem of his shirt and tugged at the handle of the *pistola* which was hidden there. He managed to pull it halfway out before the foresight snagged on the lining of his jeans and the gun discharged into his trousers.

As close as it was to the cab, the shot was an ear-splitting crack. The noise travelled straight into the pickup and rebounded from metal to glass, rattling my skull. The scream that followed it was almost as painful.

Alberto's legs folded beneath him and he fell into the dust, hitting his elbow hard against the footboard.

For a moment we were all stunned into silence, then, over the sound of Alberto's moaning, I heard Papagaio's unmistakable laughter. I looked from the crumpled wreck of the man beside me, to Papagaio who had thrown his head back and was laughing at the sky. As he then leaned forward, almost bent double, he spotted João opening the driver's side of the pickup, and he straightened up and relevelled the gun at him.

João paused as he stepped down, studied Papagaio for a

moment, then shook his head and walked around to the passenger side. 'What the hell did you do? Didn't I tell you to keep it in your pants? Who do you think you are? Charles Bronson?'

'You didn't teach him to file the sight off?' laughed Papagaio.

João ignored him and looked down at the young man who was now white in the face. The right leg of his jeans was purple and he was sitting in a plate-sized pool of blood that was growing even as I watched.

'He needs a doctor,' I said, sliding along the bench seat for a better look. 'Let me get Paulo.'

'No,' said João. 'We'll take him back to the *fazenda*.'

'You want him to bleed to death?' I asked.

João looked up at me then glanced over at Papagaio. His eyes burned. 'Stand up,' he said to Alberto.

Alberto put his hand on the footboard and tried to push himself up, but he lost his grip and slipped, this time banging his shoulder against the runner.

'He's going to bleed to death,' I said. 'There's arteries in your leg—'

'Stand up,' João shouted this time, putting one hand under the man's armpit and hauling him to his feet. 'Get in the back. I don't want you bleeding all over the cab.'

'I can get Paulo,' I said.

João turned to me and narrowed his eyes. 'Say one more word and I'll cut your throat.' His voice was laced with poison.

Once again João looked over at Papagaio who was unable to hide his amusement, then he supported Alberto round to the back of the pickup. I heard him lower the tailgate and help the young man onto the flatbed.

As João came back around to the driver's side, he stopped and spoke to Papagaio. 'Next time,' he said. 'I will kill you. But before I do, I'm going to cut out your tongue.'

Papagaio smiled at João, stuck out his tongue, then bounced over to my side of the pickup and climbed in. 'You're not going anywhere without me,' he said.

He leaned over to smile at João again, then he pulled the door shut.

12

No one spoke in the cab on the way to the *fazenda*. On one side of me, João kept his fingers gripped tight on the steering wheel, his eyes dead ahead. Occasionally he looked across at Papagaio, but that was all. On my other side, Papagaio smiled and nodded his head as if he could hear music that the rest of us couldn't. His left hand was resting across his knee, and I was surprised there was no kind of dressing on his wound. I could see the stitches pulling the skin together where João had split it the night before with his knife. It looked like it should hurt, but Paulo had done a good job with them despite being drunk, and Papagaio didn't appear to be bothered by any discomfort. He was too busy enjoying himself.

From time to time I turned around to look through the glass behind me. Alberto was lying in his own blood, but I could see he was still alive.

When we came through the *fazenda* arch, the place looked almost deserted but for three people standing near the front of the main house. And as we grew closer, I recognised Catarina Da Silva. She was speaking with two men who were dressed differently from the usual workers. These men didn't wear their weapons tucked into patched, faded trousers, they wore modern automatics in holsters, high on their hips, held snug by expensive leather belts. Neither of the men wore a hat and both were sporting the kind of shades that would have caused jealousy across the set of *Top Gun*. Da Silva clearly used the locals for her dirty work, but when it came to self-protection, she wanted something better. These men looked disciplined and well trained and I found myself speculating how they'd compare to the three men who were now working over at the Hevea estate.

As João brought the pickup to a standstill, Da Silva nodded to the two men and they moved apart, stationing themselves some distance from her, where I presumed they would watch with intensity from behind their sunglasses.

Catarina Da Silva didn't react when Papagaio was the first to climb out from the cab. He looked her in the eye, then glanced at each of the bodyguards and acknowledged them with a nod of his head.

João jumped down from the other side, immediately running around to stand in front of his employer. 'He's armed,' he said. 'And meaner than a *jacaré*, so watch out.'

Da Silva shook her head at João. 'He knows Luis and Lucas too well. Anyway, why is he here?' She looked at Papagaio. 'What brings *you* here? I asked for—'

'João was getting rough,' he said in a lazy manner as I moved to stand beside him. 'He lacks control.'

Da Silva turned to meet me, holding out her hand, asking, 'Papagaio is a friend of yours?'

'Yes he is.' I took it without thinking, feeling its softness on my callused skin. Her grip was firm but not tight, and she held my hand for longer than she needed to. As we shook, I couldn't help noticing that she wore nothing beneath her loose brown top.

'What happened?' she said, releasing my hand and pointing to my throat. The tips of her fingers touched me there, but only slightly. She smelled of soap and perfume. 'João did this?'

'He refused to come,' João blurted, attempting to clear himself before I had a chance to condemn him.

'I didn't ask for this,' she said. 'This isn't how I treat a guest.'

'He wouldn't come. Told me to tell you he was busy.'

'Then perhaps he *was* busy,' she said.

'He was asleep. He was—'

'Enough, João.' She cut him off mid-sentence and turned back to me. 'I apologise for his actions,' she said. 'João is a good worker but he's not a clever man. He's like a wild pig. Would you like me to have him punished?'

I wondered what kind of punishment she had in mind. Perhaps her people could cut him and throw him in the river for the *piranhas*. Or maybe they would put him in a ring of old tyres and set fire to him.

'No,' I said. 'There's no need for that.'

She considered for a moment, looking at my throat, concern showing on her face, but I imagined it to be an act. A show of sympathy for the benefit of the priest.

'And what happened to the other man?' she eventually said to João. 'You took another man with you.'

'He's in the back,' he replied.

She rubbed a hand across her forehead and looked to the back of the pickup. 'Papagaio?' she asked. 'You killed him?'

'He's not dead,' I said. 'And he shot *himself*.'

Catarina Da Silva looked confused.

'He wanted to shoot Papagaio,' I told her. 'Tried to pull out his gun, shot himself in the leg.'

She stifled a smile. 'I suppose we need to get him sorted out, then,' she said. 'João, take him to Zico. He'll patch him up.'

'He needs a doctor,' I said, thinking Paulo was the only medical man I knew of round here. 'Is Zico a doctor?'

'He's a vet,' Papagaio told me. 'And not a very good one.'

'He'll do what he can,' said Da Silva as João made his way

around the truck. He dropped the tailgate and started dragging Alberto towards him.

'And if you don't mind helping out, Papagaio, I'd like to talk with . . .' she stopped. 'What do I call you? *Padre*?'

'Sam,' I said. 'Everyone calls me Sam.'

'Sam.' She seemed to taste the name for a moment before her tone changed and she spoke to João again. 'Papagaio will help you, then he'll return to São Tiago with Sam. In one piece. You will make sure nothing happens to him or you will answer to me.'

Papagaio took off his hat and scratched the top of his head, thinking about whether or not he was going to help João. Then he sighed and nodded, strolling round to the back of the pickup and taking hold of Alberto's ankles.

I watched them for a moment before Catarina Da Silva put her hand on my elbow and led me towards the house. We climbed the steps and sat side by side on two of the chairs on the front veranda. We were both quiet for a while, and I looked on as Papagaio and João carried the bleeding man away, just a few metres below where I was sitting. Alberto was still now, and I suspected that it wouldn't be long before he was dead. He had been bleeding into the pickup for at least half an hour.

They took him towards the hut where I had seen the men take Eduardo not so long ago, as if this was the place such a man was taken to die. I suspected that Zico would do nothing for him, may not even come. He would be too busy with the cattle. After all, a cow was far more valuable to the *fazenda* than a man.

Da Silva interrupted my thoughts by shifting her weight and turning her chair so that it was at an angle to mine. She loosened her ponytail, running her hands through her hair, lifting it so the sun caught it, displaying a surprising mix of blonde and amber amongst the ordinary light brown. 'I wanted to ask you about Edson,' she said, scraping it back again and retying it.

'Who?'

'Edson.' She sat back in her chair and smiled, crossing one leg over the other, dangling a clean, silver flip-flop from the end of her manicured toes. 'The man you brought to me a week ago. Makes me wonder if you're always going to bring a body when you come here.'

'Alberto isn't dead.'

'No, of course not.'

'And you mean Eduardo,' I said.

'Hmm?'

'Eduardo. If you're talking about the man who was stabbed in São Tiago, his name was Eduardo.'

'Yes.' She lifted her hips from the chair for a moment and slipped one hand into a pocket of her brown shorts. 'Of course. Eduardo.' She took out a packet of Marlboro cigarettes, a brand that wasn't sold in São Tiago. She removed a cigarette from the packet, followed by a slim gold lighter, and offered them to me. I lifted a hand and shook my head.

For a moment, she didn't move. She held her gaze on me, as if waiting for me to change my mind, and for the first time I noticed how green her eyes were. A striking emerald colour that sat perfectly with her skin tone and hair colouring. On another woman they might have been beautiful, but on Catarina Da Silva, they were hypnotising. They narrowed a touch, as if something had amused her, then she shrugged and snapped open the lighter, touching the flame to her cigarette and tilting her head to blow smoke into the air above her. 'When you brought him, you asked if he had family.'

'That's right.'

'He doesn't. *Didn't*.' She leaned forward, placing her smooth, hairless forearms on her thighs, her right hand hanging loose with the cigarette, and she looked up at me. 'I had someone ask around. Nobody really knew him. Nobody really liked him.'

'Well, I suppose it doesn't matter now.'

'He doesn't even have anyone to avenge him,' she said, bringing the cigarette to her mouth. And this time when she lifted her face to blow smoke into the air, the deep neck of her vest top came forwards, her breasts falling into view. The smooth, pale skin at the top of her chest stretched a little under their weight, and I could see a darkening of the flesh towards the peaks where they fell into shadow. Part of me wanted to look away, but my eyes were drawn to them, leaving me both annoyed and ashamed that I was so easily aroused by the sight of her. 'He has no one to find his . . . killer,' she said.

I raised my eyes when she spoke again, embarrassed to find that she was watching me. Catarina Da Silva glanced down at herself before staring me in the eye and smiling. She made no attempt to cover herself, apparently enjoying the attention, so I stood up and looked over towards the corrals where Papagaio was now leaning against the hut, talking and laughing with a group of men. João was not among them.

Da Silva got to her feet and came to my side, close, following my gaze. 'Papagaio's a good friend of yours?' she asked.

'Yes,' I said, but when I caught the expression on her face I found myself protesting too much. 'No,' I told her. 'Not that kind of friend.'

She made a show of brushing non-existent ash from the front of her top, the yielding flesh moving beneath then becoming firm as if she had been struck by a sudden chill. I pretended not to notice. 'A strange choice for a man of God,' she said, allowing her fingers to linger on her chest before dropping her hand. 'You *do* know—'

'God doesn't choose my friends,' I told her, thinking that in a town like São Tiago it would be hard to find a man who didn't have something dark and ungodly in his past.

'He used to work for me,' she said. 'He was a good worker. Prolific.'

'You didn't ask me here to talk about Papagaio,' I said.

'No.' She took my elbow again, running her hand along my forearm as she led me back to the seats, pulling them nearer this time, leaning forward once more as she sat. 'I wanted to ask you about Edson.' I could smell a faint perfume on her. The scent of flowers, freesias maybe, that came from another place. A place where such colour and delicacy existed – not here, on the *fazenda*, a hard and cruel place steeped in blood and surrounded by vast tracts of ochre dirt and yellow grass.

'Eduardo.' I concentrated on keeping my eyes on hers.

'Mm. Eduardo.' She paused. 'When you brought him here, I asked if you knew who killed him.'

I felt an uneasiness creep into my stomach; a sensation which vied to replace the more licentious feelings Catarina Da Silva had so far managed to provoke.

'You said you didn't know.'

I opened my arms, hands out, indicating that she should go on.

'José was there,' she said. 'He told me what happened before you even came here.'

I looked at Catarina Da Silva, searching for malice in her eyes, but she smiled at me and took another drag on her cigarette. I should have known that Da Silva would find out the truth about Eduardo. José, our policeman, would be firmly in her pocket, and he had been there that night. He was probably one of the card players.

'He said you refused rites.'

'He needed a doctor,' I said. 'Not a priest. Like Alberto over there.' I pointed at the hut where Papagaio had taken him.

'Will you give *him* rites?' she asked. 'If he dies, I mean.'

'Rites are for the dying,' I said. 'Not for the dead.'

'Then perhaps you should be with him now?' she pushed me.

I sighed and ran a hand across my head.

Catarina waited for an answer, but none was forthcoming, so she carried on. 'I know who killed my worker. But I don't understand why you didn't tell me.'

'There was nothing to gain from it.'

'I see.' She punctuated her remark by dropping her cigarette to the ground and grinding it with one silvery flip-flop. Immediately she took the packet from her pocket and lit another one. This time I accepted her offer.

'So, what do you think I should do?' she asked. 'About the café owner, I mean.'

'What do *you* think you should do?'

She half shrugged, shaking her head. 'Maybe I should do nothing,' she said. 'No family, no friends, no one to avenge him. Edson meant nothing to me or to anyone else.'

I thought about correcting her again.

'As you can see, I am undecided. That's why I wanted to know what you would do; what you think. You must have had a reason for keeping it from me. Perhaps you wanted to punish the murderer yourself? Or did you want to protect him? To save him?'

'Do nothing,' I said.

'Nothing? A priest who would do nothing?' She raised her eyebrows.

'What's done is done. Let it stop there. He's no worse than anyone else. No *different* from anyone else.'

'He's different from me,' she said. 'Different from you.'

'No,' I told her. 'We're all the same.'

'In God's eyes?'

'In anyone's eyes.'

Catarina Da Silva appeared to think about that for a moment before nodding. 'Then I'll take your advice and do nothing.

We'll leave him be. You can consider him saved.' She held her hands wide. 'Today the church has saved another soul. *You* have saved a soul.'

It scared me that Manny's life had been in my hands. All it would have taken was one word. But it wasn't me who had saved his life, it was Da Silva, and I had an unnerving feeling that she was trying to play with my life the same way she was playing with Manny's. As for his soul, I suspected that a man like Manny was probably beyond saving. I didn't say that to Da Silva, though, I just pushed myself to my feet and said, 'Well, if that's all you wanted to talk about—'

But she interrupted me by slapping both hands on her naked knees and standing up. 'Well,' she said. 'Now that's settled, let's have some lunch.'

'Thank you,' I said, shaking my head. 'I really have to go now.'

'Something important to do? More sleeping?'

'It's been a long day.'

'Yes,' she said, a sympathetic look coming over her as she inspected my throat again, touching my skin with the tips of her fingers. 'I apologise for what João did. Are you sure you don't want me to have him punished?'

'I'm sure.'

'And you won't eat?' she smiled. 'We can go inside where it's cool. My husband is away and I'd be glad for the company. Papagaio can eat with the workers.'

'I'd just like to go now,' I said, feeling as if I were asking to be excused from detention.

'We could get to know each other better.'

'Maybe another time.'

For a second, Da Silva's smile disappeared, as if she were unaccustomed to being turned down, but it quickly returned with a flick of her hair. 'Yes. Another time. I'd like that.' She motioned with one hand towards one of the bodyguards and he walked away, out of sight. 'I'll have someone drive you back, then. Not João.'

'Thank you,' I said and began to descend the steps. When I reached the bottom, the bodyguard returned with a young man who jogged over to the pickup and climbed into the driver's seat.

As Papagaio strolled back to join us, Catarina Da Silva took my arm once more and stopped me. She put her mouth close to my ear so that I could feel her breath on me as she spoke in a near whisper.

'You're not like any priest I've ever seen before,' she said. 'There's something else inside you. Something that interests me. Something that makes me wonder if you're even a priest at all.' She paused and I heard the moist sound of her tongue wetting her lips. 'Do you even believe in God?'

'I believe in hell,' I said. 'Does that count?'

A sigh escaped her as she ran her hand down my arm before letting go and raising her voice. 'You see. All you had to say was yes or no. But you didn't. Not even a straight answer. So now you're making me think again. And I like that.'

I studied her face, as close as it was to mine, and was unsettled to find myself wondering how it might feel to put my mouth on hers. Her lips were fuller than Ana's, more pronounced, more obvious somehow. There was no denying that Catarina Da Silva had stirred me despite my intent to dislike her. She made me feel both threatened and wanted at the same time. It was a heady mix of emotions which made me view her in a new light. She wasn't the spectral figure she had always been before; a fearsome creature often spoken of but rarely seen. Now she was something else to me. She was a woman. A sleek and predatory woman.

'That's twice you've turned me down,' she said in a low voice. 'Don't let it happen again.' She kissed me on both cheeks, as if we were friends, perhaps more.

I felt myself smile.

She released me and took a step back when Papagaio reached us, but she followed me to the pickup and spoke to me again as I was about to climb in.

'I'll wait for you this time,' she said. 'You'll be back.'

13

'So what did she want?' Papagaio asked almost as soon as we'd passed under the *fazenda* arch. 'You looked close.'

'Close?'

'Yeah, like you were friends or something. I saw you two up there on high and you know what? You looked good together.'

I made a dismissive sound and turned away.

'No, really,' he persisted. 'She's a good-looking woman. I reckon you should take her. I bet she's dirty, too; would do whatever you want.'

'She's not my type.'

'Not your type? Who needs a type? Any type is good enough. You mean you wouldn't—'

'I'm not really sure what she wanted.' I cut him off, speaking over him. 'I don't know if she was letting me know she's in control round here, or if it was about something else.' I glanced at the young man who was driving us, wondering how much I should say in front of him, but his face was blank, as if we weren't even there. 'She told me she knows who killed Eduardo.'

'Eduardo?'

'At Manny's place, remember?'

Papagaio nodded and turned his face to the open window. The draught pushed up the brim of his hat.

'And that she knows I know who did it, too. It's like she was letting me know I hadn't fooled her.'

'She knows everything,' Papagaio said into the wind.

'She asked me what she should do.'

'She asked *you*?'

'Gave me the chance to save him or condemn him. Giving me a choice like she was offering beer or *pinga*.'

Papagaio laughed. 'No choice,' he said. 'It's always *pinga*.'

We lapsed into silence for some time after that, Papagaio with his face to the fields and me turning inwards with my thoughts. I wondered if the visit to Da Silva's place had been a warning of some kind. Landowners didn't like the church, everyone knew that, but it didn't feel as if she were trying to intimidate me. It felt more as if she'd been making an attempt to connect with me, even seduce me. The way she touched me, displayed herself to me. Maybe it hadn't been so much a warning as an effort to include me in something. Make me feel good about saving Manny's life. Or perhaps, I flattered myself, there was something else she wanted from me.

'Thanks for stepping in, by the way,' I said, thinking how Papagaio had drawn his gun on João and Alberto.

'Anything for a friend,' he smiled, holding up his hand to display the stitches, flexing and contracting his fingers before dropping them back to his knee. 'And anything to get under João's skin.'

'What were you fighting about last night?'

'The usual,' Papagaio chuckled. 'Drink, women, cards.' He stared into the distance as if he were remembering happier times, then he blinked and shook his head. 'Hey, I forgot, I was coming round to see you, anyway.'

'Yeah?'

'I want you to help me, Sam. All this excitement made me forget.'

I shrugged. 'As long as it's not confession.'

Papagaio laughed. 'My God doesn't like confession. No. You once said you wanted a little extra money, asking if I need anyone to help, so I came to tell you. I need some help.'

'What kind of help?'

'The kind that pays, of course. What else? There any other kind of help you're offering?'

'OK, what is it?'

'I've got some work over at Hevea.' He removed his hat, dropping it flat on his knees. 'They're building houses and they need an electrician.'

'And the first person they thought of was you?' I said.

'Sure.'

'Papagaio, you're never anybody's first choice. Not for that kind of work, anyway.' He wasn't a bad electrician, he always got the job done, but for one thing he talked too much and for another, everybody knew his reputation; who he used to work for, what he used to be, what he used to do.

'Why not?' Papagaio tried to look insulted. 'Why wouldn't they think of me? I'm good at what I do.'

'Maybe,' I said. 'But how the hell do they even know who you are?'

'Paulo told them, I guess.'

'Ah. Paulo.'

'Yeah. He's done me a favour.'

'And what do they want to build houses for?' I went on without really listening.

'Families. They want twenty houses for families.'

'Why don't they just put them in plastic tents like all the other ranchers do? Let them build their own houses.'

'This estate, it's not for cattle. It's something else, rubber I think I heard Paulo say. Anyway, they need twenty houses for families and one big place for the *chefe*.' He held his hands apart, as if he were demonstrating the size of the one that got away, or whatever might be hanging between his legs. 'It's a

99

good job and it pays well,' he said. 'I'm going to need some help.'

'I'm not skilled enough. Not for that.'

'Sure you are. It'll be fine.'

'Get someone else.'

'No, it has to be you. I'll teach you what you need to know.'

And then it clicked. Paulo had been busy while I had been out fishing. 'What do you mean it *has* to be me?'

He looked away and ran his hands around the brim of his hat.

I asked him again. 'Papagaio, why does it have to be me?'

He grinned, showing the gaps in his teeth, and then shrugged.

'What's Paulo playing at?' I asked.

'Look, Sam,' he said. 'You know how it is here. I do a few odd jobs and that's it. Sometimes I struggle to buy rice – just like you. Just like everyone else. In Goiânia or Brasilia I could make a good living b—'

'Go to Brasilia then.'

'I can't.'

'So make do,' I leaned forward, 'just like everyone else.'

'Sam, I need the work. This is a big job for me and it could be for you too. Paulo said the *gringo* would hire me if I brought you along.'

I supposed this was Paulo's way of getting me involved in something; helping me to earn a few notes. Unless he had another idea I hadn't figured out yet. 'And what's to say we'll get paid, huh? Maybe the *gringo* will burn his workers or shoot them just like Da Silva. You thought of that?' I looked at the man driving the pickup, but he gave no sign that he was listening to us.

'*Gringos* don't burn people, Sam, you know that. Shit, you're one yourself. You burn people?' He didn't wait for me to answer. 'Of course you don't, and nor will he. He's different. He's honest.'

'Then he shouldn't be here.' I leaned back in the seat.

'Sam, I need this. And so—'

'I'll think about it.' I supposed a couple of weeks' labour wouldn't be any great harm, it wasn't like taking on the responsibility of a health clinic. The extra money would be good too.

'Well, don't take too long,' he said. 'Maybe I'll find someone else.'

14

When we reached São Tiago, I told the driver to stop anywhere on the main street. I didn't want him to take me right to my place. João and Alberto had already forced themselves into my tiny piece of São Tiago and I had no intention of inviting any more unwanted intrusions.

Papagaio told me he was going for a drink and asked if I wanted to come. I said I'd prefer to be on my own for a while, so he told me again to think about the job, then he wandered back along the road, flicking up small clouds of dust as he went.

I turned and raised a hand to the driver, acknowledging the lift as I began to slam the door of the pickup, but something in his eye made me stop. He, too, seemed to falter, unsure about what he was going to do, and for a moment, both of us was frozen halfway through a movement, an awkward beat hanging in the dry heat of the afternoon. Me with my arm tensed, about to throw the heavy door, him leaning across the bench seat, his mouth open as if he were about to speak.

Then the moment passed and he spoke for the first time. 'You're the *gringo* priest.'

My arm still braced, my fingers still tight on the metal rim around the open window, my expression confused.

I nodded my head.

'The one who helped Eduardo. You and the doctor.'

'That's right.'

The man blinked a number of times in quick succession. He bit his upper lip and glanced through the windscreen before looking back at me.

'I knew him,' he said.

I relaxed my arm and moved closer to the cab, putting my toes on the footboard, leaning in but being careful to keep my distance. 'You knew him? Eduardo?'

He tightened his fingers on the steering wheel, his knuckles whitening, then he too seemed to relax a little. 'Not much.'

'He married?' I asked. 'Children?'

The man shook his head. 'I don't think children. A wife, yes, but she left him. He didn't say much about it.' Like everyone else, Eduardo was probably running from something he didn't want people to know about or he didn't want to think about. 'I reckon he missed her, though. He sometimes said her name in his sleep. Natália. Showed me a picture once, too. A big woman.'

'You know where it is? The picture?'

'No.'

'What else can you tell me about him?'

'He rides,' the man said, checking himself, '*rode*. We rode together. He worked hard.'

'A *vaqueiro*?'

'Like me.'

'You know where he was from?'

'Somewhere up north.' There was no emotion in his voice; he didn't show any concern that Eduardo was dead. Whether it was a front or whether it was genuine, I couldn't tell. He had either learned to hide his emotions, or he didn't have any. His young face was like a blank screen, white noise that disguised whatever was underneath. Perhaps he had seen things like I had. Perhaps something had hollowed him out and left him empty, too.

'What kind of man was he?' I asked.

He raised his eyebrows and stared down at the seat beside him. He thought for a second before looking up. 'He was just a man,' he said. 'Like any other.'

It was a punishing thing to say, intended or not. A man's life summed up in one sentence. Just a man like any other. Nothing more and nothing less. A man who was no longer a man. A vague memory in the minds of a handful of people.

'Thank you,' he said.

'For what?' The words took me by surprise.

'For trying to help him. You and the doctor. You're good men.'

'You liked Eduardo?' I asked him.

'Sometimes . . .' he said. 'Sometimes he was like an animal. When he had *pinga* inside him, I guess I didn't like him so much. I think he drank it to forget.'

'Don't we all?'

'But other times? When he laughed? Sure. I liked him. He was OK. He made me laugh too.'

'So he was your friend?'

He shrugged. 'I knew him, that's all.'

He moved back in his seat now, finding his driving position again, putting his free hand on the gearstick. It was about as much as I could have expected from him, and I sensed that there wasn't going to be any more. He had said what he wanted to say and it had obviously taken some strength to do that much.

'Why didn't you say something earlier?' I asked him. 'We've been in the cab with you all this time.'

He looked over my shoulder, speaking to me but keeping his eye on the road behind me. 'The man you were with,' he said. 'I've heard stories.'

'Papagaio?' I said, looking back, but he was out of sight now. 'Papagaio is a good man,' I told him. 'He's my friend.'

The man blinked again, that nervous fluttering, and pushed

the pickup into gear. He revved the engine and I stepped back, slamming the door shut.

'Wait,' I called before he pulled away. 'Tell me your name.' I leaned closer to the open window to hear his answer.

'Anderson,' he said.

'Thank you, Anderson.'

Now it was his turn to look confused. 'For what?'

'For telling me something about Eduardo.' It wasn't much, but it was something. Eduardo meant something to someone, even if it was just for them to acknowledge that he had lived, that he had made someone laugh. At least one person remembered him and cared enough to thank the people who had tried to save his life.

Anderson stared at me, probably wondering why it meant anything to me at all. Then he nodded once, put both hands on the wheel and started to let out the clutch. The pickup began to roll forwards, so I stepped back and raised a hand, watching Anderson drive away from São Tiago.

After he had gone, I went back to my quiet room and drank cold coffee. I paced, sat down, thought about Anderson and about Eduardo. I thought about Catarina Da Silva, too, I couldn't help it, so I tried to force her from my head by considering the job offer from Papagaio.

Outside, not far away, someone began strumming a guitar. It was a song I recognised, 'Mamãe Eu Quero', and after a few moments, a man began to sing. Hearing the music, I felt the need to be outside where the air was clear, so I put on my flip-flops and pulled the door closed behind me, looking up the road to see a small group of people by the roadside, drinking and singing. The guitarist was sitting on a low stool, a man beside him was banging sticks on overturned cans, offering up a tinny beat for the song. Papagaio was amongst them, taking a drink from a bottle of *pinga* and smiling his uplifting smile. One of the men, Ernesto, was scuffling a drunken dance in the red dirt, one hand outstretched and the other held close to his chest as if he had a partner. I raised a hand to Papagaio and walked towards the river, pushing away any remnant thoughts of Catarina Da Silva, reflecting on how important Ana had become to me, how strong my feelings for her had grown. I felt a great urge to be with her now. She was not a sophisticated woman, not educated in any structured way, but she knew human nature and she always made me see more clearly. This was something Paulo understood about my relationship with Ana, so if he were determined to set me up with a job at the new plantation, he would have spoken to her about it. Probably last night when they had been absorbed in conversation with the *gringo*.

I watched the river for a while, seeing the three *Americanos* from Hevea boarding André's floating hotel, carrying fancy fishing rods like nothing I'd ever seen before. I could see André up in the wheelhouse, leaning over the edge waiting for the men to climb on board before he started the engine and moved away from the bank. I could hear the engines bubbling from where I stood, and I watched the outlandish boat chug past the bend in the river, then I found myself turning away and walking back towards town. I passed the singers and declined the offer of a drink. They'd be there for a while, probably late into the night, so I could always come back later if I wanted to. Papagaio was dancing now, his hat in one hand, his hips swaying, and he tried to pull me into the party but I resisted. The others beckoned, too, but when I refused they dismissed me and went back to their singing and clapping. I left them behind, the guitarist changing to a slower tune now, the tin drums keeping tempo, and I headed for Ana's place further along the road.

Approaching the part of the street where Ana lived, I was surprised to see Manolo stepping out from her porch. He had a serious expression and his shoulders were hunched. When he looked up and saw me approaching, he crossed to the other side of the road and hurried past without making eye contact. I turned my head to follow his progress as he huffed along the road, and I noticed the revellers ignored him as he drew near. The only one who acknowledged him was Papagaio, who stopped dancing and glared at him, waiting for him to pass, and then looked to me and raised his eyebrows. Papagaio stuck out his index finger and raised his thumb in a gesture that imitated a pistol. He pointed it in Manolo's direction, and I wasn't sure if he was offering or referring to my conversation with Catarina Da Silva earlier that afternoon. I shook my head, so Papagaio threw away the imaginary gun and returned to his dance while I headed for Ana's place, going straight under the porch and knocking on the door.

'What did he want?' I asked when she opened it.

'You mean Manolo?'

'Yes.'

Ana stepped out and closed the door. 'Let's go out,' she said. 'There're some things I need from Zeca's.'

'Was he giving you trouble?' I asked as we walked. 'I can talk to him . . .'

'He's no trouble.'

'Did he try to hurt you?

'I can handle Manny,' she said. 'I can't hit him with my fists like you can, make him bleed, but that doesn't mean I can't look after myself. Mind you, you were restrained. Most men round here would have killed him.'

'Is that what you wanted?'

Ana laughed. 'No. Manolo's a nuisance but he doesn't deserve that.'

I put my hands in my pockets and told Ana that I had saved Manny's life that afternoon; that I could have sanctioned his execution, had I wished it.

She looked at me. 'You've been to the *fazenda*?'

'Hmm.' I told her about João and Alberto, about Da Silva asking my opinion.

'She must like you,' she said. 'Why else would she get you up there just to talk? Normally when someone gets dragged up to the *fazenda*, they end up in a hole in the ground. Was the Senhor there?' she asked.

'No. Just her.'

'So you were alone?' She stopped and turned to face me, a smile on her lips.

'Not really.'

'Maybe she likes you,' she said, teasing. 'Maybe she likes the *gringo* priest. I mean, who wouldn't?'

'This *gringo* priest is taken,' I said, trying not to think about the way Catarina Da Silva had displayed herself to me, and how I had found myself unable to look away. 'And she's not my type.'

'Really? You mean you wouldn't even be tempted? I heard she's an attractive woman. Rich.'

'That's true,' I mused. 'Powerful too. Maybe I—'

Ana raised her eyebrows at me, hitting my arm in a playful manner.

'No,' I said putting my arms around her waist and pulling her closer. I held her eyes with mine and smiled. 'Not even tempted.' This time it was me who kissed Ana, and as soon as I did, I knew that my vows were forgotten.

Behind us, the music stopped and the drinkers whistled and clapped. We ignored them and began to walk again, taking the side street down to Zeca's.

'Papagaio has a proposition for me,' I said before we reached the small shop.

'Oh?'

'Some kind of job,' I said. 'Over at Hevea.' I looked at her. 'Nothing to do with you and Paulo, I suppose?'

Ana pretended to zip her lips together.

'I'm going to take it.'

'It'll be good for you. After what happened with Eduardo, I think you need something like this. Maybe you should help Paulo with his clinic, too.'

'Is that what this is all about?' I asked, stopping outside Zeca's.

'Paulo wants the best for you.'

'One thing at a time.'

She took a step into the shop and turned to speak to me. 'One thing at a time? OK. That'll do for now.'

That was the first time Ana and I spent so long together. I sat with her while she worked, and later in the evening I helped clear away the cloth and the thread. We ate at the table, talking about whatever came into our heads until the conversation finally turned to Eduardo and Manolo.

'Something else happened to me today,' I told her. 'I met someone who knew Eduardo.'

'Oh?' she looked surprised. 'You didn't mention it before.'

'The moment never came.'

Ana accepted my explanation with a vague nod of her head. 'It was someone from the *fazenda*?'

'The man who gave us a lift back. Anderson. He said he used to ride with Eduardo.'

'What else did he say?'

'Not much. That he was from up north, that he once had a wife called Natália who left him, that sometimes he made him laugh. I suppose they were as close to being friends as people like that can be.'

'People like that?'

'You know what I mean. Drifters. Men who come and go.'

'And it makes you feel better to know something about him?'

I looked inwards, trying to identify exactly how it made me feel. 'It gives me another way of seeing him,' I said. 'Until now he's always been a dead man on my floor. A body wearing my trousers and shirt. A man trying to find water in the heat of my room.' I tried not to think about the way his eyes had glazed over. Instead I imagined him at work; as someone's friend.

'But now he's something else?' she asked.

'Yeah. Now he's something else. He's a person. I can imagine him alive.' I looked at Ana. 'I dream about it,' I said. 'It breaks my sleep every night.'

'You shouldn't feel guilty about Eduardo. You did what you could. I told Paulo the same thing.'

'Maybe I should be worried about how much time you spend with him.'

'And you with Senhora Da Silva.' Ana smiled.

'Anyway, it's not guilt,' I said. 'I didn't kill Eduardo, Manny did that. It's the violence, Ana. I've seen enough of it. I came here to get away from it.'

'You're talking about Roraima now?'

'Hmm.'

'You never told me what happened.' She took my hand, making me look at her face. 'Is it something you want to talk about?'

I paused before speaking. I remembered the last time I had been about to tell her. The fight I had with Manny. 'Whichever way I turn, there's something to remind me, Ana. I've seen some terrible things.'

'What things?' she said. 'Tell me about it.'

Again, I considered telling her; considered flooding her with my past. Telling her how I saw the burning every night, fresh in my mind as if it had happened that afternoon. How I smelled the smoke and the bodies, their sweet, scorched odour filling my nostrils. How I saw motherless children with flames desecrating their skin.

'Some things . . .' I cleared my throat and stared at the tabletop. 'Some things are best left unsaid.'

'And some things are best laid open. We can't bury things before they're dead, Sam. We keep them buried, they claw their way out. They leave their mark.'

I looked away. 'The mark is already there.'

'Then we should clean it, Sam. You need to talk about this.'

'I'm not ready.'

Ana sighed, an almost sensual sound in the quiet of the room. I could feel her watching me, without anything else to say. She came closer to me and pulled me to her, pressing her warmth to me, but she remained silent. We sat together like that, not speaking for some time before she stood and took my hand. 'Come,' she said. 'Let's wash it all away.'

Inside her small bathroom, Ana undressed me and gently pushed me under the shower, lukewarm water raining over me. I felt a little self-conscious, sober and naked as I was, but I enjoyed the sense of uncovering myself for her, and I watched as she unfastened her dress and stepped out of it, standing before me without any reserve. Our eyes locked for a moment, then I broke away and looked down her, seeing the swell of her rounded breasts where her chest rose and fell with every breath, her ribs quite visible beneath them. The *morena* skin across her stomach was tight and flat and there was barely enough flesh over her hips to give her the curves which almost cried out for me to run my hands over them. I studied the sinews in her arms, the fine hairs, barely visible, which dusted her forearms. I lingered over her narrow thighs and the smooth creases where they came together and touched, then moved my gaze down to soak in the entire length of her legs. I took my time, waiting for the image of her standing like that to be burned into my brain before I held my arms out to her.

When Ana came to me in the small space, we pressed our bodies against one another and brought our lips together, softly at first, then more passionately as we lost ourselves to the embrace. We kissed as the water fell over us, and we moved our fingers over each other, touching and feeling, exploring as new lovers do, until Ana stopped and took a half step back. She lifted her hands and put them on my face. 'Let me clean you,' she said. 'Let me wash it all away,' and with her own baptism, she washed me, her soapy hands moving over me, finding every inch of my skin.

When she was finished I took Ana to her room where we joined once more, the warm evening drying our skin, raising it in bumps as the water evaporated from us. Ana ran her fingers through my hair, then sat down on the end of her bed and kissed my stomach before pulling me down towards her to make love on the cool cotton sheets.

Later, we lay in the dark, naked and squeezed together in the bed that was too small for us. We drifted in a new intimacy that joined us in a way we had not experienced until now.

Ana broke the quietude, speaking in a whisper, asking, 'Was that your first time?'

'No. But it was my first time for many years.'

She seemed satisfied with the answer. 'How long have you been in São Tiago?'

'Five years,' I answered. 'Maybe even six. I don't remember.'

'And how long have we been friends?'

'Three.'

Ana shifted to make herself more comfortable. 'In all those years, this is the first time you have ever slept in my bed.'

'I'm not asleep.' For me it felt strange. For so many years I had lived alone; slept alone.

'It's good to have you here. I often wondered how it would feel.'

I waited for her to go on.

'And you? Have you wondered?'

I turned to her in the darkness, just able to make out the shape of her head on the pillow, the shadow of her hair across the white cotton. I watched her silhouette for a moment before resting my head back on my own pillow.

'Have you ever wondered, Sam?'

'Yes, of course,' I said. 'Often.'

Anna propped herself on one elbow. 'Why have you never told me, then?'

'I suppose it was hard for me,' I said.

'It was hard for me, too, Sam.' She brushed a hand across my face. 'You're so much better than you let yourself be. There's so much you keep inside. I knew from the moment I first met you.'

I turned onto my side and ran a hand over her naked shoulder, pushing the sheet down and following the curve of her breast with my palm, becoming more aroused by her involuntary gasp at my touch. 'What I am, Ana; what I *was*. And what you were.' I couldn't help smiling. 'All my life I was a priest, Ana, it's hard to change that. A priest and a prostitute. A hopeless combination.'

'A perfect combination, Sam.'

Ana lay back on her pillow and enjoyed my attentions.

The window was open but the buildings around ours retained the heat of the sun, encasing us in an old day. The intermittent hum and echo of São Tiago was muffled beyond door and walls, just loud enough for me to hear. A sporadic murmur that mingled with the drone of the cicadas.

'And now?' I asked her, moving my hand across her chest, running down between her flattened breasts and across her stomach. 'After everything that's happened. Am I still the same man? The one you thought I was?'

'No,' she said. 'You're even stronger and more stubborn than I thought you were. And what you're carrying with you . . .' her voice trailed as my caress moved on. 'I don't know what it is, but you need to talk about it, Sam. In time, when you're ready. Speaking it aloud will lift it from your heart.'

I didn't want to think about that now. I had pushed Roraima back into the shadow. *Ana* had pushed it back into the shadow, just long enough for me to enjoy this moment. And when it returned, I knew it would not be quite the same animal. Ana was right. In time it would no longer be as feral, as dark, as unspeakable. In time I would cut it from my heart. But now, in that instant, something else occupied my thoughts.

'I thought it was something I'd never want,' I told her. 'To share my life.' I felt her tense a little when I touched lightly between her legs.

'And now you're wondering if it will be possible. If there's a place where we can be together.' She almost whispered the words as her body relaxed again.

'Yes.' A little harder now.

'This is where we belong, Sam.' She sat up, pushing me back, putting one leg across to straddle me. 'São Tiago is the right place for you, just as it's the right place for me.' She reached down to hold me as she lowered herself, easing around me. 'The people here will get used to it. They'll accept it. They always do.' She took my hands in hers, lacing our fingers as she began rocking. 'But enough about that,' she said, her hair falling forwards onto my face. 'There are more important things. We have to make up for lost time.'

15

Monday morning I was waiting for Papagaio outside my place as the sun rose over São Tiago. The wide street was empty and the houses and shops were still shuttered against the night. Everything looked as it always did, but somehow it was different. *I* was different. Change was creeping over me as surely as the dry season would merge into the wet. It was as inevitable now as it was that the river would swell and that the burning would stop in the forests.

When I left Ana's house that morning, the night just beginning to lift around me, I felt as if something that had ached inside me for so long was finally beginning to dissolve. I couldn't help smiling as I opened my door and, for once, I didn't immediately think of Eduardo when I entered my room. I thought only of Ana as I washed and changed, and headed out to meet Papagaio.

I walked to the corner of the road to watch a couple of canoes coming towards the shore behind Manolo's café. I couldn't see who was in them but it would probably be Karajá Indians from Bananal coming over to buy *cachaça*. Cheap and intoxicating, *cachaça* was a good way to forget, and with a high percentage of alcoholics on the island, the Karajá would sell almost anything to get it. Fish, skins, meat, knick-knacks. Manolo wasn't supposed to trade with the Indians, they were meant to be living the indigenous life on Bananal, but he didn't care and no one ever came to check. He brought it in from Vila Rica and sold it to them for whatever profit he could make. You often saw drunk Indians, semi-naked, on the *rua* in São Tiago.

Further along, where the street came to an end at the water's edge, André's floating hotel – with enough room to sleep eight people if they dared travel on board – was moored to one of the few trees which hadn't been torn down on this side of the river. The whole thing was painted white, with a fading pale blue trim around the shutters and the waterline. At the back, by the rusted twin motors, a rickety staircase led to a top deck that was surrounded by a pale blue railing coming loose from its fixing. Lean against it too hard and you'd be swimming with the fish. There were one or two safety rings attached to the railing, but they were tied so tight they would never come off unless they were cut. It was here, on the top deck, that the main wheelhouse stood, looking like it had been dropped from the sky and just happened to land in that particular spot. It was neither straight nor well built, but it provided shelter for André, night and day, whenever he was on the river.

Down below, there was a kitchen where André did all the cooking himself, four small bedrooms, and a toilet which was nothing more than a hole in the floor. Bolted to the side of the boat was a sign painted nearly six years ago by the same man who painted the rest of the boat. Ronaldo was dead now, shot by a betrayed husband, but his legacy remained attached to the side of that boat. The sign read *André Safari Tours: Hotel Fluctuante*.

There was no sign of Papagaio yet, so I wandered over to see if André was around. I climbed aboard, finding purchase on the old tyres which he had tied around it as protection from collision, and called out, 'Oi! Anyone there?' The odour of diesel was almost overpowering at the back of the boat where the engines were housed. The smell made the air feel solid, as if

I were breathing underwater, sucking the dark stench right into my head.

André leaned out from a second floor window and peered down. 'Hey, Sam. How's it going? I hear you and Papagaio are going out to Hevea to work on the new houses.'

'Word travels fast,' I said, looking up. '*I* only found out two days ago.'

'You know me, Sam. Nothing gets past me.' André laughed and disappeared from the window. I heard wood creaking and groaning as he came down the steps inside. Everything about the boat was old, dirty and rotten, and the motors were only strong enough to take it a few kilometres a day. I had no idea how the fishing tourists ever found out about André's *Hotel Fluctuante*, but I was pretty sure it didn't appear in any glossy holiday brochures. The people who came must've heard of it from others who were keen to see real frontier life. The borders would stretch again, though, and André would have to buy a new boat or he would go out of business. Further up the floodplains of the Araguaia, and way east on Tocantins, floating hotels were more common and it wouldn't be long before foreign fishermen and eco-tourists started pushing their way towards São Tiago. There were a few more restrictions here, laws to protect the parkland around Bananal, but there was no one to enforce them, so they would come. They would come and we would all have to adapt. Unless the government went ahead with hydroelectric damming, and then we'd all be screwed anyway.

'How's business?' I asked André as he appeared from the door at the back of the hotel.

'Business? Not much of a business, Sam. How often you see me take anyone out?'

'I saw you with those *Americanos* from Hevea.'

'They're *Americanos*?' He mulled that over before dismissing it. 'Ah, doesn't matter what they are, they're just *gringos* to me.'

'Who like to fish,' I said.

André took off his cap and slapped it against his thigh, raising a puff of dust. 'Oh they like to fish, all right. These *gringos* think they know everything there is to know about fishing, but when they come here, Sam, they know shit.' He was wearing a pair of faded red trousers which were too tight for him, and his feet were bare. 'You know what they're like. They end up drinking and sleeping because they don't know how to catch big fish. They snatch too hard with *tucunaré*, too soft with *pirarara*. They want to use the wrong bait, the wrong lures, they don't want to listen, they argue . . .'

'So where are they now? What you done with them? You lost your *gringos*?'

'It's Monday,' he said. 'They went back to Hevea. When they come, it's only at weekends.'

'You sure you didn't shoot them and throw them overboard for the *jacaré*?' I pointed a thumb at the water, like I was hitching a ride.

'You must be joking,' he said. 'You know they carry pistols? Big ones, right here,' André patted his hip. 'And they got a look in their eye like they'd use them if they had to.'

'Hmm. I've seen that look. They say what it is they do over at the estate? They managers or something?'

'They didn't say. Don't say much at all, in fact. But they don't look like managers to me. What I've seen of them, they look more like bodyguards for the *gringo*.' His face lit up as he remembered something else. 'Hey, and you know what? Ernesto told me there was trouble with them on Friday. Up at the airstrip.'

I raised my eyebrows. 'What kind of trouble?' Ernesto wasn't the most reliable source of information. He had a habit of making up stories, some from his imagination and some which were embellished truths, so you could never believe much that he said. He once told me he was related to the queen of

England. One thing I did know about him, though, was that he used to be a clown in a travelling circus that pitched up in Vila Rica four or five years ago. Got so drunk one night that when the circus left, they went without him. He moped around Vila Rica for a while, made his way down to São Tiago, and got stuck here like everyone else. People said he was an alcoholic, and that's saying something, when the people of São Tiago call you alcoholic.

'What kind of trouble is it always?' André said.

'You gonna make me guess?'

'Apparently they bring their money in by plane once a month to pay the workers.'

'I heard that.'

'You and everyone else. Well, someone tried to take it, and your *Americanos*, they weren't too happy about letting them do that.'

'Anyone get hurt?'

'What do you think?'

'Well, Ernesto told you the story, so I guess there was a shoot-out, everyone got killed, the airstrip was awash with blood and the plane exploded.'

André flashed a knowing smile, then set his face with a grim expression. 'That's what you'd think. It's the kind of story you'd expect from Ernesto, but you know what? He said there wasn't any shooting at all. He ducked behind the weighing house when he saw those *bandidos* coming, but he didn't hear a thing. Not a shot. And when he got the balls to stick his head out, the *Americanos* were climbing into their pickup and driving away.'

'And the other men? The *bandidos*?'

André shrugged. 'No sign of them. Nothing. Gone like they were never even there.'

I couldn't help feeling curious. 'You sure he didn't make it up? Why would Ernesto be at the airstrip?'

'Something to do with Raul; collecting some debt money from cards, I think.'

Raul worked at the airstrip. He manned the fuel pumps, weighed the bags, sold warm drinks from a cooler box. He also stood guard with a fire extinguisher when the *Bandeirante* was preparing for take-off. The small plane came in from Brasilia once a week, landed on the dirt strip, stayed for an hour and then went back with its belly full of gas. While the passengers were boarding, Raul had to keep watching the propellers, searching for signs of fire. It was his job to douse any flames. I knew he liked to play cards, and so did Ernesto, so it was a good enough reason for Ernesto to be at the strip.

'And that's all he said?' I asked. 'That the *Americanos* drove away? The other men just disappeared?'

'That's all he said. Gone. Nothing left but dust. Probably rotting in a field with their throats cut.'

'It's a good story. I'm surprised I haven't heard it before now. I wonder if Raul tells the same one.'

'Exactly the same,' André said. 'Except he hid behind the pumps.'

'Not the best place to be hiding if the shots are flying.'

'Everyone was talking about it Friday night on the beach. There were no *gringos* at all at the *festa* that night. Not even you.'

'I was doing other things.' An image of Ana flashed in my mind, driven back by the familiar sound of Papagaio's Beetle put-putting down the street, the only car on the road. I turned around just as he took the corner up to where my place was. A few moments later the engine stopped and the horn beeped.

'That's for me,' I said. 'Better go.'

'You settle your problems with Manny?' asked André as I climbed down from his floating wreck. 'Looks like you gave him quite a beating.'

'I shouldn't have done that,' I said, stopping on the steps.

'He'll get over it. It's not the first time it's happened to him. Give him a few more days and he'll be the same as always. You know how it is. People forget quickly.'

'I'm not so sure,' I said. 'Maybe I should talk to him before he tries to stick a knife in my back.'

'Manny wouldn't do that,' he said. 'Not to you. Not to a priest.'

'You think so?' I jumped down and landed with one foot in the water.

'He's afraid of going to hell. He doesn't realise he's going anyway.'

I shook my foot dry and looked up at him. 'I think we all are.'

André laughed and raised a hand. '*Até logo*, Sam. And when I see Manny I'll talk to him. We're all friends in São Tiago.' I liked his sentiment, but I wasn't sure he was right.

'Hey, Sam,' he called after me.

I stopped on the road and turned.

'You done something to upset Da Silva?'

'What?' I raised a hand to shield my eyes from the sun as I spoke to him.

'Da Silva. From the *fazenda*.'

'I know who you mean.'

'So what have you done to upset them?'

'What you talking about?' I came back to the floating hotel, André jumping down, clearing the river better than I had done.

He came to meet me at the side of the road, one hand in his pocket. 'There were a couple of people here the other day, just before I went out with the *Americanos*. Started off asking questions about my hotel, then they got onto asking questions about you.'

'Who was it? João?'

He shook his head. 'No, some other people. I've seen them around before, but I don't know their names. They sometimes come into town on Saturday nights, that's about all I can tell you.'

'What did they want?'

André took a deep breath and let it out slowly. 'Wanted to know where you come from, who your friends are, that kind of thing. They asked if you like the women, too. It's like they were looking for dirt, Sam.'

'What did you say?'

'I told them they want to know things about you, they should go ask you themselves.'

I smiled. 'Nice.'

'Thing is though, after they spoke to me, they went over to see Manny.'

Without thinking, I looked over at the café. The awning was still rolled up on its steel frame, waiting for Manny to let it down. I wondered what he would have told them about me.

'OK, well, thanks, André,' I said, turning back to him. 'You let me know if they come round again.'

'Course.' André pulled himself back up onto the floating hotel. 'And you let me know if you need anything.'

By the time I started up the street, I could see Papagaio was out of his car and shouting at my shuttered windows. He had his hands cupped around his mouth to direct the sound of his voice between the slats.

When I reached him, I tapped him on the shoulder, making him jump. 'Where you been?' I said. 'Come on, we've got work to do.'

16

The plantation at Hevea was about thirty kilometres north-west of São Tiago, and Papagaio took the roads slowly, not wanting to risk any damage to his car. Spare parts were hard to come by, and an accident could put the Beetle out of action for weeks. We enjoyed the freshness of the early morning air, the hours between sunrise and nine when the day was at its best. They were the coolest, the quietest, and they were also the best for fishing.

'D'you want *musica*?' asked Papagaio, so I pretended not to hear him. I was wondering about my conversation with André, but he took my silence to be indecision, and put some on anyway.

The tape clunked into place when he slipped it into the player and a fuzzy samba beat immediately filled the car. He messed around with the equaliser which was bolted under the dash, until he got the sound he wanted. Seeing him fiddling with the sliders made me grin, remembering how proud he'd been when he bought the sound system last year. He'd bought the car five or six years ago, and with inflation being what it was, he'd paid more for the tape player than he had for the whole car.

Last year's carnival music thumped out from the speakers. Papagaio waggled his hand, drumming his thumb on the steering wheel. He sang the words he knew and hummed the ones he didn't.

We passed through land owned by the Da Silvas and followed the main highway through a small pocket of forest which the conservation laws had forced them to leave intact. It was refreshing to see the rich colours of the leaves after seeing nothing but soil and red dust. The foliage which stood firm against the edge of the road was tinged a rusty colour, but higher up, and deeper amongst the trees, the greens were pushing hard. The smell was warm and sweet and damp.

'André said there were some people asking questions,' I said, after a while. 'Da Silva's people. About whether or not I like women.'

'Women?' Papagaio smiled. 'I told you. She wants to find out if she can have you.'

'I thought maybe it was something to do with Ana . . .' I said, but even as I spoke the words, the image of Ana in my mind was replaced by one of Catarina Da Silva, and I couldn't help imagining the two of us together.

'He tell them anything?' Papagaio asked as we came out of the forest, climbed a gentle hill and passed the sawmill.

'No, but he saw them going over to Manny's place.' I could hear the scream of the circular blades tearing through the wood, and it was loud even over the carnival music.

'You still having problems with him?' He turned to look at me. 'You think he's going to be trouble, I can kill him if you want. You just have to say the word.'

Manny had been Papagaio's friend too, and I didn't know whether to be flattered or horrified. 'No,' I shook my head at him. 'That's not the answer.'

Papagaio shrugged and went back to watching the road. 'OK. But if you change your mind, just let me know.'

Once the mill was behind us, we were back between the

endless scrub of grazing land for several kilometres before we drove onto the Hevea estate.

The place was new and the outer ring of forest remained intact while they felled further inland. I could smell the fires and the smoke as soon as we were close, and I guessed they must've decided to start the burning early this year. I could hear bulldozers and chainsaws in the distance, and when I looked up, the blue sky was hidden by a shimmer of grey. In other places, I had seen days when the air was black with the smoke of the dying forest, and I hoped it wouldn't be the same here.

It wasn't long before the road broke into the main clearing, and on my right I saw the temporary village where the workers were living. Huge sheets of black plastic draped over wooden frames to provide makeshift tents. They were close to the line of trees, finding as much shade and shelter as possible. The front of one tent was surrounded by pots and pans and tin plates, while others were dressed with clothes that were drying in the sun.

On the other side of the road, windrows of felled trees lay in mass graves where the bulldozers had pushed them into regimented lines of tangled branches and trunks. Now they smouldered grey smoke, and even though some of the rows were still glowing from the intense heat of the fires, between them the red soil had already begun to sprout with life.

Up ahead I saw the white sign which told us we were on the Hevea estate and there was a turning to the right leading down to a warehouse and a group of office buildings. They were overlooked by a concrete water tower painted bright yellow.

'This is it,' said Papagaio. 'The new plantation.'

'So where are all the houses, then?'

'They're not ready. They only just started on them this week. Building them up there, past the dam.' Papagaio pointed to where the road continued over a newly built bridge. The dam was no bigger than fifty metres across. 'They blocked the stream so they'd have water for the new trees,' he said. 'There's a little pump on an island in the middle of it, and they hook it up to all these pipes and—'

'If they don't have houses yet, what we here for?' I asked.

Papagaio didn't answer, instead he turned the car to the right, heading towards the offices. He drove straight past them and into the line of trees where a small track led through. We followed it into a clearing.

'We're going to work on this first,' said Papagaio pulling up a few metres from an unfinished house big enough for at least three families to live in. I'd seen houses like it before, back home, but never here. Out here people lived modest.

The building was nothing more than a grey breeze-block shell at the moment, but there were workers crawling all over it. Men were fixing cherry-coloured beams on the roof, they were laying bricks, they were carrying pipes and they were fetching tiles. At one end of the house there was a flatbed Mercedes truck piled high with all the right things to build the kind of house these people had never seen before. I watched a couple of labourers lift down a white porcelain bidet. They put it on the soil and scratched their heads. Most of them had never used anything more than a hole in the ground.

Papagaio climbed out of the car and slammed the door. 'Big, eh?'

I did the same and leaned over to rest my arms on top of the Beetle and watch what was going on. The sun was warm on my back. 'Yeah,' I said. 'It's big all right.'

Papagaio stood with his hands on his hips and shook his head. 'It's *too* big,' he said. 'They'll never put a roof on that. It's not possible.'

I smiled and lit a cigarette, thinking it was going to be an interesting day.

While I smoked, Papagaio went to find the foreman. I watched him talk to a couple of dark-skinned labourers and follow their pointing fingers towards a tall *moreno* with light hair, who spoke to Papagaio and then pointed him towards the men unloading the truck. In turn, they pointed him towards a short man with a pot-belly who was wearing a battered straw hat and sawing wooden beams. He stopped what he was doing, rubbed his hand across his bloated stomach, shrugged his shoulders and then pointed at me.

Papagaio strolled back over, a big grin on his face, and said, 'Apparently *you're* the foreman. You must look important.'

'It's the colour of my skin,' I said. 'Why don't you try him?' I pointed in the direction of the front door. A tall man with green eyes was stepping out of the shadow. He had a gentle face, marred by a scar which ran from the side of his mouth and disappeared into his hairline just above the ear. He was holding what could've been plans and was talking to the *gringo* I'd seen at the *festa* on the beach. I almost expected Paulo to be the next one out of the house.

The *gringo* slipped a pair of dark glasses over his eyes and came out into the sunshine. He turned his head and although I couldn't see his eyes, I could tell he was checking what everyone was doing. Finally his head came to rest pointing in our direction. He looked for a moment and then spoke to the man standing beside him. The foreman nodded and came over to where Papagaio's car was parked.

'You're Papagaio,' the foreman said. And so work began.

17

Throughout the following days, I kept my head down, fetching and carrying and holding for Papagaio. I ran wires, I fixed switches, I installed plugs. I unloaded the car at the beginning of the day and I loaded it back up again when we were done. If there was nothing to wire or light up, I helped with other things. I carried baths, bricks, tiles, cupboards. I swept floors and I hung doors. And the physical labour made me feel clean. I slept well every night in Ana's bed, my body aching for the first few of them, and although it was hard work, it put cash in my pocket, and I could feel my muscles becoming stronger. Even the dreams were sparse, the visions of burning faded, and I was beginning to forget about Manny and Catarina Da Silva.

On the first weekend, Papagaio and I went out in the canoe, but only I baited a line. The *filhote* was mine and I was going to catch him, so Papagaio just came along for the ride. On the Sunday, we all went to Ana's place for cold beer and a barbecue. Paulo didn't say anything about his clinic and when I asked him about the job at Hevea he just winked and gave me another beer. He said he was friendly with the manager over there, so why couldn't he fix a job for a couple of friends, and I didn't bother to push it. I had a few notes in my pocket after pay day on Friday, so how I'd come by the job didn't really make any difference.

*

During the second week, the *gringo* first spoke to me. I was at the back of the house wiring sockets into a bedroom while Papagaio was finishing something off in the roof.

I had my back to the door but I heard him come in and clear his throat. '*Como vai?*' he said.

'*Bem.*' I stood up and turned around. He offered his hand so I wiped my fingers on my trousers and shook it. He gripped a little too tight, like maybe he was trying to prove something.

'Sam, right?' He said, using Portuguese. 'I'm John.'

I took my hand back.

'Paulo told me about you. He has a lot of respect for you,' he said.

'I hear you two get along.'

'We've been talking about opening a health clinic for the workers.' He propped himself against the wall. A casual pose. 'He has some good ideas.'

I felt a little uncomfortable. He was trying to be friendly, as if we had something in common. 'Paulo always has good ideas,' I said. 'He likes to share them, too.'

'He was hoping you'd help.'

'I'm very busy.' I gestured around me and he nodded, both of us falling into an uncomfortable silence which I broke by telling him he spoke good Portuguese.

'But your English is better,' he replied in our native tongue. 'Or so they say.'

I shoved my hands into my pockets, pushing them as deep as they'd go. 'And what else do they say?' I kept to Portuguese.

'That you're more than just an electrician's helper.'

'Do they?'

'Mm-hm.' He looked around the room. 'So, how you finding the job?'

'Good. Hard work, but good.' I didn't tell him it made me feel purged and that it fuelled me with more energy than I'd had in years.

'I'm wondering if it'll ever be finished. Everything's *amanha*, *amanha*.'

'We work differently,' I said. 'This isn't London. Here we have elastic time. Everything takes longer.'

He made a noise like he knew what I meant, and surveyed the room again. 'So I see.' He moved away towards the door leading into the en-suite bathroom and peered in, keeping one hand on the door frame. He came back to me, saying, '*Amanha*, *amanha*. Well, if that's how long it takes . . .'

'Everything does,' I said.

'OK, well, I'll let you get on.'

And that was it. I had met the *gringo*. My life would never be the same again.

I saw him again that weekend, only this time he had a bottle of beer in his hand. He was on the *praia*, talking to Paulo, and I was on the river, trying to catch my *filhote*. The music had started early and the beach was full of people by four o' clock. I watched them from the canoe while I waited for the fish to bite but my luck was thin and the *filhote* wasn't hungry.

I had made another bet with Papagaio and as the sun went down and I came in towards the sand, I could see him standing by Manolo's makeshift bar. He came over and helped me pull the boat onto the sand.

'You do know you're never going to catch that fish, don't you?' he said as I handed him a fold of money. 'Someone up there is trying to tell you something. Maybe he's not so happy with you. Every time you go out on the river, he whispers down to the fish and tells him his belly is full. They see you coming.'

'Why don't you just get me a drink?' I pointed at the money in his hand.

'You drink too much for a priest,' he said, starting the old routine, nudging me and adding, 'I hear you like the women, too.'

'Is Ana here?' I asked. She was hoping to make it over to the *praia*, but said she had work to finish.

'Not today. Anyway, you two shouldn't be seen together,' he joked. 'What will people think?'

'People will think whatever they like,' I said. 'Whatever they *usually* think.'

'I forgot,' he smiled. 'You're a changed man.'

'And when did you ever see a priest who didn't like women and drink?'

'I don't know so many priests.'

'Because you're a heathen?'

He laughed out loud, putting one hand on his stomach and another up in the air, starting to scuff his feet in the sand, and sway his hips in a small dance. 'At least in my religion, we know how to laugh and have—'

'Drink, Papagaio, just get me a drink.'

He danced backwards to the bar, shuffling and turning while I looked out at the river just as a *boto* surfaced and blew a jet out into the air. It swallowed hard and disappeared again.

'What the hell was that?' said a voice behind me.

'*Boto*,' I said. 'River dolphin.' I turned around and the *gringo* handed me a cold can of Brahma beer. I preferred Antarctica or San Miguel, but beer is beer, so I accepted it with a nod. I popped the ring pull with a crack-hiss, before touching it against his saying, 'Cheers.' It didn't occur to me that he had spoken in English and that I replied in the same language. It had been a long time since I'd used it out loud. Usually it was just what was in my head, and even that had begun to fade over the past year or so. 'There's a myth,' I said. 'Some people say it turns into a man at night. Comes to shore and seduces young women. Virgins.'

'Only virgins?'

'If he only looked for virgins, he'd be frustrated in São Tiago,' I said. 'Here he just has to make do.'

He smirked and watched the water, saying, 'You know the river.'

'More than some. Not as much as others.'

'And you're a priest?'

I wondered what he meant by it, and whether he intended to judge me. I knew he had met Ana but I wasn't sure if he knew of our relationship, so I let the question hang. Instead, I asked him how the house was going and he said it was going slow but I already knew that. Then he asked me how I had ended up in São Tiago, so I asked him why a man who lived alone needed such a big house. That made him laugh. 'I have a family,' he said. 'They're coming to join me as soon as the house is finished.'

I didn't look at him. I kept my eyes on the river, wondering if my fish was out there.

'They'll probably find it difficult when they get here,' he said.

'Probably.' I lit a cigarette and offered him one but he held up his hand and said no, he was trying to give up, it was hardest when he was having a drink.

'It's a primitive place for your family,' I said, glancing back at the party, seeing the *Americanos* sitting by the bar, where they usually sat on these occasions. There were only two of them tonight, though, and one of them was looking in our direction. 'It can be rough, too, you've already seen that. That why you need protection?'

The *gringo* laughed. 'Those guys? They're not here to protect me,' he said. 'They're here to protect the company's invest-ment. They've put a great deal of money into the plantation.'

'So why aren't they at the plantation?' I looked at him but he didn't meet my eye, tipping back his head and taking a long drink of beer instead.

'Because you're part of that investment, right?'

He swallowed and shrugged. 'I suppose I am. But I can protect myself if I have to.'

It sounded like he was telling me he didn't need anyone to keep his family from danger, but I couldn't tell if he was trying to convince me or himself. 'I'm sure,' I said.

For a while we just stood there, listening to the beat of the music, feeling the sand under our feet. It struck me he might feel uncomfortable, standing in silence, but when I thought about it, I didn't really care. In the house, we'd been in his place, his territory, but now we were on mine. My mind strayed back to the fish that was waiting beneath the water, waiting for my hook and my knife. Severino's catch had weighed in at sixty kilos and his hands had bled for days. My catch would be bigger. My hands would bleed for longer. Even if someone were telling him to keep away, I would find a way to catch him.

I was earning good money from the work at Hevea and I'd bought some new lines and hooks. Stronger ones. I'd been eating well and my strength was up. I'd even started to put some money aside so I could hire one of André's outboards to take me further upriver.

'I'm worried it'll be boring for my son when he gets here.' The *gringo*'s voice interrupted my thoughts and brought me back to the party. 'I don't know if there'll be enough for him to do,' he said. 'I mean, Sarah, that's my wife, she'll have a hard time trying to keep busy, so you can imagine what it'll be like for my boy. He's nearly thirteen now. And you know what boys are like at that age. It's all about the *latest things*. Keeping up with the times.'

'This isn't the best place for that,' I told him. 'There's only three things this place is good for. Fishing, hunting and drinking. Four if you count sex, but if he's only twelve . . .'

'Maybe you could teach him to fish.'

The smoke from my cigarette caught in my throat and made me cough. It wasn't a melodramatic cough, not so the *gringo* would notice. I flicked the cigarette into the river and turned to him. For the first time, I really looked at his face.

'My wife, Sarah, she probably wouldn't be so keen. She's very protective but it would do him some good. Make him stronger; give him some experiences to take back with him. An adventure,' he said. 'You think you could give him that?'

'No. I mean . . . you don't even know me. Why would you trust me with your boy?'

He drained his can and crushed it in one hand. 'Paulo speaks highly of you. He said you're the best person to ask.'

'Paulo?' I said and turned away, thinking he didn't really know Paulo either. 'No, it's a bad idea.' I looked back at the river. Paulo was trying to set me up with the *gringo* like he was a matchmaker; bringing me some home-grown therapy by passing me off as a babysitter. Maybe if he'd talked to me about it first, but letting the *gringo* spring it on me like this . . . 'No,' I said. 'I drink too much.' And the last time I'd had contact with a child, it had been to watch him die, to hear his hoarse cries of pain as his flesh smouldered and a gun was touched to the patch of bone where his scorched skin had peeled away from his skull. I didn't need to be reminded of such things.

'You and me both,' he said, not knowing the truth of it. 'We all drink too much.'

'It wouldn't work. I don't want to babysit your boy. Anyway, I have things to do.' Saying it mean, but not sure why I was being so hard on him, feeling like I barely knew myself these days. Too many changes.

He took it well, though, saying, 'OK, fair enough. Maybe Paulo will take him.'

'Paulo? Paulo wouldn't know which end of the boat to paddle from if I wasn't there.'

'Did I hear my name?'

I turned and saw Paulo standing behind us, looking as though he might've been there for a while.

'I was just saying you're a better doctor than you are a fisherman.'

Paulo opened his mouth to speak but I raised my voice to stop him. 'Did you tell the *gri*— the *Senhor* about how we saved our friend Eduardo?' It was low and I knew it. Paulo had no idea what I'd been through in Roraima. He didn't know what effect it would have on me, mentioning the boy, asking me to teach him.

Paulo's smile dropped and his lips came together. I walked past him and patted him hard on the shoulder. 'You can tell him all about it while I go to the bar.' I wanted to lash out at him for setting me up. 'I'm sure someone owes me a drink.'

I left them to talk about me and went to find beer. I took a couple of cold bottles from the bar and went to the other side of the beach. Papagaio saw me and asked if I wanted to play cards with some of the others – there were a few notes on the table, but I said no. Instead, I sat down and took off my flip-flops so I could dig my feet into the sand. It was cool now the sun had gone down. I closed my eyes and tried to forget the boy, his flesh seared, his hair gone, but the vision was replaced by another unwelcome image. Now I saw Eduardo, and I remembered how I'd taken his rigid corpse up to the *fazenda*, not really knowing who he was. Just a man who worked for Da Silva, another life which had vanished because the heart had stopped beating. It saddened me that I could no longer believe there was a paradise; that no place was big enough for all the souls that had been torn prematurely from their earthly roots.

I shook the death from my head and drank half a bottle of beer in one go. I thought about the *gringo*'s living child instead; about how positive it might feel to teach him. Twelve years old. I wouldn't be able to do it, though, for surely it would bring too many painful memories. Even now, just thinking about it, I wondered how old the child in Roraima had been.

June 1986

18

Work on the *gringo*'s house was almost complete by the beginning of June. The roof was on, the walls were up and most of the floors were down. There were one or two snags with the plumbing but that wasn't my problem.

'Ten families could live in here,' said Papagaio.

We were standing in the middle of the living room, on the black and white tiles which chequered the floor. There was some furniture in there, all of it still covered by clear plastic to protect it from the dust, and most of it appearing to be too small for such a big room. I could see it was made of rattan and fabric. At one end of the room, double doors led into a dining room.

Papagaio took off his hat and hung it on the back of a chair. 'Still don't see why it needs to be so big,' he said.

'Maybe it makes him feel more important.' I gathered a few tools and slipped them into my pockets. 'Or maybe it's just what he's used to.' I picked up some rolls of cable and took them out to the car. They were heavy and the Beetle sagged when I dumped them in the back seat. I called back to Papagaio, 'You going to carry some of this stuff or just stand there looking like you saw a two metre *tucunaré*?'

'A two metre *tucunaré*?' he shouted back. 'That's what excites you? Jesus, Sam, there's no hope for you. I never knew a man get so excited about catching a fish. Maybe if you'd said a great big pair of . . .'

I heard an engine approach and looked up to see the *gringo*'s C-10 driving into the clearing. He jumped out, shorts and a T-shirt, shoes, with socks pulled right up to his knees, and came straight over to me saying, 'Sam, I'm glad I caught you.'

I backed away from the car, standing up straight and nodding once in greeting. I'd spoken to him only a few times since that night on the beach, and even then not much more than to pass the time of day. Nothing to make him come across so friendly.

'I was hoping you'd come to a barbecue on Sunday night.' He walked over. 'My family will be here. Landing at São Tiago in the morning.'

'Some kind of party for the *camponeses*?' I said. 'So the peasants can celebrate your house being finished?'

'More like just a few people to meet my wife and son,' he replied. 'Managers, suppliers, that kind of thing. Paulo's coming. I thought we'd have a big party for the workers in a couple of weeks. Give me time to get some stuff in from Vila Rica.'

'You must be looking forward to seeing them,' I said.

'Yeah,' he smiled, a distant look coming over him before he came back to me, saying, 'Why not bring Ana, too?'

'OK, thanks,' I said, watching him. 'Sunday, then.'

I waited until he had climbed into his truck and driven away, then I turned back to loading the car.

'What'd he want?' said Papagaio coming out of the house with the rest of our tools, his eyes following the pickup as it disappeared amongst the trees and dust.

'He said you're sacked.'

'Sacked?' He turned to me. 'Why? What'd I do? He say why? Did . . . ?' Papagaio's face went blank and then he lit up like a lamp and punched me on the shoulder, saying, 'Bastard.' He was always a little slow.

'So what was it?' he said once we were in the car. 'What'd he want?'

'Nothing. Wants me to come to a barbecue on Sunday afternoon. Having a party for his family or something. Some kind of welcome.'

'Am I invited?'

'I don't know, he ask you to come?'

'No.' Papagaio was disappointed. He started the engine and drove us away, staying quiet for a while and then asking, 'So, you going?'

'I suppose.'

'But you don't want to?'

I shrugged. 'Could be a set-up,' I said. 'They want me to take the *gringo*'s boy on the river.'

'They?'

'Paulo and the *gringo*. Ana too.' I'd spoken to her about it already, the night the *gringo* first suggested it. When I asked if it was her idea, she just smiled and said that I should do it. It would be fun. 'They want me to teach him to fish but I said no.'

'Oh, I see. You turned them down so now they're having a barbecue just for you? So they can persuade you to take the boy fishing, I mean. Yeah, that makes a lot of sense.' It was a rare example of sarcasm from my friend, and it had the right effect. 'Come on, Sam, it's just a barbecue.'

'Yeah, I know. You're right.'

'Of course I am. They just can't get enough of your company. Everybody loves Sam.'

'Yeah, right.'

'Anyway, free food and beer is what matters. Free food and beer.'

And I suppose he had a point.

19

I borrowed Papagaio's car, and called to pick up Paulo on Sunday afternoon, ready to face the *gringo*'s barbecue. He was showered and clean by the time I arrived, and he looked different, like he'd grown. I noticed he was wearing shoes instead of flip-flops and it made me glance down at my own dusty feet, resting on the car pedals.

'You look smart,' I said, craning my head out of the window, pretending to scrutinise him.

Paulo grinned and shrugged as if I'd caught him doing something he shouldn't have. 'We don't want them to think we're *camponeses*,' he said.

'We are *camponeses*.'

Paulo clicked his tongue at me, then climbed in and pulled the door shut. He looked round at the back seat. 'No Ana?'

'I tried to persuade her, but she said I should go on my own. Said she has too much work to do, but I reckon she just wants to get rid of me,' I smiled. 'Get some peace.'

'Too much work?'

'That's what she said.' But I suspected she wanted me to go alone because she thought it would be good for me, and I'd told her as much. She protested, of course, showing me the piles of clothes that needed altering and fixing, but I knew that nothing was ever urgent in São Tiago. Nobody needed their clothes altered that desperately. I told her I'd stay to help, but she pushed me out the door telling me to have a good time, meet some new people. Eventually I gave in and did as she asked. She'd been right about the job, so maybe she was right about this too.

'So his family's here, then?' I said, taking a cassette out of my top pocket where it had been crushed in with my cigarettes. I turned the unmarked tape over in my fingers, checking which side was spooled, and slipped it into the deck under the dashboard.

'They were supposed to arrive on the *Bandeirante* last night,' he said, but we both knew that sometimes the plane didn't come, or there would be a delay if something happened on the stop at São Felix. 'If it landed,' he said, 'they're here.'

I pulled away from São Tiago, drums beating, guitar starting and then my old Rolling Stones compilation bringing Mick Jagger right into the car with us, telling us he lives on the ninety-ninth floor of an apartment block.

The sun was dropping in the sky and it shone in my eyes so I reached up and flipped down the visor, singing, 'Hey – you – getoffa my cloud,' and turning to Paulo, both of us bobbing our heads in time with the beat. He was singing too, overdoing the movements of his mouth because he didn't know the words or what they meant. When it changed to 'Ruby Tuesday', though, we quietened down.

'Managed to put a few notes together,' I said as we passed the endless fields of scrub. 'Was thinking of hiring a boat from André and going upriver one weekend. Sleep on the sand. Night fishing. You want to come?'

There were a couple of *vaqueiros* ahead, their tick-ridden horses mooching along the line of the fence.

'When you thinking?' said Paulo. 'Next weekend?'

The men were riding low in the saddle, both of them carrying leather pouches on their belts where their knives would be. Small, narrow-brimmed hats, with chin-straps fastened tight.

One of them had a rifle across his back. 'Weekend after,' I said, pulling the car to the other side of the road, so the horses wouldn't be startled. The riders waved us past, one of them nodding thanks.

'Looking for your *filhote*?' Paulo raising his hand to them.

'Yeah, you want to come?'

'Can't,' he said. 'I'm going to Brasilia.'

'Brasilia? How? What you going there for?'

'Going up with the wagon from Hevea. They're sending someone for supplies, so I'm going with them. I want to look into buying materials for the clinic.'

'The *gringo*'s going to help, then?'

'Not exactly. He wants to go with the idea, but his company, they don't.' He shook his head. 'I'm going to do it here in São Tiago, instead. Build it right by the river.'

'And the money?'

'I've got some from the old place. It's tied up in Brasilia, but I can get it.'

'Yeah? How much you got?'

'Some,' he said.

I gave him a look. 'You mean, all this time you had money?'

'I have *some*, Sam, not lots.'

'You have enough?'

'No. But I was thinking maybe you could help with that.'

I sighed. 'I already told you, I—'

'Wait a minute,' said Paulo. 'I'm not asking you to get your hands dirty. I wouldn't want to drag you up off your arse. All I was thinking was maybe you could go to São Felix, speak with Father Mateus. Maybe he'll give us some funding, money to buy materials. He'll help if you tell him the Indians are going to benefit. And having God on our side would be good.'

I kept my eyes on the road ahead, thinking about what Paulo was saying. He was right about Father Mateus. He and his bishop had something of a tradition in São Felix, but it usually involved upsetting the *latifundistas*. And with people like the Da Silvas living on your doorstep, that wasn't a good thing. 'What about the land?' I asked him. 'You even know who owns it?'

'Down by the river near Manolo's? That's anybody's. São Tiago belongs to anybody; whoever claims it. You know what the laws are like around here.'

'You need to be sure no one's claimed it already, then. Don't forget what happened to Father Jentel.' Some *posseiros*, farmers without official ownership of the land they occupied, led by Father Jentel, protested when their health clinic in Santa Terezinha was destroyed by local landowners. The settlers built it with their own hands, just like Paulo wanted to do, but the *fazendeiros* didn't like it, so they tore it down and bulldozed most of the village. When the people protested, the *pistoleiros* went in to burn the houses, shoot the men. Jentel went to prison for ten years for inciting the people to revolt. Brasilian justice.

'I *am* sure,' said Paulo. 'And don't talk to me about Jentel. That was ten years ago and things have changed. Even Santa Terezinha has probably forgotten about it. It's not like that any more.'

'Come on, Paulo, don't be so naïve. You know what happens out here when you try something like this. Especially when you involve the church. Landowners and priests don't mix. Out here it doesn't make any difference who you are, they shoot you if they don't like you. You remember what happened in Ribeirao Bonito.' Not so long ago, two peasant women were tortured in their cells by the police. Forced to kneel on bottle caps, pins stuck under their fingernails and into their chests. The bishop went to sort it out, so they shot one of his priests. Right in front of him. A policeman put a bullet in his face.

'Things *have* changed,' said Paulo. 'Landowners are not like that any more.'

'So how long ago was it the Da Silvas murdered their

145

workers? Three, four years? Maybe Papagaio can fill us in on the details.' I was starting to lose patience. 'The leader of the Guarani Indians was killed down in Compestre three years ago,' I said. 'A nun killed in Para less than *two* years ago. Shit, Paulo, we have *fazendeiros, garimpeiros, pistoleiros*,' I punctuated each one by slapping my palm on the steering wheel, 'and you're trying to tell me these things don't happen here any more? That things have changed?' I had no idea how many bones were bleaching out in the grazing lands, or decaying in the humidity of the forest.

'The Da Silvas have been quiet for years,' Paulo said.

'Maybe that's only because we don't hear about it.'

'All right.' He threw up his hands. 'So, things *can* still be bad, but we've come a long way from where we were and we can do something to help. This is our chance. Things are a lot calmer here than they are in other places. We're small and insignificant. When was the last time something like that happened here?'

'Three or four years,' I said. 'When the Da Silvas burned their workers.'

'OK,' he said, sounding irritated. 'So we go see them, then. We make sure it's OK to build our clinic. We get their per-*mission* if that's what it takes. They say not to, then we rethink it.'

'Who said anything about *we*?' I shook my head.

'You know her, don't you?'

'Not really,' I said, thinking how she'd displayed herself to me, and how I had been drawn to what I had seen, in spite of what I'd heard about her. The thought of seeing her again was strangely appealing and I tested myself with the notion that she was not quite what people believed her to be – that it was her husband who sanctioned the cruelty.

'You know her well enough to speak to her,' he said. 'You've met her a couple of times.'

'It's not a good idea. We should keep away from her.'

I sensed Paulo turning to look at me, but I kept my eyes straight ahead, concentrating on the road.

'She really bothered you, didn't she?' he said. 'It's not like you. Usually I see you take everything in your stride like you couldn't care less, but Da Silva really seems to have bothered you.'

'She's dangerous. The kind of person who'll make you look at her right hand while the left slips a knife around your throat.'

'She's really that bad?'

'Tell you the truth, Paulo, it was hard not to like her.'

'Then go talk to her. If you like her, talk to her. For me.'

'Just 'cause you like the look of something doesn't mean it's not dangerous,' I said.

But Paulo wasn't going to give up without a fight, so he pulled his trump card. 'Have you talked to Ana about the clinic?'

I sighed. 'Of course.'

'And what did she say?'

'I took the job, Paulo, and I'm coming to the damn barbecue, let's leave it at that.' I turned up the volume and we listened to The Stones until we arrived at the *gringo*'s giant house, no more talking, the car dipping and rising in the potholes as we drove between the trees that had been left around the building. Perhaps when the work was completely finished, they'd fill the holes, smooth the road.

I stopped the car at the front of the house, killing the engine, but the sounds of music and voices were coming from the back so we walked round without trying the front door. There were a few people on the wide veranda and more inside the house, maybe twenty people in total. A barbecue was glowing, several large pieces of beef were draped over the grill, some chicken and *paca* too, by the look of the white flesh. The smell of the meat and the charcoal was good, making me realise how hungry I was. There were crates of ice filled with bottles of Antarctica, San Miguel, some Coke and Fanta, and people were helping themselves.

The *gringo* was talking to a group of people who must have been management, they were rich-looking, wearing smart clothes. They were all getting along just fine, smiling, making all the right gestures and noises. Beside him was a European woman with pale skin. Someone who hadn't seen a lot of sun, she had a washed-out, puffy appearance as if she needed to get outside more. She was tall, like him and her face was kind. Her hair a reddish colour, light, and she probably preferred to be called strawberry blonde rather than ginger. I wouldn't blame her, though, 'strawberry blonde' suited her better.

As soon as the *gringo* saw us, he broke off his conversation and came over, his hand touching his wife's elbow. He introduced us, saying, 'This is Paulo, the doctor I told you about. And this is his friend Sam.' He made us sound like partners, a couple of *viados*, but I smiled and said enough to be polite. We talked about nothing really, him telling us about the plantation, what the plan was. As soon as the conversation slowed, though, I escaped over to one of the beer crates.

I helped myself to a cold one and took some food from the barbecue. It was good white meat and I wondered who had hunted it. *Paca* was small and well hidden in the forest, it was hard to shoot. I'd shot a few myself, spending the night in a hammock, suspended in the trees over a path worn in the forest, but it took patience. Waiting for him to come underneath, jumping at every movement, twitching at every whisper, wondering if it was him. I'd done it but not enjoyed it so much. I preferred to catch fish. Being on the water felt safer than being in the trees.

When I'd eaten, I glanced around to see if there was anyone to talk to, but Paulo was still deep in conversation with the *gringos*, laughing with the managers, and I didn't really know anybody else.

I wandered over to the edge of the veranda, following it along the line of the house, thinking how much space they had for one small family. It was a different world for people like them; they could make of it what they wanted. Burn some trees, build a house, and create a new environment. Nothing could stop them from shaping their surroundings. I stopped and looked out at the forest, maybe thirty metres away, on the other side of what seemed to be a vegetable garden. It was hard to make out what was planted, the sun was gone now and the electric lights around the house cocooned us in a small island of conspicuous civilisation. I felt that all I had to do was step out of the light, into the darkness, and I would be in another place.

'Impressive, isn't it?'

'Hmm?' I turned to see who had spoken.

'Not as big as my place, but impressive nonetheless,' she said.

Catarina Da Silva was wearing a dress. Bright pink silk, narrow straps, the skirt falling just above her knees. The colour was good against her skin, it made her look different from the way I remembered her. Her fingernails were a matching pink, perfectly manicured, as were her toenails. She was wearing high-heeled sandals, silver, which made her taller, stretching her calves, making them firm. Her hair was down, falling onto her shoulders, displaying fewer of the colours I had seen that day at the *fazenda* because there was no sunlight to grace it here. It was full around her face, giving her a softer look. I tried to remind myself that she was the same woman who was supposed to have ordered the burning of her workers, the same woman I had been arguing with Paulo about, but it was impossible to see past the way she looked. It was hard to be afraid of someone so desirable.

She was holding a drink in one hand, a cigarette in the other.

'I didn't know you were here,' I said. 'I didn't see you.'

149

'We came late. You a friend of the *gringo*?' she asked, looking me up and down, just as I had done to her.

'Not really. You?'

'Uh-uh,' she sipped her caipirinha and licked her lips. 'We supply beef, that's all. Nothing glamorous. My husband is over there talking to him now, trying to see if he can squeeze more money out of the foreigners.'

I looked over at the party but I didn't know what her husband looked like. He could have been any one of the men.

'He thinks he's in the same league,' she said. 'And you?'

'Do I think I'm in the same league?'

'No. I mean why are you here?'

I shrugged. 'I'm not really sure. I work for him, that's all.'

She nodded at me, lifting her face, showing me the smooth line of her neck, taking a last drag from her cigarette and tossing it out onto the dirt.

'Walk with me,' she said.

Catarina Da Silva put her arm through mine and led me along the line of the house. 'I haven't seen you for some time. I've missed your company.' It was a strange thing for her to say. I had only met her twice, and neither time was a social occasion.

We reached the end of the veranda and I glanced back as she led me around the corner, but no one seemed to have noticed that we had gone. When we were out of sight, Da Silva stopped and turned to face me. I had my back to the wall, just a couple of metres from the rear of an air conditioner which I knew was in one of the bedrooms. It was switched on, the humming loud, drowning the music from the party. The shutters were closed over the bedroom window, the kind of shutters I had only seen on expensive houses. The spaces between the horizontal angled slats were dark. The bedroom was unoccupied.

'Have a drink,' she said, offering me her glass.

I looked down at it. It was darker round here, no lights under this part of the overhanging roof, but there was enough light for me to see the lipstick mark around the rim. 'No. Thanks.'

'Go on,' she said. 'Take it.'

I hesitated, but sensed she would press me further so I took the glass from her hand, the tips of her fingers touching mine as I did so, and lifted the glass to my mouth. I took a sip and passed it back. Da Silva turned and placed the glass on the wall which ran around the veranda.

'I think we should get to know each other better,' she said. 'I think we could become good friends.'

'I'm not so sure that could ever happen. We're from very different places.'

'Different places?' She feigned surprise. 'No, not so different. And anyway, there are some things that bring people together no matter how different they are.'

'What things?'

'Come on,' she smiled, moving closer to me, her face level with mine because she was wearing the heels. 'Passion. Lust. Whatever you want to call it.'

'I'm a priest,' I said, an automatic response. 'Lust is a sin.'

'You're no priest.' She lowered her voice. 'I saw the way you looked at me. I know what you want.'

'We should get back to the party,' I said.

'Not this time, Sam. I won't let you run away from me this time. I know what you want.'

'I—'

'It's what we both want.' She took another step closer to me and put one hand on my hip, taking me by surprise. 'I see how you look at me.' But what surprised me most was my inaction. Like hypnotised prey, I did nothing to stop her. I allowed it all to happen as, with the other hand, she reached out and touched the side of my face, running her fingers to the back of my head and pulling me towards her. She pressed her mouth against mine, taking my lower lip between her teeth and gently biting.

Now her hand was inside my shirt, moving over my chest, making its way down to press hard against the front of my trousers, squeezing me before sliding the strap from her shoulder, taking my hand and holding it to her naked breast, letting me feel the nipple harden under my touch.

'How's that?' she asked. 'Feel good?'

Unable to stop, I allowed her to move my other hand under her skirt where she held it in the warmth between her legs as her tongue pushed into my mouth, meeting with no resistance.

And as I returned the kiss, her hand came back under my shirt and the softness of her fingers made me think of Ana and how coarse hers were in comparison. Ana, whose fingers were never manicured, whose hands were accustomed to working hard for a meagre living. With such thoughts, Ana's face came into my mind and I broke away from Da Silva, stepping back, pushing her away and shaking my head.

'No.' I looked at her, the shoulder strap hanging by her arm, her dress pulled down to the side, one of her breasts in plain view, and once again I couldn't help myself from staring at her. For all that I despised the things she had done, the things she was capable of doing, she was a captivating woman standing half-naked before me and I wanted to touch her.

'You're right,' she said, misunderstanding my reasons for breaking away. 'Not here.' She pulled the strap to her shoulder, straightened the dress and smoothed it down. 'My husband.'

'Yes.' I clung to that thought. 'Your husband.' She would stop now. *We* would stop.

'You have lipstick on you,' she said. 'Let me wipe it off.' She brushed her finger along the bottom of my lower lip, her eyes fixed on mine. 'There.'

I wiped my mouth with the back of my hand, not knowing what to say to her. I wanted to build a life with Ana and yet I was overcome with desire for the murderous woman who now stood before me.

'Stay here,' she said. 'I'm going back to the party. You should wait a few minutes.'

I nodded.

Behind me, a light came on in the bedroom and spilled around me through the slats in the wooden shutter. I moved away from the window, and Da Silva did the same, slipping to one side so that we were in shadow again.

'A little light,' she said. 'Good. You can tell me better how my lipstick looks.'

'Smudged.'

'Then I'll need to fix it,' she said and paused, looking me up and down. After a moment she leaned in again and put her mouth on mine, saying, 'Next time, *Padre*,' her breath on my lips, 'come to me at home.' And with that, she turned and left.

I leaned back against the wall and lifted my face to the ceiling. I didn't turn to watch her disappear round the corner, but remained where I was, listening to the sound of her heels fading as she made her way further along the veranda. Then I closed my eyes and allowed the noise of the air conditioner to fill my mind. Beside me the bedroom light went out and I was left, once more, in darkness.

20

After a few minutes, I rejoined the barbecue, but with a head full of passion and confusion, I couldn't look anyone in the eye, least of all Catarina Da Silva. So I made my escape, taking another beer and wandering into the house which was empty because everybody was still outside, enjoying the evening. The shutter door was smooth on its hinges, not a squeak.

I went through into the main sitting room, the one with the black and white tiles, noticing how cool it was. Not at all like my little oven back in São Tiago. I stepped out of my flip-flops and felt the tiles, smooth and cold against my feet which were hardened from years of walking on rough surfaces. The flooring in my own home was like heavy sandpaper in comparison. The furniture was uncovered now. Low, splinterless tables with glass tops, cane chairs, and a number of cardboard boxes strewn in one corner.

One of the boxes was open, so I pulled back the flap to peer inside. It was filled with paperbacks, maybe fifty in total, and I guessed the other boxes would contain books too. I squatted down and lifted out a pile so I could read the spines. Some were Portuguese dictionaries and phrase books, there were books for other languages, too, but most of them were paperback novels – some good, some bad. I'd never seen so many books together in one place since I'd come to São Tiago, and I was tempted to open the other boxes but I heard a shuffle behind me. I stood up and turned around, feeling as if I'd been caught stealing. 'I'm sorry, I was—'

The boy was wearing a pair of shorts and a black T-shirt with the name of what I guessed was a band printed on the front. His legs were skinny, his knees like knots in a piece of string. His face was pale underneath his blond hair. He looked ill, but I knew this was how most people looked where we came from, and I tried to imagine how he must see me. Lean, dark-skinned and weathered, with lines on my unshaven face and scars across my hands. Dusty feet, fingernails that were cracked and hard, hair that needed to be cut, and empty eyes that were ancient to a young boy. Perhaps I even scared him.

I looked at him for a moment and he looked back. Then I sighed and squatted down. 'You have some nice books,' I said in English.

'They're not mine.'

'Oh, I see.' I stacked a handful back into the box.

'Those are mine,' he pointed.

I followed the line of his finger. 'Do you mind if I look?'

He shrugged.

I took the knife from the back of my waistband. It wasn't a large knife, no more than fifteen centimetres on the blade, but I noticed the way the boy watched it as I slit the seal on the box.

I pulled back the flaps and studied the spines and covers which were visible. 'Some good books,' I said. 'You like to read?' Mostly they were kids' stuff.

'Sometimes.' He didn't move.

I glanced at him. 'And do you read these other books? Your parents' books?'

He looked away. 'Sometimes.'

'So which ones do you like?'

He didn't answer.

'Horror stories?' I asked.

He shook his head.

'Science fiction? Spaceships? You like that?'

He shook his head.

'Romance?'

He screwed up his face, wrinkling his brow and shaking his head.

'OK, not romance, then.' I laughed. 'So how about spy stories?'

He nodded.

'Ah, spy stories? Good. Why not? And how about some of these others?'

'Some of them are boring.'

I laughed again. He was right, of course, some of them *were* boring. 'But some of them are not,' I said. 'You should read some of these. How old are you? Eleven? Twelve?'

'Nearly thirteen.'

'OK, then you're just the right age to read this one.'

I took a book from the top of the box I'd restacked and held it out to him. He took a step towards me and glanced at the cover. 'We read it at school,' he said. 'It's boring.'

I withdrew my hand and studied the cover. 'You remember what it's about?'

'Some kids get stranded on an island. One of them dies, I think. That's about it.'

'And you read it at school, eh?'

'Yes.' Saying it like I'd accused him of lying.

'In class?'

'Uh-huh.'

'And I bet it was cold outside, maybe raining, and the desks were hard and smelled of polish. Am I right?'

No reply.

'And you had your cheek to the desk most of the time, looking out the window, trying to think of something else?' I scratched my chin like I was thinking. 'Oh yeah,' I raised a finger, 'and you were wearing a tie and it was nearly lunchtime and you had homework to do that night?'

He screwed up his face again, his nose wrinkling right up towards his forehead.

'And maybe you had a headache and you didn't like the teacher.'

'Mrs Wilkins,' he said, giving me that sour face again. 'Really boring.'

'And the teacher read a bit and then each of you read a bit in turn, and then the class ended and you'd read a bit more the next week?'

'Yes.'

Just saying those things brought memories to me – memories beyond those I was most accustomed to conjuring – and I could see myself as a child at school. Waxed desks, playground games, windy days, rain on the glass, chalk on the board. Things that reminded me of home. England. It seemed like I always had a good time at school, and even when it wasn't good, I always enjoyed having a bad time.

I held the book out to him again. 'This time read it for you. Not for class. Not for anybody else. Go outside tomorrow morning when the sun is up and the air is warm and the cicadas are singing in the forest. Find yourself a good spot in the shade where you can see the trees. Sit for a minute; open the book and smell its pages. When you've done that, start reading.'

He looked at me as if I were mad.

'Trust me,' I said. 'You'll like this book.'

Leaving the party, I shook hands with the *gringo* and kissed his wife on both cheeks. To everyone else I just raised a hand and said goodbye. I didn't know them, hadn't spoken to them, and would probably never meet them again.

Paulo and I made our way round to where we had left the car at the front of the house, but Catarina Da Silva intercepted me on the way, taking my hand in a formal manner and kissing both cheeks. But as she did so, she whispered in my ear. 'Come to me at the *fazenda*. Afternoons. I'll be waiting.'

I nodded, making it look polite and left her standing in the glare of the electric lights as Paulo and I went out to the car.

I climbed in, glancing back at her, seeing her silhouette, remembering how her skin had felt on mine. Then I started the engine and pulled away from the house.

I took us out of the trees, through the central hub of the estate and out onto the road to São Tiago. I kept my speed down; there were no lights here other than the beams from the VW and I'd had a few beers at the barbecue.

'So that was Catarina Da Silva?' Paulo said after a while, saying it like he'd been mulling it over.

'Hmm?'

'The one in the pink dress. I've never seen her before. You're right, she's hot.'

I turned to Paulo, not really seeing his face in the dark. 'That's the beer talking.'

'I saw you with her,' he said. 'And I noticed she came over to say goodbye. You must get on all right.'

I stayed quiet, wondering what Paulo had seen.

'What were you talking about? I thought you were supposed to be scared of her.'

'I am.' But not for the same reasons any more. There was something else which scared me about Catarina Da Silva now.

'She didn't look so scary to me,' he said. 'Beautiful, maybe, but scary?'

'Hmm. A jaguar's beautiful,' I said, 'and if you saw one you might be tempted to touch it, but it would be a mistake.'

'Why would you think about touching it?' he asked.

I ignored the question, deflecting it, saying, 'It might not have looked like I was scared of her, but that doesn't mean I'm going to see her about your clinic. I don't want to have anything to do with her.' And once again I had to force from my mind the memory of the feel of her skin beneath the silk dress. I wanted Catarina Da Silva, just like she said, and it had taken a great deal of strength to turn her away.

'So where did you disappear to?' he asked, sensing the conversation was over.

'What d'you mean?'

'I hardly saw you all night,' he yawned. 'Mind you, I wasn't really looking.'

'I went into the house,' I told him. 'I met the boy.'

'Me too. He seems like a nice kid. Quiet.'

'Yeah. We talked for a while.'

'So you going to take him fishing?'

I took a deep breath. 'Oh, I don't know. I don't think—'

Any further talk was interrupted by a tapir which broke out from the forest on our left, swerving and running ahead of the car, caught in the beam of the headlights. I slowed and followed it, watching it move from side to side across the road, not knowing which way to go. It was comical to see, just its rear quarters moving in the light, and Paulo and I laughed as we watched it.

After a minute or so, though, I switched off the headlights and brought the car to a standstill, giving the creature time to escape back into the forest. We continued our journey in silence, and Paulo was snoring by the time we reached São Tiago.

I dropped him home, then went to Ana's place, letting myself in. I showered, washing the whole evening from me, erasing any thoughts of Catarina Da Silva. Clean, I went to Ana in her bed. I drew back the sheet and woke her with kisses, reaffirming my desire for her by making love before finally lying back, tangled in her arms.

As I waited for sleep to take me, I thought about the *gringo*'s boy, and it occurred to me that in all the time I was speaking to him, I didn't once think about what had happened in Roraima.

July 1986

21

My contact with Catarina Da Silva stayed with me throughout the fortnight following the barbecue, and I found myself struggling to evict the visions of her from my thoughts. My growing feelings of love for Ana were clear in my mind, always feeling light and good, but Da Silva invaded me in a different, more tenebrous way. It confused and irritated me that I could be so inflamed by two such different women and that thinking about Da Silva could stir something so basic inside me, a darker lust not present in my thoughts of Ana. Like an insensible tongue that unconsciously probes a broken tooth, my attention would stray back to those moments Da Silva and I had shared in the semi-darkness. Images of her pervaded my thinking at unexpected moments – most disturbingly while making love to Ana, sometimes bringing her name, unspoken, to my lips – and the smallest thing could open a door and allow her to steal into my mind. So, in an attempt to obscure the images, to confine them to the shadows which skulked in the darkest parts of my psyche, I concentrated my thoughts on my first encounter with the boy.

I had been reluctant to have any contact with him, always mindful of my past experience, but I had met him now and I began to wonder if I would be able to teach him; that perhaps I *could* bear his company without a constant reminder of the child in Roraima and the terrible events which had occurred.

I saw him from time to time when I was labouring on the

buildings at Hevea, pale and bored with not enough to occupy his days. He occasionally joined his father, riding in the pickup while the *gringo* was working, but that was no way for a boy to spend his holiday – sitting in the overheated cab, nothing to do. Other times, if there was wiring to fix at the main house, I saw him moping around the clearing, investigating the edge of the forest, but he appeared nervous and out of place. He seemed to need direction, something more exciting than following his father or prowling the clearing without purpose. Perhaps, I thought, the boy and I might be able to help each other. I could give him experience of the river, of the wonders it had to offer, and in return he could provide me with the means to heal past wounds.

One evening, sitting outside Ana's place, at the table under the porch, I was telling Paulo about going to the plantation tomorrow to wire up the workers' houses. 'And I was thinking I might call in on your *gringo*,' I said to him.

'Why do you always call him that? His name is John.'

'Habit.'

'You should stop. He's a good man.'

'Maybe you're right,' I said.

'And you're a *gringo* yourself, you know.'

I held up my beer and nudged my arm against his saying, 'Hey, I'm more Brasilian than you are, Paulo. I dance better than you, I fish better than you and my skin is darker. Shit, I even barbecue better than you.'

He took his arm away and scoffed at me. 'You think you dance better than me?'

'I saw you on the *praia* last night, trying to samba with Ana, remember.'

'Yeah, yeah. So what do you want with John?'

'I was thinking,' I said. 'I thought I might take his boy out. On the water, I mean. I'm going on Saturday and it might be good for him. Whenever I see him he looks bored.'

'Since when did you want company on the river?'

I shrugged and looked at Ana. 'I thought it would be good for the boy to do something. He's got nothing to do over there, and he should see some of this country now he's here. He's—'

Paulo held up his hands. 'You don't need to persuade me. I think it's a great idea. For you and for him.' He sipped his Coke then bent towards Ana and lowered his voice. 'How the hell did you get him to do that? Maybe you can get him to help me with my clinic, too.'

'This isn't my doing.' Ana took her drink in both hands and shook her head.

I stood up and walked to the low wall around the porch. I ignored Paulo and looked out at the road before closing my eyes and imagining myself on the river, accompanied by the boy. It would be fine, I told myself. The boy in Roraima, what happened to him, it had been beyond my control. It was time for me to remember it, to face it instead of burying it and allowing it to consume me from the inside. Ana was right. It was time for me to accept the past and move beyond it instead of carrying it with me, allowing it to infect everything I did.

'So what brought you to this decision?' Paulo asked. 'You been thinking about it for a long time?'

I opened my eyes and turned around. 'Like you just said, Paulo, I think it'll be good for both of us.'

The following afternoon at the estate, when Papagaio and I broke off work for lunch, I went over to the house and spoke to the boy and his mother. Senhor Swan was out, she said, overseeing the burning at the northern edge of the plantation, and should she call me 'Father' or just 'Sam'? I told her that 'Sam' would be fine, that I needed to speak to her husband, and that I'd come to ask the boy if he wanted to go fishing. The boy looked excited, maybe nervous, too, but his mother was a little concerned, asking if it was safe on the river.

We talked for a while, sitting in the cane furniture like civilised people, smiling, sipping Coke from a tall glass, me finding out what it was like to be comfortable. It felt good after working all morning in the sun.

She asked me where I would take him, what we would catch and then she said she'd think about it; talk it over with her husband. I was surprised by her reaction because it was Swan who had asked me to teach the boy, but, on reflection, I could understand that his mother would be more worried about letting him go. Out here, Senhor Swan had his plantation to keep him busy but, as far as I knew, his wife only had the boy.

Later that afternoon, Senhor Swan came to where I was working and we made arrangements for the boy. I still wasn't sure why he trusted me so much. Maybe it was because Paulo had said something, because I was his countryman and because people see through rose-tinted glasses when they're away from home. Or maybe it was because he thought I was still a priest.

So that weekend we met at André's place, right where the road ends and there's nothing to see but the river and the trees on the other side. They were waiting for me, standing beside the white pickup with *Hevea* written on the side. The boy kicking his toes in the red dust, his father resting against the cab with his back to the river. Strange that, because usually people couldn't help looking at it; it had always drawn my eyes like there was nothing else in the world to see.

The boy was wearing shorts and a white T-shirt this time, again with the name of a rock band splashed over it, his skinny limbs protruding from baggy cuffs. I'd never heard of the band, probably something that was popular back home. It always took a while for the latest thing to work its way to São Tiago. He had a knife at his waist and on the ground beside the rear tyre of the pickup there was a fishing box, new, that they must have brought in from Brasilia. There was nowhere in São Tiago to buy such a thing.

I paused for a moment and watched them, father and son, not speaking. I put down the cool box and adjusted the strap of my rifle, hefted my bag on the other shoulder and then headed in their direction, passing Manolo's café.

'You don't want to put a few beers in there, *Padre*?' Manolo called, coming out from his back room. 'There's probably room for a few cans. You want Antarctica or Brahma? I can sell you a few.'

I pretended not to hear him and continued walking.

'Not like you, *Padre*,' he said, raising his voice. 'Thought you like a few beers when you're out. Antarctica, isn't it? Always thought that was a bit of a risk though, being on the river, small boat, all that beer inside you.'

I carried on past the café, watching Senhor Swan who didn't appear to have noticed Manny's shouting.

'You're taking the boy with you, eh?' Manolo persisted. 'You teaching him to drink or to fish?'

There was no way of knowing if Swan could hear Manolo, but he had his back to us now, standing with his hands on his hips and staring across the street. His Portuguese was good but maybe not enough to pick up bits of conversation when he wasn't really listening – even though Manolo was trying his best.

I kept walking until I was past the café. Manny, reluctant to stray too far from his small patch of territory, stopped shouting, but I could feel his eyes on me. I ignored him and raised a hand, calling out to greet Senhor Swan and his boy.

'Looks like you've come prepared,' I said, putting my worn canvas bag on the ground and shaking Swan's hand.

'Paulo made a few suggestions,' he said. 'I wanted to make sure you had everything.'

'I got everything we need right here.' I held up my bag and looked at the boy. 'You ready, then? You want to catch some fish?' The boy's eyes went to the rifle slung across my shoulder and then back to me. He nodded.

'You need that?' Swan asked.

I shrugged and told him, 'You never know. But I can leave it if you want.'

He mulled it over for a moment, looking down at his son and then said, 'No. No problem. Better to be safe.' He patted his right pocket and for the first time I noticed that it looked heavy. Something in there was pulling it to one side.

'OK. We'll be back some time round four o' clock. You can watch us come around the bend in the river, if you like.' I pointed so he could see where I meant. 'You sit up there. I'll tell your boy to hold up his catch so you can see it as we come in.'

Swan smiled and put one hand on his son's head, the boy appearing a little unsure.

We all headed down the street to André's, Swan and his boy keeping pace with me. I called up to the floating hotel and André came down to the bank where he had an outboard waiting for us. It was just a tin boat with an engine on the back, nothing too fast, nothing too fancy, but it would take us further upriver than the dugout.

'No holes in this one?' I said as André came over to shake Swan's hand. 'Don't want to have to swim back this time. André, this is Senhor Swan. His son.'

Swan took his hand, telling him, 'Call me John,' making me think about the way the two words sounded together. John Swan. His parents must've had a sense of humour. 'And I hope he's joking about the swimming,' he added.

'Course he's joking,' said André. 'No one could swim all that way. What you'd have to do is swim across to the side and then walk.'

Swan threw André a questioning glance. Perhaps he wasn't ready for jokes.

'The boats don't sink,' I reassured him. 'The water's flat, we have tins for bailing out, we'll be fine. Your son will be safe. I'm not big on getting wet, so I've never been in the water when I didn't want to be.' I squatted down beside the boy and spoke to him. 'You do *know* how to swim, though, don't you? Just in case?'

The boy snapped his head round at me and I winked. His face was deadpan for a second and then his smile came.

'How much do I owe you for this?' Swan took a fold of notes from one of his pockets and spoke to André. 'For the boat.'

André looked at me.

'Put your money away,' I said. 'It's taken care of.' The hire was expensive but the way I saw it, I was taking the boy fishing, showing him something of my world, so it was my place to pay. This time anyway. I told him he could pay next time.

'Why don't you put your stuff in the boat,' I said to the boy. 'Put it right in the middle, between the slats.'

While he did that, hefting the heavy box into the boat, I looked at his old man and told him what had been on my mind, saying, 'How come you're letting me take your boy out? I mean, how come you trust me?'

Swan squatted down on his haunches and opened the cool box, looking inside. 'Who says I trust you?' he said, standing up. 'I don't have to trust you to know you'll take care of him. I asked around and everybody puts you down as the safest pair of hands on the river. That and you catch a lot of fish. So if they were going out, they said, they'd want it to be with you. You know the river and you know how to fish, it's all that really matters for today.'

I nodded. 'Nothing to do with being a priest?'

'Is that a good reason to trust you?'

I smiled and shook my head. 'Not really.'

'I'm not Catholic anyway,' he said. 'And by the way, I thought you handled the guy in the café just right. If you bought beer, you'd have wasted your money. You wouldn't be putting it on that boat.'

He was smarter than I'd given him credit for. 'Thought you hadn't heard,' I said. 'Manolo pushes his luck sometimes, tries to give me a bit of trouble. We had something of a disagreement one time.'

'Maybe you can tell me about it.'

'Another day,' I said, noticing the boy coming back to us now, everything on the boat except for my old canvas pack and my rifle, which was still over my shoulder.

Swan didn't look down at his son. He kept his eyes on mine and held them that way before nodding once. 'Take care of him,' he said.

'I will.'

Then his demeanour changed, became softer and he turned to his boy. 'Have a good time,' he said, putting a hand on his head, smoothing his hair. 'And make sure you bring us back a fish.'

I left them alone and went to the boat, climbing in, turning to watch the boy with his father. Swan was saying something to him, leaning down towards the upturned face, the boy looking worried. I wondered if he was having second thoughts about coming on the river with me, but when he reached the boat, he met my eyes and steadied himself before climbing in.

When I started the engine and moved away from São Tiago, the boy looked worried. He stared back at São Tiago and waved to his father.

22

The sound of the outboard was intrusive, making it difficult to talk, but about twenty minutes out, I reached across and nudged the boy, pointing to the shore when he looked over at me. He followed my finger, seeing the exposed sand just below the line of the jungle on our left.

'*Jacaré*,' I shouted over the sound of the motor. 'Caiman.'

His eyes staying with the *jacaré*, his head turning slowly as we passed them. There were four or five of them basking in the sun, not big ones, maybe a couple of metres long. One of them was facing the water, his neck stretched out holding his chin high, his mouth wide, his teeth bared. The others had their backs to us. Just a group of caiman enjoying the sun.

'Don't worry,' I shouted to the boy. 'This isn't a Tarzan movie, and they're not crocodiles.' I overemphasised the words to make it easier for him to hear. 'They don't slide into the water and chase you. Mostly, they just eat fish.'

The boy took in everything around him, seeing the river stretch wider as we travelled up it. In some parts, during the wet season, the Araguaia could look like the sea, no shore in sight, but now the waterways were narrower, sandbanks visible everywhere. I pointed out one or two other things to him, showing him the sleek backs of the *boto* when they surfaced for air, turtle tracks left on the sand, a family of *capybara* foraging at the edge of the water, and he took it all in without giving anything away about how he felt. His little jaw set tight, his brow down, his upper lip protruding slightly. If he was impressed or enjoying himself, he didn't show it.

We'd been travelling for half an hour when I cut the engine and left the boat to slide through the water. I stayed quiet for a moment, letting the boy take in the remoteness of the river, the scale of the country. Then I turned to him, saying, 'You ever fish before?'

He shook his head.

'The best fishing is early morning, late evening,' I said. 'But we'll be OK. You like fishing, maybe we'll come another time, sleep out on the beach.'

The boy stared at me.

'That way we can catch them while it's cool.'

He continued to stare.

'You don't say much, do you?'

The boy shrugged and looked down at the fishing gear.

'You don't want to be here?' I asked him, straightening myself up.

'Sure,' he said.

'Sure you do or sure you don't?'

'Sure I do.'

I don't know if he meant it or if he thought it was what I wanted to hear. He was a difficult one to read.

'What's that for?' He pointed at the rifle which was lying behind me, in the bow of the boat. 'Who you going to shoot?'

'*Who* am I going to shoot?'

'They said there's headhunters out here, is that right? You going to shoot them?'

I laughed. 'Who said anything about headhunters?'

'Luísa,' he said, turning red in the cheeks.

'And *she* is?'

He looked down. 'The girl who cleans the house.'

'She new?'

'Just started.' He scratched the side of his nose. 'Mum says she's got a lot to learn, though.'

'I bet. And you speak to her in Portuguese?'

'Sometimes. I'm learning Spanish at school and some of the words are the same. Also, we were in São Paulo for a year, so I know some Portuguese. I'm not so good with tenses and stuff, but . . .'

'Like most people around here,' I laughed. 'Not much education, see. They're not all clever like you. You notice some of them only use one tense? Give it a few weeks and you'll be speaking better than them. Anyway,' I said, 'this Luísa? The one who told you about headhunters? She about so tall,' I held my hand at shoulder height, 'with long hair?'

'Uh-huh.'

'Long legs, short skirt, big boobs, wiggle her bum when she walks?' I could have been describing half the women in São Tiago.

'Yep.' A smile.

I nodded and turned away to stifle a laugh. I didn't want the boy to think I was mocking him, but if it was the Luísa I thought he was talking about – and I'm sure it would be – then I knew what she was like. A teenage tease who moved like a cat and looked like an angel, but wasn't much more than an airhead who drank too much and screwed too much. Many drunken fights had broken out over Luísa. I'd seen countless pistols and knives pulled as a result of her exploits. I'd even heard she wanted to move to Vila Rica, make a little money by selling herself, but it looked like she'd landed on her feet over at the Swan place. A good wage, a fair boss, probably even a clean place to live. Better than the old room I called my own. I wondered if the boy was safe from her; I wouldn't put it past her to take a fancy to the boss's son, even if he *was* only twelve.

'You want to watch out for her,' I told him.

'Why?'

I drew air between clenched teeth and tilted my head.

'Why?' he asked again.

'She's a sly one. And she likes the boys.'

'Sly? Like how?'

'Never mind.' I touched my foot to the fishing box which he'd brought with him. 'Shall we?'

The boy said, 'Sure,' so I opened the lid.

Two trays slid out on hinges. 'And this is what Paulo told you to buy?' There was a good assortment of hooks and weights and lures and leaders. Even a bright yellow bottle of Autan nestling in the bottom, ready to keep the mosquitoes away. It was all the right stuff, a couple of heavy lines, the nylon in oil-slick colours, and one or two smaller gauge rolls for catching the lighter fish. Paulo had given Swan some good advice, even if he wasn't much of a fisherman himself.

For a while, we drifted on the water, and I showed the boy how to tie the noose which was best for keeping the hooks tight. I spoke the Portuguese names for the things in his hands, so he would learn the way the words sounded. He was quick, his small fingers nimble with the rainbow-coloured line, his lips pursed, his mind intent on tying it right. He had a quiet tenacity and it wasn't long before he was doing it almost as well as I could.

While we prepared our gear, we each had a drink, cold from the cool box. I would've preferred beer, but the orange Fanta quenched my thirst well enough. When I pulled a battered packet of Carlton from the top pocket of my shirt, I noticed the boy was watching me. I took a cigarette, seeing that it was bent and crumpled, and I wondered what he must think of me in my stained shirt and my ancient trousers, nothing but flip-flops on my feet and battered cigarettes in my pocket. I shrugged my shoulders at him, straightened the cigarette between finger and thumb and lit it with the blue disposable lighter I'd found on the *rua*.

'Bad for you, you know,' the boy said, looking at me through his blond fringe.

I blew smoke into the air. 'Keep tying those lines.'

When the lines were prepared, we baited our hooks with the small pieces of beef I'd brought from my fridge. I told the boy, 'Drop your line here,' and he took one of the leader lines and plopped it over the edge.

'As soon as you feel it move away,' I said, 'give it a tug and pull it back in. Where we are now, it's that easy,' and within just a few seconds, the boy was pulling his line in, hand over hand, and dangling his first *piranha* in the air over the boat. I showed him how to hold it down with one foot and put the knife through its head.

'Sometimes,' I said, 'if the fish is a big one, looks like he's getting a bit frisky, it helps to swing him against the side of the boat a few times. Bash him up a bit. They can be slippery little buggers if you're not careful.'

The boy's face lit up. He liked the idea of bashing the *piranha* against the boat.

'Saw a guy called Josalino have half his thumb bitten out once,' I told him. 'This bit right here.' I showed him the soft flesh, where the root of my thumb meets the palm of my hand. 'Don't want that to happen to you.' And it struck me that if something happened to the boy, I would have to take him back to Paulo. Half an hour back downriver wasn't so bad, but I wondered how Paulo would cope if it was something serious.

The boy grimaced at the fish by his feet, its slick orange belly already beginning to dry in the sun. When he looked back at me, though, the expression had turned to a grin, one that covered his whole face, and I knew exactly what had brought it out. I knew how he felt and it pleased me.

'Feels good, doesn't it?' I said. 'Better than sitting in your father's pickup all day. There's not much beats catching a fish. Just wait till we move out where the big ones are. You catch one of those, and you'll go back a hero.'

By one o' clock the sun was high and I could see the boy was beginning to flag, so we wound in our lines and headed for one of the beaches. I lit a fire and soon it was ready to cook the fish we'd caught. I boiled some rice and the boy ate well, despite the gritty sand.

We sat in silence for a while, me smoking Carltons, wanting a beer but drinking Coke, and him poking the fire with a dried stick. Eventually he spoke, asking me, 'Why d'you bring the gun?'

I'd seen him looking at it and wondered when he'd ask again. 'You never know when you might need it,' I said, easing myself back into the sand, shuffling around to make an indentation for myself. 'We see something that tastes good, we'll shoot it. You ever eat *paca*?'

'No.'

'Wild pig?'

'Uh-uh.'

'Then maybe we'll go shoot some one day. Think you'll like that?'

He shrugged. 'So what sort of gun is it?' he asked, and I told him I didn't know. All I knew was that it was a twenty-two and that it was a rusted old piece of junk when I won it from Papagaio in a game of cards one time. It had taken me weeks to bring it up to anything like working condition again. Now it looked good, the wooden stock oiled and solid, the blue barrel clean and smooth.

He told me that he'd used an air rifle once or twice, so I said the twenty-two would be pretty much like that, only louder. He nodded and looked excited, like the fishing wasn't going to be anywhere near as good as the shooting, and I wondered if he knew that his father did his job with a pistol in his pocket.

Anyway, seeing that eager look on the boy's face made me feel good, so I drained my Coke and walked out towards the shore, screwing the empty can into the sand by the water. I came back to the boy, taking the rifle and collecting a handful of cartridges from a plastic box in my bag.

He looked at me when I passed him the rifle, not sure whether I was serious, so I nodded and let him take it. 'You think you could hit that can over there?' I said. The can was no more than ten metres away, the silver top catching the sun.

The boy shrugged his shoulders and lifted the rifle to look down the open sight. 'I could try.'

He seemed to know what he was doing so I took it from him and let him watch me slide the shells into the tube under the barrel. 'This is the safety catch,' I said. 'You flick that off and the gun's ready to go. When you want to fire again, pull the pump towards you and push it back again, just like they do in the films.' I handed it back to him, barrel straight up in the air, and he took it from me. 'Just don't point it at anything you don't want to shoot.'

He nodded at me, then shouldered the rifle and aimed down the barrel, holding it steady for a moment. The shot snapped into the quiet afternoon and the sand next to the Coke can kicked into the air. The boy pumped it, a little unsure, casting his eyes at me like he was checking it was OK to try again, so I smiled and he settled himself before firing a second time.

'Hold your breath when you aim,' I said. 'It takes too long, breathe out and start again.'

This time the Coke can jumped from its spot, the bullet easily cutting through the thin metal. He pulled hard on the pump, the empty cartridge jumping out towards me, and I clapped slowly, saying, 'Good shot,' before taking the rifle from him. I emptied it and put it next to my bag.

'My dad has a gun,' he said.

'Oh?'

'A pistol. Won't let me have a go, though. Says it's not a toy.'

'He's right.'

'It's for protection.'

'From what?'

The boy shrugged. 'He got robbed one time. In São Paulo.'

'I heard there could be trouble over there.' Nothing like Roraima, though. They didn't massacre villages in São Paulo, they kidnapped businessmen, or their children. For some people, it's like a profession. 'What happened?'

'One time, some men broke into the office and made Dad open the safe. Pointed guns at him and took all the money.'

'Must have been scary,' I said.

'After that, he bought a pistol. Keeps it in his pocket.' He looked across at the can he had shot. 'And it's why the Americans are here.'

'The guys who always look so serious? I've seen them around.'

The boy nodded. 'They're kind of like guards. I think they might have been in the army or something.'

'Well, there's nothing to worry about out here.' I scanned the river. 'Not a headhunter in sight.' I turned to the boy. 'Come on, let's catch some fish.'

Going back onto the water, the boy was casting his line well, striking it into the centre of the river where the big fish played. He was beginning to open up, too. He still had the serious face, the one which was either resolve or stupidity, but I was leaning towards resolve as the day went on. He wasn't the burden I had feared he would be, and I even began to think the boy and I were going to be friends.

He was happier now – especially when he caught a fish – and he talked more too. He asked the Portuguese names for the things around us; he spoke phrases in English and asked me to translate them.

'I suppose you'll want to know the dirty words,' I said.

He shrugged. 'Maybe.'

'Course you do,' I said. 'Those are the things everyone wants to know. I was the same.' I made myself more comfortable in the boat. 'Go on, then, what dirty word you want to know?'

'How about . . . oh, I don't know,' he looked embarrassed, 'how about "shit"?'

'*Bosta*,' I said, wondering if it was the first time, he'd said 'shit' in front of an adult.

'*Bosta*,' he said the word out loud, testing the way it sounded, and I watched how he stored it away for later use, mouthing it to himself a few times. 'OK,' he said, coming back. 'How about "prick"?'

'*Pica*,' I smiled. 'That's a good one.' Feeling like a kid again. 'But say "*puta*", that's even better. It means whore, but out here it sounds much worse. Like "*filho da puta*".' I spat the words to convey the meaning of the phrase.

The boy thought it over. 'Son of a whore?' he said.

'More like son of a bitch,' I corrected him, and we went on like that for a while, laughing at the different words as he opened up more and more, and each time he thought of a word, I gave him two or three Portuguese alternatives. It wasn't exactly what his father had in mind when he asked me to teach the boy, but I wasn't his father and, if he was going to hold his own against the likes of Luísa, then he was going to need all the ammunition he could get.

After we'd exhausted our respective vocabularies of swear words, we laughed about other things – music, school, his teachers, sport, fishing – and he asked a lot of questions, one of them taking me by surprise.

'Is it true you were a mercenary?' he said as I was baiting a hook, his voice sounding small out there in the open. It made me jump, though, and the tip of the hook broke the skin of my thumb. I wiped it on my shirt and then leaned over to rinse it in the river.

'A mercenary?' I said, taking some antiseptic cream from my bag. 'Who told you that?'

'I heard my parents talking.' He glanced away, watching the angle of his line in the water. 'They said you were a mercenary.'

'That's what they said, is it?'

'Yeah. Like in *The Dogs of War*.' His eyes lit up. 'There was this film we saw at school and—'

'I know it,' I said. 'Christopher Walken, wasn't it? All these guys running about in Africa with guns.'

'It was pretty cool.'

I rubbed some of the cream into the tip of my thumb. 'I look like a mercenary to you?'

The boy shrugged, like maybe he didn't know what a mercenary should look like.

I smiled at him. 'No. I wasn't a mercenary,' I said. 'A *missionary*, not a mercenary. I think maybe you heard wrong. I was never a soldier – although when I was your age, I wanted to join the army. I liked playing soldiers.' I tasted the memory for a moment before continuing. 'No, I went to Catholic school, followed my mother's faith and did what she always wanted me to do. Turned out I wanted the same thing, too; for a while, anyway. I trained to be a priest.'

The boy looked disappointed. Being a missionary wasn't so exciting for him. It would've made a good story to tell his friends when he went back to school in England. Fishing in the Brasilian wilderness with a grizzled mercenary, but even as he nodded away the disillusionment, the line twitched in his hand and it looked to me like he was going to have an*other* story to tell. His line was out in the centre of the river, starting to move off, slipping between his fingers like there was something big on the other end of it.

I moved to sit beside him on the metal slat, but refused to take the line when he offered it. 'It's your fish,' I said. 'You do it. Something to tell your dad about.'

The boy's eyes were wide, and I could feel his exhilaration, mine building to match it as we looked out at the water.

'OK, let it take some line,' I told him. 'That's it, don't tug him yet. And take a little more slack off the reel; let it sit in the bottom of the boat.'

The boy wound a couple of metres off, coiling it on top of the slack that was already there.

'OK, drop the reel down there, and when I say, "now", I want you to give the line a good tug, OK? We're gonna yank that hook right into him.'

The boy dropped the flat wooden reel into the bottom of the tin boat and I put one foot on it. 'Now!'

He gave the line a tug and it jumped in his hand, running out, taking up some of the slack but stopping before it was all used up.

'Don't worry,' I said. 'I've got the reel. It's not going anywhere. You're going to bring this one in.'

The boy looked to me for encouragement, then he began reeling the line in, hand over hand, just as I'd shown him before. 'Is it big, d'you think?' He whispered the words as if talking loudly would jinx the fish.

'Hard to tell without taking the line myself,' I said. 'But it runs like *filhote* and that's a good fish to catch.' For his sake I hoped it *was filhote*, but for mine I hoped it wasn't. If the boy caught my fish, then Papagaio would never let me hear the end of it.

The boy brought the fish closer to the boat until it struggled again and struck out for the centre of the river. He let it go for a while and then it quietened so he pulled it in again, hand over hand. As he pulled, I glanced at his small pale hands, their fingers smooth and without callus. If the fish held out too long, the boy's hands might scar like my own. The pain would be easy to bear, though, if the prize was good enough. Besides, it wouldn't hurt to have a few scars to show his friends.

'It's like *The Old Man and the Sea*,' the boy whispered, turning his head away from the river to look at me.

'Except this isn't going to be a marlin, and it isn't going to drag us out to sea.'

'And this time it's the boy who catches the fish. Not the old man.'

'Yeah,' I said. 'But don't get cocky. Concentrate on the fish.' I flicked my head, motioning out to the river, and the boy turned to look out across the water as the line slackened in his hand and he began to bring it back in again.

When the fish was no more than five metres from the boat, it surfaced and smacked its tail hard on the water, half turning, splashing and disappearing back under.

'Did you see that?' The boy was excited.

'*Filhote*,' I said. 'Maybe fifteen kilos on that fish. A good catch for your first time out.'

'I thought I'd lost it,' he said, turning his hand so he could study the red weal slashed across it. The tips of his right forefinger and thumb were red too, but they'd be fine.

'Dip it in the river,' I said. 'It'll take away some of the burn. The fish is nearly done, now. This time we'll bring him in and get him in the boat, OK?'

I knew exactly how he felt. It was the same way I felt with every fish I brought in. It was a feeling that came whenever there was a tug on the line, but with a fish like this, the biggest fish you've ever caught, then the feeling was magnified a hundred, even a thousand times. The boy desperately wanted that fish. He wanted it with every gram of flesh in his body; every drop of blood. It would fill his eyes and his ears and his mouth. His heart would be beating hard; his hands would be shaking; his whole body would be aching to catch that fish, to see it beside him, to haul it into the boat and take it home to show everybody what he had done. It was a life-mark moment that would stay with him for ever. The first time he got drunk, the first time he had sex, the first time he caught a giant fish.

When he brought it alongside the boat and we had the chance to get a better view of it, I reckoned my first estimate was low. The fish was at least twenty kilos, if not thirty, and the boy was as skinny as an eel. He had done well to bring it in.

I told him to take out his knife. The point was sharp and it would slip under the gills without any problem. I leaned over the side and showed him where to push the blade. Some of the fishermen liked to keep their fish alive, drown them in the air once they were inside the boat, but the river was wide and the fish was big. A flapping fish in the boat would paint all colours of trouble for us, so I thought it best to finish it there. And, as soon as we got back to shore we'd pack our things and head for São Tiago. I wanted the boy to hold up his catch as we approached town, to show his father what he could do. I wanted Swan to see what his son had caught.

When we rounded the bend of the river later in the afternoon, the wind in our faces and the sound of the outboard in our ears, we could see right up to the bank of São Tiago where Manolo's place backed onto the water. Swan and his wife were sitting under the shade of a tree, waiting for their boy. He would be drinking beer, I bet, and I could taste it in my mouth. Cold and crisp, straight from the fridge.

I nudged the boy and helped him with the fish. He stood in the boat, holding both arms high, his fingers under its gills, and I took its belly, supporting most of the weight. Hanging in that way, the fish was nearly as tall as the boy. I watched as his parents rose from their seats and I wished I was close enough to see their faces.

After we landed and the boy had shown off his fish, I spoke

to Swan, saying, 'Your boy learns quickly. He listens and he picks it up. He's quicker than Paulo ever was.'

'He likes you,' said his wife. 'If he likes you, he'll listen.'

For a while, the boy examined his *filhote*, rummaged in the fishing box, practised his knots, and we adults made polite conversation, getting to know each other a little better. We talked about nothing of importance, nobody wanting to offend anybody just yet.

After some time, Ana came over, saying she'd come out to stretch her legs and saw us sitting by the river, lazing about. She said it with an easy smile that slipped her into the conversation without effort and I couldn't help feeling proud that she was mine. She had a good spirit that made it easy to like her. I introduced her to Swan's wife, and when they had chatted for a few moments, Ana turned her attention to the boy.

Sarah called the boy over and he held his hand out to meet Ana.

Ana took his hand and shook it, saying, 'We have a better way to meet someone in Brasil. Here, we kiss each other. Twice. Once on each cheek.'

'I know that,' said the boy.

'Then let's meet properly,' she said, offering him her cheek so they could greet each other, Brasilian style, without any embarrassment from the boy.

'Now,' Ana said to him, 'show me what you caught.'

I watched the boy lead Ana down to the river, saw how well she related to him, saw how well he reacted to her. The way they behaved together, it was as if they already knew each other. She crouched beside him, toes in the water and listened to him describe how he had caught the fish.

'She's lovely,' Swan's wife said to me. 'And she has a way with children.'

There wasn't anything for me to say, so I went to join them at the water's edge, and showed the boy how to clean the fish.

We sliced open its white belly, cutting it from tail to chin, and removed what was inside. Ana pulled a face and held her nose, making the boy laugh, but he wasn't afraid to put his hands into the carcass, not minding the smell and the muck. I knew he would get along well with the river. We threw the guts out for the opportunists who cruised beneath the water and we cut the meat from the bones in great chunks.

'You should take some,' said the boy. 'There's too much for us.'

'This fish is yours,' I told him. 'You caught it.'

'But you helped.'

'He's right,' said Ana. 'You should let him give us some.'

I rinsed my knife and wiped it on my trousers before hiding it away. 'Well, it does go nicely on the barbecue,' I said, standing up. 'Thanks.' I looked down at the boy for a moment, thinking how much I had enjoyed our trip. 'And why don't we do this again sometime? Would you like that?'

He couldn't hide his excitement. 'Soon? You promise?'

'Sure,' I told him. 'I promise.'

'Sounds like a good idea.' Ana looked at the boy and then glanced up at me, a smile on her lips. 'But I have to go now.' She stood. 'I can't take the whole afternoon off, you know.'

Ana went back to Swan and his wife, said goodbye and then turned towards home. I followed her progress up the bank and onto the road before I turned to the boy. He was watching her, too, and he looked at me when he sensed I was studying him.

'I like her,' he said. 'She's really nice.'

'Yes. She is.'

'And she's much prettier than the woman at the barbecue,' he said.

I didn't answer him, felt a knot twist in my guts and my heart became a tightened fist for just a moment as I remembered the light through the shutters.

'Come on,' I said, trying to make his comment insignificant.

If he thought it lacked importance, he would forget it, put it out of his mind. 'Let's get your things together.'

We bagged the meat and put it onto the back of Swan's pickup, along with the boy's other belongings. I slipped the pins into the tailgate and we walked around to the front of the pickup as the boy and his mother climbed in. Her first, shuffling along the bench seat, then him, pulling the door shut. Swan stopped with his fingers on the door handle and looked at me like there was something on his mind.

'What is it?' I said. 'You can ask whatever you like.'

He pursed his lips. 'I was wondering what would bring a priest to a place like this. An English priest, especially. I asked Paulo but he said I should talk to you about it. I mean, are you working here or . . . you can tell me if it's not my business.'

'You have a right to ask,' I said. 'I was rude to you and yet you trusted me with your son.'

'And you brought him back safely. You kept your word.'

'I'm glad to have had the chance.'

He put his back against the door, raising one foot up behind him on the running board, watching me take a cigarette from the battered packet in my top pocket.

'I was a missionary,' I said. 'In a place north of here. An idealistic young missionary from England who thought he could change the world.' I lit the cigarette and stared at the ground. 'But it wasn't what I expected. I saw things . . .' I stopped. 'Anyway, a good friend told me about the mission in São Felix. He said it was quiet, the fishing was good, so I went there to get away, but it wasn't right for me any more. Things had changed. *I* had changed. Now I just fish.' I shook my head and looked at the tip of my cigarette. 'Your son tells me I shouldn't smoke.'

'He's right. Pestered me into giving up. Maybe he'll do the same for you.'

186

'Maybe.' It was an interesting thought that anyone should care.

'Is that why you don't want to help Paulo with his clinic?' he asked. 'Because it's not right for you any more?'

'I'm not sure it's right for him either.'

'His idea is a good one,' he said.

'Paulo always has good ideas,' I shrugged, 'only sometimes they're in the wrong place and at the wrong time.'

'You don't mean that.'

'You're probably right. It *is* a good idea.' I turned my head and looked at the river.

'He could use your help, you know. The support of his friend. And with a priest on board . . .'

'I'm not a priest any more. And anyway, priests are not always welcome.'

'Well, you know what Americans are like with God. And I work for an American company, remember. They won't build their own, but if you open a clinic here in São Tiago, a doctor and a priest, maybe the company will use you to take care of the workers. It's closer than Vila Rica. They'd be prepared to pay if it looked good enough.' He pushed himself away from the pickup.

'You think they'd give the workers health benefits?' I waved a fly from my face.

'Sure. These people deserve better.'

'Better than what?'

'Than what's available.'

'You sound like Paulo.'

'And it would be another way to get them to work for me.'

I blew smoke and shifted my feet. I wanted to get back to my place, have a couple of beers, some sleep, but it looked like he had something else to say.

'I had a lot of trouble getting people to work for me when I first got here,' he said. 'Something like this might help.'

'No one trusts landowners,' I said.

'Why not? I mean, I've heard stories about *latifundistas* hijacking land off farmers further north, but that doesn't happen here, does it?'

'Sure it does. That's pretty much how the Da Silvas got all their land. Guns and violence. How much land you have is down to how strong you are.' I told him what the Da Silvas did with the casual labourers a few years ago. 'When it was time to pay them, they rounded them into the forest and burned them. That's why no one would work for you. They're afraid.'

He shook his head and glanced back at his wife and son. 'I can't imagine it,' he said. 'I met them and they didn't seem like the kind who'd do that. I mean, I don't think we'd ever be great friends, but . . .'

'There are people who will do almost anything for land,' I said. 'Up north I've seen people light cigarettes from the same flame they used to burn workers. Women and children shot.' It was more than I had intended to tell him. 'Why do you think your company sent you down here with protection?'

He gave me a confused look.

'The Americans,' I told him. 'Isn't that what you told me they're here for? To protect the company's investment? It's a surprise they only sent three.'

He nodded. 'With men like that, three's enough.'

I waited for him to elaborate, wondering if he'd slipped when he implied that the *Americanos* were more than they appeared to be. Seemed like we were both intent on giving up our secrets.

'No wonder you went to São Felix,' he said. 'If that's the kind of thing you saw up north. But what about the law? I thought with the military gone, the new government—'

'They don't come here.' I cut him off. 'They don't see the farmer's animals killed, his water poisoned, his family butchered. And even if they did, they'd probably look away. It's all money, see.'

'It almost sounds as if you care.'

'It just seems like it.' I flicked my cigarette away and kicked the dirt. 'I stick to fishing. It's safer that way.'

He paused for a moment, a look coming across his face. 'Does *Paulo* know about this?' he said. 'What the Da Silvas can be like?'

'Of course he does. Why?'

'I just spoke to him. He said he was thinking about going to see them.'

'No,' I shook my head. 'We talked about it a while ago. He won't go to them.'

'That's not what he told me.'

'It's a bad idea. The Da Silvas are not like regular business people.'

'You think they're dangerous? To someone like Paulo?'

'They *might* be,' I said. 'People like them, you never know what they're going to do.'

23

I took the boat back to André's place, pulling it onto the sand by the floating hotel. Not far away, between the hotel and Manolo's café, Paulo was sitting on an unused patch of dirt. Just dust and scrub. His head was down, but he looked up when I approached.

'Still think this is the best spot for a clinic?' I asked.

'Yeah,' he said.

I glanced around. 'It's as good as any.'

Paulo sagged further and ran a hand through his hair.

I sat down beside him. 'You're thinking about Da Silva again.'

He looked at me like I'd read his mind.

'I talked to Senhor Swan,' I said.

'John? No secrets here, are there?' Paulo smiled and stared at his hands. 'If you won't go to them, I'll go myself. I need to do this, Sam. The clinic is important to me.'

'Yeah.' It was his way of dealing with what happened. There was nothing more he could've done that night, not without the right facilities, and he was carrying it with him, like I carried the things I had brought with me from Roraima. But Paulo was stronger than I was. He was prepared to bear his burden, to lighten it and make it good. It was his job to save lives and he'd failed in the one attempt he'd made in years. That's what was making him itch. He didn't want another Eduardo on his conscience.

'I ended up in São Tiago because I was a screw-up, Sam. I was happy to do nothing except fish and drink, but when Eduardo died, something changed and I can't just sit around any more. There has to be more to all this.' He opened his arms, sweeping them out.

I didn't reply.

'Whatever I am, Sam, I'm still a doctor.'

It was hard to know what to say. Paulo had been my friend for many years. I spent more time with him than most people spent with their marriage partners. We ate together, we drank together, we wasted our days together. And now he'd found something else. He'd taken to giving his life some meaning and he was leaving me behind. Now he was a doctor again and I was still just Sam. It made me feel lonely.

'Seems like we don't see much of each other these days,' I said. 'I mean, sometimes we sit outside my place, sometimes we barbecue, but things aren't the same any more. You feel that, too?'

Paulo looked at me.

'I've got Ana, my job, looking over my shoulder to see if Manolo's pointing a gun at me.' I rolled my eyes. 'Seems like we haven't got time for each other now.'

'We were never married,' Paulo attempted a joke.

'I remember you once said together we were more or less God.'

'I was drunk. And anyway, it didn't help Eduardo, did it?'

I crossed my arms over my knees and rested my forehead on them, staring at the ground below.

'I need this, Sam. Because of what happened to Eduardo. I can make a difference here.'

The sun was dropping so I told him I was going to Ana's

place, we were eating fish and rice, there would be enough for three. Paulo hesitated, so I told him I had beer, too.

We walked along the river and up past Manolo's place as we headed into São Tiago. Manolo was on his haunches outside the café, staring at the ground and chewing his nails like he was thinking hard about something. The tables inside were all unoccupied except for one. André was sitting at the back of the café drinking caipirinha from a long glass.

Manolo stood up as we approached. 'It's like you cursed me,' he said. 'You and your whore. You refused to hear me and now I have no customers.' He spat into the dust and raised his middle finger at me.

'Come on, Manny,' said Paulo. 'You two used to be friends.'

'Does a friend do this?' He pointed at his own face.

I hadn't spoken to Manny since the day he'd come to Ana's place, hadn't even seen him from anything but a distance. His face didn't look too bad, but it still bore the evidence of our fight. The yellow and blue marks just visible across his eyes and mouth even after so long.

'I'm sorry, Manny,' I said. 'I shouldn't have . . . but you said those things and . . .' I made a move towards him but he jumped to his feet and stepped back into the café, under the red awning.

'You want to hit me again, is that it?'

'No, Manny, I want us to be friends again. There's nothing for us to gain from this.' I held out my hand.

'You want me to be friends with a whore-loving priest?' Manny spat again. 'Or do you like boys now? I saw you go out on the river with that boy. That what you like now? Something young?'

I shook my head at him, not wanting to argue. 'What's happened to you, Manny?' I was tired, less angry than I used to be. I had more to lose.

Behind Manolo, at the back of the café, André stood up. He

finished his drink and came over to where we were arguing. He spoke to me, saying, 'I tried talking to him, Sam, but he doesn't listen to anyone. My advice would be to let him rot in hell.'

Then he turned to Manolo. 'You know, Manny,' he said. 'I don't think I like to drink here any more.'

Manolo glared back at him, his shoulders deflating, but André ignored him. '*Até logo*, Sam,' he said and raised a hand to me.

I returned the gesture and began to walk away.

Paulo and I continued past the café, Manolo calling after us. 'You see,' he said. 'You cursed me. No one wants to drink here any more. You weren't a priest I'd cut out your eyes. Or maybe I'll screw your whore.'

I stopped, reaching behind me and touching the handle of the fishing knife I carried in the small of my back. 'Don't touch her,' I said. 'Don't look at her. Don't even say her name.'

'Or what?' said Manolo. 'What will you do?'

I turned to see Manolo stepping towards the bar, but Paulo grabbed my shoulder and held me back. 'Come on, Sam,' he said. 'Let's go eat.'

I swallowed my anger and turned away from Manolo. 'You really think he's worth saving?' I asked Paulo, forgetting that I had already made that decision. I had already saved Manolo once before.

We ignored him calling after us, and walked to Ana's place, seeing her standing outside in the warm evening, three plates laid on the table, three glasses, a jug of caipirinha. My hands were shaking, but already I was beginning to feel more relaxed.

'How did you know to put three plates out?' I filled the glasses and took a long drink from my own, enjoying the refreshing sweetness.

'I have eyes,' she said. 'And ears.' She greeted Paulo, kissing both cheeks. 'So you and Manny still haven't made up yet?'

'He tried,' said Paulo.

Further down the street, a small group of boys was playing football, shouting to one another, kicking the ball barefoot at a goal marked out with flip-flops. I could hear the punt of their feet on the old ball.

'I'm surprised you can hear anything with them playing down there,' I said.

'Don't be miserable,' said Ana.

'My place, all you can hear is the river.'

'Your place is two minutes' walk from here,' she said. 'I bet you can hear the footballers from there too.'

I shrugged and sat down. 'She's always right,' I said.

Ana brought food to the table. Paulo and I offered to help but she told us to stay where we were. And when the food was ready, we ate in near darkness, just two candles for light.

As we ate and talked small talk, my mind opened to what I had to do. I always knew I would help Paulo. I understood that now, and I realised why I had opposed his idea; because I knew I would end up helping him, even though I had denied knowing it. If he built it, I would help. It had always been inevitable. One way or another, I would have to join him in his escape from our apathetic existence, but the truth was I had already joined him. The change had crept over me in other ways. During the past months, my life had altered beyond anything I had ever known. Sitting together with Ana and Paulo, the realisation now hit me like the changing of the season. Refusing to help Paulo was one of the last pieces of debris to which I was clinging, and letting go of it would mean beginning to let go of my blindness and turning to face who I was and what I had become. What I had ceased to be. I had stepped away from one life and I was moving towards another. The only obstacle now was the clinic and how it would throw me into the path of Catarina Da Silva once more if I decided to become involved. If I were going to join my friend's dream, I would have to see her, but I wasn't confident that I would be able to subdue my feelings for her. It would be a test of my resolve and self-discipline; a test which I did not relish the thought of, but which I knew I must take if I were to help my friend.

When I had eaten, I put my fork down on the plate and sat back. 'Out there on the river,' I said, 'I was thinking what I'd do if something happened to the boy.' Ana and Paulo both looked at me. 'Or if something happened to you, Ana.'

Paulo ran his fingers across his moustache, waiting for me to go on.

'I'll go to the *fazenda* tomorrow,' I said. 'I'll talk to Da Silva.' If any of us could seek her approval, I could. We had shared something. We had a connection.

'You sure?' He narrowed his eyes.

'I'm sure.' Memories of the barbecue came sneaking back to me from the shadows, and I hoped that in visiting Da Silva, in putting myself back into her reach, I would be strong enough to resist her. Or that I would be able to maintain a safe enough distance from her. But somewhere inside me – in the part that was ruled not by my head nor by my heart – somewhere hidden, somewhere deep, something was aroused by the prospect of seeing her again, and perhaps it was that part which had persuaded me to agree to help.

24

Paulo wanted to go with me to the Da Silva place but I told him to stay put. If he wanted my help, this was how it was going to be. Paulo hadn't had any contact with the landowners until now, and I could see no reason for exposing him to them. Instead I asked Papagaio to come, drive me in his car the following afternoon. He would be more use than Paulo. If Da Silva wasn't there, and João was the only reception committee, I wanted Papagaio at my back rather than Paulo. There was another reason for wanting him there, too. I didn't want to be left alone with Catarina Da Silva. I had been alone with her once before and I had betrayed both myself and Ana. If it happened again, I wasn't sure I'd be able to resist her, and it was possible that our relationship might become quite different. I didn't trust her and neither did I trust myself. There was something about her that threatened to burrow into my skin and run through my veins like a drug. Equally intoxicating and equally dangerous. So, for now, I chose Papagaio to be my chaperone.

Papagaio drove slowly on the way over to the *fazenda*, one of his samba tapes playing on full volume, and I wondered how he felt about going back. It was a while since he'd done anything other than run electrical wires into houses, but I remembered how he had drawn his gun, and how he had laughed when Alberto shot himself in the leg. I guessed a man like Papagaio would never change. He might have developed a set of skewed principles and a taste for hard work in the time I had known him, but I didn't doubt that he would react with calm brutality if he needed to.

As we came under the arch into the *fazenda*, I saw there were more cattle in the corrals than last time. When I had come here with only Eduardo's body for company, and a second time with João, the corrals had been almost empty, with only a few people working. But now they were filled with agitated cattle and I turned off the music to hear the lowing and the pounding of hooves washing over the sound of the car engine. There were men, too, herding the animals into the runs, steering them into the main enclosure one by one. They were shouting and whooping, prodding the cows and forcing them between the guiding fences. The smell that hung in the air was visceral and cloying, filling my mouth and blocking my nostrils, mingling with the plumes of disturbed red dirt and finding its gritty way between my teeth.

I watched two *vaqueiros* single out one animal and push it to the ground, using their weight to force it into the dust. One of them took a wide, flat knife from a pouch on his belt, unfolded it with one hand and slit the beast's testicles, removing them in one cut.

'Ouch.' I looked at Papagaio. 'I wouldn't want to have a disagreement with those guys. Could change your life.'

'You should see it on slaughter day,' he said. 'This whole place is filled with cows, even more than this, and they make such a noise after the first one is killed. The others, they can see it coming, they can smell the death and it makes them afraid. We're all the same when it comes to fear.' He was speaking from experience. 'The *vaqueiros* hold them down and cut their throats and the place is swimming with shit and blood.' He screwed up his nose. 'It stinks.'

I grimaced. I'd seen them slaughter cattle before – not here, but in one of the smaller *fazendas* on the way to Vila Rica – so I knew what it was like. Even now, just thinking about it, I could smell it; like the day Eduardo had bled all over Manolo's café.

Moving away from the corrals, though, the main house stood unmoved by the death which reeked on its doorstep. Its pale whitewashed walls surveying the blood with the same indifference the Da Silvas had for their workers.

Papagaio pulled up beside the grass and switched off the engine. 'Over to you now,' he said. 'Just take it easy though, OK?'

I nodded. 'Course. Is there any other way?' and opened the door, leaning over to spit out the taste of grit.

I took the steps up to the veranda, Papagaio a couple of paces behind me, and looked both ways at the tables and chairs which remained unused without anyone to sit in them. There were more than there had been when I last came, and everything looked cleaner. There were planters, too, the flowers bright and rich. It looked like a comfortable place; the kind of place you might come to relax, have a drink, read a book. Not what you'd expect from a working ranch on a busy day. No dirt and blood and shit here, just petals and palms. The Da Silvas did well to confine the filth to the corrals and the fields.

I turned to Papagaio, but he must have read my face because he shrugged and said, 'It was never like this when I was here. They must be trying to fix it up.'

I reached for the horseshoe knocker, but before I could put my fingers on it, the door opened and the maid stood before me. She was almost as surprised to see me as I was to see her, like she'd opened the door to leave and found me standing there. She was nearly as tall as me and wearing what appeared to be a French maid's uniform. It was an odd outfit, over-formal for such an informal place.

Her surprise turned to a forced smile.

'I'm here to see the Senhora,' I said.

She held my gaze and waited for me to speak again, standing still in the doorway.

'She in?' I asked.

She smiled again, this time a real one, and scanned me up and down in a way that made me feel wanted. She let me see her teeth, the brightness of her eyes, then stood aside to let us in, saying we should wait in the hallway. She closed the door behind us and walked away, glancing over her shoulder before she disappeared further into the house, her bare feet padding on the cold tiles. I watched her go, the way her hips swung lightly, and Papagaio leaned over to speak in my ear. 'If I didn't know better – *Padre* – I'd say you liked her.'

I shrugged him away saying, 'Less of the "*Padre*", if you don't mind,' and cast my eyes around the oversized hallway, with its double staircase sweeping from either side of the room, and its large furniture made from dark and solid Brasilian hardwood. I ran my fingers across the back of a carved bench seat. 'There must be a lot of money in cattle.'

'You see her toes?' said Papagaio.

'Hmm?'

'Her toes, Sam. The nails all painted different colours.' He whistled and shook his hand in front of him, the fingers making a snapping noise. 'And the way she was looking at you.' He sucked air. 'If only you weren't a priest, eh?'

'You're a sick man, Papagaio.'

'Hey, they paint their toes like that, you know they've got something inside them.'

'Think about something else.'

'It's like they're wild or something. They're wild and they want it. I mean, she's not exactly beautiful, but who cares? With toes like those, you *know* she'll be good. Hey, maybe she won't even care you're a priest. You could—'

Before he was able to go on, though, we heard the maid's

footsteps and turned to watch her coming back through the house. Her hips swaying a little more now, her back straighter, and I couldn't help myself from glancing down at her feet as she approached. Papagaio was right; every toenail was a different colour.

When I looked up, she was staring at me. 'Come with me,' she said, whipping around and leading us through the house, out onto the veranda at the back where Catarina Da Silva was waiting for us. There was an empty glass on the white metal table, and a jug containing a cloudy liquid that I knew would be caipirinha. Lime, sugar and *cachaça*, the drink was a religion in São Tiago. Senhora Da Silva's glass was half full and she was sipping from it as we walked out. She put it down and watched us come near, her not standing up, just indicating we should sit down at the table.

At either end of the veranda, at least fifty metres apart, a man was stationed, sunglasses shading their eyes. As before, Da Silva's bodyguards each carried a holster high on his hip, the unmistakable grip of an automatic peeping from the well-oiled leather. I expected them to intercept us, frisk for weapons, but they stayed where they were, eyes on us, confident they had corralled us as well as the *vaqueiros* corralled their cattle.

Senhora Da Silva sat back in the chair and crossed her legs, left over right. She wore a white cotton shirt, bright in the sunlight, that might have belonged to a man. It was tied in a bow at her waist, above the band of her dark blue jeans. On her wrists she wore bracelets of gold, and in her ears she wore rings of gold. Her hair was scraped into a ponytail which fell between her shoulder blades.

As we sat down, she watched Papagaio, her eyes on him like a snake. 'Sam,' she said, without looking at me. 'You shouldn't have left it so long. I was beginning to think you were avoiding me.' She waved a hand. 'Marcia, pour my guest a drink.'

The maid stepped forward, filled the empty glass. She

pushed it towards me, making it clear it was not for Papagaio, and stepped away again.

'You like caipirinha,' Da Silva said. 'I remember that.'

I felt Papagaio's eyes on me and I looked at him, awkward that she had not offered any to him. Papagaio was beneath her. He was a worker. No one of importance. I was surprised he was even allowed to sit at the same table. He nodded his head at me, once, almost imperceptible and I took it as his recognition of my discomfort but acknowledgement that I should accept her hospitality.

'Please,' she said. 'Drink.'

I replied by taking the glass and drinking. I watched her over the rim, thinking how much she looked like an ordinary person, seeing her now as I had seen her at the barbecue, not as a devil who can order men burned or shot. It would have been easier to hate her if she were ugly on the outside but, like my friend Papagaio, her manner gave no sign she was capable of brutality. Brasil had taught me one thing above all else; the savage are mundane. Everyone is capable of absolute cruelty.

'I was thinking of reorganising the *fazenda*,' she said, speaking slowly. 'Thought I might grow some sugar, make some *cachaça* of my own. Good stuff, not like that Fifty-One rubbish the workers drink.' She took her glass and held it up to inspect it. 'There's money to be made in *cachaça*.' She drank and then replaced the glass on the table and looked straight at me. 'Did you know within ten years of clearing, the pastures become unusable?'

'Yes.' I thought about the small shrub-like weeds struggling to survive in the compacted red soil.

'But did you also know that with cultivation and enough chemicals I can get sixteen crops a year? Coffee, soya bean, sugar cane. Can you imagine how much money I'd make?'

I didn't bother to answer; wasn't sure why she was telling me.

'Why are you here?' she said after a pause, her eyes flitting over to Papagaio then settling back on me. 'To see *me*?' She bit the inside of her cheek.

It wasn't the way she asked, it was the way her mind had changed direction so quickly. That's what made me hesitate.

'No, I . . . wanted to talk to you about some plans we have.' I didn't like her catching me off guard, I didn't want her to think me weak. People like her, they spot a weakness, they exploit it. They rip it out.

'What kind of plans?' Dark green eyes moving over me, studying every part of me before coming back to stare into my own.

'To build a clinic.'

'Yes, I heard about that. Actually, I'm surprised you didn't come to me sooner.' She sipped her drink without looking away and ran her tongue across her lips.

'I was—'

'I know what you think I am. Or what you *thought*. I could see it in your face the first time we met. Not so much now, I don't see it now, but then . . .' she shrugged like it didn't matter, and I felt her naked foot touch mine under the table. It took me by surprise and I pulled away. The table wasn't big, though, and she reached a little further, running her toes over my shin, moving them up to rest on my knee.

She raised her eyebrows, her head tilting to one side with suppressed amusement. She was enjoying herself, playing with me like we were sharing a private and secret game. And it was made all the more delicious for her because she was playing it out in front of others. 'You church people, you're taught to hate landowners because we're rich. They show you how to stir up trouble, encourage the peasants to occupy uncultivated land, and then you're surprised when priests are dealt with.' Something close to a smile slipped across her lips before she pursed them together, stifling it. 'But that's not how I am,' she said. 'You know that.'

I looked away, unable to meet her eyes any longer. I felt as if she were looking right into me, searching for the right button.

'I want to use the land,' she told me. 'I want to bring money to São Tiago.'

'Sure you do,' I said, wondering how that fitted in with the murder of her workers. Men with their limbs cut off, burned by the fires, shot in the head and left for the insects. I suppose she didn't do it herself, didn't see the life evaporate like I had done, but I had to remind myself that she was the one who made it happen. I so wanted to hate her. But amongst all that, I caught myself trying to believe that it was only her husband who did such things.

I took the Carltons from my top pocket and lit one, placing the rest on the table. She looked at them and then back at me. 'So you want to build a clinic and you've come to ask my permission, is that it?'

I blew smoke through my nose and shook my head. 'Not exactly. I thought—'

'You speak good Portuguese for a *gringo*,' she interrupted. 'And I heard you like to drink. Some say you even have an eye for the women. Is that right? You like women?'

I didn't answer.

'How about Marcia? You like her?' She waved a finger at the maid, who swished over to refresh the Senhora's drink. 'She the kind of woman you like? Or maybe you like someone stronger?'

'I didn't come here to talk about me,' I said, aware that Papagaio was watching us.

'I like to know who I'm dealing with.'

'No one of any consequence,' I said.

'Hmm. I wonder what brings a man like you to São Tiago,' she went on. 'What it is you're getting away from.'

'We want to build—'

'Everyone in São Tiago is hiding from something,' she said. 'Everyone has something to hide. What about you?'

'I came to be with the church in São Felix,' I offered, hoping it would be enough.

'Then why aren't you there? Why are you in São Tiago instead?'

'The fishing's better.'

'Yes, I heard you like to fish.'

'You been checking up on me?'

'You don't talk like a priest. From what I've seen, you don't act like a priest.' Again the smile, brief, hidden, just touching her lips then fading.

'I've fallen out of practice,' I said. 'What difference does it make?'

She sipped her drink. When she replaced the glass on the table, though, she changed tack again. 'So you came here to talk to me because you thought I might object to having a clinic in São Tiago?'

I was relieved she'd come back to it but I could see I was always going to be on my toes with this woman.

'Or was there something else you wanted from me?'

'No,' I said. 'The clinic. Just the clinic.'

'Why would I object?' She smiled openly now, showing all her white teeth; the kind that sparkled with dental treatment that can only be paid for by the rich. 'Why would I want to stop your clinic? Perhaps because you're building it on my land?'

'*Your* land? I thought—'

'Then you thought wrong.' Catarina Da Silva stood, pushing back her chair. She picked up her drink and walked away to the wall around the veranda.

I watched her go, seeing the flesh around her midriff, the muscle either side of her spine disappearing into the top of her jeans, and I tried not to like the way her hips moved.

'Come and look at this, Sam.' She spoke with her back to me.

I joined her, not standing too close, but close enough to smell the perfume which shrouded her. Papagaio stayed where he was, his hands palm down on the table in front of him.

'I wonder why no one calls you *padre*?' Her eyes scanned my face, reading every reaction, every sign. 'That's more normal for a man like you isn't it?' She leaned her body towards mine, the skin of her arm touching my own, and I tried not to react.

'I prefer my own name.'

'Hmm,' she looked away. 'What do you think?' She motioned with her hand, the one holding the drink, and I heard ice cubes clink against the glass. 'How about that view?'

Beyond the veranda wall, there were three or four metres of dry grass, and beyond that the ground dropped away into a shallow valley. At the base of the valley, a clear river ran dry at its banks showing strips of white sand, just like the beaches at São Tiago, only smaller. On the other side, the hill rose, every metre of it covered in good old traditional jungle. The kind that lives.

'When the rains come and the river rises, that flows deep down there,' she said. 'But you know that, don't you, Sam?'

I said nothing.

'And that's when the big fish come, so they tell me. The catfish. Right now it's good for *tucunaré*, though, and the tourists like to catch that too, don't they?'

'It's easier for them,' I shrugged. 'The big catfish, they don't catch so easy.'

Catarina Da Silva turned to me. 'People say you know fishing.'

'I know some.' She had me at a disadvantage. She knew enough about me to make me feel investigated.

'Not much else to do around here, I suppose, especially for a man like you – a priest who never gives mass, I mean. Drinking, shooting, fishing . . . sex? Which is your favourite?'

'I couldn't say.'

She looked away again, staring at the river and the forest that lay beyond it. 'Mato Grosso is opening up,' she said. 'Slowly, but it's coming. And we're in a good spot. Good seasons. Not too much land development.'

'There's enough,' I said.

'Hmm. But no miners, though, no mining towns. No mess like they've made near Marabá.'

'We'll get their mess too,' I said. 'Their mercury will come down the river towards us. It'll kill everything.'

'It won't reach this far. And one day, tourists will come from all over the world to see what we have.'

'I like it as it is,' I said. 'We don't need tourists.'

'Maybe, but it's coming. Can't you feel it?'

I thought about the tourists who occasionally came to São Tiago to use André's floating hotel and drink Manolo's beer. I thought about what it would be like if the town were teeming with them in their bright shirts and their open-toed sandals, carrying their rods and filling their fat bellies. I'd heard about the floating hotels on Tocantins, and there were some further north on the Araguaia, with their bars and their restaurants and their staff and it made me sick. It turned my stomach, but she was right. Before long, they would come. They would drift down the river towards us, they would devour our way of life and they would call it progress.

'My husband, Kiko, he's not so sure,' she said. 'He thinks the tourists will stop before they get near us, but I don't agree. He says it's too far for them to come, too *remote*, but I say they're looking for adventure. They want off the beaten track but with all the comforts of home. And when I look out here and I see the river so close, I get ideas. Maybe then things won't be so boring around here.'

'Why are you telling me?'

'You know your fish, maybe I could use someone like you. You don't do any church work, I know that, so maybe I could give you something else to do.'

'I don't need anything to do.' I had come half expecting a fight, and now it seemed that she was trying to recruit me. My life was full of people who wanted to give me things to do. 'I have enough.'

'The work at Hevea won't last for ever.' Again she glanced my way, but only a glance. 'Might change the name of the *fazenda*, though,' she said. '*Fazenda Da Silva* doesn't sound right. Not for the brochure.'

I shrugged and flicked my cigarette out onto the soil.

'I was thinking something like Clear Water. Or maybe Miracle Water. Green Hill,' she went on. 'Something like that.'

I stared up at the trees. 'Doesn't matter what you call it,' I said. 'It'll still be the same thing. It is what it is. The blood, the noise, the smell of shit.'

She shook her head. 'That'll all change. The cattle will only come here for branding, so the tourists can see what happens. They'll be killed out in the field, away from sensitive eyes. Eventually there won't be any cattle at all, just a few for the tourists to see. Instead, there will be fields of coffee, sugar cane, soya bean. There'll be horses for the little *gringo* children; jeeps, boats, fishing. There will be new people here every day. The place will be alive, not dry and dead like it is now.'

'I like it better the way it is.'

'You think I don't want you to build your health clinic.' She ignored me. 'You know I've heard your plans and you think I'll cause trouble, but this isn't Santa Terezinha and you're nothing like that man Jentel.'

The mention of his name took me by surprise but I tried not to show it.

'Besides,' she lowered her voice as if including me in a secret plot, 'I like you, Sam. It can be my gift to you.'

I suspected I knew what she wanted in exchange for such a

gift, but I had no idea how far she would go and just how much she would eventually take from me.

'I *want* you to build. It would be easier for us, you see, because then we wouldn't have to build our own. We have you to do it for us. A priest and a doctor. Everybody will trust you.'

'Sure. How could we go wrong?' I said, but the sarcasm was lost on her.

'And when you are done, you can work it for me. The clinic and the fishing. Isn't that what you want?'

'Depends on the terms,' I said.

'I'll give you a percentage of anything you make in the clinic and I'll keep you safe.'

'That's not what I meant. I don't think it'll be that kind of place,' I said, not liking the idea of squeezing money from anyone, knowing Paulo wouldn't like it either even though he'd already mentioned it himself. 'It won't be unsafe and it's not about making money.'

'It will be.' She paused, deliberately unspecific. 'Our . . . *relationship* . . . warrants you some kind of special treatment, Sam, but my husband will still want to see a return. We'll help, though. Get you on your feet. You'll need money for materials and labour, isn't that why you came to me? To use me?' She turned to look at me again, showing me she was serious, and suddenly she was not the same person who had been at the barbecue. She had changed from flirtatious and passionate to businesslike and controlling, but if I'd had time to think about it, I would have realised that these things were all part of the same act. Without such a luxury, though, I was confused that this was the woman who, just moments ago, had been touching me under the table. And now I began to feel a mixture of anger and embarrassment at being here, asking her for permission. For help.

'When our tourists come,' she said, 'they'll need someone to take care of them. Someone to take care of their sunstroke, patch them up when they stick a hook through their finger, fall off a horse. The clinic you build for me will be perfect. I only wonder if it shouldn't be closer to the *fazenda*.'

I turned around and sat on the wall, glancing over at Papagaio. He was still straight up in his chair, the palms of his hands still flat on the surface.

I drained my drink and put it on the wall beside me.

'Talk to your doctor friend,' she said. 'See what he says about my proposal. You don't build the health clinic, someone else will. I can always bring someone in, but I'd rather it was you, Sam.'

'I'll talk to him.'

'Good. Come back and tell me his decision. At least this way he gets to do what he wants.'

'In a manner of speaking.'

Da Silva smiled again and nodded. 'The maid will see you out.'

Marcia led Papagaio and me away from the veranda and through the house. She opened the front door and moved to one side to let us out, but as I stepped into the sunlight, I felt a hand on my arm.

'Go ahead,' Da Silva said to Papagaio, 'wait in the car.' Then she looked at Marcia who immediately understood and disappeared back into the shadow of the house.

When we were alone, she spoke to me, saying, 'I wonder exactly what you will get out of this clinic.'

'Peace of mind.' I shrugged.

'Mm. Or maybe something else,' she said. 'I think we're going to be good friends, Sam.'

'Do you?'

'You don't think about what happened? At the barbecue?' The Catarina Da Silva from the barbecue was back now, as flirtatious and alluring as ever. It was as if two women resided within.

I pursed my lips, tried not to remember how she had looked in the silk dress, the way her soft skin had felt.

'I do,' she said. 'All the time. I can't stop myself. The way you kissed me. You're no priest. Just now, back there, I wanted to have you. But if someone were to see . . . if Kiko were to find out . . .'

I turned to leave, but she tightened her grip on my arm and held me back.

'I like you, Sam,' she said. 'I intend to have you. When you come back, make sure you're alone.'

25

'We can't trust her,' Paulo was saying. 'She's a snake.'

We were on the *praia*, all of us sitting on the white sand by the water. It was early evening and the sun was dropping behind the trees across the river. Behind us, closer to the edge of the foliage, Manolo had set up his bar, and one or two people were already dancing to the music. He seemed to have attracted a few customers, but most of them were Indians from Bananal. I hadn't asked anybody to stop drinking at his place, but business had been slow for him these past weeks and I couldn't help feeling a little pleased that people might be avoiding him because of what he had done. Manolo was never going to pay for Eduardo's murder, and slow business for a few weeks might be the only punishment he ever received.

'She's worse than a snake,' said Papagaio. 'She's a snake with tits. Or maybe a *piranha*.' He looked at Ana and shrugged. 'Sorry but it's true. The biggest red belly you ever saw, with teeth that would cut you in half.' He came back to the rest of us again. 'What's to say she won't just take over? Start telling you what to do, get upset when you don't?'

'She's already doing that. We shouldn't trust her,' Paulo said again. 'It's not what I wanted.'

'Who said anything about trusting her?' Ana said. 'You don't have to trust her; just take her help.' She was sitting beside me, her arm touching mine.

'You mean you think we should go with it?' Paulo was going to take some convincing.

'From what Sam said, it looks to me like you don't have a choice,' Ana told him. 'If you want to build a clinic, then this is the way it's going to be done.'

'Maybe we shouldn't have told her. We hadn't told her, she wouldn't know, it wouldn't matter.' Paulo trying to make sense.

'And where would you get all the money you need?' I said. 'You'd run out eventually. Anyway, she already knew. If you'd gone ahead with it, she would've either taken over *then*, or pulled the whole thing down. You piss her off too much, she'd send her people to cause trouble.'

'She's bad news.' Paulo rubbed his forehead in despair. 'This isn't how it was supposed to be.'

'It doesn't have to be bad news,' I said. 'Just go along with her. She's even going to help you build it; supply materials, workers. What's the problem? And once it's built you can run it pretty much how you like.'

'So long as she's happy,' said Paulo.

I shrugged. 'It was always going to be this way. You wanted your clinic in São Tiago, and out here the Da Silvas are everything. We're nothing. It sounds like a good deal to me, but it's not my decision. This is for *you*, not us.'

'You're in on it too, now.' Paulo's whole face saying he needed us to back him up. 'This is all of us now. We're all in it.' He leaned forward to see around me and look at Ana. He knew she was the best way to get to me.

'Sure,' I said, moving to block his view. 'We're all in it, but we're just helping out. We won't let you down, Paulo, but you *own* this. The clinic is yours.' What I'd brought back from the *fazenda* wasn't the solution he wanted, but it was the best one he was going to get, and I wanted the decision to come from Paulo. I'd go along with whatever he wanted, but it had to come from him. 'Look,' I said, shifting back again on the sand so we were in a rough circle and Ana was included more. 'Da Silva's put a deal on the table you can't refuse.'

'So I end up in her pocket? They run the clinic, they take the money, they supply the patients, what else they do? They *make* patients? I end up looking after people who get shot?' He shook his head. 'Uh-uh. No way. I don't want to work for them.'

'I know it's not what you hoped, but there are changes up there,' I said. 'You're the one always saying things change, well maybe you're right. I think things might be a little different before long. Come on, Paulo, you're not in this for anything other than to make sick people better, so what're you worried about? This is about Eduardo, isn't it? So what's the difference between treating a man shot on the *fazenda* or a man stabbed here in a café? A life is a life, Paulo.'

'Besides,' Ana interrupted, 'you won't be working for them, so don't look at it that way. The way you should look at it, they'll be working for you.'

Papagaio wasn't convinced and he eyed Ana like she didn't know what she was talking about. She was a woman, what the hell did she know about people like Catarina Da Silva? 'How d'you figure that one out?' he said. 'The Da Silvas don't work for anybody. Hardly even work for themselves, for Christ's sake.' He gave me a small nod, a kind of apology for taking the name in vain.

'It's all in the way you think about it,' she argued. 'Sam says they'll provide money, land, materials. They're giving you everything you need. And Paulo will be running it. He'll be the doctor, he'll take on the staff, he'll order the supplies,' counting them off on her fingers. 'So who's running it? Who's working for who? All they want is a cut of the money.'

'Yeah, but it shouldn't be about money.'

'Paulo, *every*thing is about money,' I said. 'And you knew *this* would be. We already talked about it.'

'True,' he conceded.

'So when she brings her tourists down here, you charge them what you need to and send Da Silva what's hers. That's all.'

'And if there's no tourists? I can't charge our people tourist prices.'

'Then we'll make sure she understands that,' I said. 'We can worry about these things later. For now, just get it built. Take her money. If you don't do it, she'll get someone else.'

'I still don't like it.'

'OK.' I threw my hands in the air. 'It's the best I could do. She wasn't handing out free cash. You have a better idea, I'd like to hear it.'

We were silent for a while, each of us looking out towards the river, Paulo sighing a lot and probably realising he didn't have much choice. Eventually he stood up and paddled into the water, wetting his feet, then coming back to sit with us.

'I could use the money,' he said. 'And I suppose it'll mean you can do more overtime at Hevea. If I get wages for workers, I won't need you two. You can get the work finished over there.'

'They're paying me well,' Papagaio agreed. 'And if Sam goes to work for Da Silva, I can keep the lot for myself.'

They all looked at me at once.

'You heard what she said?' I glanced at Ana, watching her reaction.

'Sure I heard it,' Papagaio said. 'I had my hands on the table, not over my ears.'

'Hear what?' asked Ana. 'She offered you a job, Sam?'

'Senhora Da Silva laid it on thick for the priest,' said Papagaio. 'I think she and her maid fancied a bit of holy *gringo*, the pair of them sniffing round him. It was all they could do to keep their hands off him.'

Ana turned and stared at me, eyes widening, about to speak, but Papagaio went on. 'Maybe the Senhora likes a challenge,' he said. 'She saw a priest and thought she'd see what she could get him to do. Her maid, too, I saw them both looking at you like . . . well, like they wanted to do more than just look at you.'

'Hang on a minute,' said Ana. 'What kind of job?'

But Papagaio was on a roll now, saying, 'You should've seen her, Paulo, the maid. She was tall. Tits like a carnival queen and legs like a dancing girl.' He shrugged at Ana like he was saying if she wanted to sit with the men, she was going to have to put up with his conversation. 'And she had a different colour on every toenail. I mean, if I had a maid like that—'

'Shut up, Papagaio,' said Paulo, turning to look at me. 'What did I miss with Da Silva? What's this about a job?'

I took another swig and shook my head at Paulo. 'You didn't miss anything. She—'

'She offered him a job,' said Papagaio. 'For when she turns the *fazenda* into a holiday place.'

'A holiday place? What kind of holiday place? And what the hell would she want a priest for?' Ana glanced at Papagaio, then looked back at me, almost as if she were accusing me. 'Why does she need a priest?'

'She doesn't,' I said, holding my hands up as shadowy and lustful images of Da Silva leapt into my mind, squeezing blood and heat into my cheeks. 'She wants someone to handle the fishing.' I hoped I didn't sound too defensive.

'Or handle something else,' Papagaio added, making me glare at him.

'You're not helping,' I said to him.

Paulo looked worried now. 'But you're not interested, right? I mean you don't want to work over there, do you?'

'Of course I don't,' I said. 'Papagaio's making it sound a whole lot worse than—'

'Not even for Senhora Da Silva?' Ana asked, a piqued tone washing over the edges of her words. 'And her maid with the

215

painted toes?' She raised her eyebrows at me, more than just a little irritated by the direction the conversation had taken.

'No.' I put my hand on Ana's and held her eyes. '*Especially* not for Catarina Da Silva.'

26

Catarina Da Silva was surprised to see me back the next morning, probably startled by how early it was – Papagaio and I arrived a little after six o' clock. I half hoped she'd be asleep, unable to see me, but she was up and ready, like she'd been awake for hours.

Da Silva had told me to come alone, so I made Papagaio stay in the car when we arrived at the *fazenda*. He tried to protest, saying something about me being a priest and them being mad bastard killers, so I reminded him it was just a business arrangement. I said Senhora Da Silva wouldn't hurt me, I was sure of that, so he sat back in the Beetle and sulked.

She was on the rear veranda, where we'd met her the day before, and the table was laid with an assortment of fruits and cheeses and cold meats most of her employees would have killed for.

Just like before, there was a man perched at each end of the veranda – Luis and Lucas she had called them – each wearing his cleanest jeans, his whitest shirt and his best-oiled automatic. This time, though, she wasn't alone at the table. A man, pale-skinned like herself, clean shaven, but with a profusion of tangled hair bursting from the open neck of the dark blue polo-shirt he was wearing. I had seen him at the barbecue, but not known who he was. He wasn't a tall man, possibly shorter even than his wife, although it was difficult to tell because he was sitting down, and he carried a excess amount of weight on his small frame. Not at all how I imagined the husband of a creature like Catarina Da Silva. His hair was thinning around his crown and even though it was still early morning, there was already a film of sweat forming on his brow.

'You're early,' Da Silva said as Marcia of the painted nails ushered me onto the veranda.

'On my way to Hevea,' I replied.

She studied me for a moment, our eyes locking, then I glanced at the man sitting opposite her. Catarina Da Silva blinked. 'My husband, Marco,' she said.

The man remained seated but extended a hand for me to shake. I was a little taken aback by the gesture and I hesitated before I took his hand. When I did shake, of course, the grip was firm. I also noted Catarina had introduced him as Marco, not Kiko as she had called him yesterday. Marco was his official name. When he released my hand, he indicated an empty chair.

I shook my head, saying no thanks, I didn't want to sit down. 'I won't keep you,' I directed my comments to both of them, not sure who was in charge. 'I've come to confirm what we talked about yesterday. We'd like to accept your offer of help.'

'Good.' Catarina dabbed at her mouth with a linen napkin and sat back in her chair. An odd gesture, the thing with the napkin; like she was genteel, this woman who ordered men to be beaten and burned. This woman who gave herself to priests. Again I had the notion that she was not just one person, but two.

'Good,' she said again. 'I'll arrange for someone to come to you this afternoon. You can give him a list of any materials you need. We'll get what we can and give you some money for the rest. You can get timber from the mill; bricks from Vila Rica.'

'Within reason, of course,' Kiko said.

'Of course,' I agreed, knowing that I'd have to tread carefully. We were in their pockets now, making a deal that could go in almost any direction. 'Will there be enough to pay some workers?'

'I'll send workers.'

'We can find men of our own,' I said. 'We don't need to take your *vaqueiros*. Leave it to me and you won't have to trouble yourselves.' I knew it would make the people in São Tiago nervous to have Da Silva's men building the clinic. If they knew she was involved, the people wouldn't dare use it. They would rather suffer their illnesses than risk crossing paths with Catarina Da Silva.

She thought for a moment. 'OK. I'll make sure you have enough. The man who comes this afternoon, though, will come to *you*,' she said. 'No one else.'

I shook my head again. 'I won't be there; it's not my project. He'll have to go to Paulo. He's the doctor, he'll tell him what we need.'

Catarina looked at her husband and then me. 'I'd prefer it if you were to do this. I trust you. You came to me, so the deal is with you.'

'No, I have other—'

'If my wife says it must be you, then it must be you.' Marco Da Silva not even looking at me, his voice daring me to say no again, but his wife held up her hand and smiled at him.

'Let him finish,' she said to her husband before inclining her head at me. 'You were saying?' I didn't know who was the boss in this particular household, although I suspected that when Kiko was home, Kiko called the shots. But the clinic, I guessed, was his wife's project. Something for her to get her teeth into.

I sighed and rubbed a hand across the stubble on my chin, my eyes meeting Catarina's. 'I have a job,' I said, but she already knew that. This was her way of making me understand who was in charge; *she* would be making the decisions.

'At Hevea?' Saying it for her husband's benefit, pretending not to know so much about me.

219

'Right.'

Catarina Da Silva put a tiny piece of thin cheese in her mouth and nodded while she mulled that over. After a moment, she swallowed and dabbed her mouth again. 'OK,' she said. 'But I want you to come here every morning on your way to Hevea. I will expect a daily account of the work you're doing.'

'I don't have my own transport. I have to rely on—'

'Then something will be arranged for you,' she said, making it clear there was no avoiding her. 'Something will be brought to the site this afternoon. It won't be anything special, but it'll have to do.'

'OK,' thinking Paulo was going to owe me big time. 'If that's how it has to be.'

'Good enough.' She pointed to the food on the table. 'You sure you won't have any breakfast?'

I'd been hungry when I left São Tiago, but now, 'I don't have much of an appetite this morning,' I said. Kiko was tucking into his food, ignoring me, picking at the meat on his plate. A thick piece of pink beef, and it made me feel ill just looking at it. 'Thanks all the same.' He was like a boar rooting in the forest.

Catarina glanced at her husband, an almost imperceptible curl touching the corner of her mouth. Then she looked back at me and smiled. 'Your friend, the doctor. What did you say his name was?'

'Paulo.'

'Hmm. Well, this is my project now, not Paulo's, and I expect you to keep me up to date,' she said. 'Come by tomorrow. A little later, though, I have a busy morning planned.'

I wondered what a busy morning was for her. Maybe painting her nails or brushing her hair. Ordering a couple of shootings. I glanced at her husband, still ransacking the breakfast spread, and considered trying to convince myself that perhaps it was just Kiko who was responsible for such things.

'You're working for me now,' she said, and the conversation was over. She dismissed me, her eyes going out to the trees beyond the river at the back of the house. She raised a small cup to her lips and drank. It made me feel like I should bow and back away from their company.

In the car, I told Papagaio what Da Silva had said. 'So it looks like I'm working with Paulo on the clinic after all. I might need to take a few days away from Hevea from time to time, and I'll be a little later in the mornings, but it shouldn't be too much – Senhor Swan shouldn't mind about that. I can go to the clinic every evening when we get back, see how things are going, then let her know the following morning.'

Papagaio shrugged like it was no big deal. 'Morning meetings, eh? So you get to see more of Senhora Da Silva.' He turned to me. 'Nice.'

I sighed.

'And the maid with the toes,' he added with a whistle. 'Shit. You want to be careful they don't try to keep you there.'

When we reached the plantation, the smell of burning was strong. There was almost no breeze that day and the smoke hung in the air over the furthest border of the estate. So many trees that had taken years to grow were now turning to ash in man-made rows.

'They cut much more down,' I said, 'the dry season will last for ever.'

Papagaio took us along the road leading through to the main office area. Either side of the track stood telegraph poles made from stripped-off tree trunks painted white around the bottom. Coming into the hub of the plantation, the buildings were arranged in a squared horseshoe. The offices, painted pale yellow, were directly alongside the road, four single-storey blocks with shining new corrugated-iron roofs. It struck me that during the rains, when they finally came, the sound would be almost unbearable. On the other side of the road, along the line of the trees, three manager's houses stood in a row.

Opposite the offices, on the other leg of the open square, fifty metres away, a pale blue warehouse loitered on the red dirt. A tractor was ticking over in the loading bay at one end, blue-black exhaust fumes bruising the air. Two wiry men wearing caps and open shirts were loading the trailer with sacks and irrigation pipes. A mechanic's workshop completed the cluster of buildings. Inside, a bright yellow bulldozer, its treads full of mud, was sitting idle.

Usually, at this time of day, the workers would be out in the fields and this part of the plantation would be fairly quiet, but today was pay day, so many of them were forming a line outside the accountant's office, waiting for their packets to be brought out and distributed. There was a hatch at one end of the building, where the accountant would sit, flanked by the two of the *Americanos*, handing the small brown envelopes through the window and accepting signatures from those who could write, thumb prints from those who could not.

Papagaio pulled over by the first office and we climbed out.

'Come on, then,' he said. 'Let's get paid.'

'You go ahead,' I told him, wanting to collect my thoughts. 'I'm going to stand here a while.'

'I'll join the queue,' he nodded, walking away. 'Save you a place. But you take too long, you lose it.'

I watched Papagaio join the line, speaking with the men in front of him, sharing a joke and laughing.

I stayed where I was, taking time to enjoy the growing day, leaning against the car and lighting a cigarette. After a few moments, the hatch in the accountant's office opened and I saw the man's face appear behind the counter. He was saying something, I couldn't hear what, and he was raising his hands

222

to the worker at the front of the queue. Behind him, I could see the pale faces of the two *Americanos*.

The worker at the front of the queue was obviously not pleased with what the accountant was telling him and he started gesticulating, growing more agitated, removing his hat and throwing it to the ground. The men behind him began breaking ranks, moving round him, pushing to gain access to the hatch. Within a few seconds the line had completely dissolved and all I could see was a crowd of bodies, maybe thirty men, surrounding the hatch, raising their fists, their voices shouting to be heard.

Papagaio separated himself from the crowd and came back to where I was standing. He sat on the bonnet of his car and took off his hat to wipe his brow.

'What's that all about?' I asked.

'No money,' he said. 'Least, as far as I can tell.'

'No money?'

He watched the crowd of men pushing and shoving, vying for a position in front of the hatch, the opportunity to have their say.

'No wonder they're unhappy,' I said.

'Yeah. Me too,' said Papagaio. 'I need *pinga* money for the weekend.'

'You'll survive,' I said. 'Anyway, there must be an explanation. Senhor Swan always pays us.'

As I spoke, I heard the sound of an engine heading down the road and I turned to watch Swan's pickup approaching. He drove straight into the centre of the open space within the horseshoe of buildings and came to a halt. He pipped the horn three times and jumped down from the cab. Immediately, the workers turned on him, running over to the pickup. Swan climbed up onto the bonnet and held up his hands.

It seemed to do the trick. He had gained enough respect from his workers for them to give him a chance to speak.

While he waited for the men to settle, I noticed the accountant slip out and scuttle away to his house – one of the three built on the other side of the road, not far from the offices. As soon as he was out of sight, I turned my attention back to Senhor Swan who was looking around at the faces below him. He shook his head and began to speak, raising his voice so that everyone could hear him.

'There's no other way to tell you this,' he said. 'We've had a problem with the pay.' He paused and allowed himself to make eye contact with some of the men, looking for those he knew best. He would be trying to pick out the crew leaders, the men who would reassure the other workers. 'Everything was ready to be sent through from São Paulo, but there were problems with the transport and . . .' He shook his head again, probably knowing that most of the men would not care about his excuses. Banks, transport difficulties, logistics, these were things which meant nothing to them. They were drifters, fugitives, men who could not even sign their own names. All they cared about was having enough notes in their pocket to buy a little rice, some meat, plenty of *pinga*.

'We have enough here to pay you half,' he said. 'You will get the rest as soon as—'

'Pay us,' someone shouted, sending a ripple through the crowd. 'Pay us what you owe.'

I pushed myself into a standing position and glanced at Papagaio who had done the same.

Some of the men were moving now, driving through to the front of the crowd, a few more shouts of 'Pay us,' rising from them.

Swan climbed from the bonnet onto the cab of the pickup, wanting to be higher, and stood tall, raising both hands again. 'We'll pay you what we have.'

'Pay us.' A few more voices now, more people pushing to the front, one man breaking from the crowd and climbing onto the bonnet of the pickup. Surprised by the surge, Swan stepped backwards, one foot slipping from the cab, but he managed to regain his balance. When he was upright again, his hand went to his heavy pocket, unconsciously seeking the reassurance of what lay within.

Papagaio and I remained where we were and watched as the man I now recognised as Fernando, one of the irrigation crew workers, took two steps across the bonnet of the pickup and began pulling himself up onto the roof. I was about to move, thinking I should do something to help Senhor Swan, but Fernando only took two steps before he was stopped.

As if from nowhere, one of the *Americanos* appeared in the crowd, reaching for the attacker, grabbing his shirt tail and hauling him back with one hand so that he slid face first onto the bonnet. The *Americano* then took a stronger grip, holding the waistband of Fernando's trousers, hoisting him from the pickup. Fernando tried to hang onto the vehicle, but his fingers found no purchase on the smooth metal and he came off, the *Americano* twirling him onto his back as he threw him down hard in the dirt. The *Americano* kicked him once in the ribs, then climbed up onto the bonnet himself, standing in front of Senhor Swan.

I had only ever seen the *Americanos* either in São Tiago or as faces behind the hatch at the accountant's office, and I was surprised to see that this man was armed not with a pistol, which I assumed they carried at all times, but with something far more fearsome. This man carried a carbine, a shortened assault rifle, with a plastic stock and a carry handle over the top. He presented the weapon in front of him, angled towards the crowd, and became still.

There was a moment of silent indecision, and then the crowd began to move again. A group of men pushed towards the pickup, but when the first of them attempted to climb onto the vehicle, the *Americano* kicked him hard in the face, his nose spraying flecks of blood, knocking him back amongst the surging bodies. The second man received the same treatment, but then more men were trying to scale the vehicle at the same time. In one swift movement, the *Americano* brought the butt of his carbine down on the first man to actually make it onto the bonnet, hitting him hard on the top of the head, then he raised his weapon to the sky and fired a burst of shots in rapid succession before pointing it at the crowd once again.

The workers immediately stopped pushing and fell silent.

It was only then that something behind the crowd caught my eye and I looked away from the hub of the action. On the periphery, I saw a second *Americano* take a step back to improve his scope of fire and then, as if they had materialised like ghosts, I spotted another, in position, the three of them now covering as much of the crowd as possible. I wondered how I hadn't seen them before, and I didn't doubt that, had they wanted to, they could have killed every man around the pickup.

I spoke without looking at Papagaio. 'They're good.'

'Better than me. Better than Luis and Lucas, even. See how they work together like predators?' he said. 'The one at the front, he draws their attention, while the two at the back . . . shit, no one even knows they're there. They're the ones who're most dangerous right now. Any one of those men looks like he's going to pull a weapon, they'll open holes in his back, I'm sure of it. And those rifles they're carrying? Soldiers' weapons. I never saw guns like that carried by anyone but soldiers.'

It made me think about the time the boy asked if I had been a mercenary, excited at the prospect, when all the time there had been three of them much closer to home.

The crowd of workers was quiet now, looking up at the two men standing on the Chevrolet. I knew that many of them would be armed. Most would carry knives, one or two would even have pistols with them, but they were not drunk and they were not here to kill. They were here to work. Some to feed their families. And now they had seen the *Americano* at work, heard the rapid report of his weapon, they would not want to risk their lives.

Once again, Swan spoke to them, saying, 'Please, you'll get your money. As I said before, we have enough to give you half. The rest should be here in the next few days. Be patient. I promise you'll get your money.' He was making calming motions with his hands now, his voice loud, but I could detect a nervousness to it. I don't suppose he had expected to be involved in crowd control when he took the job.

The men who had been hit were picking themselves up, Fernando coming round to the front of the crowd, looking up at the *Americano* standing over them, his weapon still raised.

'Look.' Swan dropped his hands now and stepped down from the cab, onto the bonnet. 'There is no point getting angry,' he said. 'There's nothing I can do about this. The money will come soon. Until then, we'll have to make do with what we have. As I promised, you will all get half what you're owed, and the rest as soon as we have it.'

A few men shuffled in the crowd.

'And this afternoon, I'll open the store,' said Swan. 'Every man will get rice for himself and his family. Free.'

A few heads nodded, some faces smiled, and there was a general murmur of agreement amongst the men.

'And I'll go to the farm,' he said. 'I'll get pigs and chickens for us to slaughter. We'll have a party.'

Voices chatting now, heads nodding.

'Tonight. Right here.'

The men growing louder now, the money forgotten, the promise of a party looming on the horizon.

Senhor Swan had to raise his voice further to be heard over the growing sound of the workers. 'Bring your wives and your girlfriends,' he said. 'We'll have free beer and music. Tonight.'

A cheer now, some of the men even punching their hands

into the air, Fernando stepping away as the *Americano* slipped down from the cab, the workers surrounding Senhor Swan, patting his back, giving him the thumbs-up.

Papagaio looked at me. He pretended to wipe his brow and flick away the sweat. 'Close,' he said. 'I thought there was going to be blood.'

'There *was* blood,' I said, glancing at him.

'Mm-hm, but not much. Nobody died.'

'He knows how to handle a crowd,' I said, feeling a growing respect for John Swan. He had played the men just right, turned down the heat. But I had also seen him reach for the reassurance of the weapon in his pocket. I wonder what he would have done if he had not been able to placate the men.

'Just one thing,' said Papagaio.

'What?'

'How's he going to get pigs and beer if he doesn't have any money?'

I shrugged. 'He'll get it on account. You think Manny won't give Senhor Swan beer?' I looked back at the crowd, seeing how happy the workers were with the promise of beer and food.

'True,' he replied. 'I reckon Manny would sell his own heart on account if he thought he'd get enough for it.'

'Not sure it would be worth much,' I said, studying the crowd, looking for a trace of the *Americanos* and their guns, but they had disappeared. They seemed to have dissolved as quickly as they had materialised, leaving almost no trace of ever having been there. Just as André had said. There was nothing left but dust.

Papagaio wanted to stay for the party, but I persuaded him to drive back to São Tiago that evening after work. I was keen to see what Catarina Da Silva had provided for the clinic.

Arriving in town, we went straight down to the river to see how things were going. Paulo was there, surrounded by building materials, and it looked as though things had started to move. It wasn't anything like the Swan place, not by a long way, and it was slow work, but it was already coming on. Paulo told us someone came over from the *fazenda* late morning, brought a truck full of materials and tools. There was a roll of cash, too. So Paulo rounded up a few men and put them to work. Poor guys had no idea they were working for Da Silva and that if the clinic wasn't finished, the only thing stopping them from having their hands cut off were a pitiful priest and a deluded doctor.

'At this rate, we'll be finished in a month.' He was pleased. 'And that,' he pointed at a white Chevrolet pickup, 'is for you.'

It wasn't new and it was probably the same truck that Alberto had bled out in, but it would do me just fine. Even better, it was free. Or, at least, that's the way I told myself to see it, because nothing is ever free.

'From Da Silva?' said Papagaio. 'Shit, you really must have done something right. That old bitch up there doesn't do favours like this for just anyone, you know. You sure you're not offering her a little extra something on the side?' His eyebrows went up and down, his tongue going to the side of his mouth making a visible lump. 'That why I had to stay in the car this morning? I'm waiting outside while you give Senhora Da Silva some holy *pica*?"

'Try thinking about something else,' I said to my friend. 'Just for one second.'

'Like I always say, what else is there? Round here, not much. So what was it you did that made her want to give you a car, eh?'

Paulo winked at me, getting in on the joke. 'Well, whatever it is, it sure as hell must be good. She give you a car for nothing or she make you pay up in some other way?'

I tried not to see Catarina Da Silva in my mind, feel the rush of passion I had for her that night in the darkness. I tried, too, not to see the look on Ana's face, the mask of betrayal, if she were to ever find out such a moment had passed between us. Instead, I played along, forcing a smile, taking the ribbing on the chin, 'Well, you guys know how it is; when you've got it, you've got it. They just can't keep away.' I dusted down the lapels of an imaginary jacket. 'And don't forget the one with the painted toes.'

'Hey, listen to the priest,' said Papagaio. 'He gets one woman to give him a car and suddenly he's the ladies' man. Mind you, whatever it is you got, I could do with some myself. These São Tiago girls just aren't in my league.'

'You're right about that.' I put my hand on Papagaio's shoulder. 'They're way too classy for you.'

Papagaio went quiet, thinking about that for a second, then took a step back. He pointed at me. 'You made a joke, right? You saying I'm not good enough?'

'Papagaio,' I said, 'I was a woman, you'd be, well, maybe second on my list.'

'So who'd be first?' said Paulo. 'Me?'

'Uh-uh,' I shook my head. 'Couldn't handle the moustache. I was thinking maybe Reginaldo over there. There's something about the uniform.'

We all looked over at Reginaldo who was leaving his post at the bank. His shirt was coming untucked around his belly, his trousers hanging lower than they should have been, dragged down by the weight of the *pistola* in his holster. The underarms of his khaki shirt were stained dark with sweat. He saw us laughing, and raised a hand.

'Oh, and by the way, Paulo, I'm supervising your building work. I'm in charge.'

'What?'

'It's the way Da Silva wants it. I have to see her every morning, let her know what's happening.'

'Why?'

'God only knows. Maybe she just can't get enough of me.

But you're all going to have to do without my expertise tomorrow, I have a promise to keep. I'm taking the boy out, but I won't need your car, thanks,' I looked at Papagaio. 'I have transport of my own, now.'

My friend's face dropped and he looked at me. 'What about Senhora Da Silva? She's not going to be happy if you're supposed to be here. She might even—'

'Don't worry about it,' I said. 'She doesn't expect me to be here all day every day. I just have to let her know how it's going. I'll see her tomorrow, give her what she wants.' I made a move to walk away, then stopped and turned back to Paulo. 'You do your part, I'll do mine. I'll keep her happy.' I tried to sound as if I knew how to handle her, I wanted my friends to enjoy the way things were falling into place, but I knew Da Silva was dangerous and I was divided at the prospect of spending time alone with her. Despite knowing how unpredictable and cruel she could be, and despite my feelings for Ana, I still felt myself drawn to her, like a man standing on the edge of a precipice, wondering how it might feel to free-fall through the air.

27

The following morning, not too early, I called in at the *fazenda* as ordered. I drove more slowly than usual, not noticing the day, telling myself I could handle this situation. Catarina Da Silva was just a woman. I could deal with her in a businesslike and distant way.

When I rang the bell, Catarina Da Silva came to the door herself; no sign of Marcia this time. Her hair was down, like it had been at Swan's barbecue, and she had make-up on her face; not a lot, just a little eyeshadow to bring out the colour, a touch of lipstick to swell her mouth. She was wearing a light cotton dress, emerald green to match the colour of her eyes, low cut around the neckline, high on her leg. I was surprised to see her dressed in such a way; at the *fazenda* I had only ever known her in short trousers and shirts, with her hair scraped back in a tight and vicious manner.

'*Bom dia*,' I said, but she didn't reply, she simply pushed the front door wide and slid back into the hallway, her bare feet silent on the tiles. No bodyguards stood to attention when we entered, but they'd be there somewhere, out of sight and waiting for trouble.

I followed her into the sitting room, and went straight to the window to look out. There wasn't anything to see that I hadn't already seen before, but I wanted to keep my distance from her.

She may have been sporting happy colours, but so does a coral snake.

'Come and sit down,' were her first words.

I hesitated, turned away from the window, and saw her sitting on one of the sofas. But this was not the woman who had been eating breakfast with her husband, brokering a business arrangement only yesterday. This was the woman who had been at the barbecue.

The short dress had ridden further up her legs and her thighs looked bigger like that, the soft flesh splayed out on the seat, pale and smooth. One hand was fanned open on the cushion beside her as if she had just patted it down. She watched me, her chin out, her face tilted upwards, every inch of her looking like a woman who expected to get what she wanted.

'I'm fine right here,' I said.

She parted her legs a little and ran her fingernails over one knee. 'Are you afraid of me, Sam?' She smiled, the expression slight at first, but spreading as she went on, saying, 'Or are you afraid of yourself?'

'Neither. Are we here to talk business or to talk about me?'

She pursed her lips as if she were killing the smile. 'To business then. Did you get everything you need? Money?'

'Yes.'

'The materials arrived as promised?'

'They did.' I felt more comfortable now that we were talking business again, but my eyes were drawn to the tightness of the material across her chest, the way her fingers were caressing her knee, the way the dress had risen high on her leg to cast a shadow over the spot where her thighs came together.

'And the vehicle,' she asked. 'It's to your satisfaction?'

'Yes . . . thank you. It is.'

She pushed herself to her feet, coming over to where I was standing. 'And is there anything else you need?' she asked, reaching out to touch my face.

'No,' I said. 'Nothing.'

'Nothing at all?' She moved her fingertips across my skin. 'You're sure?'

'What about your husband?' I said, turning my head away from her.

'He's not here. Won't be back until this afternoon. He's out every morning. Just about the time we're going to have our meetings.' She looked directly into my eyes.

'Senhora Da Silva,' I said, taking her hand away, feeling my own desire for what I knew she was offering. 'I am a priest. Not a very good one, I admit, but a priest nonetheless.' It was the only thing I had left to hide behind.

'Lucky then, that you're exactly the kind of priest I like,' she said. 'Not too many hang-ups.' She made a contented sound and moved closer, pressing herself against me, placing her hands on my hips this time. 'Not afraid to touch a woman in the right places.' She circled her arms around my waist, sliding her hands under my shirt, touching my skin, bringing us together like lovers. 'You *do* remember that don't you? The barbecue?'

'I shouldn't have . . .'

'I want to begin where we left off.' She ran one hand up my leg, circling from back to front. Once again, I was disturbed to find myself aroused. Not because I liked her, but because she was warm and soft, and she smelled so good. Like freesias and honey and chocolate. She smelled *expensive*. Her touch was seductive and she was making herself available to me in a way no one had ever done before. I found the mixture of submission and force almost mesmerising.

'What I'm saying is I made vows,' I managed. 'Sacred vows I don't want to break.' I didn't know how long I could resist, and it was all I could think of to make her stop. 'I don't want to ruin my reputation with the people of São Tiago.' I sounded ridiculous, floundering and nervous, but she couldn't know the truth;

the real reason for my resistance. That my vows to God were empty, broken for another woman. That there was something else I didn't want to betray now. Something more important. But Catarina Da Silva didn't need to know that. She didn't need to know about Ana, because while her husband could be dismissed and God could be ignored, a seamstress would be crushed.

I tried to push her away, without too much force, knowing I should stop, wanting her to continue, but she only persisted with more excitement. Her breathing intensified. Her fingertips stroked my spine. She slid one knee between my thighs and I attempted to take a step back but I was against the wall now, nowhere else to go.

'I remember how you kissed me that day at the *gringo*'s place,' she said, her painted nails raising bumps in my flesh. 'How you touched me. And I remember how you looked at me. I saw what was in your eyes, Sam. You want me as much as I want you. You want to do things to me that would make your God turn his back in shame.'

'No,' I heard myself say. 'This isn't what I want.'

'Isn't it?' She removed one hand from beneath my shirt and drew it along the inside of my leg, bringing it up to press hard against the front of my trousers. I flinched, and then relaxed into her touch.

'See?' She narrowed her eyes. 'I know all about you. I know all about that reputation you're so worried about, Sam. I might not live in São Tiago, but I make it my business to know what happens there.'

I felt a tightness in my stomach. She knew.

'That's right.' She sensed my reaction. 'I know about your whore,' she smiled. 'The one who calls herself a seamstress.'

Her words were like ice. I should have realised sooner. 'You've been checking up on me,' I said, remembering the conversation I'd had with André.

'Of course. I hear how you like to spend the night at her place. Often.'

'No, she's . . .' I wanted to say that Ana was unimportant, that she was meaningless, anything to make Da Silva leave her alone, but I knew the denial would achieve nothing. She knew everything and she controlled everything. She would have what she wanted. She would *always* have what she wanted.

'That's how sacred your vows are, Sam.' She moved her hand, reaching to the back of my head, pulling me towards her. 'So why not stop fucking around and just give me what I want. What we *both* want.' She bit at my lower lip, as she had done that night, her hold tightening when I tried to move, making it clear there was no option.

'I'll make it easy for you, Sam,' she said, her mouth against mine. 'Just give me what I want and, in return, I'll give you your clinic.' She ran her tongue across her lips and opened them a little wider, moving her head forward, brushing them against mine, still talking. 'Do it, Sam, and I'll leave your whore alone.' I felt the heat of her breath in my mouth, and the tightness of her grip over my world as I yielded to her. 'Your friends, too. You can have everything,' she said into me as she reached down to unfasten me, sliding her warm hands over me. 'You can have your clinic, your woman, your friends. And you can have me too, Sam. You can have everything you want.'

'Don't talk about them.'

'I don't want you to love me, Sam. I don't even want you to *make* love to me. Keep that for your whore if it's what she likes. I want something different from you. Something more basic. I just want you to fuck me.'

Backed against the wall, tasting Da Silva's waxy lipstick, her tongue seeking mine, her fingers encircling me, my head began to spin. There was no choice for me to make. There was nowhere for me to turn. She owned me. Away from her, I wanted to resist Catarina Da Silva, but here, at the *fazenda*, when she was giving herself to me, she was right about what I wanted. Something wretched inside me ached to take her and use her in the way she intended to use me. She knew she didn't need to threaten me, she was just giving me an excuse to do what I wanted.

I was weak in body and I was unfaithful in spirit. I was betraying myself and I was betraying Ana when I told myself I had no choice, because I knew that there is always a choice. I was incensed with myself in that moment, and I let my anger surge through me as I put my arms around Da Silva's waist and pulled her against me, our bodies grinding together. I ran my fingers through her hair, seizing it tight with both fists and yanking her head back to kiss her, forcing my mouth against hers, feeling her lips push hard against her teeth.

I took the straps of her dress and I pulled at them, ripping one side as I forced them down her arms, dragging the dress from her body, seeing that she wore nothing beneath. I pushed her forwards, away from me, naked but for the green nail polish which so perfectly matched her dress, and I studied her the way I had studied Ana that first time. I looked at the curves of her body, the surplus flesh over her hips, the slight bulge of her stomach, her heavy breasts, the tips tightened in anticipation. Then I went to her again, angry and lustful, crushing my mouth to hers, taking her shoulders tight in my hands and turning her around, pushing her forwards onto the table, making her put out her hands to stop herself from falling on her face. I unbuckled my belt and used my legs to separate hers, shoving her feet wider apart, gripping her hips, pulling her towards me as I thrust myself into her. Somewhere in my vehemence I heard Da Silva cry out either in pleasure or pain, I didn't care which, and in the moments when the complications of head and heart were drowned by the intensity of passion and lust, I felt good and primitive and strong.

*

Later, leaving the ranch, Da Silva ran her fingers down my back. 'You surprised me,' she said. 'You had more energy than I expected.'

We were outside, both of us standing at the top of the steps. She was wearing shorts and a T-shirt now, the enticement complete. Once again, I was nothing.

'I'd be willing to bet it's a side of you your whore has never seen. Maybe I should go see her. We could compare notes.'

I stifled the urge to hit her. I wanted to tell her never to speak of Ana again, but it would only give her a stronger hold over me.

'Come back on Monday,' she said. 'Same time.'

I nodded without looking at her, and began my descent.

'You want me to wear the pink dress?'

I went straight to the pickup and climbed in, glancing at my fishing gear lying in the flatbed. The boy would be wondering where I was.

28

I took the road down towards Swan's house, not wanting to go fishing today. Instead I wanted to go home, wash myself clean.

I drove by the hub of the plantation where the trouble had been, and I passed through the trees into the clearing that held the Swans' new home. To my right as I approached, a water tower and a small pump house flanked six or seven rows of corn. The plants were young, still small now, but when fully grown, they would hide the pump house from view. Beyond this, four smaller buildings. Three were completed, homes for the *Americanos*, but the fourth was just a shell. Once the inner walls were up and we had run in the wires, I guessed the maid would live there. Luísa was probably bragging to her friends even now, saying she was going to live next door to the *chefe*.

I stopped the pickup and climbed down from the cab, hearing the cicadas creaking in the forest. I took a deep breath, inhaling the earthy smell of dirt and plants, of trees both living and dying. There was a tinge of black smokiness to it which I tried to ignore. I went straight to the front door and lifted my hand to knock when I heard a noise to my left. I looked across and saw the boy come out of a path cut into the jungle. He stopped when he saw me, just for a second, and then came towards me without smiling.

I turned to meet him, saying, 'You OK?'

He shrugged. 'Fine.'

'Sorry I'm late.'

'Doesn't matter,' he said, sounding like he didn't mean it.

'What you got there?' I pointed to the book in his right hand, so he held it up for me to see. 'I thought you'd already read that,' I said.

'I have.' Not looking at me. 'Twice now.'

'And was I right? It's better the second time round?' I took the book from his hand, flicking through the pages, seeing how well used they looked. 'Reading it for you, and not for the class?'

'Yeah.'

'So you go out there to read, do you?' I asked.

'There's a place where I can sit. It's quiet.'

'And you don't get scared?'

He ran a hand through his hair and glanced up at me. 'Sometimes. Saw a spider there once. Sitting right on the tree where I go to read. About this big, it was.' He opened his hand wide and held it out for me to see.

'So what did you do?'

'Chased it off with a stick.'

'You need to watch out for those,' I said. 'They can bite.'

'Would you die?'

'No, but it would hurt a lot. And when they get mad, they shoot tiny hairs at you. Itches like hell.' I studied the cover of the book he'd been reading.

'That happen to you before?' The excited look coming over his face now. I preferred it to the sullen one.

'The hairs, yeah. The bite, no.' I made a biting gesture with my hand, watching the boy, and neither of us said anything for a moment.

I pushed the backs of my legs against the low wall running around the veranda. 'So what's the best bit, then?' I handed him the book. 'Which bit do you like the most?'

'Dunno,' he said. 'I suppose the end, where Ralph gets

rescued.' He flicked the pages, the papers rasping against his thumb.

'You like it that he gets rescued, then?'

'Of course,' he said, creasing his brow. 'And there's this other bit. I mean, I got a bit confused at first. I didn't really know what was going on, but the part where they kill the beast.'

'Where they're dancing? And the storm is coming and they're pretending to kill the pig?'

'Yeah, and then it comes out of the forest, doesn't it? And they're shouting "kill the beast" and they're hitting it and there's blood.'

'But it's not the beast.'

'No, it's not.' He let the hand holding the book fall back to his side. 'It's one of them, isn't it? One of the boys.'

'Simon.'

'Mm.' The boy turned his head away from me, tightening his chin. 'He's ill. Going mad. Dying maybe. He climbs the hill and sees they're all wrong.' He was speaking quietly now. 'There *is* no beast, it's just them. So he comes to tell them, and they kill him.' He looked back at me and I wondered if I saw wetness in his eyes that hadn't been there a few moments ago.

'That's right.'

'I think it's even sadder than when Piggy dies,' the boy said. 'Because it's an accident, they didn't mean to do it, and they never really know. They think Simon just disappears, so they forget about him and he gets washed out to sea. It's like he was never there.'

The boy rubbed the palm of his hand across one eye.

'Is there something you want to talk about?' I said, but he shook his head so I asked him to walk with me, and we moved off.

'I'm sorry I'm late, you know,' I said. 'Things happened and . . .' I let my voice trail off. Life seemed so much more

241

complicated now. There was a simpler time when I had nothing to fill my days.

The boy shrugged, didn't say anything, made out like it didn't matter to him one way or another. It made me feel worse.

'You think you can forgive me?' I asked.

'I suppose.'

'Sometimes we have to do things we don't want to,' I told him. 'You know that, right?'

'Like when they make you do stuff at school you don't want to do.'

'Yeah, maybe. A bit like that. Sometimes it's worse, though.'

'I thought when you grow up, you don't have to do things you don't want to.'

'That's what I always thought,' I said.

'When I'm older, I'm not going to let anyone tell me what to do.'

'It never works out like that. Some things . . . well, there are some things you have to do.'

We carried on walking, out to the line of the trees, the spot where I had seen him emerge from the forest.

The boy stopped. 'Doesn't matter. I go back to school in a few weeks anyway. After that, you won't have to feel bad about not taking me fishing.'

He probably didn't mean them to, but his words cut into me. 'Hold on,' I said. 'Are we talking about different things here? I'm not saying I don't want to take you fishing.' I squatted down so that my face was level with his. 'The thing that made me late today. *That's* the thing I didn't want to do.'

'Mum and Dad said I shouldn't bother you so much, asking you to take me fishing all the time.'

I put my hands on his shoulders. 'Normally it's me asking you, remember? I don't like fishing on my own, not any more.'

'Mum doesn't even like me going; doesn't like me doing anything that might be dangerous. She said—'

'We're partners, you and me. It's not the same if you're not there.'

The boy tried to stop the smile but it came anyway. 'Really?' He narrowed his eyes.

'Yeah.' I stood up, keeping one hand on his shoulder, and turned him around to come back to the house. 'Let's get your gear. There's still time today.'

And as we walked I thought about what he had said. 'You go back to England in a few weeks, eh? That soon?' I thought for a moment. 'Tell you what. Your mum and dad both at home right now?'

'Yeah.'

'You get your gear then, and I'll have a word with them. Tell them we need to plan a few more trips.' I stopped, an idea coming to me. 'And you know what? Let's take Ana with us on some of these trips. It's about time she learned how to fish.'

29

Sunday was always a good day. Ana and I would sleep late, lie together with the shutters closed and listen to São Tiago come to life around us. The mornings were lazy, a few hours spent together sitting at the table outside her place. If I had a book, I would read it, or I would watch her with a pad and pencil, drawing designs for new dresses she would never make.

I didn't sleep well that night, though, the first night after sex with Catarina Da Silva. When I did manage to sleep, I had the dreams again. The burning, the women and the children. Except now it was Ana who was burning and it was the boy who was lying in the ashes, his head half missing, me holding the gun, Da Silva standing beside me, one hand on my shoulder, a smile on her face. But for much of the night I lay awake, staring at the ceiling, mulling it over, thinking how Ana would feel if she knew what I had done. I tried to persuade myself that I had done it for her; that I was doing it for the sake of my friends and the clinic, but when you hold a mirror to your face, you can't avoid looking yourself in the eye. I had done it for me as much as I had done it for them. I had wanted Da Silva from the first moment she made it obvious she wanted to have me, and what we did yesterday made me feel powerful. For those moments she was no longer the mistress, and I was no longer the slave. I had something she wanted and, when she was naked and exposed, I felt there might be a time when I would be able to use that power for my own gain. But once we were finished and the sweat had dried, I was reminded that when she had finished with me, she would flick me away like a cigarette butt. I had signed my pact with her now, there was no going back.

So it surprised me how easy I found it when Ana turned to me that morning, raising her head from the pillow and pulling me to her. I had no difficulty making love to her, and afterwards I held her tight, my face buried in her hair, words of love hanging on my lips, unspoken. My feelings for Ana had not been damaged by my infidelity with Catarina Da Silva, and it crossed my mind that perhaps it would not be so difficult for me to have what I wanted from both women. And for both to have what they wanted from me.

After breakfast, we went out to sit at the table. Ana with her drawing and me with a book borrowed from Hevea. Everything was normal. Here, in São Tiago, everything was as it should be. Catarina Da Silva could be kept separate. What happened at the *fazenda* would stay at the *fazenda*. It would be a small, distinct part of my life which no one else needed to see. I was accustomed to putting things away in my mind, and this would be no different. When I was with Ana, I would be myself.

Somewhere around twelve o' clock, the sound of a vehicle on the road made us both look up. It was the first engine we had heard all day. A pickup, the Hevea logo on the side, was bouncing along the street, popping in and out of the potholes, the tailgate rattling. As it drew closer and began to pass, I noticed Senhor Swan and his family in the cab, so I lifted a hand to wave to them.

The vehicle slowed to a stop and backed up in front of Ana's place. Senhor Swan put his elbow on the window sill and leaned out, saying, '*Bom dia.*'

The door on the other side of the cab opened and the boy came round the front of the vehicle. 'Hi, Sam.'

I nodded to him and winked.

Swan followed suit, opening his door and climbing down, his wife stepping out behind him. They came over to stand at the edge of the covered porch.

'Senhor Swan. You got business in São Tiago?' I asked him.

'Please, Sam, call me John.'

I nodded. 'John.'

'Not really. Pick up a few things from Zeca's place, that's all. An excuse to get away from the plantation more than anything. Hi, Ana.'

Ana returned the greeting and invited them to join us at the table, telling them to come into the shade. The sun was at its highest and it was cruel to pale skin. She cleared away her drawing, took my book inside and came out with cold beers and Coke for the boy.

Swan looked surprised, maybe a little embarrassed because Ana hadn't asked if they wanted anything, but the boy was happy to be with us. He pulled a chair between me and Ana and dragged the Coke across the table towards him.

'I hear you're becoming quite a fisherman,' Ana said to him. 'Sam told me you caught more fish than him yesterday.'

'Yeah, and we didn't even have that much time,' he said.

'Oh?'

'Sam was a bit late,' said Sarah.

'So by the time we got to the Crisostomo, there wasn't much time for fishing,' the boy added.

Ana tilted her head to one side and gave me a questioning look. 'Late? How come? You didn't say you were late.'

I suppressed the feeling of cockroaches scurrying in my stomach and took a drink of beer to give myself a few more moments. 'The meeting with Da Silva,' I said. 'She wants to know everything that's going on, every last detail. Sometimes it's hard to get away.'

'She keeps you that long?'

'Sometimes,' I said. 'It's part of the deal. I have to go.'

'So how *is* the clinic?' asked John.

Ana was still watching me as if she were studying my reaction. I glanced at her and then looked back at John.

'Um, yeah, pretty good,' I said. 'We get most of what we need.'

We discussed the clinic, then turned to small talk while we finished our drinks. When John drained the last of his beer, he stood up and said they'd better be going, they had a few things to pick up and then they were going over to the café for lunch.

'Why don't you come with us?' Sarah asked. 'We can have lunch together.'

The boy was excited by the idea but I said no thanks, telling them I didn't use the café any more, not since Manolo and I fell out.

'You never did tell me what that was about,' said John.

'Another time,' I said.

So John and his family turned to leave, the boy looking disappointed that he wasn't going to spend more time with Ana and me. I saw Ana watching him, not liking the way his face had fallen when they left the table, and then she was moving forward, calling them back, asking, 'Why don't you have lunch here with us? I was about to make something.'

John and his wife looked at each other, as if discussing it between them, making a decision without needing to exchange any words.

'That would be lovely,' his wife said eventually. 'We'd love to. But only if you'll let me help.'

I was proud when Ana led Sarah into her house and invited her into her kitchen. I was proud that she was not ashamed of who we were and where we lived. Next to these people we were poor and had very little and it would have been easy for a woman in Ana's position to be embarrassed.

When they had gone inside, the boy following them, John and I settled back into our seats at the table.

247

'I thought you handled yourself well,' I said. 'On Friday.'

He lifted his eyes skyward and sighed. 'It was a close call.'

'Could've been nasty.'

'Hmm. I had to fire a few men, some of the troublemakers, but I did it quietly. Worked out OK in the end.'

The boy came out of the house with two beers and put them on the table. I ruffled his hair and thanked him before he went back inside.

'Those men of yours,' I said. 'They look like they know how to handle themselves.'

He steepled his fingers on the table in front of him and studied them. 'Yeah. Not exactly the kind of men I want to have around, but they have their uses, I suppose.'

'You reckon you could've managed OK without them on Friday?'

John took a deep breath and looked at me. 'I don't know. Maybe. A situation like that, maybe. It's not what I signed up for when I came here, but I'm learning fast. There are other things, though; other times when I need them. I don't like it but it's the way it is.'

'They collect the pay, don't they?' I said, remembering the story André had related to me. 'From the airstrip.'

'You heard about that?'

'I heard something,' I said, putting both hands around my bottle of beer. 'A story, that's all.'

'What exactly did you hear?'

'A third-hand story,' I said. 'That someone tried to take the money. That no one knows what happened to them. That they just disappeared.'

'I heard that version, too.'

'From them? From your *Americanos*?'

'No.'

'But you asked them?'

'Yeah.' He pulled his fingers into tight fists, the knuckles whitening before he relaxed them. 'They said nothing happened; that someone tried to hold them up, they fired a few shots and the men went running in all directions. It's no great secret we bring the money in on the *Bandeirante*, anyone could try to take it if they wanted.'

'So which version do you believe?' I asked him. 'The one where the men run away or the one where they disappear?'

'It's easier to believe their story, Sam.'

'The *Americanos*?'

'I sleep better that way.'

I nodded and took a sip of beer. I guess São Tiago was taking Senhor Swan too. Darkening his soul. It was giving him cause to lie to himself − a reason to keep him awake at night. I considered saying something to him about there only really being one truth, no matter which version of the story he believed, and that after seeing his *Americanos* in action on pay day, I felt more inclined to believe the version I had heard from André. But he didn't need me to tell him that. He knew that men had been hurt in his name, and for the sake of the job he was doing. He knew that it would probably happen again, in this remote place where such things were an integral part of our daily life. Out here it was too easy to look the other way when such things happened. There was no one to act for your conscience, no law to be afraid of, no priest to take your confession. I suspected that a man like him would not last long in a place like this. The more I had come to know him, the more I realised that he would not stay long. It was not a suitable place to raise a family, and bad deeds sit like heavy demons on the shoulders of good men.

'Your boy goes back to school in a few weeks,' I said. 'I'll miss his company.'

John smiled down at his hands. 'You've been good with him. He likes you. Ana too.'

'I suppose it's a strange place for a boy his age,' I said. 'He needs a friend. A brother maybe. I always wished I had a brother or sister.'

He looked up with a quick flick of his head, his brow coming down, his eyes narrowing.

'Did I say the wrong thing?'

John's face softened and he turned his head away. 'No.' He was staring at the road. 'It's just . . .' He looked back at me and took a deep breath. 'He did have a brother. Older.'

'Sorry,' I said. 'He never mentioned anything.'

'He doesn't talk about it. I think he hardly even remembers him. It was a long time ago.'

'Can I ask what happened?'

Behind me I heard the door open and Sarah came out using both hands to carry a bowl. She set it down on the table, saying, 'I hope you two are hungry. Ana's made quite a feast for us.'

Indeed, Ana had done a good job with the food, putting on the table almost everything we had. There was fish, beef stew, rice, beans, even some tomatoes. We squashed together like friends, eating from mismatched plates and using mismatched cutlery, and Ana sat beside the boy, telling him what everything was. She made him taste it all and laughed loudest when he turned up his nose at the *feijoada*.

It was good to see them together. I liked the way she brought a smile to his face. I never saw him smile like that for anyone else.

August 1986

30

For so long I hadn't wanted to be involved with Paulo's clinic, but everything had conspired to push me in that direction. Now I found that the more time I spent with him, seeing my friend's enthusiasm for what he was doing, the more *I* started to believe in what he was doing, and the more I admired him for it. I could almost taste my friend's dogged resolve driving him to make his vision real, and I wondered how I could have been so opposed to his wishes. I had been deliberately awkward and obstructive, but seeing the clinic rise from the baked dirt and witnessing Paulo's relentless labour made me understand he had always been right. Without people like Paulo, nothing would ever improve, and I was proud to call him my friend. He had shown, in so many ways, that he was determined to press ahead, not least by the shedding of his own sweat and blood, and I couldn't deny him my help.

Papagaio and I joined Paulo to work on the clinic most evenings. Often, when we arrived back from the Hevea estate, or when I came back from fishing with the boy, Ana would be there too. When she was finished at the sewing machine, she would go down to the clinic and work as hard as the men. Already I could see a change in her, feel the further toughening of her skin and the increased tautness of her muscles.

One evening, The Stones on the car stereo after I'd banned Papagaio from playing samba all the time, I came down from the wooden scaffold and stood with my hands on my hips, looking at what we'd accomplished so far. The outer walls were up, the inner structure was taking shape, and the roof was tiled. We enjoyed the moment, our muscles aching from the labour. At this time of day, without the other workers present, the clinic was truly ours, and an unspoken sense of brotherhood settled among us. We were proud of what we had done.

'Looks like we'll make it,' said Paulo, acting like he had it all under control.

I put my hand on his shoulder. 'You're doing the right thing, you know. I'm sorry I gave you a hard time.'

Paulo pretended to be shocked. 'First you take a job, then you take the boy fishing. You even agree to help me build. And now?' he said. 'Now you're *apologising* to me?' He raised his hands. 'My God, will wonders never cease?'

'He's a strong man,' said Ana. 'Strong enough to apologise; strong enough even to resist Da Silva's attentions.'

They all laughed, and I made a show of laughing with them, but Catarina Da Silva was the one part of the clinic with which I was still uncomfortable. She owned every one of us and could destroy us on a whim. I had seen how easily she dismissed Eduardo's death, and I knew she would not hesitate to have our blood spilled if we failed to please her. I was, however, tied to her in a way which no one else could know about.

Each day I went to her as instructed, always wondering what mood she would be in, apprehensive about how I would be received. If her husband were there, she was businesslike and abrupt, but when she was alone, she pulled me further into her web and willingly I went with her. She would come close to me, touch me, probe me with questions I didn't want to answer, and it would always end the same way. Naked and sweating from our exertions. Basic and primitive, exactly as she wanted it. And for a while I would feel that she was mine and that I could do with her as I wished. Those were the moments I enjoyed.

'She bothers you,' Ana said, seeing through my reaction.

'No,' said Paulo, 'Sam's got her under control, haven't you?' His face continued to smile, but his eyes asked for reassurance. We all knew she was a risk, that she might turn at any moment, but none of us wanted to say it aloud, as if airing it might bring us bad luck.

'She's fine,' I told him. 'A little testy sometimes, but yeah, she's OK.'

'You sure?' Papagaio wanted to know.

'If there was another way,' I said. 'Someone else . . .' I shrugged and looked at Ana. 'Yeah, of course she bothers me. We all know what she can do, but she likes me, if that's the right word. She's *interested* in me.'

'Interested in what, though, that's what worries me,' said Ana.

'Well, as long as she feels that way, she'll fund the clinic.' I didn't want to think about what she might do once she had grown bored with it, or if the tourists never came. Burn it, perhaps. Turn it into a brothel.

'I appreciate what you've done, Sam,' said Paulo, becoming serious. 'Dealing with Da Silva, helping with the clinic.' He glanced around at each of us. 'You've all done so much.'

'Yeah, yeah,' I brushed it off. 'Don't get sentimental on us, Paulo. Just build the clinic and save some lives. That's why we're doing it, right?'

I looked over at Manolo's place and thought about the night I found Eduardo lying in his own blood. The lights were on under the awning and two men were sitting at one of the tables. Manolo was standing behind the bar, leaning over the counter and staring across at us as if he were trying to hear what we were saying. The air was still, our voices would carry.

'You should clear things with Manny,' Papagaio said, following my gaze. 'You used to be friends. And it's all that's left now. Everything else is good. Shit, when was the last time life was this good?'

He was right. Forgetting Da Silva, forgetting Manny, I couldn't remember a time when everything seemed to fit into place like it did right now.

'You should tell him what you think,' Papagaio went on. 'Get it all out in the open.'

'He already knows what I think. He killed a man in cold blood,' I said, making Papagaio look away and scratch his nose.

We fell into silence as the sun disappeared over the river, listening to the water and the cicadas and the scraping of chairs as one or two more people drifted into the café.

'The clinic's coming along, though, don't you think?' Paulo changed the subject, looking back at our building.

Papagaio met my eyes and we watched each other before I turned to Paulo. 'Yeah,' I said. 'It is. I really think it's going to be good.'

The expression on Paulo's face suggested he had everything he wanted in life. 'We're making it happen,' he smiled. 'And I couldn't have done it without my friends. Just a few more materials to get, and we'll be well on our way.'

'I still have money,' I said. 'What do you need?'

'Timber mostly. We'll get what we need from the mill.'

'Then we'll go tomorrow,' I said to Paulo. 'As soon as I'm done with Da Silva.'

31

The sawmill was built on a rise in the land, a pregnant swelling that distended from the red earth. The hill was smooth, almost perfectly rounded, with one road leading straight up to a wide, open area of dirt. At the back of that space, maybe sixty metres across, was a wooden building so old and tired it looked as if it might've been standing there when the forest was cleared from around it. This was the mill itself; the place where forest trees that weren't scorched were dealt with once and for all. The intermittent noise that came out of the building was tremendous. A sound which stretched to the end of the world and echoed right back again; the shrill scream of giant blades tearing through hardwood trees.

On the far side of the clearing there were piles of timber, planks carved from ageless trees brought in by trucks from the areas where they were deforesting. There were trunks, stripped of their branches and leaves, now nothing more than naked telegraph poles, and there were other lengths, these ones cut into neatly stacked beams and planks bound with dull, crimped metal. In front of the structure, a couple of pickups were parked in no particular way at all, and an empty flatbed stood idle. There was no sign of human life. I pulled alongside the other vehicles, our own clattering and rolling on the uneven road before we came to a stop. We climbed down into the rich smell of cut wood and looked about.

To one side of the mill there was a smaller brick building, painted yellow, with a sign across the top telling us it was the office. Once Paulo and I had stretched our legs, we headed straight for it.

Inside, the cluttered room was hot and still. On the wall behind the desk, there was a map of Mato Grosso, Brasil's Lost World; Its Heart of Darkness. Some of the towns were circled in red, and there was handwriting scrawled across parts of the map. There was a calendar, too, but not like the one I had in my room. On this one, the photograph was of a milk-chocolate-skinned girl with almost perfect breasts. She was standing under a gentle waterfall, her hands in her hair, her brown nipples hard and round.

The man behind the desk was nowhere near as pleasant to look at. He was maybe fifty, with a belly the size of a well-fed hog and a moustache which had never been trimmed or cleaned. On his head, he wore an American-style cap, the kind with the perforated back that sits high on the head and has enough space inside to keep your lunch. Apart from the stains, it was red and white, the logo on the front was Marlboro. The top three or four of his buttons were undone, showing a profusion of wiry hair, and breasts which were close in size to those of the calendar girl, but lacked their shape and firmness. The dark discolouration around his armpits suggested the acrid smell of body odour filling the room was coming from him.

When we entered without knocking, he took his feet off the desk in a hurry. The chair thumped forward as the front two legs made contact with the floor. He grunted with effort as he pushed himself to his feet, looking us up and down with suspicious eyes.

'You're the *gringo* priest,' he said, one hand moving up to tip back the peak of his cap.

I told him we wanted to buy wood.

He looked from me to Paulo, saying, 'How much you want?'

I nudged Paulo with my elbow and he told the man how much we wanted. It didn't sound like a lot.

The man scratched his whiskered chin before coming round from behind the desk that was littered with printed papers. 'Come with me.' He pulled the cap down.

He led us out of the office and across the front of the mill towards the piles of timber we'd seen earlier. The smell of saw-dust was welcome after the unwashed stink of his tiny office. 'How you planning to take this?' he said. 'You're not going to carry it on your pickup, that's for sure.' He glanced back, sizing us up with something worse than contempt before turning away again.

Paulo pulled a face at me and shook one fist behind the man's back.

I tried not to laugh. 'You have a truck we could borrow?' I said. 'Or maybe one of your people could bring it over for us. It just needs to go to São Tiago.'

Sweaty man stopped and thought for a while, pushing his hat back again like he needed to give his brain room to breathe. He lifted it from his head and ran one hand across his balding crown, then he grinned and said, 'Sure, I have a man who'll do it for you.' He pointed to a dirty old truck. 'I'll get Bruno to drive for you. You'll like him. Everybody does.'

He told us we'd have to pay the man, though, he wasn't a delivery boy, so we agreed a price for the driver, gave him some money for the timber, then set about loading the wood into the back of the Ford F-4000 that was parked up by the mill.

When we were done, Bruno came out from the main build-ing and sauntered over, looking at Paulo and asking, 'You ready?' His eyes shifted across to me and then back to Paulo. 'You got the money?'

Paulo handed him a fold of notes. 'We'll give you half now. Once it's delivered, you get the rest.'

Bruno pocketed the cash and beamed, showing us the gap at

the front of his teeth. He introduced himself, taking Paulo's hand and asking his name. Then he looked at me and spoke to Paulo saying, 'Who's the *Alemão*?'

Paulo didn't answer him, so the man held out his hand to me, saying, 'Bruno.' I took his hand and shook it, telling him my name. He said it once, mispronouncing it 'Ess*am*' like most people did, and then he smiled again. The gap in his teeth was so wide, there must've been at least two missing, but it didn't seem to bother him and I don't think he even noticed me looking. He was probably used to it.

Bruno shielded his eyes from the brightness and indicated the F-4000 'You want to go now?'

The blue cab was in need of paint, and the bare wooden flatbed on the back was old and rotten, but it started up first time and once it was on the road, we followed close behind in the pickup.

I allowed my mind to wander until I was thinking about Ana. She made me feel comfortable, like being with her was the right thing. Life was more complicated for me now, but the responsibilities didn't feel like a burden. None of the things that had come into my life weighed heavy apart from my relationship with Da Silva. If I forgot about her, everything else made me feel more alive.

I took my eyes off the road in front of us and looked at Paulo. His face was turned towards me, like he'd been watching me for a while.

'You're thinking about Ana,' he said, as if he'd read my mind. 'You always get that look when you're thinking about her.'

I couldn't help smiling. 'Yeah.'

'You're a lucky man, the way she sticks with you.'

'I know.'

'She waited a long time for you.'

'Yeah.'

'I've seen a good change in you, Sam. Ana makes you stronger. She makes you happy.'

I concentrated on the cloud of dust ahead.

'I'd like to meet someone like her. It's like being given a second chance.'

'I'm not sure I deserve a second chance.'

'Everyone deserves a second chance,' he laughed. 'Even you, Sam.'

I put on an unconvincing charade of laughing along, but I was thinking about the boy in Roraima. I wondered what kind of a God would give me a second chance but not him, and I realised Paulo had used the right word. Chance. It was what ruled our lives. It was what had led me to Ana and it was what had led me to Catarina Da Silva. There were no higher forces at work here.

Paulo read me well, though. 'Maybe you should leave São Tiago,' he said. 'Take Ana away. Live somewhere more civilised.'

'I've been thinking about that,' I said.

'And?' He sounded surprised.

'I like it here. Anyway, I don't want to miss out on your clinic,' I said. 'Or lose my *filhote* to Papagaio.' But once the clinic was finished, once Paulo had what he wanted, it might be the only way for me to evade Catarina Da Silva and put my life in order once and for all.

Paulo shook his head. 'There are better things than catching fish.'

We were a few kilometres from São Tiago now, coming to the small pocket of trees where the narrow plank bridge spanned the gully before continuing into town.

'And it's too dry here,' said Paulo. 'Too hot. Why in God's name doesn't it ever rain? You think the dry season's getting longer?' He lifted the bottom of his T-shirt and used it to wipe sweat from his face.

'It'll rain,' I said. 'And then—'

'I'll complain. I know.'

As we approached the pocket of trees, we saw a white pickup, the same type as mine, parked across the mouth of the bridge, three men leaning against it, facing towards us. A fourth man was still in the cab, sitting at the wheel.

Bruno slowed the F-4000 and I followed suit.

'Looks like someone needs help,' Paulo was saying, but as we grew closer, the men pushed themselves away from the pickup and I saw one of them was carrying a shotgun.

'Bandits?' Paulo said.

'Don't know.'

'After the truck maybe?' he looked worried. 'The wood?'

'Bandits who steal wood?'

'Could happen out here.'

Bruno brought his truck to a stop and I did the same. We watched the three men approach him.

'Hunters, maybe,' I said, attempting to reassure us both. 'Probably their pickup broke down.' But one of the men went straight to the driver's side of Bruno's truck, reaching up and pulling open the door, showing a flash of revolver.

'Shit,' Paulo muttered beside me, and somewhere behind a prickle of fear, I thought about dropping the pickup into reverse but I knew it was no use. The other two men were quick, coming towards us, one of them going to Paulo's side, and the other coming to my open window raising his shotgun. He motioned the barrel of the gun, making it clear he wanted us to get out.

I stared at the wide bore and swallowed. 'Just do what they want,' I said, to Paulo, climbing out, showing them my hands.

The man moved back, maintaining a safe distance, but keeping the shotgun pointed at me. It was single-barrelled, the notched wooden stock attached to the blued steel by a length of copper wire. Wrapped around and twisted at the ends to keep it

262

tight. A cheap, home-made weapon, brandished by a cheap, home-made thug. Like everybody else round here, he probably used the gun for hunting *paca*, duck, whatever he could find to eat, whatever might earn him some money. He would make his own cartridges, guessing at how much powder and shot to pack into the brass shells. I'd seen weapons just like it do no more than fizz and spit, and others belch balls of flame and lead. With any luck, he'd put too little in, but there was always a chance he hadn't.

He had short, bow legs, the kind that wouldn't stop a pig in a corridor, we used to say, and a hard pot-belly which pushed out the waist of his trousers. He was like any person who might walk down the main street in São Tiago, except this one was pointing a gun at my face, and the look in his eyes turned me cold, the way they widened and narrowed, jittering from one direction to the other, searching for his partners. His hands tightened and loosened on the gun. Sweat stained the front of his pinstriped shirt. It was the same look I had seen in Alberto and it scared me. He wasn't used to this kind of work.

Paulo stumbled alongside me as the third man pulled a machete from his belt and shoved him hard. He pushed Paulo into me, the two of us close, our shoulders touching, the gun now trained on both of us.

The two men said nothing.

Paulo and I kept quiet, exchanging anxious glances, but in the truck Bruno was swearing loudly, using colourful words to tell them they weren't going to take his ride, there was no fucking *way* they were going to take his ride. There were a couple of slaps, the sound of metal hitting flesh, then the man with the pistol backed out of the cab, dragging Bruno with him. The driver came out head first, twisting onto his back as he fell out of the truck. When he hit the ground, the man kicked him in the ribs, then pulled him to his feet, keeping the weapon pressed hard against him. He moved around behind Bruno and kicked him towards us.

'*Vai tomar no cu.*' Bruno spat on the floor, and bit the end of his thumb, putting it together with his forefinger and showing them the circle which it made. This earned him another beating, the man with the pistol whipping the barrel into Bruno's face. He hit him once either side, splitting one cheek and knocking him to his knees. He then raised the weapon to shoulder height and was about to bring it down on the top of Bruno's head when I said, 'What do you want?' I had to force my voice out, it didn't want to work, but if I didn't say something, they were going to beat Bruno to death in front of me. 'Please,' I said. 'You want the truck; take it. Take whatever you want.'

The man stopped with the weapon raised and looked at me. He lowered the pistol and came close to me, his face inches away from mine, making me flinch back. 'Nothing else comes into São Tiago for you.'

'No more building, you got that?' said the one with the shotgun, getting in on it. 'You try again and . . .' He lifted the shotgun higher and raised his eyebrows. 'I think you know what happens, eh?'

I wasn't sure I heard them right. 'What?' My tongue clicked in my dry mouth.

'Why don't we show them?' said Shotgun, sounding calm. 'Show them what happens.' And as he spoke, the pickup across the road started to back up. It left the track, swinging in an arc so it was facing us.

'Yeah, we should show them what happens if they try again.' The one with the pistol ignored the vehicle, holding the weapon in his left hand, letting it hang limp at his side, just inches from Bruno's head. I could make out the blood and pieces of skin on the raised sight protruding from the end of the barrel.

264

Shotgun pointed at me. 'Let's do this one.'

I closed my eyes and wished I still believed.

'Not the priest.' Pistol spoke up, his voice thin and high pitched. 'The others, they don't matter so much, but not the priest.'

I opened my eyes to see the other two nod as their partner stepped forward, tucking the pistol into his belt and grabbing Paulo by the front of his shirt. 'Do his hand,' he grinned and pushed Paulo to the ground in the same way I'd seen the *vaqueiros* do it at the ranch. Machete went to help him while Shotgun took a step back, training his weapon on me with renewed vigour, but his attention was drawn to what his friends were about to do.

My whole body felt stiff, frozen in place, but I couldn't allow Paulo to be harmed, so I took the distraction, forced myself to move. I lunged for the barrel of the shotgun but my movement was clumsy and the man spotted me with ease. He circled the weapon away from my reach and brought it back round to poke the barrel at my chest, with enough force to knock me off balance and make me stumble back against my pickup. Then he moved right away from me, so I was well out of his reach, and levelled the weapon at my head, but my fear was gone now, chased away by my actions. I looked him in the eye, let him see my anger.

'Leave him.' The voice came from the pickup, making them all glance up. 'It's time to go.'

They paused for a moment, but the one with the pistol shrugged and tightened his grip on Paulo. Bruno's blood was not enough for him. His lust was up and he wanted to see more.

'Get in,' the voice shouted again. 'We're done here.' He revved his engine. 'Come on.'

Pistol ignored him and put his full weight on Paulo, forcing his body down, while Machete took my friend's arm and pulled it out and away at a right angle from his body. He put his knee across Paulo's forearm and raised his dirty blade to shoulder height.

'Let's go.' The impatient voice from the pickup called again. 'We're done here.'

Machete looked at Bruno, then at me, and spoke over the sound of the revving pickup. 'You wanna watch this hand come off, or you wanna close your eyes?'

Rage boiled inside me now. I wasn't going to stand by and allow these men to mutilate my friend. I had stood by once before and carried it with me for the rest of my life. So, ignoring the man pointing the shotgun at me, I dropped low and grabbed for the machete. I took the man's hand in both of mine and twisted his arm as hard as I could. In my furious mind, I hoped this was a good plan. The way I saw it, Shotgun wouldn't shoot at me because his friend would be in the way. Paulo and Bruno would have the sense to tackle the other one before he had time to draw the pistol he'd tucked away. The one in the pickup, I was sure, wasn't going to get involved.

What happened, though, the one with the shotgun *did* squeeze the trigger. There was a numbing bang, a bright flash, a cloud of smoke and I heard his body hit the ground as he went down screaming. He was on his back, his broken face a mask of blood, his hands wanting to go to it but causing him nothing but more pain. The backfiring weapon had splintered some of the stock into his eyes, and the blast had seared much of his skin. It looked like I was right about the home-made cartridges.

Paulo and the man who was still holding him were so stunned by what happened they were left frozen in time, just long enough for Bruno to reach into the man's waistband and pull out his pistol. He pushed it against the man sitting on Paulo, right into his belly, and pulled the trigger. Another bang, this one not quite so loud, and the man collapsed, hitting his head on the chromed bumper as he fell.

Machete relaxed his arm, allowing his weapon to drop. He

tugged his hand from my grasp and used his full weight to push me away from him, knocking the breath from my body. He stood, stumbled, collected himself, and broke into a run, ignoring the sickening screams from his friend with the blasted face, and the moans from the one with the bullet in his stomach. Bruno chased him out into the road, swearing and firing twice as Machete scrambled to open the passenger door of the accelerating pickup. One of Bruno's shots caught the man somewhere in the back, dropping his dead weight to the ground between the front and rear wheels of the pickup. The vehicle jostled when it rolled over his body, the tailgate clattering, the wheels spinning, but the tyres bit into the dirt once they were past him, and the driver escaped in a flurry of dust. Bruno hurried to the broken, bleeding man lying in the road and watched him for a moment, deciding he wasn't worth another bullet. Instead, he kicked the body between the legs and spat on him.

I stayed where I was, propped up against the C-10, catching my breath, and watched Bruno come back, blood thickening on his cheeks. He was walking with purpose, his back rod-straight, his eyes fixed ahead of him, the revolver gripped tightly in his right hand. He ignored me and Paulo, instead going straight to the man who had fired the shotgun. Still howling in a high pitch, the man was writhing on his back, unable to see, his hands flailing the air over his face. Bruno shot him in the head and put an end to his horrific screaming.

Satisfied with the result, Bruno marched over to the owner of the pistol. The man wasn't dead, but he was in pain and he was bleeding out quickly. He could manage little more than a monotonous groan. Bruno squatted beside him and pressed his gun hard against his mouth, so I could hear the steel raking against the man's teeth as Bruno forced the barrel between them.

'That hurt, *puta*?' I heard Bruno say. 'I hope it fucking hurts.

Trying to take my truck, take my fucking money. *Coma a merda.*'

'That's enough,' I said and turned away so I didn't have to watch. 'Leave him.'

He fired once more and then I heard him open the chambers of the pistol and drop the spent cartridges onto the dust. When I looked back at him, he stood and snapped the pistol shut, saying, 'Didn't think about that, did they, huh? Didn't think I could do that? Just thought I was some stupid fucking driver. No brains, huh?' He tapped the side of his blood-spattered head.

Bruno crossed himself with the pistol still in his hand, fumbled a packet of Hollywood from his top pocket and lit one up. He took a drag from it and then collapsed onto his backside, wavering for a moment before keeling back into the road. He crumpled into the dust beside the man he had just executed.

I looked at him, stunned, and tried to take it all in. It was quiet now, as if nothing had happened. Just another day at the office. I shook my head and picked up the packet of cigarettes Bruno had dropped. I took two out, lit them both and passed one to Paulo who had dragged himself from the dirt and come to stand beside me. I took a deep breath, exhaled and went down on my knees to put an ear to Bruno's chest. His heart was hammering so fast it was almost humming. I sat down on the road and glanced over at Shotgun, just long enough to see there was blood all down the front of his shirt and almost nothing left of his face. I dry-swallowed and shifted my gaze to look at the trees. I didn't need Paulo's skills to confirm the men were dead.

'Shit.' Paulo squatted beside me. 'What now?'

'Don't know.' I thought for a moment, then said it again. 'Don't know.'

Paulo put his hands together as if in prayer, and put them to his lips.

268

'*He* won't help us,' I said, raising my eyes to the sky. 'He's not listening any more. All we can do is wake Bruno up, drive back into town.'

'What about these three?'

'Leave them.'

'*Leave* them?'

'What else can we do?'

'We don't tell anyone?'

'Who d'you want to tell? What Bruno just did . . . shit, he might be a maniac, Paulo, but . . .' I tried not to think about the final shots he'd fired. Seeing him put the gun in someone's mouth and hearing him pull the trigger reminded me too much of something I had once done myself.

'You're saying we owe him?' he asked.

I stared.

He shuddered. 'Just a couple of dead guys on the side of the road, I suppose. No one will care.'

He was right. No one would care. Three more dead men were nothing in a place like this.

'Maybe we should roll them off the road,' Paulo said.

I looked at the man with no face and closed my eyes. This was what I had run away from in Roraima. This was the life I wanted to escape.

It took us close to an hour to move the bodies. In silence, we shifted the one closest to the car first, me taking his shoulders and Paulo grabbing his feet. We hauled him to the side of the road and heaved him over the wire fence. The undergrowth amongst the trees was too thick here for us to penetrate even a short distance, so we dragged him out and laid him in the dry grass, close to the edge of the forest, fifty metres or so from the road.

Moving the man who had brandished the shotgun was more difficult. Holding his shoulders, I tried not to look at what was left of his face, but I felt my eyes drawn to it, seeing the patches of bone around his forehead and cheeks where the skin and flesh had completely come away. We were tired now, too, finding it more strenuous to manoeuvre him over the fence, his clothing catching on the barbs because we no longer had the strength to lift him high enough. We laid him alongside the first body and threw his splintered weapon into the trees.

We were both breathing heavily when we came back for the third man. He was sprawled in the road where the pickup had driven over him, blood pooled around him in the dirt. As I crouched down to straighten him and take the weight of his shoulders, though, the man's chest hitched and his eyes moved beneath the lids.

I shuffled backwards and fell onto my behind. 'Shit.'

'Can't be.' Paulo went down on his haunches, about to put his fingers to the man's neck, when the man opened his mouth and breathed out, blood bubbling on his lips.

Paulo drew his hand away and stared at me.

We remained that way for several minutes, listening to the cicadas and the quick rasping breaths of the dying man, searching for the right words. I imagined Paulo would be struggling hard to know how to react. The man who was now fading slowly in the road was the same man who had intended to cut off his hand, and yet Paulo was the only person who had any chance of helping him. Even though I knew almost nothing about Paulo's profession, I knew he would be sworn to an oath that would compel him to help the man. But, as I had learned, oaths could be broken.

When Paulo moved, pulling up the man's shirt, searching for a wound, he said, 'Too much blood. We haven't even got anything to wipe it away.'

'Can you fix him?' I asked.

Paulo examined him further and shook his head. 'He's been shot. And God knows what damage the pickup did. Broken pelvis, maybe, probably crushed his spine. No, he's going to die.'

'Let's move him with the others then.'

'We can't just leave him to bake alive in the sun.'

'It's shaded by the trees,' I said. 'What *else* can we do?' But I knew what this was leading to. I made my voice calm. 'What would you do if we had the clinic, Paulo?'

'I still couldn't save him,' he said. 'He needs a hospital, but he wouldn't get to one before he died. And even if he did, he wouldn't have much chance.'

'So what *would* you do?' I asked, already knowing the answer he would give me. 'If we had the clinic, I mean?'

Paulo rubbed the sides of his head and pursed his lips. He closed his eyes and took a deep breath. 'Assuming we got him there in time . . .'

'Yes.'

'. . . I'd give him something for the pain; make him comfortable and let him go in peace.'

'That's it?'

'That's it.'

I understood what Paulo was saying and I thought about the knife at the small of my back, pictured myself leaning over the man and drawing it across his throat. I stood up and took a few paces away from him, hanging my head, looking up at the sky, putting my hands on my hips, on my head, on my face.

'Nothing you can do?' I said, coming back to them. The dying man gasping, Paulo sitting beside him, shaking his head.

'OK,' I said, 'then I'll do what I can.'

With an overwhelming mix of emotions, I made the decision to free my friend's conscience. He couldn't leave this man to suffer and there was only one way to avoid such a thing. I did what I knew he wanted to do but could not. But not with my knife. I couldn't include myself in the violence. I couldn't spill more blood. Instead, I placed my hand over the man's mouth and pinched his nose tight with my forefinger and thumb. No rites, no prayers, just a touch of human mercy.

I don't know how long I stayed like that, looking only into Paulo's eyes, but it felt like an eternity. And in all that time, the man didn't move once.

Paulo broke the spell by reaching forward to put his fingers to the man's neck. He waited a moment, then lowered his eyes and took my hand away.

'Come on,' he said, hauling the man up. 'There's nothing else we can do for him.'

So we took him and put him with his companions, side by side in the dry grass on the edge of the forest.

32

Back at the car, we acted without speaking. As if we knew exactly what had to be done, we took off our flip-flops and used them to scrape dirt over the blood on the road. Much of it had soaked into the dry earth already, and what was left became a coagulated mess when we covered it with dirt. When the blood was gone and all the bodies were laid together, we were both sweating from our efforts under the severe sun. I could feel the beads forming in my hairline and running down my forehead, catching in my eyelashes, and I could taste the saltiness on my lips.

Paulo eventually spoke, keeping his voice quiet, almost a whisper. 'I never saw anyone killed before.'

I closed my eyes. 'What about Eduardo?'

'Eduardo was already dying when I got there. I didn't see the violence, just the effect of it; didn't have to see the moment of . . .' He searched for a word and then shrugged. 'I don't know what you call it. It's like it's not even happening when you see something like that. Like your brain doesn't want it to be real. Or maybe it's just that you'd expect it to be worse, and you're disgusted with yourself because you don't feel more.'

'How d'you mean?'

'It seemed so matter-of-fact,' he said. 'I felt nothing for them at all. Nothing. Bruno shot them and they died.' He leaned against the car. 'And that's it. Another life gone and nothing changes.'

I didn't know how to reply. Another life gone and nothing changes. It wasn't true. Something always changes. Death always changes something, no matter how small. Eduardo's death had changed us all.

'What now?' Paulo dusted himself off.

'We get Bruno away from here.' I looked over at the man who had saved my friend's hand – probably his life.

Together, we dragged Bruno towards the truck. He stirred as we did it and he burped, a strong smell of alcohol wafting out.

'He's been drinking,' I said. 'Go check the cab, I bet there's *pinga* in there.'

While Paulo went to the cab, I pulled Bruno closer to my pickup and propped him against one of the wheels. Once that was done, I collected the empty cartridges which he'd ejected from the gun and I tossed them out into the field, just as Paulo returned, holding up a half-empty bottle of Fifty-One.

'You were right,' he said.

'Give me some. I need it.' I tucked the empty revolver into my trousers and took the *pinga* from him. I wiped the top of the bottle and took a slug.

'In a day they'll be gone,' I said. 'Something'll eat them.'

'And there's nothing to connect us,' Paulo replied.

'Except the one who got away.'

Paulo looked at me. 'He won't talk,' he reassured himself. 'And even if he does, who'll listen? I mean, a priest and a doctor? No one would believe him would they?'

'Course he'll talk, Paulo. Those men weren't trying to steal from us, they were warning us. They'll go straight back to whoever sent them.'

'Who?'

'There's only one person I can think of.'

'Da Silva?' It was the most obvious suggestion, and I could

understand why it had come to him. Organised violence could normally be traced directly to them; they were the main land-owners in the area. But this wasn't their work.

'No, they wouldn't sabotage their own clinic. Not Da Silva.'

He looked at me, not understanding. 'Someone who doesn't like Da Silva, then?'

'Not sure anyone would be that stupid,' I said. 'No, this is someone who doesn't know Da Silva is involved. Someone who doesn't like you and me.'

'I still don't—'

'Manny,' I said. 'He's the only one I can think of.'

'Manny?' he sounded surprised, but he didn't look it, so I guessed the thought must have crossed his mind.

'Who else? It's the only thing that makes sense. He must have been listening yesterday. When we were at the clinic talking. He must have overheard we were going to the mill. How else would anyone know to wait for us here?'

All he said was, 'So what are we going to do?'

'We forgive him.'

Paulo gaped at me as if I were insane.

'We talk to him, we forgive him and we put this behind us. I'm tired, Paulo, and it's the only way to make it all stop.' I took another drink of Bruno's *pinga*. 'Either that, or we'll have to kill him.'

Paulo stared at me. 'You think you could do that?'

I shook my head.

'But back there . . .' Paulo looked over his shoulder at the spot on the roadside where I'd smothered the man. 'How . . . ? I mean . . .'

My hands were shaking now. 'I did it for you, Paulo. For us.'

'What about God?' he asked.

'God?'

'How do you square it up? Can you ask for . . .'

'Forgiveness? You mean will God forgive me?' I shrugged.

'To hell with him.' I slid down into a sitting position, my back against the wheel of the pickup. Paulo came down beside me.

'But you're a priest,' he said.

'I was. When I was a different person. In a different place. Not here, though. Not any more.'

Paulo took the bottle of *pinga*. He drank and passed it back.

'Anyway,' I said. 'He doesn't care. If he's even there, he's blind, or dead or just plain ignorant.' I looked up at the sky and raised my voice as I spoke, angry that I'd had to smother the man, been forced to make another human being die.

I lowered my eyes to the ground and hung my head. 'It's not the first time I've taken a life,' I told him.

Paulo said nothing.

'You know, I went to Roraima to make a difference?' I spoke to the fine red dirt. 'I never told you that, did I?'

'I figured you'd talk about it if you wanted to.'

'Ministering to the privileged back home left me cold and discontented,' I said. 'Living was easy, I was doing nothing, helping no one. Not in the way I wanted, anyway. I became a priest because I wanted to do some good, not so I could pander to the spoiled. A priest. My mother would have been proud; it's what she wanted. Never saw it, though. Cancer. God's will, as priests always say.'

I didn't look at my friend but I could tell he was waiting for me to go on. 'Anyway, I was naïve enough to think there was something bigger, Paulo, a better way for me to serve God . . . It was my grand gesture.' I swigged from the bottle and looked out at the field where we had left the bodies.

'Others had come,' I told him. 'People I'd heard about who came to places like São Felix but made no difference. Not like me. I'd go to the heart of the problem. I *would* make a difference. I *would* change the world . . .' I took a deep breath and shook my head. 'In the end I didn't change anything at all,

276

though. No one can, I don't think. Not here. Not in a place like this. Instead, the country changed *me*.'

'Roraima changed you, Sam, not Brasil.'

'What's the difference?' I said.

'It's bad up there. It would change anyone.'

'And everything's fine here, right?' I held out my hands.

Paulo sighed.

'Anyway, I went to Roraima to work with a man called Father Machado. To defend the rights of the Yanomami to live on their own land. They didn't know the ways of the people who were taking their heritage and destroying their culture, so we tried to help them. I was young and stupid and thought I could change things, Paulo. I thought I could stop the people who wanted to cut the trees and sell them. The people who wanted the gold. I thought people respected the priesthood and respected God enough to listen to us, but I was wrong.' I stared at the bottle of *pinga* for a moment, seeing the road through the clear liquid.

'They drove the people out of their homes and they mined the land. You've heard the stories. No one could stop them. Not even Father Machado, and God knows he was a man who demanded attention.'

For a moment it was like I was there, on the bank of the Rio Branco listening to samba playing over the sound of the water; fishing and drinking Black Label with Father Machado, talking about what the *garimpeiros* were doing to the land. Those things were a small escape from the violence and the cruelty.

I looked down at the bottle in my hands.

'You want to tell me what happened?'

I remembered what Ana had said; that I shouldn't keep it buried inside, that if I let it go, it would feel as if something had lifted from my heart. I hadn't been ready then, but now – after what I had just done – *now* I was ready.

'I went there because I was idealistic,' I said, knowing I was giving my confession. 'Came to Brasil because I thought it was what I was supposed to do, that it was what *God* wanted me to do.' I stared at the bottle and remembered how I had run. 'But I couldn't stay in Roraima because I didn't believe in what we were doing any more. And because I was afraid.' I had abandoned my friend and the shame of it, the violence, the indignity, were all things I had tried to forget. Since coming to São Tiago, my life had been dedicated to wiping the horror from my mind, numbing it, but now it felt right to remember. After everything I had experienced in the last months, I knew this was long overdue. I had lived blind for so many years, and only now did I see that I owed it to Father Machado. I had come to understand it was my responsibility to keep it fresh in my memory, no matter how appalling. I needed to learn from these things, not force them into limbo and ignore them, allow them to decay inside me. If I forgot the events of Roraima, then it would be like they hadn't taken place, and everything would have been for nothing. The clinic, the boy and Ana, had all been instrumental in leading me to realise that. And they were all a part of my healing. The only thing which surprised me was that it was now, here with Paulo, that I was able to let the truth go. I had always imagined I would be with Ana when the moment came, but this was the right moment. After what I had just done, what we had just been through, Paulo would understand. He would be in no position to judge me.

'The Macuxi, Wapixana, Yanomami, all of them were threatened by the constant removal of land. Miners, loggers, ranchers, everybody wanting their own piece . . . and in the middle of it all, Father Machado was there to protect their rights, have a presence in a place without law. He kept good relations with the incomers so they might listen to him, leave the Indians to their way of life.'

'But they didn't?'

I shook my head. 'Father Machado and I became good

friends in just a few weeks. Living in each other's pockets, it was hard not to. We fished a lot, Father Machado teaching me the river, and we drank to pass the evenings when the light was gone. He talked about the mission at São Felix, told me about fishing in the Araguaia, said we'd go some time; that together we'd catch the biggest *filhote* anyone had ever seen. Life was good for a while.'

'At that time, there were just a few miners, prospecting a little gold for themselves, keeping away from the Indians. They were OK – illegal but just trying to make a living, I suppose. Mostly they *did* listen to us and they respected the people, but Father Machado was afraid that more prospectors would come, and when they eventually did, they came with machines and hoses and explosives and they tore the place apart. And people get greedy when they've tasted something they like, Paulo, so they kept on going, trying to get more. More trees were cut and burned, more gravel was taken out and sifted. The waters were polluted with mercury, the fish died, and then the logging and mining moved on to areas where the Indians had made their villages. No one was consulted or asked, they just told the Indians to move out, and when they refused, they forced them out, did whatever they had to. You know how it is, Paulo, you've heard the stories, you've seen things, it's touched your life too. Violence, no law, land belongs to those who take it. Sometimes they bulldozed whole settlements,' I said. 'Or set fire to them.'

'Whole villages? Women and children?'

'Women, children, men, animals, they all burn equally, Paulo. And the *pistoleiros* waited for them to run from the trees. Shot at them for sport, laughed over their screams like they were nothing. Sometimes they took the children to the mines, raped the women and sold them into prostitution in Boa Vista. Villages were burned, Paulo, and the land was littered with blackened bodies. You could smell them in the air.'

Paulo shook his head and stared out at the field where the dead men lay.

'After the first village was taken, we did what we could. We went to the owners of the mines, and told them it had to stop. We told them we'd make sure they had to account for their actions. We'd go to the Church, we said, the press, the government, the Pastoral Land Commission, anyone who would listen. We told them the courts would prosecute them, but they were empty threats. We knew no one would listen – that we could do nothing to stop them from taking the land – and they knew it, too. We were nothing more than a nuisance. A pest. So they punished us.'

Paulo looked at me, studied my face, not understanding. 'Punished you?'

I closed my eyes and turned my face to the sun, feeling the heat, speaking to the sky. 'The *pistoleiros* from the mine took me with them one night. Dragged me from my bed and marched me through the forest until we came to the spot their employers wanted to mine. Gave me a can of gasoline and held a gun to my head.' I paused and squeezed my eyes tighter. I opened them again and looked at my friend. 'They made me help them, Paulo. Pointed guns at me and laughed when they forced me to set the fire. Me. I burned people. They made me a part of it.'

Paulo remained silent, there was nothing for him to say; nothing he *could* say.

I cleared my throat and made myself continue. 'I saw people on fire, Paulo. My fire. You can't imagine what it's like. To see people consumed by my flames, desperate to free themselves of the pain that *I* had caused them. To hear their screams and their crying and their pleas for mercy. They ran in circles, some of them, burning, and the *pistoleiros* laughing as they shot them down. And afterwards when they combed the village making sure everyone was dead, they dragged me with them, putting a pistol in my hand, pointing it, making me shoot the bodies, seeing the bullets puncturing the bloated flesh. And when they found a survivor, they were like excited children, forcing me to put the gun to his head. A young Indian boy. Hardly even looked human, he was so badly burned, but I recognised him straight away. Round his neck a crucifix that Father Machado had given him, almost fused to his chest.'

I lifted the bottle of *pinga* to my lips and filled my mouth, taking more than I should, swallowing it all down, feeling the liquid scorch my throat. When I spoke again, my voice was hoarse and strained.

'His name was Davi. Maybe ten years old, I don't know. Used to hang around the mission, asking for whatever we'd give him, which wasn't much. Sometimes we had sweets, maybe some Coke, something like that. He stole the crucifix. Pulled it right from Father Machado's neck. Just yanked it right off, snapping the chain and running away. I went after him, but Father Machado pulled me back, told me to let him have it. I remember I was angry at the boy for stealing, but later we laughed about it. It was a trinket. Just a *thing*. But there it was again, round the boy's neck, and the boy was trying to breathe air into lungs that were probably burned solid. Charred and ready to crumble into dust.

'They were thrilled at the prospect of seeing a priest take a child's life,' I continued. 'He was dying anyway, they laughed. Burned like that, his hair gone, his skin gone, he wouldn't survive long. Not even a doctor could save someone from such burns, they said. I'd be helping him; putting him out of his misery. It would be like shooting a lame mule, they told me. I would be saving him from the wild animals attracted by the smell of his cooked flesh.'

Once again, I looked at my friend. His face was blank, no expression suitable to register the horror of what I was telling him. Instead, he reached out and put a hand on my shoulder.

'I pissed myself,' I told him. 'I pissed myself when I pulled the trigger, and it made them laugh even louder.' I shook my head now. 'They laughed when I did what they wanted me to do; what no God would ever make his servant do. I murdered a child, Paulo. And later, when the men had taken me home, I fell to my knees in the dust before Father Machado, my streaked and blackened face streaming as he offered me undeserved forgiveness.

'After that, I couldn't bear it any longer. So I ran away and left Father Machado behind. I came to São Felix because he spoke about it all the time. It was an important place to him. I begged him to come with me but he wouldn't. He said he had a job to do, but he told me to go; told me to tell people what had happened. Tell the bishop in São Felix. He made me promise I wouldn't let people forget what was happening.' I paused for a moment, allowing my last words to settle over my conscience. 'Perhaps if I'd stayed with him things would've been different. Maybe he . . .' I shook my head. 'News came to us that Father Machado was killed. You know as well as I do, those who claim the land don't welcome people like him. They don't like priests telling them what to do.

'So I stayed in São Felix a few months, but everything had changed. I wasn't the same any more, I didn't want the same things . . . I didn't want to think about anything. I wanted to forget. So I came here to São Tiago where the fishing was good and no one would bother me.'

I stopped speaking now and listened to the sound of the land around me. I felt its air on my skin and I breathed its scent into my lungs. I let Brasil seep through my pores and fill every part of me. There was so much I hated about this country and yet there was even more that I loved. Despite what it had done to me, I couldn't imagine myself anywhere else.

Paulo chewed his bottom lip and looked at me. For a long

time he didn't say anything. Then he shook his head and spat into the dirt.

'And I let you get involved with Da Silva,' he said. 'God forgive me.'

'No.' I shook my head. 'There *is* no God. The things that happened in Roraima . . . No God would do that to his people.'

33

We stayed a while on the road, neither of us speaking much, both of us lost in our own thoughts. Me hoping that Ana was right – that my heart would grow a little lighter – and Paulo, perhaps, with his a little heavier. And when we heard a vehicle moving somewhere in the distance, the sound of an engine coming to us across the vast kilometres of open land, we shuffled to our feet, went to the trucks and put ourselves through the motions of carrying on with life.

I'd never driven a truck like the F-4000 before, so it took me a while to get the hang of it. I lurched and stalled it back to São Tiago, while Bruno lolled on the seat beside me like an old dog that's ready for the needle.

We came into town at dusk, me in the truck, Paulo trailing in the pickup. Glowing over the whitewashed buildings there was an orange light that I didn't expect to see. An orange light that was giving off a thick, black smoke into the darkening sky. I picked up speed along the *rua* and headed straight for the riverside where Manolo's café and the clinic stood. I hoped I was wrong, but I was certain I knew where the flames would be.

Our clinic was on fire, disappearing more quickly than it would take to drink a few bottles of beer. There wasn't a part of the building that hadn't been swallowed by flames, and the crown of it was the roof frame and the scaffold, the perfectly laid timbers now burning perfectly in the dusk. A small crowd of people had gathered to watch the flames, and I spotted Papagaio standing to one side. His shoulders were slumped as he watched. Beside him, Ana shook her head in disbelief.

Paulo and I jumped down from the vehicles and went to join them, but there was nothing we could do. We, too, stood idle as our wood turned to ash, our brick blackened and crumbled. No one bothered with water, the fire was too far gone already. Before long everything would be destroyed and it would burn itself out, leaving nothing more than an oversized barbecue of dying coals. All we could do was watch the fire play in the sky, tiny sparks of our hard work being carried away by the smoke and the heat.

'How'd this happen?' said Ana. 'How could it?'

The smell of burning wood was strong in my nostrils, my eyes were stinging from its sweetness. 'Everything's so dry. Wouldn't take much more than a cigarette.' I could feel the intensity of the heat, its thickness around my face.

'All that work.' There was despair in Paulo's voice. 'All that time; all those materials; all that money. Everything wasted. The whole damn thing.'

Papagaio put his arm around Paulo's shoulder. 'It can be rebuilt, you know. It's not so bad. We'll do whatever we can.'

'We've come too far. Too much has happened for us to allow this to change anything,' I said to Paulo. 'We'll rebuild it.' I wanted it for myself as much as I wanted it for my friend. It was more than just a clinic; more than bricks and wood disappearing in front of us. Too much had happened, too many sacrifices had been made and too much blood had been spilled. The clinic was a symbol of everything that had happened since Eduardo's death and if we allowed it to fail, to crumble into nothing but ash and dust, then everything would have been for nothing.

Paulo closed his eyes and rubbed one hand across his forehead.

'We have what's on the truck,' I said. 'And I can go to Da Silva for more materials.' I glanced at him long enough to see him nod. 'I'll go to her tomorrow. The workers can start clearing up first thing.'

I turned around now, looking back into the town, and spotted Manolo standing under the awning of his café, smiling, arms folded. I stared at him for a while, until his eyes met mine.

'What?' Papagaio asked, turning away from the fire. 'What're you . . . ?' He looked over to the café, following my gaze, and his face dropped. 'Manny thinks this is funny?' he said. 'Shit. You want me to go over there and kill him?'

Beside me, I sensed Paulo was about to speak, so I nudged him hard to make him stop and I turned to Papagaio, his black skin shining in the glow of the fire. His eyebrows were raised and he was tapping the wooden handle of the revolver hidden beneath his shirt. 'I could do it now if you want.'

All I had to do was say one word and my friend would've taken Manolo's life, but I put my hand on his and shook my head. 'No, Papagaio. It wouldn't help.' I turned back to Paulo and gently shook my head, warning him not to tell Papagaio what we knew. Not yet, anyway. If Papagaio knew what Manolo had done, he would kill him for sure. 'We'll make a start on it first thing,' I said. 'There's nothing for us to do here now except watch the fire. You should all go home.'

'And you,' said Ana. 'Where are you going?'

'I'm going to talk to Manny,' I said.

Papagaio watched me like he was trying to make up his mind about something. He glanced over at Manny, and then back at me. 'Is there something I should know?'

'I just need to talk to him.'

'He's got something to do with this,' said Papagaio. 'Tell me, Sam.'

I spoke to Paulo. 'The fire, it doesn't change anything we discussed. The blood stops. We forgive him, just like we agreed. Take Bruno to my place,' I added. 'Make him comfortable. Papagaio can help you. And when you've done that, tell him what happened on the road. But don't let him go anywhere near Manny.'

I turned to Ana and touched her face. 'I'll come later,' I said. 'I won't be long.' And then I walked away from my friends, leaving them surrounded by the warmth of the flames.

Manny stood up as I came close, and he hurried into the hut at the back of his café. I rushed after him, pushing my way in through the door, taking the *pistola* from my waistband as I went in. Inside Manolo was reaching up to take a shotgun from its rack on the wall, so I pulled him away, spinning him around and pushing him back against the table.

'Sam. Listen—'

I bent forward, touching the muzzle to Manolo's forehead, saying, 'It was you.'

He didn't speak, he just stared, the whites of his eyes perfectly round.

I allowed my finger to drop down onto the trigger. 'It was you,' I said again. 'The fire. The men on the road. It was all you.' I pressed harder, pushing the muzzle tight against his skin. 'Wasn't it?'

His head nodded an inch. Up and down, just an inch.

'They were going to cut off Paulo's hand.'

'No,' he said. 'No. They were going to scare you. They—'

'They're dead,' I said, seeing myself sitting over the man in the road, holding my hand tight over his mouth. 'Shot with this revolver.'

'What?'

'All three of them. Is that what you wanted? More blood? *My* blood?'

'No . . .'

I heard footsteps behind me. Someone shuffling in the doorway, but I kept the revolver tight against Manny's forehead.

'Sam.' It was Ana's voice. 'Sam, what's going on?'

I released some tension, and Manolo must have felt it, relief showing, daring to blink. There was dampness in his hairline, around his neck, the collar of his Brasil football shirt starting to darken. The smell of fear and sweat coming off him was rank.

'Sam? What's going on?' Ana came further into the room and stood beside me.

I relaxed a little more, allowed my finger to find its way from the trigger, allowed the muzzle to move from Manolo's head leaving a perfectly round indentation on the skin between his eyebrows. I could feel Ana close to me, her hard breaths, the beating of her heart.

I stepped back and lowered the weapon. 'Why, Manny? Why would you do that?'

He moved his mouth, no sound coming out.

'Why would you do that?' I repeated.

'Do what?' said Ana. 'What has he done?'

'The fire,' I said. 'It was Manny. He sent men to attack us on the road, too. They were going to kill Paulo.'

'No,' said Manny. 'They were supposed to warn you. To make it difficult.'

'Because I wouldn't take his confession. Because I hit him.'

'Manny?' Ana looked past me.

'I don't need to dirty myself with him,' I said, tucking the revolver away. 'We've got Da Silva to do that for us.'

'Da Silva?' Manolo managed to whisper the name through his fear.

'You didn't know this was her clinic, did you? Everything you burned. The tools. The materials you tried to stop us bringing in. Paulo, me. Even you, Manny. *Every*thing belongs to Da Silva. Should have paid more attention to our conversations, shouldn't you?' I said. 'This is Da Silva's clinic. Not mine, not Paulo's. Shit, all I have to do is give her your name. She already offered once before. When she found out it was you who killed Eduardo.' I turned my back on him, just like I did that night under the awning when my feet were sinking in Eduardo's blood. 'The only reason you're still alive is because I told her to spare you.'

'You were supposed to be my friend. You refused my confession.'

'Just as you knew I would. The only person who could have forgiven you was Eduardo.'

'I didn't mean for anybody to get hurt. I told them no one was to get hurt.'

I stayed where I was, looking at Ana.

'I just wanted to make it difficult for you,' he said. 'You have to believe me. No one was supposed to get hurt.'

I turned back to Manolo again and watched him cowering. I shook my head and sighed, pulling a chair away from the table.

'Sit down with me, Manny. You too, Ana. You might as well stay now you're here.'

They joined me at the table, both of them confused.

'I want us to be friends, Manny, like we used to be.' I took out the *pistola* again and opened the cylinder to show him it was empty. 'I wasn't going to shoot you, Manny.' I dropped it on the table, the metal sounding heavy and brutal against the wood. 'I wanted you to see how far this can go. We can carry on for ever, hating each other, making life hell, maybe until one of us kills the other, but neither of us wants that.'

'You refused my confession. You drove my customers away.' He stared at me. 'You beat me.'

'You killed a man.' I raised my voice.

'You're supposed to forgive me.'

'It was unforgivable.' I banged my fist on the table.

Manny lowered his eyes. 'It's your job.'

I spread my fingers and forced myself to relax. 'Not any more,' I said, almost a whisper. 'I'm just a man. Like you. And as a man it wasn't my place to give you what you wanted. But as a man I can forgive you what you've done today. To me. But you must pay a penance.'

'What kind of penance?'

'I want you to help us rebuild the clinic. I want you to be a part of it. The labour will make you feel clean.'

'And if I refuse?'

I shrugged. 'Then Da Silva will know what happened here today.'

'You would tell her?'

'Why would I want to protect you?'

Manolo put both of his hands on his face and rubbed his eyes. 'Can we really be friends again, Sam?' He watched me through his fingers. 'After all this?'

'Yes,' I said. 'We can.'

Coming away from Manny's place, passing the last few people still watching the fire, Ana took my hand.

'I was afraid you were going to shoot him,' she said. 'And part of me thinks he would've deserved it. You've all worked so hard on the clinic.'

'So have you.'

'You want to tell me what happened on the road today?'

I recounted it to her as we walked back to her place, and she listened to my words without speaking; not flinching when I told her what I had done. When I had finished, she squeezed my hand. 'You must have been very scared,' she said.

We stopped outside her porch and I turned to face her. I put my arms around her and thought about the man I'd smothered. I felt no guilt for it.

'It was a good idea,' she said. 'Making Manny help with the clinic. Making him part of it. It'll be hard to work with him after what he's done, but . . .' She stopped mid-sentence and held me at arm's length, looking into my eyes. 'Let's not talk about it any more,' she said. 'Let's go inside. Let's forget about everything for a while.'

'Not yet.' I broke away and went to the table under the porch. 'Let's sit here a while,' I said, lowering myself into one of the chairs, beckoning for her to do the same. I wanted to be outside when I told her about Roraima. It seemed like the best place to be.

Ana didn't interrupt as I told her the same thing I had told Paulo earlier, but I saw the pain she felt for me. There was enough light from the moon that night for me to see the tears glistening in her eyes as I spoke. Only now did she understand the weight of what I had been carrying with me for so long, but she was right that it needed to be spoken aloud. When I had told Paulo, I was giving my confession, but telling Ana was different. A cathartic process that lifted something invisible from between us. I had always been afraid what her reaction might be – that she would find me repellent, knowing what I had done – but Ana was too strong and had seen too much. She knew the tumescent illness which corrupted this beautiful land, and she knew that no one was untouched by it. I had been a victim of the disease, just like she once had, and telling her, cutting it from between us, left me in no doubt about my feelings for her. Ana knew me now, she knew everything that decayed inside me, but she did not step away, shocked. Instead, she came closer. She listened to me, then put her arms around me and touched her cheek to mine. Her actions were enough. There was nothing she needed to say.

Afterwards, we went inside, washed the day from our bodies and held each other in the darkness of Ana's bedroom. For the first time in my life I truly understood what it meant to make love, and I knew that Ana would never judge me for what I had done.

34

When I went back to my place in the morning, Bruno was still there, sweaty and snoring like a sick animal. He opened his eyes when I nudged him, and I pointed to a small cup of coffee on the bare, unfinished table. It was strong and sweet, and I was sure a few cups would bring him round. 'Drink it,' I said. 'As much as you want.'

He pushed himself up onto his elbows and looked around.

'You're in São Tiago. My place. When Paulo gets here, we'll go down and unload your truck. After that you can have your money.'

Bruno worked his mouth, stretching it open and wincing. He ran one hand around his jaw.

'You remember what happened?' I asked.

His fingers moved to the dressing on his left cheek. 'Yes.'

'It's all taken care of. Paulo patched you up and we brought you back here.'

'And the men?'

'Forget them.'

Bruno narrowed his eyes, about to speak again, but someone banged on the door and I went straight to it. Paulo was standing on the step, unshaven, his moustache and hair uncombed.

'Take whatever you need,' I said to Bruno. 'My house is yours.'

I went outside with Paulo and closed the door, telling him what Manolo and I had agreed last night.

Paulo kicked the dirt. 'You want him to help us? After everything he did?' He was still angry, and I couldn't blame him.

'Things got out of hand,' I said. 'Manolo didn't mean for all this.'

'Of course he meant it, Sam. He set fire to the clinic as sure as he stuck a knife in Eduardo.'

'So what do you want to do? Kill him? That's the only other way to deal with this.'

'I want to punish him.'

'That's what we're doing. You think he *wants* to help us? You know Manny; he just wants to sit around all day. This is the only punishment he's going to get unless you want violence,' I said. 'How else will he ever pay for it? You know how things work around here. I hit him, he hits back harder. It'll go on and on until someone gets killed – probably you or me.'

'But you're still using Da Silva as a threat,' he said. 'The threat of violence.'

'Yeah.'

'So he's not doing it because it's the right thing or because it's some kind of penance; he's doing it because he's afraid of Da Silva.'

'That's how his religion works. He needs to fear something and he needs to believe there's a way out. That's why he wanted to confess. Because he's afraid of damnation and he thought I'd forgive him.'

'Make him say a few prayers to buy his ticket to heaven?'

'Exactly.'

'Doesn't seem like he's too worried about damnation any more,' said Paulo. 'Sending those men after us, burning the clinic.'

'Things went wrong,' I replied. 'But we've given him something more real to think about, anyway. You and me, Paulo, we're not God, we never were. But Da Silva? Da Silva is the closest thing we've got to God in São Tiago. Let him be afraid of her.'

When Bruno was on his feet, he joined us by what was left of the charred clinic. He was happy to see his truck untouched, abandoned beside the ruin. I half expected it to have been stripped, but everything was intact.

As we began unloading the materials, Manolo appeared from the hut behind his café and came over. Looking like he hadn't slept, he waved a sullen greeting and stood rubbing his chin. Then he sighed to himself and reached up to help me take down some heavy roof beams. Paulo eyed him with suspicion, but continued to work.

'I have to go,' I said to Paulo once everything was unloaded. I had taken the day off, promised another fishing trip, and the boy was excited. I would not let him down. It was a part of my life over which I seemed to have some degree of control and I wanted to make sure it remained that way. 'I have my morning report to make, too. Da Silva's expecting me.'

I sensed Manolo stiffen when I mentioned the name.

'Don't worry,' I told him. 'I'll deal with her. You just worry about helping to clear up your mess. The men will be here in an hour or so, but as long as the sun is up, there's work to be done. Paulo will tell you what he needs.'

It was good to talk to Manny without malice. As a man, I had forgiven him for what he'd done, and I felt that I could put behind me the things that had passed between us. The destruction of the clinic was a tragedy, but we would build it again, faster this time. Paulo said that some people had even offered to help for free after they'd seen our efforts disintegrate into the darkness the night before. I was glad to have Manny's help, too.

The clinic would belong to all of us now, it would be a true part of São Tiago.

I threw my fishing stuff into the back of the Chevrolet, stowed my twenty-two behind the seat, and turned the engine over. Looking across at Manny beginning work, I began to feel apprehensive. I'd have to tell Da Silva what had happened, there was no way around that, but I didn't want to give her Manolo's name. If she knew what he had done, she'd kill him. I would have to persuade her that a violent reprisal was not the right action, and that I would deal with the problems we'd had. I needed to make her understand there was no need to search for a culprit.

As I drove, though, I tried to put everything to the back of my mind. I didn't want to think about Da Silva and the complications of being involved with her. She was a new guilt which gnawed at me. Every time I heard her name or saw her face in my mind I had been torn between two violent emotions, but now things were changing and my bond with Ana was becoming stronger than ever. Ana did not judge me for my actions in Roraima, as I had feared she might, but if she learned of my betrayal with Da Silva, things would be very different. Ana was too important to lose and I knew that I would have to end my relationship with Da Silva. I *wanted* to end it. Not just for Ana's sake, but also for my own. I wanted no one other than Ana and I was ashamed that I had been too weak and blind to realise it.

The moment I arrived at the *fazenda*, tyres crunching on the stones around the driveway, the front door opened and Catarina Da Silva stepped out. Luis and Lucas followed her, stepping to either side of the door where they stood to attention. She waited for me to climb down from the cab, and then she came over, passing me and moving out towards the pens and runs where I'd seen them castrating the cattle. Luis and Lucas remained where they were, but I assumed she wanted me to follow her, so I did, noticing her tight jeans, the way they hugged low on her hips. She was working herself, or that's the way it seemed to me, displaying herself, showing what she had. Only thing was, though, I wasn't sure if it was for my benefit or just anyone who might be watching.

This was what passed for God in the lost world.

'We're slaughtering cattle today,' she said as I came alongside her. 'Walk with me.' Her pace was slow but steady.

We went away from the main house, towards the cattle runs, like civilised friends out for a morning stroll, listening to the cicadas in the dry grass. Several *vaqueiros* on horseback, João among them, were forcing a group of cattle forwards with a lot of whooping and shouting. There weren't many cows. Five, maybe six, bony creatures with dirty hides and empty eyes.

Catarina led me towards the nearest fence and stopped, leaning forward against the top rung, saying, 'Kiko is here this morning.'

I couldn't help feeling relieved, but then a thought occurred to me. 'Why?'

'I'm not sure,' she said. 'But we won't be able to go inside the house yet.'

'You think he might know?'

'About us?' She shook her head. 'If he did, we'd both be dead already. Or something worse. He's very possessive.'

I allowed her words to sink in, wondering what could be worse than being dead. I imagined that the Da Silvas both knew many different answers to that.

'Well, maybe we should stop . . .'

'Only when I say it's time.' She looked at me and smiled. 'I haven't finished with you yet.' It wasn't a friendly smile. 'He'll be leaving later, before lunch.'

'I have another list of materials we need.' I tried to change the subject, taking Paulo's paper from my pocket and holding it up. I didn't want to come straight to the trouble we'd had.

'We kill once every two weeks,' she said, 'and sell the meat to the workers.' I looked for a point in what she was telling me, but couldn't find one. 'Sometimes I come to watch them work. It gives me something to do.'

Once the animals were in the main pen, one of the cowboys closed the gate and dismounted from his horse. Now there were three men standing inside the corral with the cattle, and from the look of the animals, they must have picked the skinniest, saddest creatures they could find. Da Silva was probably thinking it was better to carve them up and sell them to the workers than let them die out in the fields, left to be picked at by vultures and insects.

'You ever watched them do this?' Da Silva asked, taking the list and stuffing it into a back pocket. 'It's fascinating how quickly they do it. You know, I once saw João over there kill four cows when he was drunk? Never missed the spot.' She raised a hand and pointed a finger at João, as if I didn't know who he was. He was wearing a black and white checked shirt and a pair of faded orange trousers. 'And how are things in São Tiago?' She turned to me. 'You're working hard?'

I said, 'Yeah,' and watched as two of the cowboys huddled against a cow, putting all their weight behind it, forcing it to the ground as the men had done to Paulo on the road the day before. Once it was down, a small cloud of flies rose from its hide, circled and then settled again. João took a long thin knife from the sheath on his belt and rubbed it once across the leg of his trousers. He crouched down beside the animal and looked into its eyes before glancing up at us. He grinned at me and nodded.

'We had some trouble,' I said, ignoring him.

'Three dead men at the roadside,' she replied. 'One with his face missing, another all messed up like he was run over.'

'You know about it?'

'I know there was a fire too.'

'And you know who they were? The dead men?'

'They used to work for me.' She held both hands out in front of her and inspected the nails.

'*You* sent them?' I pretended not to know the answer.

'Of course not.' She watched João crouching beside the cow, struggling now to keep it on the ground. 'Why would I send men to sabotage my own plans?'

'But you knew them?

'Not personally, they only worked here. Men who will do anything for money.'

'So you know who paid them?'

'Not yet,' she said. 'But I'll find out. I always find out. And when I do—'

'No.' I stopped her. 'No violence. Not over this. Not over the clinic.'

'I will do what I have to. I've spent money on this. I will do what I must to protect my investment.'

'But it's my time and labour,' I said. 'I'll sort it out. I'll deal with it another way.'

'Out here,' she said, 'there is no other way.'

'There is now,' I told her. 'It's your clinic but I'm running it. I'm not a stupid labourer who needs to be told what to do. Let me do it my way.'

'You telling me to back off, Sam? Telling me to do nothing, like before, with the café owner? You don't like the blood-letting?'

'There's no need for it. I don't want any more blood on this clinic. Its job is to *stop* the blood.'

Now she turned to me, seemingly impressed. 'I like your forceful side,' she said. 'I don't often see it in conversation. Usually it's only when you're fucking me.' Catarina raised her hand to João, stopping him as she continued to speak. 'Spend

299

the afternoon at the *fazenda* with me. Kiko will leave soon. We can have lunch together, talk about the problems you've been having.'

'I'm dealing with them.'

'And afterwards I'll take off these clothes and get on my knees. You can put it in my mouth and make me use my lips.'

'I have a commitment,' I said, glad that the comment did more to repulse me than arouse me. My heart was finally beginning to drag my lust into line.

'Shame.' She turned back to João and nodded. João smiled at me again and slipped the knife into the cow's throat, sliding it into the flesh as if it were a saggy bag of red wine. He kept his eyes on me as he whipped the blade out in a flash, the steel being followed by a full gush of thick, dark liquid that sent the hungry flies into a frenzy.

'What kind of commitment?' she asked me when the flow became just a trickle.

'It's unavoidable,' I said. I didn't want to discuss the boy with her. It was not her business. 'I made a promise.' My mood starting to worsen.

She nodded again to João and then turned back to me. 'A promise? And you have to keep it, right? Because a priest has to keep his promises?'

'Right.'

'Another time, then?'

'Sure. Another time.'

She stood away from the fence and sighed. 'Don't you ever get bored here, Sam? Nothing to do but fishing and drinking? There's always the soap operas, I suppose, but I doubt you even have a television.'

As far as I knew, there was only one television in São Tiago, but without a private mast, the reception was poor.

'There are other things,' I told her. 'Not just fishing.'

'But you've been to other places. There must be more for you there.'

'I like it here,' I said. 'It suits me.'

She put her hands on her hips. 'I hate it. I hate the people, the land, the heat.'

'Then leave. Go somewhere else.'

'I wouldn't know where to go.'

'Where are you from? Why don't you go back there?'

'I married Kiko and came here from São Paulo when I was sixteen. I couldn't go back now, I'd be too afraid.'

The notion of Catarina Da Silva being afraid of anything was strange. São Paulo could be a dangerous place, but she didn't have a gentle reputation and meeting her told me her infamy was justified. I was sure the Da Silvas had enough money for a good life in São Paulo, but I didn't know what kind of a tether her husband used on her, and alone in the metropolis she would be a nobody. She wouldn't have workers to subjugate and *pistoleiros* to do her bidding.

'Get your husband to take you,' I said.

She paused and stared at me, her glare making me uncomfortable, like she was trying to see right inside me. 'I wonder if you were *ever* a man of God,' she said, reaching out to take the front of my shirt between her forefinger and thumb. 'I mean, look at you.' She let go. 'You don't look like a priest; you don't act like a priest. You know what to do with a woman. When was the last time you said mass? Took confession?'

'I don't hold much with those things.'

'You have callused hands, sharp eyes, a lean look I never saw in any kind priest before. Or any kind of man. There's something about you makes you different.'

'I'm just the same as everyone else,' I said, thinking how the hell was I going to get away from here.

'No, that's just it. You're nothing like the other peasants

round here. People like João.' She waved a hand. 'Papagaio. Even your doctor friend. You're not like them.'

'Sure I am.'

'No. There's more to you. You've seen things, been places, I can see it in your eyes. There's nobody else here like you. I wonder what it is that makes you stay.'

'What about your husband?' I said. 'He's not like these people.' I hated saying it like that. These 'people' were my friends.

'Kiko?' She swatted at a fly which settled on her cheek. 'Kiko's like a native. He's not much more than a peasant with money. A *camponês*. He bores me as much as this place does.'

I wondered if the fly had been feeding in the cow's blood.

'And anyway, he's never here. Always off chasing something or another. Women, money. He's always hungry for something. That's why I need you, Sam.' She moved a little closer to me. 'Stay here with me now. Come inside and screw me, Sam. When he's gone. Put it inside me and make me scream. I know it makes you feel like a man.'

I took a step back from her, shaking my head. 'I can't.'

Da Silva stared at me now, a dangerous expression flashing over her face, just a glimpse of thunder before she forced a smile. Without taking her eyes off me, she raised a hand to João who slit another throat, spilled more blood into the corral.

I turned away and went back towards the house, while João and the others slaughtered the rest of the cattle. I walked to my newly acquired Chevrolet, trying to get away from the smell of death and the sight of Da Silva, and I changed the subject as I went, raising my voice, saying, 'Those materials, you think you can get them for us?'

I reached the truck and she came round to stand in front of me, dipping into my top pocket and taking the cigarette packet. It was battered and crumpled, but she took one anyway. 'Don't walk away from me, Sam,' she said, placing the unlit cigarette between her lips. 'You're mine now. You belong to me. Don't forget that. Nothing is over until I say it's over.'

'I have to go,' I told her. 'I have a promise to keep.'

She looked over my shoulder at the gear in the back of the pickup. 'You're taking the *gringo*'s boy out again,' she said. 'You and he have become friends, am I right?'

'I suppose so.' It didn't surprise me that she knew I took him on the river. She seemed to know almost everything else about me.

'Your contact with civilisation. And now he's more important than me. You take him fishing when you should be here with me.' She smiled and propped herself against the truck, one elbow resting on the rim of the flatbed. 'Light me.' She pushed out her lips.

When I offered her the flame, she used both her hands to steady mine and came close to me, allowing the smoke to melt from her mouth towards my own. Her hands were soft and warm, as always, but stirred little in me. 'The river can be a dangerous place for a young boy,' she said as she tucked the pack into my top pocket.

'Why's that?' I asked. 'Is that some kind of threat?'

She made a small sound like laughter and waved a hand. 'Why would I make threats, Sam? We're friends.'

'Yes,' I said. 'And the boy is my friend. His father too.'

'Of course.'

She'd made the threat without thinking, trying to impress her ownership upon me, but I knew that of all the people in my life, the boy was the only one she would not dare harm. To us, the small and unimportant people of São Tiago, Catarina Da Silva was a god, but only to us. The foreigners were not part of this place, not yet, and she had no power over them. If she did anything to upset the American investors, her world would turn to dust. If she harmed the boy, she would be faced with the might of the company, the corruptible police, and John Swan himself. A man who currently had three well-trained soldiers at his disposal.

'We need more timber,' I said, trying to hide my contempt for her. 'Bricks, cement. Some tools need to be replaced. You can arrange that?'

'You'll get what's on the list.' She reached round behind and patted her own flanks.

I popped the door of the pickup and stepped up into the cab.

Catarina Da Silva put her arms on the rim of the open window and blew smoke into the cab. She paused for a moment, holding my eyes with her own, then she stepped back, saying, 'Go on then. Go to your boy. Keep your promise. Then come back here tomorrow. You make sure you keep your promise to me too, priest.'

'I will,' I said. 'And I'll find out who sent those men, so make sure you leave it to me.'

'I'll do whatever I think is best,' she said.

I crunched the pickup into gear and fled the *fazenda*, looking forward to the safety of the river. *Piranhas*, caiman, and *candiru* were going to be a soft touch after dealing with Catarina Da Silva. I'd been in São Tiago long enough for it to seem like a lifetime – a whole *new* lifetime – and since coming down from Roraima, I'd never felt threatened and exposed in the way I did now. That's why I came to São Tiago; because people left me alone. No one ever asked me why I was here. It just wasn't the way we did things. Until Catarina Da Silva.

São Tiago had been Father Mateus's idea, him saying it would give me the escape I needed. He saw what was happening to me and understood I needed somewhere quiet. In São Tiago people would leave a priest alone no matter how strong or weak his faith, he said. A small, insignificant place full of runaways who care nothing about your past. A place where a man may own nothing more than what he can hold in his hand, and still be like everyone else. They accepted a priest just as they would accept a teacher or a mechanic. A doctor or a *pistoleiro*. But I wasn't invisible. From time to time there were unavoidable expectations, just as there would be for a doctor or an engineer. A doctor would be called upon to fix a broken bone; an engineer to fix a broken car.

To a man like Manolo, I was a convenient way out. He wanted me to pardon his murderous act, absolve his guilty hands. He wasn't ashamed of what he'd done to Eduardo, he was just a superstitious killer whose watery faith made him fear what his God might do to him if he didn't confess. For him, it was basic survival instinct, not atonement. The way he saw it, everything would be squared up if I gave him the forgiveness he asked for. All debts would be paid.

To other people I deserved respect, no matter how I led my life. Even men like Severino, an ageing *pistoleiro* with the blood of others splashed across his soul, could see my life was empty, that my back was to the Church, but they still held Father Mateus's view of the priesthood. To most people, though, until they needed to think otherwise, I was nothing more than a lonely man who spent his days fishing and trying to forget. To them I was a man who had lost his faith, whatever it had once been, and in many ways they were right. All my old faiths had been broken and buried; those that I held when I came to Brasil, and now those that I'd first embraced in São Tiago. All those beliefs were gone, dissolved from the moment I accepted the truth of my feelings for Ana. Feelings which had run fast and long for months, but now ran deeper than ever. No one knew more about me than she did; no one could heal me like she had. No one meant more to me than her.

To Catarina Da Silva, though, I was fair game. I was a new toy, and it worried me. She was threatening my new way of life.

35

The boy was waiting outside his house, sitting on the front step, skinny legs stretched out in front of him. He raised a hand as I approached, and then stood, collecting his fishing box from the ground beside him. As soon as I pulled up, he hefted it over into the back of the pickup and reached out for the door handle, turning as his mother emerged from the shade of the house. She allowed the screen door to bang shut behind her and took a few steps towards us before the boy went back to her.

While she said a few words of farewell, issuing the expected safety advice and orders to be careful, I caught her attention and waved, letting her know we'd be fine. Reassured, I looked away so the boy wouldn't feel awkward when his mother kissed him, and when she was done, she stepped away, leaving him to climb up onto the footboard. He pulled the door shut and rested his elbow on the open window, relaxing back into the sun-heated mock leather, acting like a seasoned pro.

I waved to his mother, calling '*bom dia*', and dipped my head so I could look past the boy. She stayed where she was, returning the greeting but didn't move away from the house. I assumed the boy had asked her to stay put; he didn't want her cramping his style. After a couple of moments, though, she couldn't help herself and held up a hand, coming over to my side of the cab. Beside me I heard the boy sigh and I imagined him rolling his eyes.

'Back for seven?' she said.

'Probably more like eight, eight thirty,' I told her. 'Ana's making dinner tonight. Cooking the fish we catch.'

She pursed her lips and creased her brow.

'I spoke to John,' I told her. 'He said it would be OK.'

'Mum,' the boy protested, 'can we just go, please?'

She looked at us both in the cab, considered for a moment as she glanced at the rifle on the shelf behind us. Then she sighed, just as he had done, and stepped away from the vehicle. 'All right,' she said. 'Have fun.'

I noticed Luísa, the maid, standing behind the screen door, her face green and blurred by the mosquito netting. I smiled to myself and put the Chevrolet into gear.

'No later than eight thirty, though,' she reaffirmed.

'Of course,' I agreed. 'No later.'

I let out the clutch and followed the main road through the plantation where the sky was grey with the smoke from the burning trees. As we left, I checked my rear-view mirror, watching both women wave at him through the dust, but the boy remained face forward.

'You shouldn't be so embarrassed,' I said.

'Hmm?'

'Her wanting to kiss you goodbye; the fussing. Mother stuff.'

He looked at me as if he didn't understand.

'It's good she cares,' I told him. 'You should make the most of it. My mother was always the same. I remember telling her not to kiss me at the school gate, like everyone else I suppose, but now I wished I hadn't. It meant something to her. I reckon they care more than we ever know.'

It felt fresh to use my own language, as if I were taking a step away from everything, leaving it behind. I didn't need to think about Catarina Da Silva when I was with the boy and we were using our own words. I could think in a different way, as if all the bad things that happened in Roraima happened to another man.

'I might see if I can get a rifle like yours,' the boy said. He meant 'ask permission' of his mother, but I suppose it made him feel more grown up not to say that.

'Like mine?' I said, looking over at the warehouse as we passed.

'That way, I'd have something to do, wouldn't I?' he said. 'I could shoot cans or something.'

'I suppose.' I nodded to one of the workers I recognised. 'But don't you think you're a bit young to have one of your own?'

He bit his lower lip and his eyebrows came down and together in a frown. Like many of his expressions, it was one which I'd become accustomed to seeing. I was getting to know the boy well, and I knew I'd miss him when he was gone.

'Maybe in a couple of years?' I said. 'You can have a go with mine for now.'

We came out of the estate and turned onto the road which ran back to São Tiago, driving into the area where a pocket of trees had been left standing. I was just starting to accelerate now, the pickup slowly responding to my firmness on the pedal, when a Red Brocket deer stepped out of the line of trees on our right and walked into the road. Immediately I braked and the pickup lurched, stalling to a standstill, throwing us both forward in our seats. The boy reached out to brace himself against the dashboard as my chest came into contact with the oversized steering wheel. Everything in the back of the Chevrolet slid up the flatbed, slamming into the back of the cab with a clatter, and my rifle twirled and collapsed onto the seat behind us.

The deer stayed where it was, startled by something it had never seen before, paralysed in the road just ten or fifteen metres away from where we'd come to a halt. It was a beautiful creature, a well-nourished adult. I could see the softness in its dark brown eyes, the rich chestnut of its hide, the smoothness of its skin, the strength in its flanks. I watched it through the windscreen and it watched me. And then I leaned back, feeling for the stock of my gun. My fingers touched the old wood and I lifted the twenty-two into my hands, straightening myself up in the seat. 'Open the glove compartment,' I whispered to the boy, keeping my eyes on the deer. 'There's a small box in there. Open it, and pass me some of the cartridges. One at a time.'

As he opened the glove compartment, I unlocked the magazine and slid out the inner tube. I did it without looking, keeping my eyes on the deer, then holding my hand out, repeating 'one at a time', and as the boy handed me the cartridges, I slid them into the loading port until the magazine was full. I locked the tube, keeping the muzzle pointing away towards the open window, and cocked the weapon. I looked at the boy, just for a second, seeing the wideness of his eyes, the tightness of his fingers around the box.

'Put them back now,' I whispered and reached for the door handle. I opened the door as slowly and quietly as possible, shifting my bodyweight so that I could step down from the cab.

With one foot on the red dust road, and one foot still up on the floor of the cab, I leaned forward into the window and, now that the door was wide open, rested one elbow on the edge for support. I raised the weapon, bringing the deer's head into the sight, and thumbed off the safety catch. I breathed in, held it, and squeezed the trigger.

Click.

Just a click, and the spell was broken.

The deer glanced away to the forest, looked back at me. Then, without any sign of haste, it continued its journey. It stepped into the trees and was gone. I kept the gun trained on it as it disappeared amongst the red-tainted foliage at the roadside and then the cartridge fired, a loud pop in the stillness, and a spit as it cut into the undergrowth where the deer had disappeared. 'Damn.' My shoulders relaxed. 'Hang fire.' The smell of gunpowder mingled with that of the smoke which clung to the air even here, a few kilometres from where they were burning.

I watched the place where the deer had melted into the forest and then turned to the boy. 'That's Zeca selling me duff cartridges, that is.' I unlocked the magazine and let the bullets slip out, turning them about in my palm. I smiled at the boy, aware that my hands were shaking a little. 'He owes me one for this.'

The boy didn't smile back. He was still in the cab, his fingers tight around the small, unmarked cardboard box which I had asked him to put away. He was watching the spot where the deer had been standing a few moments ago.

I climbed back into the cab and offered him the shells. He held out both hands and caught them, fumbling them back into the box, replacing it in the glove compartment.

'We'll have to try a few more,' I said, stowing the gun and settling myself behind the wheel. 'Better not all be like that.'

I felt the boy watching me. 'What?' I said, turning my head to see him. 'What's wrong?'

'You were going to kill it.'

'That's right,' I said, driving away. 'It's good meat. People would pay for it. I need the money.'

He weighed that in his mind for a moment, as if putting everything in order. 'You allowed to shoot things like that?' he said. 'I mean, are priests allowed to shoot things?'

'Sure they are,' I said. 'Why not? It's no different from catching a fish, is it?' It wasn't the reaction I had expected.

The boy shrugged. 'Feels different.'

'How does it feel different?'

'Well, I suppose a fish is just a fish, isn't it? But that deer . . . well, it looked alive. Like it was going somewhere, doing something.'

I nodded and kept my eyes on the road, saying, 'Maybe

you're right. Maybe it *was* going somewhere,' and I was thinking that when it came to hunting, a pair of brown eyes was sometimes all it took to put you off for life. 'So you don't like hunting,' I said. 'That's fine.'

'I don't know if I like it,' he said. 'I don't think I do, but . . . I don't know.'

'Is it because I'm a priest?' I asked him.

He mulled that over for a while, making me look across at him, my expression asking him for an answer.

'Maybe,' he said. 'It just doesn't seem right, somehow.'

'Why's that?'

He shrugged. 'Don't know. Just doesn't.'

I nodded and we drove in silence for a few minutes before I said, 'Well, we're just fishing today. We won't shoot anything unless you want to have a go with some cans, OK?'

The boy smiled. He liked that idea.

When we came to São Tiago, I drove us straight to the water's edge, where André kept his boats. Paulo was still at the clinic, clearing away the blackened remains, making way for the rebuilding. I called to him, beckoning him over as we unloaded our stuff.

'Everything OK?' I said as he came close.

'We'll manage.' He looked tired.

'And Manolo?'

'Only stopped working a couple of times. If someone comes into the café he goes over to serve them, that's all.' There was a film of sweat on his forehead and his shirt was covered with grime. Paulo wasn't one to let other people do all the work.

'Make sure he stays at it; it'll be good for him. We'll be back this afternoon,' I said. 'There'll still be light for me to help. And when it gets dark, we can use the headlights from the pickup.'

'Take your time,' he said. 'We have enough men here for

now.' He looked down at the boy. 'And how about you?' He spoke to him a little more slowly. 'How many fish you think you're going to catch this time?'

'Ten, maybe.' The boy lifted his fishing box from the back of the pickup and stepped down. 'More than Sam, anyway. Maybe I'll even catch his *filhote* for him.' He put the tailgate back into place and locked it with the pins as Paulo laughed out loud.

'Yeah, yeah,' I said to the boy. 'Keep on dreaming.'

I held out the pickup keys to Paulo. 'Never know if you might need some wheels.'

He came to take them and when he was close, I spoke quietly.

'She already knew about the trouble we had.'

'She knows it was Manny?'

'I don't think so, but it won't take her long to figure it out.' I half wished I wasn't going away. 'I've done what I can to put her off. I told her to leave it to me, but it's hard to know what she'll do. Hopefully she *will* leave it to us, but she doesn't like her money going up in smoke.' I glanced over at Manolo who was sifting through the ruins, collecting bricks that could still be used. 'We're not careful, this could get nasty.'

I handed the keys to Paulo and lingered while he dropped them into his pocket. 'I better go,' I said. 'The boy's waiting,' but when I made to leave, Paulo stopped me.

'Thanks,' he said, thinking about the words he was going to use. 'For what you did out there. On the road, I mean. I don't know if "thanks" is the right thing to say, but . . .' He broke off. 'That man . . .' His eyes glazed.

'We did the right thing for him, Paulo. He was going to die anyway.'

'Yeah.'

'It wasn't our fault.'

I could tell that Paulo still had something to say, so I waited.

'Yesterday,' he said. 'After what happened. You told me about Roraima?'

'Uh-huh.'

'You said that no one can change this place, that no one can make a difference . . .'

'Just talk, Paulo, that's all.'

Paulo forced a smile. 'It's not true,' he said. 'We *can* make a difference, you know. That's why we're doing this.'

'Yeah.' I looked over at the boy. 'I think you're right.'

'And I couldn't do it without you.'

36

On the water, the boy asked what happened to the clinic. Coming to São Tiago for our fishing trips, he had watched it grow, talked to Ana and Paulo as they worked on it, so now he wondered why it was nothing but a blackened ruin. I sat down on my spot in the boat and marvelled at how simple my life was just a few months ago. 'It's a long story,' I said.

He glanced around him as if to ask where I was going in such a hurry that I didn't have time to tell him. His face was tanned, no longer pasty and puffy, his sun-bleached hair falling over his brow creating a curtain for him to look through. His hands were stronger, his eyes keener, his whole manner more comfortable with the way of the river.

'Something for another time,' I told him. 'We're supposed to be fishing.' My moments on the river were fewer now than they used to be, and I enjoyed the tranquillity of it. I didn't want to think about the realities of my life. 'I keep meaning to ask Ana to come with us one day,' I said, watching a bird I didn't know the name of swoop across the top of the river, dipping its beak into the water as it flew. 'She likes you.'

'I like her too. She's nice.'

'It would be good for us to spend some time together. Just the three of us, don't you think?'

'Yeah.' The boy looked keen on the idea and he showed me

that smile, the one Ana always managed to conjure from him. 'Can she fish, though?' he asked.

'I don't think she can. Not very well, anyway. Maybe we can teach her together.'

The boy shrugged, 'OK,' and looked away at the riverbank.

I enjoyed the feeling of contentment and turned my face into the breeze which was whispering over the flattened plains, dropping down the white sandy banks and playing across the surface of the river. It felt cool and I recognised the signs. The river seemed a little higher that day, the beaches a touch shorter. Somewhere, the rains had started. The river system was beginning to swell and we were seeing the effects. There was no way of telling how long it would be before the rains reached us, but they were coming. Of that, I was sure.

'Is Ana your girlfriend?' The boy spoke into the breeze, making me turn to face him.

'Yes,' I told him. 'She is.' Almost without thinking, I pulled at the line between my forefinger and thumb, playing the bait on the riverbed, tempting the catfish without even realising I was doing it.

'Is that allowed?' he said. 'For a priest, I mean.'

The boat drifted and I felt the hook and bait drag across the silt, trailing over the hidden debris beneath. For a moment it snagged, pulling hard and then freeing itself, so I began to reel it back in, pulling the line hand over hand, flicking drops of river water across my forearms.

'You mean like am I allowed to shoot deer?' I laughed.

'No, not like that.' He was serious.

'OK,' I said, giving him my attention. He had asked a question and it deserved an answer. 'No, priests are not allowed girlfriends. But then, I'm not really a priest any more.'

'Why not?'

I sighed, giving myself time to find the best way to reply. 'Well,' I said, 'sometimes things happen that make you change

315

your mind about something. It just wasn't right for me any more.'

'I didn't know you could stop being a priest.' The boy concentrated hard, like he was formulating his next question, trying to get it just right. 'So does that mean you don't believe in God any more?'

'You don't have to be a priest to believe in God,' I told him.

The boy looked down at his feet, an inch or so of water flooding the soles of his flip-flops. 'That doesn't really answer my question.'

'No. I suppose not,' I admitted.

He had come a long way from being the timid boy I had first met at the barbecue. He seemed to have grown in so many ways. He was still calm on the surface, introspective and quiet, but he was no longer the fearful child who had looked back at his father with a worried expression as our boat travelled away from São Tiago. I hoped John was as proud of his son as I was.

'I had a brother.' He was still staring at his feet, acting almost as if I wasn't in the boat with him. He was alone, sorting through his thoughts, ordering his mind. 'He died, though. Hit by a car when he was eight. I was six. We were playing with a ball and I kicked it too hard. It went on the road and Simon went after it, running between the parked cars. One moment he was there and the next he was gone. I could see him and then I couldn't.' He looked up at me now, tears in his young eyes. 'I don't really remember much after that except thinking it was my fault because I kicked the ball and I should've gone after it and . . .' He stopped, rubbing a hand across his eyes, trying to wipe them clear, but only making room for more tears.

'His name was Simon?' I asked. Simon. Like the boy from the story. The one with the fever who eventually had a moment of clarity. The boy who was killed, murdered by his friends, and washed out to sea, forgotten.

316

'I remember Mum and Dad said he went to heaven. That he went to be with God.' He sniffed hard. 'Is that really true?'

I sighed and closed my eyes. When I opened them again, the boy was watching me, hoping for an answer from a man who should know. But I was lost for words. The truth was that I didn't know and I didn't understand. The things I had seen and the things I had done had shaken my faith, destroyed it and cast it down, made me lock it away in the darkest part of my soul. But here I was, faced with the tears of a young boy who was desperate to know the answers to things which holy men tried to explain with words. But there are some things that cannot be explained with words. Some things are too heavy for the words which try to carry them.

'There's no answer to your question,' I told him. 'There are so many things we don't understand. Things we'll *never* understand. We just have to heal ourselves and carry on. Think about what you have, not what you've lost.'

'So there *is* no God?'

'I don't know. But sometimes it makes people feel better to think that there is. It's one of the ways people help themselves to heal and there's nothing wrong with that.' And as I spoke, somewhere inside me, in the place which hadn't seen light in a long time, something whispered and a brief feeling of illumination came over me. What I had said to the boy was true. I didn't need to be a priest to believe, and I had a sudden, fleeting recollection of the comfort given to me by my faith.

After that, we were quiet for a while, both of us lost in our own thoughts. The silence was not awkward between us, but we both recognised that sometimes it is necessary to say nothing. We cast our lines, we drew them back, we baited hooks and replaced ones which were lost on the river bed. As the day drew on, we paddled closer to São Tiago, letting the current take us the rest of the way.

*

'I was thinking,' I said to the boy as we came closer to town. 'You go back to school soon, right?'

The boy nodded. 'Yeah.'

'So then, let's have one big fishing trip before you go.' It would be something for him to look forward to. A grand finale to his holiday; an adventure to relate to his friends.

'How d'you mean?'

'How about a whole weekend fishing? We'll find a good beach, make a tent out of some sticks and an old tarpaulin I have, build a fire, fish at night. You want, we can go look for turtle eggs in the morning. Eat them for breakfast.'

He looked excited and disgusted at the same time, so I told him we could look for them and then leave them right where we found them if he preferred.

'What do they taste like?' he said. 'Turtle eggs?'

'Who knows? Never brought myself to eat one. It's such an effort for them to find a place to lay. They dig for so long, and then when they hatch, most of them are eaten by the caiman. Doesn't seem fair for us to eat them, somehow. We'll take chicken's eggs instead.'

The boy smiled and nodded like he knew exactly what I was talking about.

'So how about it? We'll get Ana to come. Just the three of us. We'll have a great time.'

'Not sure Mum'll let me,' he said. 'She always thinks something's going to happen to me.'

'That's understandable.'

'Maybe if you speak to her, though. She *might* let me.'

'You leave it to me.'

The boy lifted a hand to his brow. 'Is that someone waving to us over there?'

I squinted over at São Tiago and saw a figure on the bank waving both arms. 'Looks like it,' I said. 'Come on, let's paddle over, see what they want.'

When we arrived back at São Tiago, Paulo was waiting for us, standing on the bank taking the front of the canoe as we slipped into the shallow water.

'What's all the excitement?' I asked.

'You've got some business to see to,' he said as he helped us pull the boat ashore.

'What kind of business?'

'Important business.' Paulo used his thumb to point over his shoulder at Manolo's café. 'I just met God.'

I looked over to the café and saw a nervous looking Manolo placing a drink at one of the tables. The table was flanked by men with pistols on their hips, Luís and Lucas. On the other side of the road, I saw João in a bright green T-shirt, loitering in a doorway, providing some kind of back-up. There were other men, as well, two or three of them further down the street, but I didn't recognise them.

The only occupied seat under the Coca-Cola awning was taken by a woman. Catarina Da Silva.

'I better go see what she wants,' I said, dusting off my hands and looking at the boy. 'Why don't you run over to Ana's place. You can wait for me there.'

'I thought I'd come have a look at my clinic.' She started speaking as soon as I stepped under the awning. 'Check on my investment.' She twirled her glass on the table. 'It's a long time since I've been to São Tiago. It's a very dirty, dull little place.'

'A matter of opinion,' I said.

She let it pass. 'And the trouble you had?' She pushed her sunglasses up onto her head. The sun had begun its descent but there were still a good few hours of life left in it yet. 'Have you dealt with it?' She wanted me to see her eyes.

'It's in hand.' I resisted the temptation to glance at Manolo. 'It won't happen again.'

She twisted in her seat and stared directly at Manolo, who looked like he wanted the earth to swallow him whole, then she turned back to me. She showed me a knowing expression. Nothing escaped her. 'No, I'm sure it won't.' She touched her cheek with the fingertips of one hand. 'And the promise you had to keep? You kept it?'

'You've been here a while.' I pointed at her half-empty glass. 'You'll have seen me come back.'

She motioned to the men flanking the table and they moved away, pushing Manolo back to the bar, giving us some privacy.

Now that we were alone, she smiled in a suggestive manner. 'I wanted to see you.'

'You couldn't wait?'

'No. I couldn't.'

Her answer surprised me. As far as I knew, I was nothing to her but someone to satisfy a basic requirement. She had never expressed the need for anything else from me. And yet here she was, acting like a woman who was missing her lover. She looked almost as if she were excited about something that she was unable to keep to herself. It was a side to Catarina Da Silva I hadn't yet seen and I hoped there weren't too many more undiscovered facets to her personality.

'He's going away,' she said, keeping her voice low. 'Kiko. He's going on one of his trips next week.'

I waited.

'That's why he was still here this morning. Preparing. He'll be gone a whole week. You could come to the *fazenda*. Stay. Keep me company.' A thin smile crossed her lips as she considered the possibilities. It was a look that made me think of insects that eat their mates. She shifted in her seat again, both feet on the floor now.

'I'm not sure that would be a good idea,' I said.

'It would suit us both for you to stay with me a couple of

days. No need for morning meetings . . . well, not in the business sense anyway.'

'What about your husband? Someone would tell him.'

'*I'll* tell him. I'll say you're coming to stay as our guest; to discuss what you can do for us when we open to tourists.'

'You think he'll believe that?'

'I'll *make* him believe it.'

'I wouldn't be any kind of company,' I said. 'I drink too much.'

'We could drink together.'

'I don't think so.'

She put her forearms on the small table so that her knuckles touched mine. I withdrew my hands but she came closer, lowering her voice, her actions suggesting an intimacy between us.

'We'll have some fun, Sam. You and me together for all that time. Think of the things you can do to me.'

I remained impassive.

'Think of all the different ways you can have me,' she said.

She was wearing a low-cut top and the part of her chest that was on show began to flush, as I had seen it do so many times before, the redness spreading to her neck. Seeing her aroused like that made me wonder how it would feel to take her now, push her across the table and humiliate her in front of the whole town.

'I can't,' I said, forcing myself to put away the images which were coming to mind. 'There are too many risks. We should keep things as they are.'

She sat back, her face clouding. 'You're worried about losing your whore?'

With those words, the images were stripped from my head as if someone had opened a blind and let the sun back into a dark room. 'Keep her out of this,' I said.

'She's already a part of this,' she answered. 'And if she

becomes a nuisance to me, I can have her taken care of. Very easily.'

I stared at Catarina Da Silva, not sure how to reply. It was the first time she had made a direct threat, and her words were ones that I could not take to mean anything else. I did not want to risk angering her but what I wanted more than anything at that moment was for her to leave São Tiago and never come back. Until now, she had remained separate, sitting up on high in the *fazenda*, waving her hand, answering prayers and changing lives. I had been happy to be with her in her own kingdom. I had been willing to dominate our God in the way that she had wanted me to, but now she was here, walking among us, and it scared me. A God should not walk among her people.

'Leave Ana out of this,' I said through my teeth, struggling to keep my voice low. 'You touch her and I'll—'

'You'll what, Sam? What will you do?'

I searched for a suitable threat, wondering what on earth I could possibly do to Catarina Da Silva that would bend her to my will. I'd had plenty of time to consider this moment. The thought that Catarina Da Silva might turn on me had always been present at the back of mind – you keep snakes, you expect to be bitten – but I had never given myself the time to think about what I would do when it finally happened.

'There's nothing you can do, Sam. Anyway, what do you care? She's nothing more than a backstreet whore. And you're just another customer.'

It enraged me to hear Da Silva speak that way. Ana was superior to her in more ways than I could grasp. 'You know that if you do anything to her, you'd lose me.' I tried not to spit the words, but I couldn't help clenching my teeth as I spoke. Even so, it seemed to arouse Da Silva more.

'I could live with that.' She was enjoying this. She was revelling in the hold she had over me.

'And if I get to your husband first? If I tell him about us? About *you.*'

For the first time since I had known her, Catarina Da Silva's face fell. The redness around her neck and chest immediately drained, as if João had stuck his knife in her and bled her out. She took a deep breath and glared at me, her green eyes on me like a cobra ready to strike.

'What did you say he'd do?' I said, my heart thumping in my chest like a diesel engine, running fast enough to give light to São Tiago for a month. 'You said he'd kill both of us. Maybe even something worse.'

'You dare to threaten me?' she said, finding her voice again. 'After all I've done for you and your friends.'

'What?' I said. 'What have you done for us?'

'I'm giving you your clinic,' she replied, but I was beginning to wonder if we still needed her money. I'd saved a little from my job at Hevea and there was always Father Mateus in São Felix. I had disregarded Paulo's previous suggestion of asking for help, but things had changed. I was more eager to help now I had invested much of myself in the clinic. And perhaps even John Swan might persuade his American company to invest if they knew that the Church was involved. It always looked good for foreign companies to be seen putting something back into the land they were stripping.

'And don't pretend you don't enjoy our mornings together,' she added.

'I *did* enjoy them, but—'

'And now you're threatening me with my husband?'

'You threatened Ana,' I said.

'Maybe I need to show you what I can do, Sam. An example. Some kind of lesson?'

I held up my hands in surrender. I had used my bargaining chip, my only counter-threat, by mentioning her husband, and I was beginning to sense now that it was not enough; that perhaps it had made things worse. 'Let's calm down,' I said. 'Please. Let's talk about this some more.'

'I could have my men cut you down right now,' she said. 'How would you tell my husband about us then?'

Now it was my turn to drain of colour.

'Then I could send my men over to your whore's house to rape her and cut her throat. Or maybe I'll have her dragged up to the *fazenda* so that we can watch the men rape her one by one.'

I stood and looked down at her.

'Sit down, Sam.'

I hesitated, staring down at her, wanting to take my fishing knife from the back of my waistband and plunge it into her chest. I wanted to thrust it into her over and over again, spreading her blood across the concrete floor, spilling her life into Manny's café.

'Sit down,' she said again.

I forced myself to sit.

'But of course, you're right.' She had regained her composure completely now. She was back in control, the balance had been restored. She was in charge again. 'We should talk about this,' she said. 'But not here.' She shook her head. 'Not now.'

I fought to restrain my hammering heart.

'Let's sleep on it. Think about it for a while. Come to me on Monday and we'll speak about it again. See if I can't do something to persuade you.' She reached out and put her hand on my arm, sending shivers through me and making me want to recoil, wondering how I had ever wanted to touch such a creature; how I could have betrayed Ana, the one person who was so perfect for me. 'I know we'll come to the right decision.' Da Silva was no longer the beautiful, dangerous jaguar I had seen through a deceptive haze of lust. Now she was something else. Now that my eyes were clear, I could see her for what she really was. A Wandering Spider. Aggressive, venomous and deadly.

She stood, motioning to her men who came to her side.

'I'll see you on Monday, then,' she said. 'It's been nice talking to you. Always a pleasure.'

37

Ana was fixing a shirt when I pushed open the door. She glanced up and took her foot from the pedal of the sewing machine. 'Good catch?'

I looked at her, taking in everything about her, reminding myself what it was that meant so much to me. I had stayed at the café for a while after Da Silva left, drank a beer and collected my thoughts. I still didn't know what I was going to do about Da Silva, but I pushed her from my mind. I wanted to be calm when I went back to Ana. So when I was ready, I drove the pickup over to her place and went in, pretending that nothing was wrong.

'Did you have a good catch?' she asked again.

'Yeah. Not too bad.' I nodded to the boy, who was sitting at the table drinking a Coke and reading a book. I took the fish to the sink. 'Didn't he tell you?' I rinsed them under the tap.

'No *filhote* again,' she said.

I washed my hands with soap and went to Ana, kissing the top of her head. 'No sign of him. I've almost given up hope.'

'You smell of fish,' she laughed and pushed me away.

I pulled her from her seat and held her to me. 'I told the boy we should take you with us one day. We're going to stay on the beach. Fish at night.'

'And dig for turtle's eggs,' said the boy.

'Yeah, that too,' I agreed.

I broke off my embrace with Ana, holding her at arm's length to look at her. I wondered how I could ever have betrayed her. 'You know, I realised something today,' I told her. 'Father Machado would have been proud of our clinic. He would have said we're trying to make a difference; that we're trying to make life better for the people of São Tiago. I think he'd be proud of what we're doing. In some ways, it's a memorial for him.'

'Even with Da Silva's involvement?' Just the mention of the name dulled my spirits, but I fought to hide it.

I looked at the boy, his nose still in the book and I wondered if he was listening to us. 'Why don't you go read on the porch for a while,' I said. 'I'll be out in a minute, we'll drive down to the clinic, see if Paulo needs some help. Maybe do a little fishing from the *Hotel Fluctuante*.' I waited until he was outside, sitting on the other side of the screen door.

'We couldn't do this without her help,' I said keeping my voice down, not wanting to involve the boy. 'Father Machado wouldn't have liked it, but he would've understood.'

Ana broke away and went back to her sewing. 'I saw you with her just now. At Manolo's.'

I felt my mood sink further as I watched her work the pedal again, the clattering filling the room. It was an old machine and when I had enough money, I planned to buy her a new one.

'It's good you're happy, Sam, but she terrifies me. I don't think you can handle her like you thought you could, and this whole thing with Manolo makes her more dangerous.' She paused, turned the cloth, continued.

'She won't harm him. I've spoken to her ab—'

'Her coming to São Tiago today frightens me. People like her don't come to places like this.'

'She came here because she sees the clinic as an investment,' I said. 'She wanted to see it for herself. And to satisfy herself that I'm dealing with any problems. Manny, the fire.' I was

327

lying to her now, trying to soothe her. It was the first time I'd been forced to do such a thing, and my strained good manner was giving way to my true feelings as I struggled with all types of emotions; emotions which followed me wherever I went. Guilt, shame, fear. Ana was right to be afraid of Da Silva, she was a dangerous woman and I thought that I could manage her, but I was wrong. And now my association with her had begun to creep between the relationship I had with Ana. Had I been stronger, more able to resist my lust for Da Silva and thought more carefully about my actions, I would have known that this moment was inevitable.

'It's you she wants,' Ana said, her pinpoint intuition making my stomach lurch. Ana had judged Da Silva well from what she had seen. 'She doesn't want a clinic. I've always thought it, but now I *know* it. I'm only glad you're as strong as you are.' She didn't look up from the fabric, but stopped the machine as if she were waiting for me to confirm this last statement. She wanted me to reassure her, but I didn't know what to say.

I watched Ana's fingers hold the material taut as she passed it under the needle. The muscle in her calf tightened as she worked the pedal again. I glanced at the boy sitting outside, still deep in his book. 'She doesn't want *me*,' I said, putting my hand on her shoulder. 'What would she want me for? Why would you say—'

'I saw, Sam, I was watching. The whole *town* was watching. *Every*one saw her touch you and whisper to you.'

'Maybe she's like that with everyone.' A weak attempt to steer her away from any unwanted conclusions. She couldn't find out. I couldn't bear to see the look on her face, to face her rejection if she were to discover me. Da Silva I could lose, *wanted* to lose, but not Ana. Not Ana.

'Surely you're not so blind that you don't know when a woman is interested in you. You may have been a priest, Sam, but you're still a man. Anyone could see what she wanted.' She stopped the machine again. 'Didn't she tell you she's bored? That her husband cheats on her? Maybe she's looking for something to occupy her time. Or maybe she wants to cheat on *him*.' Perhaps she suspected already, wondering about my relationship with Da Silva, but afraid to voice it, afraid to ask me directly, afraid that it might be true.

'No. There must be other things, other people,' I protested. 'I mean, what the hell would someone like her see in someone like me?' It was as much a question that I needed her to answer, as it was a question that was intended to misdirect her.

'God knows what a woman like her wants. The same things I do? The sensitivity you try to hide. Your strength.'

I felt myself flush and I was unable to speak. I had deceived Ana most horribly, lying to myself and persuading myself that I had done it for her, for my friends and for the clinic, and here she was, telling me my virtues.

'Or maybe she just sees you as a challenge. A prize to be won. Something to own.'

'Da Silva already owns me. She owns all of us,' I said. 'So how do I put her off? You're a woman. How could I put *you* off?' Perhaps there was a way to push Da Silva aside without appearing to. Perhaps Ana could think of something; something which had not occurred to me.

Or perhaps I should tell her the truth right now.

'Coming home every night smelling of fish might work,' she suggested, maybe seeing the need to lighten the mood. 'But I'm not Catarina Da Silva. I'm not even sure what kind of a woman she is. She might not be the sort who's easily put off.' Ana stood and began clearing her things from the table. 'But you need to do something.'

'Like what?'

'Perhaps Papagaio could help.' She stopped and looked at the boy through the screen door, as if she'd just realised what she'd said. Her arms were crossed in front of her, rolls of material held tight.

'What're you suggesting, Ana?'

'I don't know. Nothing.' Despite everything that Ana was, she was still a product of São Tiago, and in this town, lead and steel were always waiting, whispering from just below the surface, asking to be put to use.

'It's not the answer.' I was telling myself as much as I was telling Ana. It was, after all, a possible solution to my predicament. With Da Silva dead, I would no longer have anything to fear from her. Of course, the money for the clinic would stop, but I'd already thought about that. If the church at São Felix would endorse us, give us a little money – which they were more likely to do with the Da Silvas gone – the Americans were sure to follow. I almost found myself hoping for Da Silva's death, but knew I could never be involved in such violence.

'I was wrong to say it, Sam, I'm sorry,' Ana shook her head. 'I wasn't serious anyway, not really. You know me better than that.'

I took the rolls of fabric from her arms and dropped them to the floor. I held Ana tight and waited for her to do the same. 'We'll be OK,' I said. 'I'll do something. It'll all be fine.' We stayed like that until Ana broke away and reached up to put her hands on either side of my face.

'Perhaps you need to remind her you're a priest,' she said.

'But I'm not. Not really.'

'Then lie, Sam. You can do that, can't you?'

'I can try.' I looked down at the rolls of material on the floor, my eyes going to a bundle of clothing under the table. I immediately recognised the green dress on top. It was the dress Catarina da Silva had worn that first time. I could see that the shoulder strap was torn and I remembered how I had ripped it in my urge to remove it, to lay my hands on her flesh.

'She's been here?' I said, feeling anger rising in me again.

330

Ana followed my gaze. 'Da Silva? Yes. She brought some work.'

'And you took it on?'

'How could I say no, Sam? What would—' She stopped. 'How do you know that's hers?'

'Hmm?' I looked up, realising my mistake, thinking quickly to cover my tracks, almost wanting to tell Ana the truth. 'She wore that to the barbecue,' I said. 'The one at John's place that time.'

Ana looked up at me. 'And you remember that?'

I shrugged.

'She must have made an impression,' she said.

'Oh,' I replied. 'She certainly does *that*.'

Ana kept her eyes on me as if she were searching for something, suspecting me of hiding something from her, so I smiled and turned away. 'I better go,' I said. 'I can't leave him sitting there all afternoon.'

Ana didn't reply immediately.

'We'll go see if Paulo needs help.'

'Yeah. OK.' She spoke slowly. 'I'll see you later.'

I kissed her and called to the boy as I let the screen door bang shut behind me. I could still feel Ana's eyes on my back as I climbed into the cab.

I started the engine as the boy ran round to the other side and climbed in, slamming the door and turning to look at me. 'That lady at the café today?' he said. 'She's Da Silva?'

'Yes.' I looked at him as I pulled away and steered us down towards the clinic.

'I remember her from the barbecue.'

'Oh?'

'I saw you with her.'

'Did you?'

'Mm. But she was wearing a pink dress, not a green one.'

I stopped at the junction with the *rua*, looking both ways

before starting to pull out, turning left, heading to the clinic where I could see the men still working. Closer, the café, a few men coming towards it, the first one stepping under the awning. I looked at the boy, wondering what else he had heard. 'Oh,' I said. 'Was she? I don't remember.'

I was about to give it some gas, head out onto the road, when something distracted me and made me stop. The man who stepped under the café awning just a few moments ago was wearing a bright green T-shirt. The same colour that João had been wearing just an hour before.

It made me think about the way Catarina Da Silva had looked at Manny, and I remembered what she had said to me earlier that day. *Maybe I need to show you what I can do? An example. Some kind of lesson.*

38

I lurched the pickup to a standstill, throwing us forward in our seats.

'Get out,' I said to the boy.

'Why? What's wrong?' His eyes were wide, his expression frantic.

'Get out. Go to Ana's place. Now.'

He hesitated, one hand going to the door handle, his head still turned in my direction. He'd be wondering if he had done something wrong, but I didn't have time to explain my urgency.

'Run.' This time I shouted, no doubt scaring him, but needing him to get out and run to safety. If I was right about what was going to happen at the café, it was something I didn't want the boy to see.

The boy was shocked into action, throwing open the door and jumping down from the cab. As soon as he was on the dirt, I started moving, the open door swinging to click shut as I sped away.

Reginaldo, the guard, looked up from his post at the bank as I passed, one hand half raised in greeting. Behind him, the bank was deserted; the manager the only person inside, his feet up on the desk, his head turning to follow my progress. On the floating hotel, André was scrubbing the top deck with an old mop. Jeans rolled to his knees, bare chest and bare feet. He stopped mopping, one arm cradling the wooden shaft, his spare hand lifting to shade his eyes as he watched me approach the café, sounding the horn, calling Manolo's name from the open window. Paulo and Papagaio stopped what they were doing and looked up, along with the other workers at the clinic.

Beneath the Coca-Cola awning, Manolo was unmoved by my efforts to attract his attention because he was already concentrating on the three men in his café; the three men who now faced him, standing about him in a semicircle, like wolves preparing to make a kill. As I slowed the pickup to a halt, João struck out at Manolo, hitting him directly in the face. Once, twice, knocking him to the ground, while the other two squatted down to restrain Manolo's arms and bare his throat to João's knife. Manolo was to be bled, like a beast, right there in his own café.

I jumped from the cab, covering the red dirt in a second, and hit João at a run. I balled into him, lowering my shoulders to catch him, and knocked him onto the bare concrete, his knife skittering away under one of the tables. His two friends turned their attention away from Manolo, making a grab for me, but I pushed them away and faltered backwards as Manolo saw his chance and shuffled away on his hands and knees.

I stood firm, breathing heavily as João and his men got to their feet, coming to face me.

'Go back.' I made the words sound strong. 'Go home. There will be no killing here.'

The men stepped closer, hands reaching under their shirts, fingers curling around well-used revolvers, one of them staying his hand for a heartbeat as our eyes locked. I hadn't recognised him. He'd had his back to me and my attention was concentrated on João, but now I had time to look at him, I recognised him immediately. Anderson. The man who had given me a lift back from the *fazenda* on the day that Catarina Da Silva had laid Manny's life in my hands. The same man who had thanked me for trying to help Eduardo. He blinked

334

hard, recognition evident, then looked at João as if waiting for his instruction.

'She wants him punished,' João said before I could speak. 'For burning her clinic.'

'I've spoken with the Senhora,' I told him, watching Anderson a moment longer before turning my attention to João. 'I'll deal with this myself.'

Paulo and Papagaio came to stand with me as João levelled his big revolver at my face and moved the barrel from side to side. He aimed it first at my right eye, then at my left.

'She said to teach you a lesson. Show you what happens by making him sorry.' He brushed the steel against the tip of my nose, pointed it at my mouth. 'And that means only one thing.' His voice was calm, but there was an edge to it. I could tell he was excited by the thought of killing me.

'I can do that without needing to cut his throat,' I said.

'Not what the Senhora wants.'

'I'll talk to her.'

'She wants me to bleed him like an animal and hang him from your clinic. I'll do my job, and then I'll be gone.' He glanced around at the café, searching for his prey. 'Don't get in my way, priest. Not again. God can't help you here. He doesn't see São Tiago.'

'And what about you?' I looked directly at Anderson who blinked again, his eyelids flicking up and down a number of times in rapid succession. A nervous twitch that I hoped betrayed his confusion rather than demonstrated his agitation. 'You want to see a man bleed?'

Anderson shrugged his shoulders and frowned at João.

'What are you talking about?' asked João. 'What difference does it make what he wants?'

'You want another man to die here?' I persisted. 'You want *me* to watch another man die? Bleed to death right here in front of the whole town?' I looked around, but there weren't many

335

people to be seen. 'In front of this man?' I indicated Paulo standing beside me. 'The doctor who tried to save Eduardo's life. The *good* man. That's what you called him the first time we met.'

'He killed my friend.' Anderson spoke with a quiet voice. Almost like he was trying to convince himself this was the right thing to do. As if he felt the need to punish the man who had taken his friend from him, but knew this was not the way to do it. I thought it significant, too, that Eduardo was now his friend, as if Anderson had spent time considering what his relationship had been with the dead man. The day he had brought me back to São Tiago, Anderson had said that Eduardo was just a man, that he knew him and that was all. But time had made him realise that Eduardo was more than that, and it gave me a good feeling despite my current predicament.

João glanced at him, a quick flick of his eyes. 'What's he talking about?'

'So now you think *he* deserves to die?' I asked, sensing something better in Anderson; something deeper. 'Another life gone. And then who kills you? Where does it stop?'

Anderson stayed quiet.

'And why haven't you come here before now? If you knew it was him. If you knew it was Manny, I mean. Why didn't you come to kill him before?' I shook my head. 'It's because you're better than that, Anderson. I can see it.'

'What do you know about who he is?' João sneered. 'You don't know what he's done.'

'I know he's a good man,' I said. 'He thanked me for trying to save his friend.'

'What friend?' João spat the word, as if it were venom on his tongue.

'No killing,' I said, still watching Anderson. 'No more wasted lives. Go home.'

João grabbed the neck of my T-shirt with his left hand and forced the barrel of the gun under my chin, the steel pressed hard against my flesh. 'Enough of this shit. This isn't the first time you've got in my way, given me orders. Don't tell me what to do, *gringo*. No one tells me what to do.'

'Except Da Silva,' I said, all my focus on João. 'And she won't be pleased if something happens to me.'

'Don't be clever.' He pushed the pistol hard enough to restrict my breathing. 'I can make you bleed just the same as anyone else. Don't push your luck. You want to be even closer to God?'

I wondered if I would have the chance to share my life with Ana; if I would ever fish again. 'But if you kill me,' I managed, 'how will I build Da Silva's clinic? How would she like that?'

'She'll get someone else.'

'Who?'

He shook his head at me. 'You think anyone would care if I shot you right here, left you to bleed in the dirt?'

'I'd care.' The voice came from somewhere behind me, and when João loosened his grip, I turned my head to see André still on the top deck of his floating hotel. He was looking down at us, along the barrel of the twenty-two he used to shoot *paca*.

I called to him. 'It's all right, André.' I was grateful for my friend's help, but I didn't want any violence committed in my name. 'Put it down.'

'Not a chance,' he replied.

João stared up at André for a moment and then looked back at me. He pushed me away, but his gun stayed level, still close to my face.

The other two men raised their weapons and pointed them up at André. He was protected by the barrier that ran around the top of the floating hotel, but I still didn't rate his chances. Those *pistolas* looked quick and light, and the men holding them were eager to use them. I'd seen the same look in the eyes of the men on the road back from the sawmill.

'So what happens now?' I said to João.

The crease on his brow deepened. 'Maybe I tell my people to kill your friend up there.'

'And you? Will he shoot you first? Or maybe you?' I spoke to Anderson. 'You want to die here today? Put your gun down, Anderson. You too, João. You don't want this.' I wondered if André would even do it.

Anderson blinked again, squeezing his eyes hard like he was trying to block out my voice.

I glanced at Papagaio and Paulo beside me. Beyond them, I saw movement and I focused away from my friends to see Reginaldo, the fat bank guard, coming towards us. His hand slipping down to his holster, removing the catch and lifting out that big old revolver with surprising dexterity. His footfall was heavy, though, and as he approached, one of João's men turned, stretching his gun out in front of him, turning his aim to meet the new threat.

So now nobody was in control. Not them and not us.

And then Manolo straightened it out.

'For Christ's sake,' he said. 'Will you people put away your guns?'

Manny was a sneaky bastard, I'd always known it, and he'd taken a chance when he saw it. I thought he'd run away to cower, but now he was standing just a few metres away from João. Manolo was holding a shotgun. It wasn't the best shotgun I'd ever seen, and if he'd fired it from where he was, he probably would have killed me too, but it didn't really matter because it had the effect he wanted.

João paused, lowered his weapon. 'I'll come back for you,' he said to Manny, motioning to his partners, waving his hand downwards, telling them to do the same. 'You too,' he pointed at me. 'On the river, on the street, or maybe some time when you're sitting outside your place with your bitch whore. Maybe not to kill you, eh? Maybe I'll just hurt you.'

I could feel the adrenalin surging through my body. My heart was thumping in my throat, my head was pounding, my arms and legs were tingling, but I stood my ground. I did what I could to look unafraid.

'And you,' he looked at Papagaio. 'I'm going to have your tongue.'

Papagaio raised his middle finger.

João turned to me and stared for a moment, then grunted and walked away. His men followed him, Anderson desperate not to make eye contact, but unable to resist a quick glance before he turned away. I wondered, if it had come to it, whether the young man would have been able to take a life. Perhaps he would have placed his loyalty in João and his men – gritted his teeth and pulled the trigger – but part of me wanted to believe that when the time had come, Anderson would have thrown down his pistol and walked away.

We all watched them go, none of us saying a word until they had climbed into their vehicle and driven out of São Tiago.

When I turned to Manny, he shrugged, touching the fingers of his left hand to his throat. 'Thanks,' he said, and he tried to smile.

'And you,' I said, looking at the shotgun in his hand, wondering if Manny had learned anything from what had happened over the past few months.

39

When they were gone, and our hearts had recovered their true pace, we went over to Manny's café and he opened a few beers telling us they were on the house. He made a joke about not threatening to shoot us if we didn't offer to pay, but none of us felt much like laughing. André came down from his boat to join us, Reginaldo too, Papagaio asking who was going to look after the bank if he wasn't there.

'I can see it from here,' he said, like he didn't care. 'Anyway, I've been guarding that bank more years than I want to remember and there's never anyone tried to rob it. Don't think there's even any money inside. And now I have the wild bunch to help me out, so there's nothing to worry about. I'll have a beer, then maybe I'll go back.' It was more words in one sentence than I'd heard him say in years. 'First time I ever pulled my gun,' he added, patting the worn leather holster.

'Well, you must've been practising at home in front of the mirror, because you drew it like Clint Eastwood,' said Paulo, putting a hand on Reginaldo's shoulder before quickly removing it and looking at it. 'All that tension made you sweat, huh?'

We pulled a couple of tables together and sat down, none of us saying much as we took our first gulps of beer and lit cigarettes. We didn't want to believe how close to death we had just come.

I took a seat at the table that gave me a view away from the river. Usually I liked to look at the water, but today I wanted to be able to see Ana's place. I kept my eyes on it, seeing the door open after just a few minutes, watching Ana step out into the street. She raised a hand to her brow and looked over at us, the men sitting in the café drinking beer. I got to my feet and stepped out from under the awning, waving to Ana, showing her that everything was OK. I tapped my watch, indicating that I would join her in a while. She held her hands out at shoulder level then threw them down as if she wasn't happy with the situation. But when I gave her a thumbs-up, she shook her head and went back inside. She couldn't leave the boy alone, not after seeing the men with guns, and she wouldn't want to bring him down to the café where the danger had been.

When I came back to the table, the others were all watching me.

'Thank you,' Manolo said. 'For what you did. For stopping them like that. I'm sorry for what I did to you. Ana too.'

I exchanged a glance with Paulo and Papagaio. It struck me how a tense situation can bring people together, make friends out of enemies, force people to do what's right. It wasn't so long ago I had held a gun to Manolo's head, and yet today I had saved his life. And he had saved mine in return.

'It's a good thing, what you just did,' I said to Manny. 'I thought you'd run away.' And, perhaps worse, he could have tried to kill those men – sneak up on them and shoot them dead with his shotgun – but he hadn't. If Manny had decided on a different course of action, the main street of São Tiago might now be thick with blood. Mine included.

He flushed, trying to laugh it off, saying, 'They came in as customers. They didn't pay for their beers.'

I acknowledged his attempt at humour.

'You think they'll come back?' said Paulo, to no one in particular.

'Let them come.' Manolo was brimming with bravado. He

was sitting with one hand on the barrel of his shotgun, the butt planted firmly on the ground. Now he yanked it up and took it by the stock, brandishing it before him.

'They won't come,' I said.

'They'll come for me,' said Manolo. 'They'll come to do what they were told.'

'No,' said Papagaio. 'They'll come for all of us. You 'cause it's his job. Me, because João lost face and he'll take any excuse to come after me. Reginaldo and André for pointing guns, and Sam? Shit, Sam pissed him off more than anyone,' he said. 'No one likes to get stopped by a smart-arse priest. This is about something else now, Manny, not just you. They'll come and there will be more than three of them.'

I looked around at my friends, seeing the mixture of fear and excitement on their faces. I saw the way their attention switched from Papagaio, the man with a reputation for killing, to me, the man who was supposed to respond to a higher authority. I wondered if I should tell them I believed Papagaio's gun to be more effective than my prayer.

'What do you suggest, Papagaio?' I said. 'What would you do?'

'We should take this right back to them,' he said. 'I wouldn't give them a chance to regroup. Stop João before this goes any further.'

'Then I say we get ready to go after them,' said Manolo, still hefting his shotgun. 'Right now.'

'You'd fight?' I asked. 'Kill, even?'

'Whatever I have to do. There are six of us here, we can make enough noise.'

'What if he's called more people? What if they're now ten men?' I said to him. 'Ten guns? Twenty?' There had been enough violence. Everywhere I went it was waiting for me. 'We can't stop that many.' I looked down at my hands and studied the nicotine stains on my fingers.

'They have ten guns, then we have to be ready for that,' Manny said. He had killed at least once before; perhaps it wouldn't be so hard for him to kill again, even after everything that had happened between us. For me it was different. I had no taste for it.

'We have, what?' said Paulo. 'A shotgun, a rifle and a pistol? You think that'll be enough?' He turned to Papagaio who was watching me, studying the expression on my face. 'Maybe we can curse them? You think that'll be enough, Papagaio? You think that'll chase them off?'

'No.' Papagaio was still watching me. 'It won't. We need to take this to them right now. Find João right now while he's just one man. Three at most. Sam here has his twenty-two, and I have one of my own. A *pistola*, too. I've seen Sam shoot, he's pretty good.' He turned to Paulo. 'You? You can't shoot for shit, so maybe you should take my shotgun.'

'How many guns you got?' Reginaldo this time.

'Enough for us all.' Papagaio drained his beer.

'I'm with you,' said Manolo. 'We go now, finish it tonight. Reginaldo?'

Reginaldo closed his eyes and nodded his head. 'OK.'

'Paulo?'

Part of me wanted to give them my blessing and send them out with their guns and their dark aggression. João was a dangerous man and he frightened me even though I had stepped up against him. He had threatened my friends and he had threatened Ana, but while I had to find a way to stop him, I couldn't sanction my friends to take up their weapons and use them to destroy life. There had to be another way to settle this. There *had* to be.

'There won't be any killing,' I said. 'I can't believe you're even talking about it. And you, Manny, after everything that happened? I'm going to talk to Da Silva, and I'm going to sort this out. It's ridiculous, talking like we're killers. None of us is like that. Not any more.' I looked at Papagaio and then at Manolo.

'What about Jose?' asked Paulo. 'Shouldn't we tell him what's going on? He *is* supposed to be a policeman.'

'When was the last time you saw him do anything?' said Reginaldo.

'When was the last time I saw *you* do anything?' Paulo replied. 'Ever since I've been here, I only ever saw you standing outside that bank. I've seen you grow fatter, never heard you say more than "Good morning", and never once seen you lift a finger to do anything.' He stared at Reginaldo who was leaning back in his seat as if Paulo were about to physically attack him. 'And yet today I finally meet you, talk to you, I see you draw your gun and point it at another person, and now you're talking about killing a man?' Paulo paused. 'So maybe people can surprise you. Maybe we should let José do his job.' Reginaldo eased a little in his seat and Paulo half smiled at him. 'Was it loaded, by the way?'

Reginaldo opened his mouth to speak, like he was going to say of course it was loaded, but he stopped himself and closed it again.

'Jose is no use to us,' I told them. 'As far as I can tell, he's in Da Silva's pocket. It's standard practice. The law and the landowners walk hand in hand. Anyway, he's just one man.' I looked round at my friends, realising that I needed to restore some sense to our situation. They were agitated and I wanted to offer a solution that would not make them afraid for their lives. I needed to reassure myself, too.

'I'll go talk to her,' I said again, hoping I might have some influence with her. 'I'll sort it out.'

'I have a wife,' said Reginaldo. 'You think she'll be safe if we don't go after them? Or even if we do?'

'You have a wife, Reggie?' I said, looking over at Papagaio. 'I never knew that. What's her name?' Papagaio was watching

Reginaldo now, then looking away and pinching the top of his nose, squeezing his eyes shut and rubbing them.

'Eliana.'

'Nice name,' I said. 'I never even knew you were married. You don't wear a ring.' I pointed at his hand.

'Couldn't afford one,' he said. 'Other things seemed more important. We don't have much.'

'What the hell has this got to do with anything?' said Manolo. 'What I want to know is whether we're going after them or not.'

I looked at him. 'I already told you, Manny; I'm going up there to sort this out. No blood lost. After that—'

'It's my fight, Sam. They came for me. I should do whatever I have to.'

'No, Manny, it's not your fight any more. They threatened all of us. Even Ana. This belongs to all of us, now. And *I* am going to put a stop to it.'

It wasn't late, not long after five, but it was starting to get dark now and Manolo had switched on the lights under the awning, the bare bulbs hanging from wires strung from one side of the café to the other. Already, the bugs had begun to dance in the halos.

'You gonna go up there on your own?' Manolo asked.

'Yes,' I said, looking over at Ana's place, reassuring myself that everything was quiet. I wondered what the boy was doing. If he was still reading, or if he and Ana were doing something else.

'You really think it will make a difference? You think those guys who were here today will just forget about this?' Manolo looked at me. 'Even if you *do* sort something with Da Silva?'

'Yes.' I made myself believe it.

'I reckon it's gone further than that now,' Manolo said. 'She hasn't got that much control over those men. They lost face today, they'll be back. After what happened here, they won't care what Da Silva tells them. We should do what Papagaio says. Go after them and finish it.'

'I agree with Sam.' Paulo looked at Manolo. 'No fighting.'

'I can make her stop them,' I said, glad for Paulo's support. 'Maybe now it's time for us all just to calm down and get some rest.'

'Rest?' said Manolo. 'With João out there? I don't think I'm going to rest until—'

'That's enough, Manny. No more beer. Come on, you should all go home. Get some sleep. Reggie, your wife will be worried.'

'I'm not sleeping,' said Manny.

'Maybe you should pray for us.' Reginaldo looked up. His eyes were half closed and weighed down by heavy bags.

'I will,' I lied.

'Pray for us and we'll be OK. Maybe they won't do anything knowing you're a priest. It might even put off a man like João. What d'you think, Papagaio?' He looked over at Papagaio and I did the same thing, wondering what my friend would answer.

Papagaio shook his head and reached out to put a hand on Reginaldo, then he looked at me, saying, 'You're wrong, Sam. You can't send us home. João will come back to finish what he started. Not because Da Silva told him to, but because he likes it. I know him, Sam, remember that. I've seen João beat a man until he came apart. Took an axe handle and beat him until you couldn't even tell he'd been a man.' I'd heard the story many times, but never before had it made me feel as cold as it did that night. 'I've seen him swing his machete into a woman's head, shoot men in the mouth, throw people in the river with their hands and feet tied.'

Manolo put his head in his hands and looked down at the table. Reginaldo just shook his from side to side.

'I saw him cut out a man's tongue,' Papagaio went on. 'Said

the guy talked too much. I've seen him press his thumbs into a man's eyes, push a knife into—'

'OK, Papagaio, I think we all get the picture now.' I didn't need to hear any more, and I was annoyed at him for stirring us up again. He'd scared me, too, now, and I couldn't shake the image of João creeping into Ana's house and murdering us both in our beds.

'We should go after him, Sam. You don't have to come. I'll go with Manny.'

Manny nodded.

'But you have no way of knowing where he is right now,' I argued. 'Where would he go?' Papagaio could be decisive when it came to matters of violence and brutality, but did not have a great capacity for forward planning. 'There's no point just arming ourselves and running out into the fields.'

Papagaio thought for a moment. 'Then we need to stay together,' he replied. 'Stay together and wait for him. I'm sure he'll come tonight.'

'Why tonight?'

'He's not a thinker,' said Papagaio. 'He's a man of action. He'll want to do this now; tonight.' He looked around the table: a café owner, a fat guard, a hotel owner, a failed doctor and a failed priest. 'We don't exactly have an army, do we? So we need somewhere to go. Somewhere to defend.' His eyes rested on André. 'The *Hotel Fluctuante*. That's where we'll go. It's the safest place for us. We should go there now, wait for João to come back.'

I put my hands over my face and shook my head.

'I'll go and get my guns,' Papagaio said.

'You won't need them,' I told him.

Papagaio shrugged. 'It'll make me feel better.'

I sighed and stood up. 'OK, then I'd better try to put a stop to this before—'

'You should stay here, Sam.' Papagaio put a hand out, trying to make me sit down. 'It would be safer.'

I shook my head. 'I have to take the boy home. After that I'll go to the *fazenda*.'

'You're driving up to Hevea?' said Papagaio.

'I have to.' I didn't relish the idea of driving out of São Tiago when I knew João was somewhere out there, but I had to take the boy to safety, and I had to get to the *fazenda* before things escalated. I had already resolved to give Da Silva whatever she wanted. For the safety of Ana and my friends, I would do anything she asked of me in return for her promise that no harm would come to them. I just hoped that she would be receptive to my pleas.

Papagaio pulled me back down into my seat. 'You need to speak to Senhor Swan. He's your friend. Tell him what's happened. Tell him you want to borrow his men.'

I found myself nodding.

'We need men like that,' said Papagaio. 'With those men and those guns . . .' He whistled. 'That's exactly what we need tonight.'

'I'll see what I can do.' I would certainly feel safer with such men around me, but I knew I wouldn't ask for their help. I would find a resolution that did not allow for bullets and blades. I would settle my differences with Da Silva.

'And don't stop on the road. Not for anybody.'

Paulo held up his hands and hushed us, saying, 'Shhh.'

We all fell silent, noticing that the cicadas had stopped singing. We listened to the low hum of the generator, audible now the insects were quiet.

'Rain,' said Papagaio.

'It's too early,' I replied. 'It shouldn't come like this for at least two weeks.'

'What is it then?' said Paulo.

We heard the sky moan somewhere beyond the town, saw a

flicker of light, and we sensed the steady fall of rain beyond São Tiago. Within a few minutes, the sheet came into view above the low buildings. A curtain of downpour like a misty wall advancing towards us, obscuring the town as it came. We stayed silent as it approached, the sound of the heavy drops penetrating the red dust, beating the bricks and tin roofs like a hail of stones.

And then it was on us, battering the Coca-Cola awning with the ferocity of a wet-season storm. The grazing lands would welcome it, soak it up with an intense thirst. The river would rise again and the beaches would sink beneath its surface. The Araguaia would break its banks and the fish would spill out. The rains would bring new life. And in the forest, the burning would stop.

I breathed in the heavy smell of the wet earth that was pushed under the awning by the force of the torrent, and I enjoyed the vitality it carried with it. I listened as it passed over us and around us, battering the corrugated roof of Manolo's kitchen and stirring the waters of the Araguaia into a froth.

'Bloody rain,' said Paulo. 'When it comes, there's always too much.'

I nudged my friend. 'I said you'd complain.'

I waited a few minutes before I got to my feet and took the pickup keys from the table. I asked Paulo to come with me, ride up to Ana's place and bring her back to the *Hotel Fluctuante* with the others. I wanted to keep her with me, not let her out of my sight, but I couldn't take her to the *fazenda*. Especially after what Da Silva had said that afternoon. Papagaio came too, saying he'd go back to his place, collect his guns and head straight back to André's.

We nodded goodbye to the other men, who were already getting to their feet, and we stepped out into the rain. We didn't bother to run; just a few seconds in a downpour like this was enough to soak you through.

'I should come with you,' Paulo said, coming alongside me. 'To Hevea. The *fazenda* too.'

'No.'

'It might be better with two of us. Safer.'

I looked at my friends, standing with me in the rain. 'They know about Ana,' I told them. 'You heard João.'

'I heard,' Paulo said.

'I can't take her with me, it's too dangerous. That's why I need you to stay here with her. You too, Papagaio. Take her to André's with the others. Keep her safe. Protect her for me.'

Papagaio came forward and put his arms around me, the brim of his battered hat rough against my cheek. The rain made a hollow drumming sound as it battered the crown of straw. He smelled of damp sweat and wet dirt, but it didn't matter. 'I'll die for her if I have to,' he said. 'For you too.' He slapped me hard on the back, then released me and opened the cab door. He climbed into the pickup without looking at me.

Paulo wiped his soaking hair from his face, messing it up even more than it was already. He was dishevelled, drenched to the core, but we stayed where we were, feeling the cool water on our skin.

'She called her a whore,' I told him. 'Said Ana is a backstreet whore and I'm just another customer.'

The rain was fresh and clean, but there were many things it could not wash away.

'It's not true, is it?' I looked at him.

'What you and Ana have is good. Don't let Da Silva crawl inside your head.' He wiped the drops from his eyes. 'You know, teaching John's boy wasn't my idea, Sam; it was Ana's. The job too. She put you right, not me. Ana fixed you like no one else could.'

'I think I love her.' I didn't know what else to say.

Paulo nodded and looked at Papagaio sitting in the cab. 'We've known that for a long time.'

40

I could see that Ana was frantic when she opened the door to us.

'I didn't know what to do.' She came outside and closed the door behind her, not wanting the boy to hear. 'I came to see what was happening and I saw those men with guns. What's going on? Are you all right?' She glanced at Paulo, standing out of the rain, then at Papagaio who was jogging into the darkness, heading back to his place.

'We're fine,' I told her. 'For now, anyway. But you're going to have to leave the house, Ana. Go with Paulo. He'll tell you what's happened.'

'And you? Where are you going?'

'I need to take the boy home,' I said. 'It's not safe for him here right now. Not with us. I'll take him home and come straight back.'

'I'm coming with you,' she said. 'I'm safest with you.'

'No.' I was abrupt. 'You need to go with Paulo.'

'Why?'

'I have to go to the *fazenda*. Those men you saw, that's where they're from. Da Silva's people. They came to find Manny, punish him for what he did to the clinic but now . . .' I didn't have time to explain it all to her. 'I have to go to the *fazenda*, get Da Silva to call off her men.'

'I'll come with you.'

'No. You can't come to the *fazenda*.'

'Why not? Maybe she'll listen to another woman.'

I put my hands on her shoulders. 'Not to you. Please, Ana, just trust me. Go with Paulo.'

Paulo came closer, his hand reaching for Ana's arm.

'Why can't I just stay here, then? What have *I* got to be afraid of?'

'I'll explain everything when I get back.'

Ana looked at me as if she suddenly understood. She took a step back from me, my arms falling to my sides, and she pulled open the screen door. 'Go,' she said. 'Do what you have to do.'

I went in and called to the boy, telling him to get in the pickup.

When he was in, I leaned into the cab, taking hold of my rifle and handing it to Paulo. He shook his head. 'You take it,' he said. 'You might need it. Papagaio has enough for all of us.'

I hesitated, looking at Ana, then replaced the rifle behind the bench seat.

'Take care of her,' I said to Paulo. 'Go straight to the hotel. Run. Don't stop.'

Ana came to me as I was about to climb in, pulling me back, kissing me and holding me tight.

'Come back to me,' she said. 'Whatever happens.'

I drove straight out of town, leaving the whitewashed buildings behind, and headed onto the fence-lined road. In the night and the rain, there was nothing to see but the blurred cone of light from the headlamps, filled with the torrential downpour. The wipers struggled to keep my vision clear and I sat forward in my seat, keeping as close to the glass as I could. The once dry road quickly became waterlogged and the ground was soft under the pickup. The tyres spun in the mud, the vehicle sliding from side to side, so I eased off the accelerator and kept a firm grip on the wheel.

Beside me, the boy asked what was happening, but I ignored his question, telling him to take my rifle from behind the seat and load it. 'You know how,' I said. 'The shells are still in the glove box.'

He did what I asked without hesitating, his small fingers working the shells into the rifle. He did it without difficulty, even in the dark and with the lurching movements of the pickup. When he was done, I told him to pump one into the chamber and leave the rifle between us, butt on the floor, barrel pointing to the roof. And while he did what I asked, I concentrated hard on the road.

As soon as I was aware of the trees on either side of me, I slowed even further, taking the pickup to a crawl because I knew the bridge was close. I couldn't afford to take my eyes off the road for even a second. If I came to the bridge without realising it, there was every chance I would pitch over into the gully.

When I reached it, I came to a standstill and squinted into the night. Before us, the road ended in blackness, beginning again a few metres beyond. It was a blackness that I needed to avoid. I crunched into gear and crawled towards the channel, my eyes scanning ahead, searching for the ends of the beams so I could line up my tyres. But, as the wheels came closer and closer to the emptiness of the gully, the headlights failed to pick out the bridge. Nothing.

Not wanting to risk moving any further forward, I stopped the vehicle.

We sat for a moment, just the sound of the rain beating on the roof of the cab. I remembered how Papagaio had told me not to stop. Not to stop for anything.

'You see anything out there?' I asked the boy.

He leaned forward, like me, almost pressing his face to the glass. 'Nothing.'

'Wait here,' I said, stepping out into the rain and taking hold of my rifle. With the light behind me, I walked to the edge and peered out at where the wooden beams had once been. There was no longer a way across. The beams were dislodged, skewed at an angle, the far end of each one lying in the bottom of the creek below. It would take a bulldozer and a few strong men to lift them back into place.

I jogged back to the pickup and stowed my rifle between us.

'It's gone,' I said. 'The bridge is gone.'

'The rain?' asked the boy.

'Maybe,' I replied, but I knew the rain was not responsible. In the rainy season, the gully sometimes had water creeping along its bed, but never more than a few inches. No. Someone had brought down the bridge. And I had a terrible feeling I knew who it was. João didn't want any of us to leave town.

I backed up, turned in the road, and drove back into São Tiago as the rain began to fade. I headed directly for André's place. I needed to get to the *Hotel Fluctuante*, find the others, warn them and prepare to meet João head-on. It looked as if Papagaio was right. There was going to be blood tonight.

Entering town, I took us onto the *rua*, wanting to drive faster but afraid that I would lose control of the vehicle. I fought to calm myself, my mind spinning, knowing that I would not be able to live with myself if something were to happen to Ana or the boy. I had to protect them at all costs. In my haste to get to the *Hotel Fluctuante*, though, I failed to notice the pickup lying in wait on one of the side streets which ran off from the *rua*. As I passed Zeca's store, the vehicle revved its engine and sped from the side road, slamming into us, catching us just behind the cab, at the front end of the flatbed section. The boy and I were thrown together at one end of the bench seat as the tail of our pickup spun in the road, swinging around and hitting the front wall of Zeca's store.

Dazed, I looked down at the boy who was now lying across my lap, and then up at the windscreen to see two men climbing out from the vehicle which had hit us. The way I felt, I wanted to stay where I was, regain the breath which had been punched from my lungs, but I knew there was no time. Instead, I pushed myself up in my seat and threw open the door beside me. I dragged the boy across my lap and dropped him onto the ground.

'Run,' I said to him, turning my attention away, looking into the cab, searching for my rifle. It was lying under my feet, across the floor of the cab. I looked back at him. 'Run as fast as you can. Find somewhere to hide and don't come out.'

'But—'

'Just do it,' I screamed at him, glancing back through the windscreen at the two men who were approaching. 'Run!'

Full of fear, the boy began to run, his small legs carrying him into the shadows. As I watched him disappear, I reached down into the footwell and put my fingers on the stock of my rifle. I began lifting it into my hands when the first of the two men reached me. He leaned in and pressed the barrel of his revolver against my neck.

'You should come see the others,' he said.

They pulled me outside, dragging me from my flip-flops, and beat me down into the dirt. I curled myself into a ball and tried to protect my head as they kicked and punched me, and after a while, too weak to protect myself any longer, they rolled me onto my back and ground wet mud into my face. When they were done, they ushered me, barefoot, along the street, grit raking my eyelids every time I blinked. I repeatedly spat out the earth until my tongue was dry and dumb.

The rain was gone now, but the air was fresh with its scent, despite the persistent taste of the mud in my mouth. The wet dirt was soft under my hardened feet, but from time to time I felt a sharpness as I stepped on a stone, a nail, a shard of glass. It didn't matter, though, I wasn't thinking about my feet. I was thinking about my friends.

My breathing was heavy, the fear forcing my lungs to work harder. My legs beginning to feel weak, my footsteps faltering as we came towards the place where Manolo's café backed on to the river. I could see a brightness coming around the edges and over the roofs of the low buildings which blocked my view. As we came closer, I heard the sound of an engine ticking over and I saw the glare of headlights.

André's *Hotel Fluctuante* was on fire. The shell was still intact, but the rooms inside were burning, flames licking at the broken windows, smoke rising to the heavens and blotting out the stars. Soon the entire vessel would be aflame. The road in front of it was lit up like carnival. Two or three pickups, one with its engine idling and its roof crowned with an array of dazzling beams which spotlighted my friends like actors on stage.

Papagaio was dead. As I rounded the corner, seeing him lying face down, still, broken, twisted, I knew he was gone. I had known him for as long as I cared to remember, but now he was nothing more than a wrecked and lifeless body.

João was standing over him, staring down at his sodden, wretched corpse. He looked up as the men dragged me forwards, and he smiled. He was wearing the same clothes he'd been wearing when I saw him last, except now they were soaked in Papagaio's blood. As was the machete that hung in his left hand.

I closed my stinging eyes but couldn't look away. I had to open them again, feeling them drawn to my friend's shape lying in the dirt. The shadows from the bright lights and the flames played tricks across his body, bloating the darkness around him, shining in the blood that had pooled around him and thickened in the wet earth. The way the shadows fell made him appear fragmented, and I imagined it must have been the disturbance in the mud creating troughs and peaks which were responsible for the strangeness of the shadows. But when they brought me closer, I saw Papagaio's feet and hands were no longer attached to his arms and legs. His face was twisted up and to the side, and his mouth was wide and bloodied. João had cut out my friend's tongue.

The men stopped dragging me when we were just a metre away from the broken body, and they released my arms. My hands collapsed to my side and I stared into João's eyes. He held my gaze, not speaking.

'He only fired a couple of shots,' said João after time. 'But he got two of my men.' He kicked the corpse at his feet. 'The others, though, they came out running once they saw him fall. That's all it took. That, and a few bottles of gasoline,' he laughed. 'They ran into the night like frightened animals.'

I wondered where Ana was now and wished I had listened to Papagaio. I desperately wished I could go back to a time earlier that evening, so I could take my friend's elbow and give him my blessing; send him out into the evening with a gun and a stony heart. I had so wanted to avoid such an atrocity. I wanted only to protect my friends; to prevent them from committing such an act themselves, and to stop such an act from being committed upon them. In my desire to do what I thought was right, though, I had left all their lives at risk. Perhaps the awful truth was that they had been right. There was only one way to deal with men like João.

João shook his head, then turned a fraction and raised a hand in gesture to the men who were standing behind him. There must have been four, five, maybe even more; it was hard to tell with the darkness and the brightness mingling to make shadow. When they stepped forward, they brought Reginaldo from the night. He was held, like I had been, and the men pushed us both to our knees.

'Ana?' I whispered to him. 'Where's Ana?'

'With Paulo—' he managed before João slapped him hard, saying, 'You brought his gun?'

João dropped the machete, point first, into the ground before holding out his hand. One of the men slapped the handle of the revolver into his palm and João tightened his fingers around it. He lifted it into view, opened the cylinder, looked into it and snapped it shut. 'You keep it very clean,' he said to Reginaldo. As he spoke, there was movement around us as more men arrived, dragging André and Paulo into the circle, knives to their throats.

I threw Paulo a questioning glance but he just shook his head and lowered his eyes.

'And the other one?' João's voice breaking amongst us but not severing the looks that we passed. 'Where's the other one? The one this is all about.' The four of us now sensing this was the end. Knowing it, tasting the scent of Papagaio's blood in the air, our bodies weak with fear. We were cattle on slaughter day, breathing the smell of death.

'The one from the café. The one we came for. Where is he? Where's the one who runs the café?' He demanded it of us, but he knew we wouldn't tell him.

I didn't know where Manny was. Perhaps he had run away, put himself as far from danger as possible, or perhaps he had taken further steps to defend himself, but even if I knew, I wouldn't tell João. There was nothing for me to gain from it. He was going to kill us. Whatever we did or said, we knew João was going to kill us. There was nothing we would give him; nothing we would tell him.

'I have him.' A voice spoke from the darkness and another two figures appeared. Anderson was holding a revolver in one hand while his other hand was gripping Manolo's arm, pushing him towards us. As they came closer, I could see that Manny had been beaten and I guessed that Anderson had punished him for what he had done to Eduardo. Punished him but not murdered him. Not yet. Something must have stopped him.

Anderson shoved Manny to the ground beside us and took a

step back, deferring to João. I tried to make eye contact with him, but his gaze was focused on Manny and I somehow knew that he was refusing to look at me, understanding that if he did, his resolve would be broken. He knew what he was doing was wrong, but Anderson was part of a pack, and João was the pack leader.

Paulo spoke to me in a whisper. 'It isn't your fault.'

'Ana?' I asked him, but again he just shook his head.

I closed my eyes, squeezing them shut, praying for the first time in years. Praying that the boy had run fast and long; that Ana was safe; that Papagaio was in a better place; that my friends would not be butchered like animals. All these thoughts passing through me as one entity.

'Don't close your eyes,' I heard João say as he touched Reginaldo's gun to my head. 'I've got a treat for you. Come on. Open your eyes. I've been saving this one for you.'

It was Ana's voice calling my name that made me look.

'Sam.'

I opened my eyes and saw her, watched as João's men pushed her down like one of the herd, pinning her arms even as she fought to push them away.

'You know what the Senhora wants me to do with your whore?' João said, watching her struggle. 'She wants me to fuck her. Did I forget to tell you that?'

'Don't let this happen.' I spoke the words under my breath, not sure to whom they were addressed. To João? To myself? To God?

'What did you say?' João leaned over me.

'Don't let this happen,' I said again, this time louder, looking up at João and then past him. My eyes settled on Anderson, and I knew who I was talking to. I was talking to all of them. I was speaking to every man there in the light of the vehicles and the flames. To every man standing in the rain-sodden dirt.

'Don't let this happen,' I said again. 'It doesn't have to be this way.'

Anderson met my eyes now, staring long and hard. No blinking. A sense of something passing between us.

From the corner of my eye I saw João nod to one of his men who went to Ana and stood over her. I turned my head to see the man stop and study me as if he were considering my words, then he looked to João.

'Go on then,' said João. 'What are you waiting for?'

The man raised his eyebrows, hesitated, moved his head as if to shake away an unwanted thought, then reached down and ripped open Ana's dress, tearing the buttons that ran down the front, pulling it open to reveal her.

Ana struggled harder before submitting, becoming limp. She spoke to the man standing over her. 'Please,' she said. 'Please don't.' Appealing to his better nature, hoping that *he* may have one, for we knew that João did not.

The man looked over her exposed flesh, saw the expression on her face, then turned his head with the air of someone unable to witness their own actions. Perhaps these men were not the butchers that João was.

João grinned and stared down at me, one hand holding the gun. He put his other hand under my chin and lifted my face, forcing me to look at him. 'You know what, though? I think your friend likes her.' He moved so the pistol was pointing at Paulo now. 'I think he wants to screw her first.' He released me and looked round at his men. 'Shall I let him have first go?' The men didn't respond immediately. Instead, they looked to one another as if perhaps they were waiting for one of them to have the courage to oppose João; as if this wasn't what they had expected. Perhaps this had gone further than they intended.

'OK then,' João said. 'Maybe someone else? How about you, Anderson?'

Anderson snapped his head round to look at João.

'No,' I said. 'No.'

João went to where Ana lay in the mud and looked down at her. 'Or maybe I'll just shoot her now.' He turned to look at me. 'How would you like that?'

It crossed my mind that perhaps Ana was better off dead. I was sure that João intended to kill us all anyway. He had come under Da Silva's orders to make an example of Manny – to make an example of Ana, too, as it turned out – but now he had found his own agenda. He was having fun, that was clear enough, and he meant to go on having it until he'd had his fill.

I wanted to close my eyes, to remove the vision of Ana lying in the dirt from my mind. I wanted to close my eyes so that everything would disappear but I knew that it would still be there when I opened them again. There was no way out of this now. João was going to kill us all.

'Anderson.' I looked up at the man who had thanked me for trying to save his friend. 'You can't let this happen. She hasn't done anything to you. None of these men has harmed you.' I looked beyond him to the other men, pleading now, begging for our lives. 'You men. You have families. Friends. Brothers, sisters. What would they say if they could see you now? Are you going to let him kill us all? Are you going to *help* him?' I could not believe that amongst them there was not one man with an ounce of goodness and compassion within him.

'What else are they going—' João's sentence was punctuated with a single popping noise and his face took on an expression of surprise.

At first it seemed to me that the sound had come from the *Hotel Fluctuante*, a piece of wood expanding and bursting in the fire, but I realised that the noise had come from behind us, which explained why João was now staring over our heads. And when I saw a fresh flow of blood slip from the cuff of his T-shirt and run down his arm, I knew what the sound was. It was the sound of a single twenty-two cartridge being fired.

I turned to look behind me, knowing what I was going to see, but willing myself to be wrong.

I was not wrong.

About twenty metres away, perfectly lit by the flames from the *Hotel Fluctuante* which was now crowned with fire, the boy was standing at the side of the road, my rifle tucked hard to his shoulder. I could only imagine why he did not fire again. Perhaps he was too shocked by the thought that he had fired a weapon at another human being. Perhaps he could not understand why João had not fallen to the floor, dead, as people always do in the movies. Perhaps he was beginning to think that João could not be killed. Perhaps he was just too frightened. Or perhaps he *had* fired again, and the propellant in the cartridge had once again failed to ignite. Whatever the reason, I saw the boy's eyes widen further and he dropped the rifle, throwing it down, turning to run.

The first shot which João fired took the boy's feet out from under him, making him stumble and fall to his knees with his back towards us. The next two, in quick succession, thrust his torso forwards, throwing him face first into the mud. His legs straight out behind him, his arms limp at his sides. The boy twitched once and then became still.

41

I fought to gain control over my mind and my body. A blackness was descending on me which threatened to blind me and deafen me to the world. I felt my senses dulling, my entire being wanting to shut down, to shrink itself into nothing, to crawl into the smallest, darkest place and fade into non-existence. I was in a living nightmare. A nightmare which never wanted to end. A nightmare which had stretched from Roraima to Mato Grosso; which had begun with fire and blood and went on burning and bleeding for eternity.

I tried to push myself to my feet, but my mind refused to communicate with my body. It was as if every different part of me was trying to find its own unique way to cope with what I had just witnessed.

I stared at the boy's lifeless form, lying in the dirt, and my head spun as I turned it, reeling like a drunk, taking in everything that was happening around me. Papagaio dead at my side, Ana lying exposed before me, her mouth wide in silent scream. João standing over me, a pistol in his hand, still pointing at the spot where the boy had fallen. He was speaking to his men, shouting at them, his voice distorted in my ears by the ringing from the gunshots.

'Shot by a kid,' he was yelling. 'Shot by a fucking kid.' His face almost hysterical, his attention going to the blood which was flowing from him. His whole body seemed to sag, the weight of the pistol in his hand forcing his arm to drop to his side.

'Don't just stand there,' he said to his men, his voice beginning to calm now as the blood drained from him. 'One of you do something.'

But his men were rooted to the ground, their leader dying, none of them knowing what to do. The two who were holding Ana released her, not caring that she shuffled away from them, clasping her dress. In my daze, I watched her get to her feet, stumble, staring past me at the boy. Anderson saw her too, but stayed where he was, choosing instead to watch João's life slipping away.

João looked around at them, confused. 'Do something,' he said again, but still they remained impassive, so he turned to us now, managing to lift his revolver high enough to point it at Paulo. 'You. Doctor. Do something.' But as he spoke, his voice weakening, he saw Ana move past us, going to the boy. João turned his head in her direction, mustering the strength to raise his revolver higher and I knew that he intended to kill her too.

So my body finally began to move. But it moved before my mind even knew what I was going to do. My hands reached out for João's legs and I pulled him to the ground, throwing myself over him, smothering the weapon. He fired twice in Ana's direction before he went down and I fell across him, leaning heavily on his hand, forcing myself on him, trying to take the gun for myself, but the steel was slippery with João's blood and my fingers found no purchase on it.

As we fumbled, João fired his weapon over and over but the cartridges were all spent now and the pistol did nothing more than click and spin. He swore, searching the ground around him as I tried to pull myself to my feet, but finding no more weapons to hand, he took his pistol by the barrel and swung it hard at my head.

He was weakening, but João was a strong man. The handle

of his pistol struck me hard, rattling my teeth and sending a grating pain through my skull as the bone seemed to crack under the blow. I put out my hands, grasping João's shoulders to steady myself as he pushed me away and hit me again. I tried to stand, but the darkness was too heavy, descending like a shroud as I collapsed to the soggy ground beside Papagaio.

I dreamed of fire again. The popping of wood, the ugly screams of the dying and the blackened face of a child. And in the strange way dreams merge into one another, I ended on the river, with Ana and the boy. The heat, the gentle shift of the boat on the water, the dryness of my skin, my thirst. These were of no importance. The boy had caught the fish, my fish, the fish that Father Machado and I were going to catch, and he was presenting it to me. His words were slow, too quiet to understand, and yet I knew what he was saying. He wanted me to take the fish, to claim it as my own, but I turned away from him and held up my hand. I told him there would be other fish, and I looked up into the sun, closing my eyes against its radiance and feeling its warmth on my face, as Ana took my hand.

It was the brightness that woke me. And the pain. My head burning. I opened my eyes and looked about me. Paulo's face leaned in, his mouth was moving, but I couldn't hear any sound other than the droning in my head. Then André was there, looking into my eyes and moving his gaze to the core of the pain that burned through me. Paulo's hand touching my head.

I pushed them away and struggled to my knees.

The *Hotel Fluctuante* was an inferno. The heat which exploded out from the burning mass of wood and rubber was intense on my skin, and the flames lit the night, licking into every shadowy corner, crackling and spitting their glowing embers into the air around us.

Beside me, João was bleeding to death, his lungs rattling as he drowned in his own fluid. Anderson was looking down at him with a blank expression of indifference. He put out one foot and nudged the dying man's shoulder. He nodded once, then turned around and walked away, joining the other men who were climbing into their pickups and leaving São Tiago.

Several metres to my left, Reginaldo was sitting in stunned silence, his eyes fixed on a place somewhere beyond my shoulder. Manolo was close by, his hands covering his face.

'Ana?' I said, remembering the last shots that João had fired.

'Stay still,' said Paulo. 'You need to—'

'Where's Ana?'

Paulo lowered his eyes.

'No,' I said. 'Not her too.'

Paulo looked away and I turned my head, dreading what I might see.

Ana was sitting beside the boy. With one hand, she was holding her dress about her, and with the other, she was stroking the boy's head.

I stumbled to my feet and went to her, crumpling into the dirt and staring down at the boy. Ana had cleaned the mud from his face. She had used the rainwater to wash his features clean. He looked pale now. Pale and fragile. Just a child whose eyes were glazed and dead. Whose mouth was twisted in fear.

He would never smile again.

I took Ana's hand away from the boy and placed my own on his head, resting it gently on his hair. I kissed his forehead and looked up into the sky. I closed my eyes and I whispered to the stars. 'I ask that . . . that you receive this child into your arms . . .'

And as I floundered, searching for the right words to say, the rain began to fall again.

42

The tears in my eyes were washed away by the rain as I carried the boy to my pickup. Ana tried to pull me back, begged me to let her go with me, but I told her it was something I needed to do alone. I still had to take the boy home.

His body was small and light in my arms. His weight was nothing to that of the last person I had taken home. Eduardo. The man whose death had started it all.

I walked the length of the road, going to the spot where I had abandoned my pickup, the rear bumper crushed against the wall of Zeca's shop. Ana and Paulo kept pace beside me, not speaking. Faces came to windows, doors opened now that the shooting had stopped, but I ignored them, kept my eyes forward, set on fulfilling my final promise to the boy. I was going to take him home, no matter what it cost me. Nothing else mattered any more.

Paulo stepped ahead of me, pulling the cab door open, and I laid the boy on the bench seat, settling him, straightening him, making him comfortable for his journey. When I was done, Ana climbed in, looking down at the boy once more, touching her hand to his face, brushing his hair from his brow. She kissed him on the forehead as I had done, and looked up at me climbing into the other side of the cab.

'Let me come,' she said. 'Please.'

I studied her face, seeing how much it meant to her, and finally nodded my consent.

Ana lifted the boy's legs and slid onto the seat, lying him across her, and we drove out of São Tiago together. Three of us in the darkness and the rain.

When we reached the bridge, it was just as I had last seen it. I stopped the pickup and cut the engine. I left the lights on and turned to Ana. She asked me what we were going to do so I told her we would walk. It was the only way.

'What about the others?' she asked, her voice hollow. 'Da Silva's people?'

'Turned off further back,' I said. 'Driven across the fields. There must be tracks.'

'Can we—'

'It's their land,' I said. 'I don't know it like they do.' I wouldn't be able to find a safe path with just the narrow cone of the headlights.

So together we carried the boy down into the gully, our feet sliding on the mud and the stones, but we didn't once drop him. We rested a moment at the bottom, neither of us knowing any words to say. We crouched in the mud, the boy lying across our knees, away from the ground. I stared at the shallow stream that was forming around us because I couldn't bear to see the way Ana's face was contorted with grief, the way her shoulders hitched. Instead I watched the ripples in the moonlight.

When we began scaling the other side, moving upwards in the wet dirt was more difficult. Many times we slipped, but each time we got to our feet and we began again. We were determined. And in that determination, I saw strength in Ana beyond anything I had ever seen before. Her tears were gone now, driven away by her need to take the boy home.

I don't know how long it took us to make it to the other side of the ruined bridge, half an hour, maybe more, and when we were at the top, we went down on our knees to catch our breath. My arms and legs were burning from the effort, my heart almost unable to cope with the strain, threatening to burst. I could tell that Ana, too, was exhausted. I looked at her, covered in mud, her hair plastered to her head, her dress drenched and clinging to her, her breath coming in small short gasps.

'I don't think I can carry him any further,' I said between breaths. 'I'm not strong enough.'

'Yes you are,' she said, taking my hand, squeezing it once before letting go and preparing to stand.

I pushed myself to my feet and lifted the boy into my arms.

Together we walked along the side of the road, trudging past the grazing lands until we saw headlights in the distance coming towards us. I kept my arms strong, holding the boy across them despite the pain that burned through them.

'They'll be looking for him,' I said. 'He should be home now.'

We continued walking as the lights grew closer and it became apparent that there were two vehicles approaching us, not just one.

When they were half a kilometre or so away from us, we stopped and waited at the side of the road, neither of us knowing what we were going to say; how we were going to tell them what had happened to their boy.

The beams from the first pickup spotted us straight away, and the vehicle slowed to a halt in the middle of the road. The second truck followed suit.

John and Sarah jumped down from the first cab, one on either side, and stopped by the doors, watching Ana and me standing by the road.

'Sam?' John called. 'Is that you?'

I stepped towards them, the light blinding me, and Sarah let out a short gasp. From the truck behind, the three *Americanos* ran around to stand behind her husband, raising rifles at us.

John stayed where he was as his wife approached me, slowly at first, not wanting to face what she knew to be true, then faster as if to assure herself that she was wrong.

'What . . . ?' She looked at her son and then up at me.

She took him from my arms and went down into the mud, holding her boy to her chest, speaking his name and letting out a low moan. The sound of ultimate suffering. The sound of a mother mourning her child.

John came to her now, crouching beside her, putting his arms around her, but she pushed him away, unbalancing him, sprawling him in the mud as she began to shout at him, blaming him for bringing them to this godforsaken place, for letting me take responsibility for him, for trying to make him a man instead of wrapping him up like a precious possession and cherishing him and loving him and protecting him.

When she had vented her anger, she grew silent again, taking her boy to the pickup and sitting as Ana had done; with the small body across her lap, waiting to take him home.

The *Americanos* helped John out of the mud, but he brushed them off, standing on his own and staring at me. 'What happened?' John asked, his voice cracking. 'Sam. Who did this?'

I shook my head and stared at the ground. I couldn't look him in the eye.

'Who?'

'Da Silva,' I said. 'It was Da Silva's people.'

'You're sure?'

I nodded.

'Why?'

'They came to hurt us. To hurt Ana. Your boy, he . . . he was trying to protect her.' And in giving his life, he had saved us all. A small boy, not even thirteen years old.

For a long time, John did not speak. When he did, his voice

was strained and hoarse. 'Burn it,' I heard him say to the *Americanos*. 'Kill them and burn it all.'

And with those words he returned to his vehicle and drove into the night, closely followed by his three avenging angels.

Ana and I watched them leave, saying nothing, then sat alone by the road and held each other in the darkness. There was no light other than that from the stars and the moon. The rain had stopped now, but the air was still cool and our clothes were still wet. We stayed like that for what felt like hours, shivering in the mud, not speaking. And in the distance I heard the faint rattle of gunfire.

After some time, I noticed an orange glow hanging in an arc beneath the stars, but it was too early for dawn; the glow was not from the sun.

'It's the *fazenda*,' I said to Ana. 'The last burning of the season.'

If you enjoyed
DRY SEASON

Don't miss
DARK·HORIZONS

Dan Smith's latest thriller
available soon in Orion hardback
Price £18.99
ISBN: 978-1-4091-0824-5

1

I had never before witnessed the exact moment at which life passes from the body; the instant it becomes nothing. With only twenty-five years behind me, I had collected just a few experiences of death which I kept hidden in a place I rarely visited. A neatly dressed body lying in the velvety folds of fabric in the confines of a carefully chosen box. The wax-like effect of once living skin now tended by the mortician's expert hands. I had stared down at the sunken features of a mother I had loved and cared for; empty now, reduced to a motionless collection of skin and wasted bone. Mourners dressed in black. Sombre faces, hands shaken, drinks taken. These were my experiences of death. I had participated in the act of farewell, but I had never seen *that* moment. The exact moment at which life evaporates.

But I saw it that day. Sprawled on my stomach, with my head turned to one side, pressed to the hot tarmac, I watched life disappear. I saw it vanish as if it had never existed, leaving nothing but the ruined shell it once inhabited.

For a while before I opened my eyes, I was content to be where I was. The sun warm on my back, the air quiet around me. My head was filled with a pleasant, bleary feeling, as if I were just waking from a long, deep sleep. But the silence was punctuated by the first stunned groan, and as consciousness clawed its way back into my mind, I became more aware of the sounds around me.

A child crying. A man moaning, or perhaps it was a woman, it was hard to tell. Both, maybe. More than one person. More than two. Then the world popped into focus and I heard many people. Many voices. Shouting, crying, screaming. The sound of twisted metal settling into place.

I opened my eyes, alarmed that I could see nothing more than a blur of light around the periphery of what I should be looking at. My whole body was numb. A wave of nausea swept over me and I retched. Disorientated and muddled, I was shamed as my stomach heaved and I vomited so publicly.

Blinking hard, I tried to move but was unable to do more than shuffle a few inches before another wave of nausea came over me. I closed my eyes tight and fought the feeling, pushing it back down.

When I opened them again, the world came to me in a bright flash of light and colour. The first thing I saw was the bubbles of tarmac which had bloated and popped under the intense heat of the sun. A smell of oil and petrol crept into my nostrils and clawed into my lungs, making me retch again, forcing me to fight it. I wriggled my fingers, moved my hands, brought my arms up towards my face. I planted my palms on the road, trying to push myself up, but the effort was too great, so I let my head fall back onto the warm tarmac and shifted my eyes to take in the scene around me.

I'd been lucky, that much was clear. I had survived, but others had not been so fortunate. An old woman was facing me, her mouth opening and closing, her voice producing little more than a weak, breathy moaning. Blood ran from her nose and formed tributaries as it slid into the wrinkles around her lips and chin. Her eyes were wide, her hand outstretched towards me as if she knew she was dying but refused to relinquish her life without the touch of another human being. To me, she was an unfamiliar face in an unfamiliar land. Her skin was different from mine, her eyes were not shaped like my own, and our culture was not shared. Yet there are some things which we all have in common. No one truly wants to die alone.

I watched her for a moment, keeping my eyes on hers, summoning my strength, then I manoeuvred my right arm up and reached across to take her hand. But she was too far away. There was a space of an inch or so between the tips of our fingers, and yet we continued to stretch towards each other, desperate for that last moment of human contact.

I began to pull myself towards her, dragging my weight along the tarmac so that I could take her hand. I struggled to close the gap between us, seeing that she was unable to move. The weight of the bus pinning her to the road was far too great.

Around us, the sounds of suffering grew. The ringing in my ears and the fuzziness in my head was dissipating, and my eyes didn't hurt so much anymore. I tried not to listen to the creaking metal, the screaming, the crying, the moaning. I tried to ignore the smell of oil and petrol and blood that saturated the thick, hot air. I tried not to notice the other people around me. The dead, the dying, and the dismembered. I tried only to concentrate on the old woman, her mouth opening and closing like a fish left to die in the sun, her final ounce of strength channelled into the act of stretching her fingers towards mine. I pulled myself closer and grasped her hand, squeezing it so that I felt the bones rubbing together beneath her thin, leathery skin. Old life and new life.

She squeezed my hand in return, closed her eyes in relief, then opened them again and looked at me.

And *that* was the moment. A life-changing moment. The moment when her deep brown eyes emptied in front of me as if her body were a vessel and her life were a liquid that had been poured from her. Her eyes died. One moment they were alive and a person lived behind them. A woman with memories, a place in the world, a purpose. And the next she was just lifeless skin and bone and flesh. In an instant she had changed from something of incredible value to something of no importance at all.

I was still holding the old woman's hand when I forced myself to look around once more.

The bus in which I'd been travelling was lying on its side, its rusted orange and green markings looking up at the cloudless azure sky. Its nose was crumpled, the windscreen shattered into crushed ice spread across the soft tarmac. Skewed at an angle in the dirt at the side of the road was another large vehicle, this one a truck. The cab had come away from the flatbed.

Seeing the rotting monstrosities like this reminded me of the moment they had collided. I'd been sitting at the front of the bus, in the 'death seat' as I have since heard it called. After waiting almost four hours in the terminal in Medan, and after two failed attempts to board other buses, I had followed the crowd onto this ill-fated vehicle, only to find myself pushed down into the backless seat beside the driver, my face only inches from the windscreen.

I'd heard that bus travel in Indonesia was a game of Russian roulette, but I hadn't expected to find myself in such a position on my first day in the country – in an overcrowded bus, surrounded by a foreign language, baskets of chickens, screaming babies, sitting beside a driver for whom life was a race. For an hour I'd tuned out the whining, high-pitched eastern singing that blasted from the internal speakers. I'd persuaded myself not to care that some travellers were actually *outside* the bus, clinging to the sills around the windows and the roof-rack. I'd ignored the open door beside me and I'd tried not to think about what would happen if the bus were to come to a sudden and terrifying stop. But I was certain that of all the passengers in the bus, I would be the first to die.

As it happened, though, I was wrong. Our collision was not head on, as I'd expected it to be. Travelling with my eyes half open, I'd assumed that when the impact came, as it surely would, it would be at the moment when our driver made one of his reckless overtaking attempts – at high speed around a blind corner, giving only a toot of his horn to indicate he was on his way. I was wrong. Our contact came, in fact, at a fork in the road, and the oncoming Mitsubishi truck hit us at the front side, knocking me from my seat, propelling me through the open door before the bus twisted, slid, turned and toppled.

The people who had been clinging to the near side of the bus were crushed immediately, leaving a ragged red stain across the potholed grey tarmac as the vehicle slid to its final resting place.

I could see the tide left by the runaway bus. It was a gruesome wake of crushed bodies, dismembered limbs, blood drying in the sun.

I lingered over the sight for longer than I wanted to, unable to take my eyes from it. I wanted nothing more than to rub it from my mind, to reach inside my head and disinfect such a view, but I was compelled to look. I'd never seen such a thing before. I imagined that it was how it might look if a bomb had exploded. Bodies separated from limbs. A head. An arm. A leg protruding from beneath the overturned bus. A man whose lower body was so crushed that he had split, burst like a wet balloon, and his viscera had spilled onto the road. The flies had already begun to feast on the shiny mass of grey and red which had emptied from him.

I turned away and looked back at the old woman, then I forced my arms to move, pushed myself up onto my elbows, brought my legs around and dragged myself into a sitting position.

My head swam as I scanned around me. Chickens running in the road. People strewn all about. Thirty, thirty-five bodies that I could see. Many of them dead. One or two people were dragging survivors away from the wreck. Others were wandering in a dazed stupor as they searched for relatives.

At the side of the road, a few onlookers, unable or unwilling to help.

People's belongings, too, were scattered around the wreckage. A suitcase burst open, clothes distributed across the tarmac. A shoe. A basket full of chickens, intact. A soft-drinks crate containing only glass and the last fizz of what had been contained within. My backpack, bright blue, spotted with blood. It held everything I'd brought with me except my passport and the money which I kept hidden beneath my shirt in a thin canvas belt.

I stared at my backpack, trying to focus on it. It had made it all the way here from England. From a small camping shop on a steep street in Newcastle. I'd bought it on a wet Thursday afternoon, the sun already set, the street lights on and blurred behind the rain. A cold, wet, ordinary afternoon marked by the purchase of a bright blue rucksack that was to be my travelling companion for the months to come.

Only now it was lying on a bloodied road under an intense sun in an alien world.

A motorbike passed me, its engine chugging as it made its way around the wreckage. The rider weaved in and out of the people, the body parts, scanning, witnessing, then picking up speed and heading back onto the open road. Somebody had somewhere to go and a crash wasn't going to stop them from getting there. They'd seen it before and they would see it again.

I tried to get to my feet, but once more the nausea surged over me and I waited for it to subside before I began shuffling towards my backpack. My one symbol of home. The only thing I had that made me who I was. I kept my eyes on it, focusing on nothing other than the bright blue canvas.

On my hands and knees, I made my way past the old woman, not looking down at her as I struggled forwards, keeping my eyes only on the bag, until I was distracted by a young boy who came into my peripheral vision, making me turn my head to follow the movement. The boy, maybe twelve years old, had come from the side of the road where a small gathering of people had grouped to stare, none of them making any effort to come to my assistance. He stepped over a piece of debris which lay between me and my goal, then headed for my backpack. He stopped beside it, glancing across at me before bending at the waist and picking it up. He felt its weight, and then used both hands to swing it around and drape it over his back. He hunched under its load as he began to move away. I tried to call out to him. He was taking my bag. Perhaps he was moving it to a safer location, perhaps he was helping to clear the road. Or perhaps he was just stealing my belongings. Whatever he was doing, I called out, but my tongue was lazy and my mouth was dry. My confused mind rebelled against me, refusing to send the right messages to any part of my body. I was unable to stand and now I was unable to speak. The only sound I heard myself utter was a fumbled one, as if my tongue had grown too large for my mouth.

The boy stopped and stared at me, the way I mouthed my words, the way I held out one hand in protest. He watched me for a moment then came towards me. He had seen sense. He realised I was trying to tell him the rucksack was mine.

I lowered my arm, fell back onto my knees and waited for the boy to come closer. When he reached me, he placed the back-pack on the ground and squatted beside me. He waved a hand in front of my face and I tried to smile, nodding like an idiot. The boy looked around, glancing up at the people who'd gathered to survey the mayhem, then at the mayhem itself. When his eyes came back to mine, he reached down and took my hand. He lifted my arm, slipped my watch from my wrist and put it around his own. He smiled at me before standing again and slinging my backpack over his shoulder.

I stared, helpless, as the boy disappeared among the spectators.

I slumped, my shoulders sagging under the weight of my head, and I felt a mesh of darkness creeping across my mind. There was pain behind my eyes which reached up and spread its fingers around the top of my brain, squeezing in rhythmic pulses, tightening its grip. I felt woozy again, the sounds of the crash fading in and out. I struggled to a sitting position, leaned back against whatever was there to support me. My vision began to swim and I closed my eyes, wanting to stay right there, curl up and go to sleep. I wanted to enjoy the warmth of the sun, to find a comfortable spot to lie in.

I felt a tugging at my feet, and opened my eyes enough to allow a little light to needle in. Everything seemed brighter than it ought to be, the glare from the sun forcing its way into my eyes, shaded only by the figure crouched at my feet, tugging my shoes from me.

Then a voice, shouting in a language I didn't understand. Nasal, foreign, not sounding like words at all, but more like a staccato attack of consonants and vowels being fired from a rifle. The tugging at my feet stopped, my shoes slipped away, and the shadowy figure disappeared from view, replaced by another image, this one looming close to me, running a hand over my head.

An angel. An earth-bound angel, or a heaven-bound one, I wasn't sure, but an angel nonetheless. She took my head on her lap and she lifted a bottle to my lips. I drank the warm, sour water, grateful for the liquid on my parched and raw throat. I complied with her every touch when she moved me onto my side, brought my legs up and turned my head. I let her manipulate me and move me, and then my mind slipped away into the abyss as she ran her hand across my forehead and spoke in her soothing tone. Then, darkness.

2

A warm breeze on my face. A large ceiling fan above me, churning the air over my head, wafting the smell of disease and affliction, swirling it around me. The blades spinning without sound, the stalk swivelling in its fixing.

I watched the predetermined motion of the fan, allowing my eyes to adjust to the afternoon light, collecting my thoughts into a coherent pattern. I'd been in a crash. I remembered that. I remembered the old woman, and the angel, too. Although, she couldn't have been an angel because I wasn't dead. At least, I didn't think so.

I moved my toes against restrictive sheets which were pulled tight across me and tucked into either side of the iron bed. I pushed my feet up, loosening the stiff cotton, giving myself room to move. I looked around at the other beds in the ward. Ten in total. Five on my side and five on the other. All occupied.

To my left, a man with a bandage across one eye, the centre of the gauze rusted brown with old blood. To my right, a man with one of his legs kept from under the sheets, the limb wrapped in bandages, again with the same coloured stain seeping through the cream material. All of the other beds were occupied by men in similar states of disrepair. Bandages and stains seemed to be the requirement for accommodation in this particular ward, and I found myself lifting a hand to check for injuries. Sure enough, the top of my head was bandaged.

I pushed up, manoeuvring into something close to a sitting position and studied my surroundings. A plain ward, with white walls and a green painted concrete floor. No tiles, nothing fancy, everything functional. The smell of full bedpans evaporating in the tepid air. Ten iron beds with tight white sheets. Two windows on the opposite side of the room, both filled with green mosquito netting, the shutters thrown open to the day. I could see a glimpse of foliage outside, the top of a tree which might have been a palm. The mosquito netting gave everything outside a strange fuzzy hue.

None of the men in the other beds was talking. They either slept or sat and stared. The man beside me, the one with the bandaged face, caught my eye as I looked around the room, and he smiled, nodding his head once. '*Salamat siang.*'

I processed the words, remembering them from the phrase book I'd bought before leaving England just a day or two ago. I waited for them to digest, turned the sounds into written words inside my mind, searched for the translation as I remembered it from the pages of the book. Once that was done, I returned the words, pronouncing them as best as I knew how.

'*Salamat Siang,*' I replied. Good afternoon. A polite formality, but contact was made.

The man smiled at me again, 'Ah, *salamat siang,*' he said again, giving me a thumbs up before launching into another sentence which, to me, was nothing more than a jumbled collection of sounds.

The brown stain in the centre of his bandage was looking more and more like a strange and sinister eye, so I tried to concentrate on his good one.

I held up my hands. '*Saya . . . tidak . . . bisa . . . bicara . . . bahasa . . . Indonesia,*' I said with my best accent, telling him I couldn't speak his language.

He stopped talking and nodded knowingly, '*Baik, baik.*'

After that we just looked at each other, smiling and nodding, sharing the common experience of being strapped beneath tight sheets with bandages wrapped around a part of our body.

Then he had a thought. He leaned across and offered me his hand. 'Muklas,' he said. 'I Muklas.'

I took his hand, surprised at his limp grip. 'Alex,' I told him. '*Saya* Alex.'

Once again we fell into an awkward state of smiling and nodding before his face lit up again as if he'd come to a sudden and significant conclusion. He took a hand of small bananas from his bedside table and ripped one from the bunch. He passed it to me saying, '*Pisang. Pisang tuju.* Ba-na-na.'

I took it from him. '*Terima kasi*,' – thank you – words I'd committed to heart – and opened it immediately, my stomach grabbing for the food. It occurred to me at that precise moment, though, that I didn't know where I was, nor how long I had been there.

It was a strange realisation that dropped into me like a weight, especially when I remembered the fate of my rucksack. I stopped, with the banana touching my lips, and I put my free hand to my waist where my money-belt had been.

Gone.

I dropped the fruit on the sheets and turned to check the table beside my bed. I leaned down to open the small door, feeling the blood racing to my head where it pumped and pounded, beating in my ears. The cupboard behind the door was empty. The weight that had dropped into my stomach began to mutate. It was no longer just a weight, it was now a living thing which was expanding and rising inside me, threatening to cause panic in every cell of my body.

The man beside me was speaking again but his voice sounded different as my breathing quickened. I had lost everything that gave me any identity. I had lost myself. *Everything*.

I wrestled with the constricting sheets and swung my legs from the bed. My ankles skinny and pale, dangling from the mattress as I lowered my feet onto the floor. The glossy paint covering the concrete was cold under my soles as I pushed myself up to stand. I crossed the ward as quickly as I was able to, my head numb and the sickness returning to my stomach. I didn't know where I was going or what I would do, but I needed to do something. My clothes had been taken from me, somebody must have undressed me, put the gown over me, and that meant someone must know where my belongings were. My money and my passport. Without them I was nobody.

I leaned on the swinging doors, pushed my way into the corridor and stopped. I put out a hand, leaning against the wall for support and looked around. One side of the long hallway was lined with beds and trolleys, many of them old and broken, all of them full. Men and women, some with limbs missing, blood draining from their bodies as ill-equipped doctors and nurses struggled to help them. The other wall of the corridor provided a place to lean on for yet more patients. They were sitting in the stifling heat, no fans above their heads to break the air.

I stayed where I was, taking it all in, the sounds and the smells and the sights overloading my mind. I put my free hand over my eyes, my head swimming, wondering where I was and what I was going to do. When I took it away again, a middle-aged man in a long white coat was standing before me. He put his hand on my shoulder and spoke, but his words meant nothing. I shook my head. 'I don't understand.'

He tried to look sympathetic, nodding, still talking, but the look in his eyes was unfamiliar. His expressions were not like those I was used to. I tried to move away from him, but he smiled, taking my arm.

'No.' I snatched away. 'No. I need to . . . I need to . . .' I needed my life back. I needed to know where I was, but I didn't know how to ask him and he didn't know how to tell me.

Once again he reached out and took my arm, a reassuring look that I recognised.

'No.' I pulled away again, but with less conviction this time. He was trying to help. So I held up my hand and nodded, letting him take me and lead me back into the ward. He helped me to my bed and waited until I was beneath my sheets before he held out both hands, palms towards me.

'You want me to stay?' I asked him. 'Wait here, is that it? You want me to wait here?'

He backed away, still keeping his hands up, making small movements with them, reinforcing the idea that he wanted me to wait.

So I waited.

For how long, I don't know. From time to time I glanced at my wrist, forgetting that my watch had been taken from me on the road. So I waited a while longer, and a while longer still, staring at the door, wondering when the doctor was going to return, hoping he would bring my identity with him.

I ignored Muklas, the man in the bed beside mine. I avoided any contact with him, keeping all my attention on the swinging door.

When the doctor returned, he was not alone. This time he was accompanied by the angel I had seen on the road. But of course, she wasn't an angel. She was quite real, and she brought with her a breath of fresh air, a relief and a beauty which made her the next best thing to an angel.